THE WOODCARVER'S SECRET

Connie Shelton

Books by Connie Shelton

THE CHARLIE PARKER SERIES
Deadly Gamble
Vacations Can Be Murder
Partnerships Can Be Murder
Small Towns Can Be Murder
Memories Can Be Murder
Honeymoons Can Be Murder
Reunions Can Be Murder
Competition Can Be Murder
Balloons Can Be Murder
Obsessions Can Be Murder
Gossip Can Be Murder
Stardom Can Be Murder
Phantoms Can Be Murder
Buried Secrets Can Be Murder
Legends Can Be Murder
Weddings Can Be Murder
Holidays Can Be Murder - a Christmas novella

THE SAMANTHA SWEET SERIES
Sweet Masterpiece
Sweet's Sweets
Sweet Holidays
Sweet Hearts
Bitter Sweet
Sweets Galore
Sweets, Begorra
Sweet Payback
Sweet Somethings
Sweets Fogotten
The Woodcarver's Secret

NON-FICTION
Show, Don't Tell
Novel In A Weekend (writing course)

CHILDREN'S BOOKS
Daisy and Maisie and the Great Lizard Hunt
Daisy and Maisie and the Lost Kitten

THE WOODCARVER'S SECRET

Connie Shelton

Secret Staircase Books

The Woodcarver's Secret
Published by Secret Staircase Books, an imprint of
Columbine Publishing Group
PO Box 416, Angel Fire, NM 87710

Copyright © 2015 Connie Shelton
All rights reserved. No part of this book may be reproduced or
transmitted in any form or by any means, electronic or mechanical,
including photocopying, recording, or by an information storage and
retrieval system without permission in writing from the publisher.
Printed and bound in the United States of America

This book is a work of fiction. Names, characters, places and
incidents are either the product of the author's imagination or are
used fictitiously. Any resemblance to actual events or locales or
persons, living or dead, is entirely coincidental.

Book layout and design by Secret Staircase Books
Background illustration © Rolffimages
Box illustration © Rkasprzak

Publisher's Cataloging-in-Publication Data

Shelton, Connie
The Woodcarver's Secret / by Connie Shelton.
p. cm.
ISBN 978-1945422263 (paperback)

1. Ireland, 12th century—Fiction. 2. Germany, WWII—Fiction.
3. Paranormal artifacts—Fiction. 4. Spanish Inquisition—Fiction. 5.
Camino Real, Mexico—Fiction. 6. Magical items—Fiction. I. Title

Samantha Sweet Mystery Series : Prequel.
Shelton, Connie, Samantha Sweet mysteries.

BISAC : FICTION / Historical

813/.54

As always, my deepest gratitude goes to those who have helped make my books and both of my series a reality: Dan Shelton, my partner in all adventures, who is always there for me, working to keep the place running efficiently while I am locked away at my keyboard. My fantastic editing team—Susan Slater, Shirley Shaw, and proofreader Kim Clark—each of you has suggested things that help me see something new in my writing.

And especially to you, my readers—I cherish our connection through these stories.
Thank you, everyone!

*In the early twenty-first century a woman in Taos,
New Mexico, falls heir to an extraordinary mystical
artifact, a carved wooden box, which she discovers has
a long and complex history. What follows is a glimpse at
that history.*

Chapter 1

Lightning Strikes

Heavy, lead-colored clouds hovered ominously at the
horizon, stealing the last scrap of sun that had peered
tentatively around them half the morning. A frigid wind
came off the waters of Galway Bay, whipping the gray
waves to a foamy froth that licked at John Carver's feet. He
studied the clouds as the next wet salvo washed over his

thick leather boots, filling the left one, draining out through the hole near his big toe. Maggie would give him the devil for his carelessness the same way she reminded the children to care for their things. "An' where do you think we'll be gettin' a new pair of boots?" she would surely prod.

Already this morning his wife had thought of a dozen chores he might do at their small hut—sweep up his wood shavings, clear his wares to the outdoors so there would be more space, watch the children while she kneaded bread. The woman always became demanding of him when she was expecting another one, and by the size of her belly the new mouth to feed would arrive within a few weeks.

He pulled his woolen cloak tighter to his shoulders and walked away from the shoreline, staring at the two tall alder trees on the rise beyond the gray stone city walls. Both were long dead, gnarled old things whose smaller branches had been stripped and taken for the fires in a dozen homes. The last of the leaves had blown to the far corners of the county four or five seasons ago. The trees interested him, though, far more than anything else in his life right now. He put his walking stick ahead of him and began to make his way toward the stately silhouettes, black against the billows of cloud. Thunder rumbled somewhere behind him.

Plates. Bowls. Cups. The words drummed through his head as he walked. Common kitchen utensils comprised his work these days. People had no money for niceties or trinkets in these times. They bought wooden plates and cups because the pieces were durable, wouldn't break like real crockery could. Each week at Market Day, John managed to sell a piece or two, enough to buy flour that he hoped would not turn out to be infested with weevils. Sometimes there was money enough for some carrots or potatoes, or he simply bartered for what they needed. Four weeks ago the butcher's wife had fancied one of John's bowls on which he'd applied a simple inlay pattern, and the man grudgingly traded a half leg of lamb for the bowl. Maggie had given him no trouble on that day, when he showed up with the prize.

If only he could make another desirable object like that bowl, something one of the wealthy merchants' wives would take a liking to, something which could command a handsome price. He stared again at the two dead snags— some fine wood there, nicely dried already. He would not have to store it for months before beginning to work it. He would need to first cut the wood, then examine it. A piece of quality wood always told him what object it was most suited to become.

A figure interrupted John's concentration. The man walking along the hilltop was someone he recognized. Tyrel Smith spotted him and crossed the hill, raising a hand in greeting.

"Greetings—fine morning!" Tyrel always had a way with irony, John thought as a spatter of rain grazed his cheek.

Perhaps his friend was right; being out in the open, no matter the weather, made for a better beginning to the day than performing household tasks at the whim of a woman. Tyrel waited in place until John caught up.

"I've given some thought to my next piece of woodcraft," John said, not admitting his pleasure at selling a single, artistic piece rather than the utilitarian ones he normally made. "And I'm thinking ... these trees are doing no one any service up here on the hill."

"That one's worm riddled," Tyrel said, pointing at the southernmost of the two. "It will not be suitable for any fine pieces. The other, however—that one would catch my fancy. If I were in the business of wood carving."

John patted the side of his carry-bag, assuring himself that he had brought his axe. He walked up to the huge tree, admiring the jagged arms it sent skyward. It would take a mighty effort to fell it. Perhaps he could climb up, take the large limbs one at a time. He touched the trunk; most of the bark had fallen away, leaving a smooth surface and an indication of the beautiful bowls that could be carved from this wood. One limb of decent size was within his reach. He drew his axe from his pouch.

Tyrel had moved down the slope, and he shouted something to John now. But the woodcarver didn't catch the words, lost as they were to the rising sounds of wind and storm. He hefted the axe.

Crack!! Thunder shook the earth and brilliant light blinded him. He felt his feet leave the ground.

* * *

"By the gods, man. Wake up!"

John's eyes flickered open. A familiar face hovered over him, a rough hand slapping at his cheek.

"Carver! Wake up!" The rough hands pushed John's hair away from his eyes. "The rain's coming, we have to get out of here. Can you stand?"

John reached for his friend's shoulder, thinking to pull himself up. But his arm refused to rise. He willed it to move. His fingers tingled, as if he'd fallen asleep with the arm pinned beneath his body. Tyrel took him by the forearm, tugging at him, but John barely felt the contact. His legs felt similarly unconnected from his wish to make them move.

"Can't you move, John?" Tyrel's face had a look of alarm. "Come on, man, try again."

"What happened?" John looked around but could not see beyond the bulk of his friend kneeling beside him.

"Lightning. It struck the tree and flung you down the slope. I feared you were dead."

John stretched his fingers. This time they responded, tingling painfully.

"Nay, I'm not dead," he said, trying to put a chuckle into it.

Heavy raindrops struck his face and he rolled to his side. Feeling rushed back into his arms and legs, jabs of pain that made him grimace and catch his breath. When it subsided he rolled to his hands and knees, wondering if the limbs could take his weight, frightened that he might have been rendered a cripple.

Tyrel placed an arm on John's shoulders, bracing him as he hung his head. Finally, like a dog, he shook himself and then sat back on his haunches. With numb fingertips he brushed the hair away from his face. One hand came away bloody.

"You've got yourself a nasty splinter there," Tyrel said, plucking the shard of wood from John's temple with a delicacy incongruous with the size of his thick, calloused fingers. "There—it's out. You'll want Maggie to tend to that when you get home."

Maggie. John wondered at the reception he would receive. "How long have I been here?"

"A few minutes," said Tyrel. "Looks like we've missed the worst of it."

He tipped his chin to the north, where the furious black cloud blasted the earth with rain only a mile or two away.

John shook his arms once more, started to rise, reached for the support of his friend's shoulder. One at a time he stretched each leg before requiring it to take his weight.

"I was about to take my axe to the—" He looked toward the hilltop.

The magnificent old tree with the snaggled arms was gone. A smoldering stump marked its location and pieces lay about—from entire limbs to tiny shards like the splinter taken from John's own face.

"Well, you'll not be havin' to cut him down now, will ya?" Tyrel said.

John couldn't speak. Surrounding the debris field he saw a brilliant orange aura. He stared as it faded to yellow and then transformed itself to deep red. He squeezed his eyes shut and pressed his dirt-crusted fingers to the lids.

"Carver? What is it?"

When John opened his eyes again he saw only the wisp of smoke from the trunk and the profusion of fragments covering the ground. The colors were gone. The air smelled of freshly cut wood. In the distance, the purple-black clouds had dissipated to gray, the storm quickly becoming only a memory.

"John Carver?"

"It's nothing. Just a mite dizzy for a minute." He knew he could never tell anyone of this experience, not unless he wanted to be branded an idiot—or worse.

Tyrel nodded. "Well, as there's two of us here, shall we take up some of the wood, carry it home for your work?"

John's legs ached with the first few steps, but as he approached the abundance of wood lying on the grassy hill he felt his strength return. He examined a few of the larger pieces. By god, he had a treasure here, enough wood for a decade's work if he saw fit to use it. He began to envision how to use these pieces to best advantage.

"I'll borrow a cart," he said. "I can—"

He paused, unwilling to divulge his plans. Tyrel Smith was his friend, but word had a way of spreading through the village as quickly as a flash flood. Competitors would arise from the men who had little work in these hard times. Or, worse yet, the overlord would appear and claim the bounty as his own, creating a method for taxing John until any profit was gone.

"Never mind," he said. "I'll take a log or two. But let's not mention this to anyone."

Tyrel shrugged. A smithy's trade, with its requirement for special tools and years of apprenticeship and training, never seemed in jeopardy, whereas every man in the land with a knife or chisel could claim to be a woodworker.

"How about that one over there?" John said, pointing out a section of the tree's trunk that was nearly a meter long and several inches thick. "Carry it for me? I'll get this other."

John's imagination went to work as the two men walked back toward the village. Perhaps a wooden box of some sort. One of the fine ladies had mentioned such an item to her friend when they browsed at his market stall a few weeks ago. He could add decorative carving, perhaps something inspired from nature or from the rich fabrics the women wore. With the two pieces of wood, he could use one to make a practice piece and the other for a finely done one. Surely, the wife of the lord would appreciate such an item. And if not one of the titled ladies, certainly it would catch the eye of the butcher's wife or the mistress of the sheriff. With the right buyer John could make more money than he had in many months. That would surely quiet his wife's nagging tongue.

The storm had unleashed rain in patches. The two men crossed fields where the earth was completely dry, only to come upon a gushing stream where water poured from higher ground and formed in puddles at the lower roadway. In the bay, the surf pounded the shore in muddy, foam-topped anger, as if to make the point that a mere batch of clouds was no match for the sea. The men spoke little, each concentrating on finding the path of least difficulty while walking with his sizeable burden hefted to his shoulder.

On the outskirts of town lay a huddle of small cottages, John's home only by virtue of the fact that Maggie's brother farmed a few acres of the nearby land. Tenant farmers were provided a home in exchange for dawn-to-dusk labor and the baron receiving an outsized share of the food they produced. If the day came that Sean chose to marry, John and Maggie and the wee ones would have to either take up farming to earn a home of their own or move into the town in order for John to keep up his woodcraft.

He preferred to watch his children play and work out here where there were grass and plants, rather than in the winding, muddy streets of Galway where household waste was tossed from upper story windows into the shallow gutters and sickness ran rampant. For now, his brother-in-law showed no inclination toward women and seemed content to abide among the extended family with his sister as housemaid and cook. John put the thoughts aside; making radical changes to their living situation was something they did not discuss.

Outside the one-room stone structure with its roof of heavy thatch, John spotted his young son Ethan, the eldest of the four, loading his arms with blocks of peat from the stack near the door. When the six-year-old saw his father, he abandoned his chore, dropped the peat and came running.

"Da', da'! Look what I found!" The boy reached into the pocket of his woolen trousers to bring out his treasure, but pulled out only a few fragments of pale blue shell and a slippery mess of yolk. His small face crumpled and a tear threatened to slide down his face.

"Oh, a robin's egg," John said gently. "I'll bet it was beautiful!"

Ethan nodded.

"No matter. We'll find another, you and me together."

Ethan noticed Tyrel and went quiet, rubbing the remains of egg on his pants and lowering his gaze to the ground.

"We've found some beautiful timber," John said. "Go, finish helping your mother and I'll show them to you when I set them down."

He led the way to the lean-to structure he had constructed against the side of the stone cottage, a place where he could keep his wood pieces dry and work in relative quiet outside the house where seven people, a cow and two goats provided nothing in the way of the solitude needed for creativity. Inside, he'd made shelves for finished wares. For pieces of wood that he'd not yet worked, there was a small bin, empty now.

"Put it there," he told Tyrel, nodding toward his small bench.

He set his own length of the alder on the three-legged stool where he sat when working and stared at the two. These were fine pieces with a unique grain and no knots. He could create something worthy with them.

"And what's this?" Maggie's voice came from the narrow

doorway behind him. "You've not stolen that, have you?"

"And bring the sheriff down upon my neck? No, woman, I'm not stupid."

"It was given by God," Tyrel said. "He sent it directly to John."

Maggie's tired eyes squinted, her mouth tightened. "What are you sayin'?"

John wished Tyrel would keep quiet but there was no way to caution him without creating a bigger scene.

"The tree was on common land," John said. "Not the baron's."

"He's right about that," Tyrel said, facing Maggie's skepticism square-on. "Your John faced it with bravery, even when lightning tried to strike him dead. He's due this tree."

Maggie looked past Tyrel, facing John with a mixture of fear and anger.

"Lightning? And what were you doin' out there in the storm, John Carver? What kind of fool are you, with a family to feed?"

Tyrel sensed he'd perhaps gone too far. He edged out of the workshop, past the woman whose fists were planted firmly on her hips, and set a brisk pace toward the stone wall of the town a quarter mile away.

John faced his wife with a firm gaze. "I'll not speak of it. That's final."

Maggie's eyes flashed, but she said no more.

* * *

The fact that John wanted the lightning incident

forgotten had little bearing on the townsfolk of Galway. No sooner had Tyrel returned to his blacksmith shed than the widow O'Connell happened by. An imposing old woman of fifty, she was known for her direct ways.

"So then, Tyrel Smith, weren't you one of the men I saw walking up the hillside this afternoon? It wasn't a minute before the bolt of God came down, strikin' that old tree, breakin' it to bits."

With his tongs Tyrel picked up a rod of iron and held it to the fire. He worked vainly not to meet her eyes.

"Ah, I knew it," she said. "A wonder you're not dead, the two of you. Who was the other? Me eyesight's goin,' you know."

Tyrel busied himself with the bellows; the fire had gone low in his absence and he'd not be accomplishing anything today if he didn't bring up the flame.

Mrs. O'Connell glanced up the narrow street. "That Carver fellow, I'd wager. The man's got no friends but you, thanks to that wife with the mouth on her. She's angered every merchant in the village, haggling over their wares and insultin' 'em to their face."

Tyrel watched the flame in his forge roar to life. "John Carver's a good man, an honest worker."

The widow grunted. Her late husband, a baker of fine quality breads, was the one who'd had words with Maggie. Of course, he'd had words with half the townsfolk, and no one was so awfully surprised when he dropped dead, clutching his chest. It was only sad fortune that Maggie had left his shop not five minutes earlier. The widow O'Connell would forever blame her.

She touched the horseshoe beside Tyrel's door, for luck, then lifted her skirt above the smelly rivulet of mud that ran down the street and proceeded on her way to torture the wool merchant.

Tyrel drew the red-hot iron rod from the fire and pounded it mercilessly until he felt better. He should have never mentioned the misadventure in front of Maggie; the woman and her shrewish tongue would be the death of John Carver yet. He'd simply been unthinking. He would buy his friend a pint of stout next time he saw him.

A fortnight passed before that occasion and when John Carver passed the blacksmith's barn, he seemed preoccupied.

"How goes the woodworking?" Tyrel called out.

John turned away from the street and entered the warm, smoky shelter. "Well," he said with a smile. "It's going well."

Tyrel thought of the pint of stout he meant to offer, but the set of gate hinges he was working at the moment couldn't wait.

"And the family? Everyone's all right?"

"The little bairn's learning to walk. I suppose she'll be toddlin' toward the fire, just about the time Maggie's got her hands full with the new one. Her time's gettin' close now."

Tyrel nodded as if he knew anything about that sort of thing. He'd been the youngest of four, and never knew his mother. The two sisters were so much older that they'd moved off, as far as Limerick, with husbands. He'd grown up in a house with a rowdy brother and a father who drank all the time and muttered about the unfairness of his wife dying like that and leaving him with a worthless baby to care for. All of Tyrel's hard work in learning a useful trade earned him no points with the old man, who'd finally done the world a favor by dying two winters ago.

John stepped closer and looked at the hinge Tyrel had

finished, the first of four.

"It should have a lid," he mused, picking up the large hinge and studying it. He set it back. "First things first. Better get back to it. Tomorrow is market day—I'll see you then."

He hurried off without another word.

"Odd one, that Carver," said a man who had bumped shoulders with John as he rushed away. "They say he's become even stranger since the day of the lightning strike."

Tyrel felt a jab of guilt. Had his careless comment in front of Maggie started a raft of rumors through the town?

"Last market day," the man continued, "my wife wanted to buy two plates. The man would barely speak to her. Sat there under his measly awning, carving away at some square thing, like a moody artist. I say artistic genius is one thing, but in this town a man's not going to make his living from that foolishness. He'd better be selling useful things to his regular customers."

A square item. So, John Carver must indeed be working on the wooden box he'd mentioned to Tyrel as they carried the broken tree parts down the hill.

"Don't understand it, myself," the man said. "Carver always seemed personable, friendly."

"Maybe it was just a mood that day."

"Moods—ha! Got no use for no la-di-da *moods*. Sell me a pair of horseshoes, would you, Smith?"

Tyrel busied himself with fitting and shoeing the man's horse, putting aside his concerns about the change in John Carver. A personality changed by a lightning strike? It seemed preposterous. Most likely it was exactly what John had hinted at—his wife was about to present him with a fifth child and was giving him hell about bringing in more money. He got an idea.

* * *

John put the last of his finished wares into the small handcart and bent over to lift the yoke. Once it began rolling, the burden moved along easily enough. Maggie had asked that he bring bread, vegetables and candles when he came home. She made a point about the candles—he'd been burning far too many of them, working late into the night in his shop at the side of the house. Making matters worse, her brother Sean added to the discussion by disparaging the work of an artist, saying John should instead do something useful with his time, helping out on the plot of farm land.

He put his brother-in-law's comments aside and turned to wave at his wife, feeling a rush of emotion at the sight of the thin woman, hugely pregnant now, with little Siobhan perched on her hip and the next two hanging on to her skirts. Her old smile briefly lit her face, bringing back memories of their courting days. Ethan had begged to come with his father, but the six-year-old didn't yet have the stamina to make it through the long market day without becoming tired and whiny. Maggie was a good mother and an excellent cook, given what she had to work with. It was no wonder her temper ran a little short these days. He turned to the rutted road that led the half-mile to the side gate of the town wall, hurrying, as he was already getting a late start.

At the gate a stream of patrons were making their way toward the open square where tables and blankets were spread with food and wares. A butcher displayed cages of chickens, squawking wildly, and sides of meat. Someone else showed piles of dirt-crusted potatoes and carrots; one woman's table was laden with lengths of cloth. The women who paused there looked longingly at the pieces dyed in reds and blues, but purchased the plainer tans and grays which must have been less expensive. An old man under a wooden shelter hammered at a strip of tin, forming the handle for a teapot.

John hurried to his customary spot. Pushing his cart up against the wall of a two-story stone building, he whipped out two blankets and began setting out his display of plates and kitchen implements. A section of tree stump made a stool, and his box of chisels afforded him the ability to work when he wasn't waiting on a customer. He looked at the sky. Clear, for a change. If the clouds began to threaten rain, he would need to get out the poles and tarpaulin of oiled cloth and erect a shelter over his work area.

His interest quickened as he came to the cloth-wrapped packet that held the wooden box he'd begun making two weeks ago. From the smaller of the two lengths of alder branch he'd blocked out the rough shape of the piece with his hatchet—a rectangle about two hands in length and one hand wide. The depth would be sufficient for a lady to store her bits of finery; a man might use it for his pipe; an important courier could use it for the safe keeping of letters. Perhaps one day a letter to the king would be carried all the way to London in this very box!

He set the parcel on the open end of the cart, the place that afforded a reasonably stable surface for working, then dragged the stump-seat near to it. Peeling back the cloth covering, he felt a moment's disappointment.

In his mind, the lidded box was a fine, polished piece, worthy of that letter to the king. But in reality the carved quilt pattern had not turned out as well as he had hoped. He had made the mistake of applying a stain to the entire piece without testing a small bit first. The walnut oil was too dark in places where it had run into the deeply carved grooves, and he had been interrupted by the children before he could properly wipe it down and distribute the color more evenly. It would be difficult to rework it at this point, but he felt he could do it.

John became aware of someone standing nearby.

"Good market day," Tyrel said.

John looked around. No one had stopped to examine his wares yet, so he could not quite agree with the statement, but he gave his friend a smile anyway.

"What's this?" Tyrel was eyeing the unfinished box.

John wanted to flip the covering over it once more, but Tyrel had already seen it.

"It isn't finished," he said.

"Ah, yes. You mentioned some hinges for it." Tyrel reached into his pocket and drew out two small bits of metal. "A gift. I felt badly for the way my mouth ran off that day."

John had long since forgiven Tyrel's mentioning the lightning to Maggie. He looked at the metal pieces. The hinges were of fine quality, working smoothly, and just the right size for the box.

"Now that I see it, I'm thinking a clasp to latch it closed would be nice too," the blacksmith said. He held his fingers up to the place where box and lid came together, measuring. "I shall come back by the end of day, provided the demand for wheels and tools isn't too great."

John started to protest that he had no money for metalwork, but the smith had rushed away and two women approached his display. He diverted his attention to make the sale, pocketing the small coins the younger woman gave for two of the plates. The money would provide enough for a half-dozen new candles, the tall ones. He stretched his fingers, working them to get rid of the residual tingling that still often plagued him, and sat down to mount the new hinges to the box.

Shouts and a clatter of hooves grabbed his attention. Two boys, no more than twelve years old, ran through the market square and ducked into a narrow alley before reaching John's place. Rounding the bend in the High Street, came a dark horse. The rider wore the livery of the Sheriff.

"Where did they go?" the man demanded from the great height of his saddle, staring down at the shoppers in the street. "Those two thieves! Where did they go?"

John lowered his gaze and studiously worked at his hinges. When the sheriff's man pulled his horse up in front of John, he glanced up disinterestedly and shrugged. The man rode on.

He supposed that if the thievery had happened with his own wares he would have welcomed the sheriff's intervention, but he doubted this was the case. More likely, one of the wealthy ladies was missing a small trinket and had reported the two lads as culprits. Or, they were simply taking something to eat—a loaf of bread or piece of cheese. They'd looked hungry enough.

This current sheriff—the baron's newest appointment— had won no friends here, cultivating a climate of distrust and practically forcing people to cheat when he imposed dozens of onerous taxes at the time he took office two years ago. This deputy would find no one in Galway willing to turn in two young boys who only needed food. John watched the black horse disappear around a bend in the road as he picked up his smallest chisel and worked to smooth the rough edges of the box.

The sun was low in the sky by the time John looked up from his work. A few customers had put some coins into his pocket but he'd spent the majority of his day adding small touches to the wooden box, realizing that it would never become the beautiful piece of craftsmanship he had imagined. He still had several pieces of wood at home, however, and rather than feeling discouraged he was looking forward to attempting another.

His cart loaded, he remembered Maggie's requests and rushed along to the remaining vendors, finding their stocks depleted. The baker had only one loaf and since it was a little moldy on one side, gave it to John at no charge; the supply of vegetables was reduced to a small pile of potatoes, rejected ones with bruises. Maggie's favorite gardener who raised herbs had also departed. It said something of his good fortune, he decided, that the candle maker had a nice supply. He spent the majority of his coins there, tucking the heavy wax sticks deeply in among his tools.

A shout caught his attention as he picked up the cart's handle, turning toward home.

"You! I've one last chicken," called the poultry woman.

He pulled up short beside the stack of empty cages.

"You're John Carver, aren't you? I noticed you trying to round up some food." She nodded toward the lone hen. "She was not my largest but maybe she'll provide the children with something."

John felt his face redden. Was this the new rumor about the village, that his children were going hungry? He started to decline her charity.

"It'll be ten pence," the woman said.

He reached into his coin pocket and discovered that ten

was all he had. He tossed it to her. She expertly grabbed the chicken and wrung its neck in one quick move.

"There. All ready for tonight's supper." She stacked the empty cage onto her hand-truck and started off in the opposite direction.

John fumed, wanting to shout something about how his children ate quite well, thank you very much, but what would be the point? At least now he had a decent meal to soothe Maggie's likely complaint about how much he'd spent on candles.

His legs ached as he pulled the cart home, the rising moon lighting the double track by the time he caught sight of the cottage. He stopped beside the lean-to workshop and secured the tarpaulin against a possible night rain before picking up the dead chicken and small net bag of potatoes.

Inside, smoke rose to the peak of the thatched roof, a little of it wafting out the hole at the top, most of it filling the room. Maggie stirred a pot that smelled like boiled cabbage, balancing the eighteen-month-old baby on her hip and ignoring the pitiful whines of the next two. Her brother sat on the bench against the wall, scraping thick mud from his boots, making no move to help. She brightened slightly when she saw the chicken, but her brows knitted together in worry only a moment later. John followed her gaze.

On the floor in the corner young Ethan lay on his straw pallet, his eyes closed. John started to tease his oldest son for being lazy but noticed that the boy's face was unnaturally red, his breathing shallow.

"He's taken worse and worse all day," Maggie said, leaving the cookpot long enough to take the new food from John and set it on her work table.

He marveled at how she handled it all one-handed and kept the toddler under control with the other, and he wondered how she would manage once the new infant came. Soon, Ethan would be strong enough to lend a hand. But a second glance told him the six-year-old was not doing well.

"What's the matter with him?" he asked.

"Fever, and now he's got some spots on his skin."

"Better not be bringing the Black Death in upon us," Sean piped up from his corner.

John felt his stomach tighten. Surely, here in this little village ... even in town, a half mile away ... surely, the dreaded plague had not come this close. He rushed to the bedside and knelt down. Ethan's skin was hot and dry to the touch.

"He's burning up! Why haven't ye done anything?"

Maggie's face tightened. How much could one woman cope with, he supposed. He found a scrap of cloth lying beside his son's head.

"It's slipped off," Maggie said. "Dampen it with cold water. Try to cool him."

John dipped the rag into a crock of stream water they kept beside the door and returned to dab at the boy's face. Ethan barely responded. Meanwhile, the others began to wail and Maggie ordered them to the table where she set out bowls of cabbage soup. Sean joined them, John noticed, while Maggie tended the baby and he continued to press the wet cloth to Ethan's face.

"I'd best bring in the animals," Sean said a few minutes later, wiping his mouth after he stuffed in a sizeable chunk of bread. "We'll have milk for the little ones soon." He walked out into the moonlight.

"Every time I get ready to give him a piece of my mind,

he does something like that," Maggie said, "offering the first milk to the children."

Unless John wanted to start farming, himself, and get his family into their own cottage, he would have to live with Sean—his unhelpfulness and his moods. And the truth was, right now there were no new tenancies available. Unless the baron opened up new lands, their lot in life was set.

He went outside to dampen the cloth again and when he came in Maggie took it and made him take her place at the table, setting out the last bowl of soup for him. She placed the cool cloth on Ethan's forehead before turning to the others, washing their faces and hands and telling them to go use the privy one last time before bed.

In the adjoining room, John heard the sounds of the two goats bleating as Sean penned them into their corner, followed by the crisp sound of milk from the cow hitting the bottom of a wooden pail. Maggie spread two more straw pallets on the floor and shook out blankets. She dipped warm milk from the bucket and gave the three- and four-year-old each a small cup before settling them onto their beds. Sean had climbed the ladder to the small half-loft above the room, and they could hear him groaning as he settled himself for the night.

"You rest," John told his wife, nodding toward the only real bed in the house, the wooden frame standing against the far wall. "I shall sit up with Ethan and watch him."

"Wake me if he gets worse. I can walk to Mrs. O'Sullivan's for some herbs."

"You'll do no walking about in the dark," he told her, placing a kiss on her forehead. She smelled of sweat and smoke from the peat fire, but then everyone did. "I can go for help if we need it."

Even among the two-dozen similar cottages clustered together in what was known as the village, there was always a woman who specialized in cures. She would be the same one who would come when Maggie knew the new baby was arriving. The nearest real doctor lived in town but it cost money to bring him out and, aside from drawing blood from the sick child, John doubted the man knew any more than Mrs. O'Sullivan about making their Ethan well. He knelt again beside the boy and felt his face—not a bit cooler. He found a second cloth and wet it from the cool water in a bowl, switching it with the overheated one.

Settling himself against the wall near the child's head, John dozed then woke. He replaced the cloth again and found himself more alert now. He thought of the wooden box he had worked on all day. With the hinges, it seemed a nicer piece, more finished. He rose quietly and went out to the cart where he pulled it from under the tarp.

The design consisted of diagonal cuts at ninety-degree angles to each other resulting in a quilted look. The high points between the X-shaped intersections rose in soft pillowy curves. At the bottom he had smoothed a border around the base, and at the edge of the lid he'd made a precise row of small raised dots, like beadwork carved of wood. In the moonlight the piece was nearly beautiful, the uneven effects of the ill-chosen stain adding depth now. He smiled and opened the lid.

He would smooth the inside a bit more and perhaps add a fine cloth lining if he could get the right material. He ran his index finger around the inner edges of it, starting in the upper corner and moving down and around, feeling for any small unevenness. When his finger completed the circuit of all four sides, a jolt shot through his hand, up the arm to the elbow, and into his body. Blinded and dizzy, he fell to his knees, dropping the box on the ground.

* * *

His breath came in short bursts; panting, John sat up. He held his head in his hands for a minute or more, willing the dizziness away. What in the Lord's name had happened just now? How much time had passed? He blinked and dared a glance at the moon. It had not moved, so he'd not been out very long. He rubbed his hands down the sides of his face and flexed his fingers. The tingling that had intermittently plagued him since the day of the lightning incident was gone.

He stood. The pain in his legs had vanished.

His arms. They no longer ached.

He looked around at the other cottages in the village. No lights showed under doorways, no human shadow appeared in the moonlit meadows. He prayed no one had witnessed the event. There was talk enough in the village and in town about his escape from the lightning bolt that had felled the massive tree. He took a step and felt ... he felt good! Young, spry!

He retrieved the carved box from the ground. Did the ugly brown stain take on a golden glow when he touched it? He held it at arm's length and decided it was only a trick of the moonlight. He started to set the box back on the cart but at the last moment changed his mind and carried it into the house.

Inside, sounds of sleep filled the small space. Overhead,

Sean's loud snores echoed through the rafters, while Maggie moaned lightly as she rolled over, adjusting to find comfort for her large belly. In the corner, Ethan was quiet—too quiet. John knelt and held the lamp above the pallet in the corner. The boy's face now had a rash of dark spots against the heat of the fever. John's heart lurched. He held the back of his hand near the boy's open mouth, hoping to feel breath. It was there, but very shallow.

Should he wake Maggie? Should he start for the O'Sullivan place?

"I don't know what to do for you," he whispered under his breath. "Son, I don't know what to do."

He leaned forward and pulled Ethan's limp body into his arms, hugging the boy to his chest, stroking one puffy, hot arm with the hand that was accustomed to discerning every knot in a piece of fine wood. Ethan stirred, his eyelids fluttering.

"Da'?"

"Hey, boyo, how are you?" John kept his voice low, rubbed a fingertip across his son's forehead. It seemed a little cooler than a moment ago.

"Da' I don't know what happened."

"You're a little bit sick. Your mother's been here all afternoon but she needed to sleep."

The flush drained from the child's skin, and John could barely tell a difference now between his own temperature and the boy's. Ethan struggled in his arms and sat up.

"I'm hungry, Da'. I missed my supper, I think."

John nearly laughed aloud, tears of joy threatening to spill. "Aye, you did that. Supper's long over, but I'll find you something. Wait here."

But when John stood to look for something to feed the child, Ethan got off his pallet and skipped to the table. "There's bread," he said gleefully, "oh, and fresh milk!"

Maggie sat up. "What's this noise about, then?"

John found himself speechless. He moved the lamp to the table and watched his son scramble around, picking up and munching whatever he spotted to eat. Maggie stared at John, almost accusing.

"You let him out of bed!"

"He got up. The fever's gone and look at him!"

She couldn't argue with the happy face and exuberant energy of their son. But she gave John a long, hard look.

"We'll not be repeating this story," she said. "Not unless you want to see me burned as a witch."

He nodded somberly. There was one suspected witch who lived in the town, and she'd gained that reputation for an event very similar to this. When a young girl had fallen ill two summers past, the gray-haired woman had brewed a concoction—she protested that it was a tea of herbs but no one else, including the doctor, knew of these herbs. When the little girl began to sing and dance about, the old woman's friends had all stood at a distance, denying that they knew her. Twice, the church had sent men to get her, to put her to the stake, but the woman had a disappearing-spell and knew how to stay away from them.

Maggie had no spells, no way to escape. They would take her, for certain.

* * *

At daylight, Sean woke early and left for the day. John

and Maggie sent each other signals across the table as the children ate their breakfast of bread and goat cheese. When the young ones had been sent out with little chores to fulfill, they spoke of it for the last time.

"We must proceed as normal," John said. "Sean is the one person who might ask. Tell him only that the fever broke during the night and our Ethan has recovered."

He left her to pluck the chicken and he picked up the carved box and made his way quickly to his small workshop.

In the light of day, sitting among his other carvings, the piece was as ugly and benign as ever. Somehow he had expected it to have retained that near-translucent glow. He lifted the lid, letting it rest open on the new hinges. Nothing about the plain interior gave a hint as to how it came to contain such power. He tentatively touched the inner edges. Nothing happened.

Last evening he had sat for a long time at his son's bedside. Perhaps he had dreamed the episode. Maybe Ethan had gotten well simply because the disease ran its course. He picked up the box with both hands, examining the workmanship, contemplating whether to make another one, a finer one. After a minute, the wood began to warm to his touch and the brown stain turned to the color of dark honey. His heart quickened. The thing did possess some sort of power!

He set the piece on his work table where it quickly lost the glow. In the corner, on the floor, sat more chunks of wood from the lightning-struck tree. He picked one up and laid it on the table, contemplating its size and the direction of the grain. It would certainly be adequate for a second box. He took up his hatchet and went outdoors to rough out the shape.

The sun was a high white orb behind a solid bank of cloud when he heard the hoofbeats. John had become so absorbed in fine-tuning the basic shape of the new box and its lid that he'd not realized how the day was getting along, nor the fact that it would probably rain within the hour.

Three men on horseback approached, the large English animals thundering along the small cart track from town, slowing only as they came close enough for John to recognize faces. It was the sheriff—a man called Dunmoor—and two deputies, one of whom was the blonde-haired man chasing those two boys through town yesterday. Dunmoor, a heavyset man with official attire and a face showing an indulgence for rich food and strong drink, dismounted and walked to the back of John's handcart.

"You—farmer!" the light-haired deputy called out. "Why are you not out tending the baron's fields?"

John explained that Sean was the family tenant farmer, that he was himself a craftsman. Maggie, hearing the voices, had stepped out the doorway of the cottage and the men eyed her for a long moment.

"How many are living in this dwelling?" demanded the sheriff. "Too many, I'd warrant, for the ration of food earned."

"Sean Farmer provides for himself and the animals only," John asserted. "I provide for my wife and children and myself."

He had set the new box on the back of the cart and Dunmoor picked it up now.

"Piss-poor work. I'm amazed you can sell this sort," he said, holding up the rough-cut shape.

John wanted to protest that the piece wasn't finished, that his kitchen utensils actually sold quite well, but that part of it was not quite true. Besides, there was no winning an argument with a sheriff in these parts. He merely gave a small nod and lowered his gaze.

"Where is this man, Sean Farmer?" demanded the deputy.

"Out working." John said. Instantly regretting the impudent tone, he added, "I mean to say, I believe he planned to till the acreage beyond the stone wall."

Dunmoor clutched the unfinished box between his meaty paws, as if he meant to crush it. John held his breath, hoping the piece would not show a reaction to the man's touch; he would die a slow death in prison if that happened. But the sheriff's attention had gone toward the other small cottages in the village. He dropped the box back to the cart and mounted his horse. The three spurred their horses, laughing over the clods of mud that struck John's chest.

"Pigs!" Maggie hissed once the men were out of earshot.

"Careful," John warned under his breath. "They have supporters here and there."

He turned back to his work, carrying the new box and its lid to his table where he could begin to lay out the quilted design and start the finer work with his chisels. The wood took shape under his hands, responding to his tools, somehow feeling different to his touch than the first one.

* * *

The second box was more pleasing to John's eye. He had taken more care in the sanding and finishing, smoothing the surfaces cautiously, applying his walnut stain with more restraint. He carried it outside and held it up where the morning sunlight could show it to advantage. Perhaps the box would find a buyer today, he hoped, as he loaded the cart and began the walk toward town.

But, hours later, he'd had no such luck. Four wooden spoons and a pair of bowls had comprised the day's sales. He'd made a good trade for some fine cheeses early in the morning and Maggie would be happy to see the four good loaves of bread—those would mean no hours of kneading dough for a few days, now that her back was constantly in pain from the heavy burden at her belly.

He arrived home to find the children gathered outside, fussing with hunger.

"What's happened? Where's your mother?"

The little ones looked at him with large eyes and Ethan spoke up. "The midwife's come for her."

Poor little ones, they had no idea what that meant. John knew he was not to be allowed into the cottage's one room, so he took the children into his workshop, cleared a space on the table and made places for them to sit. Breaking the bread and cheese into chunks, he satisfied their immediate need. While they ate, he walked back to the house and stood at the doorway, calling to the midwife that he was home now, asking whether she needed anything of him.

He expected a shouted "no, thank you" so when the woman appeared at the door, he knew it was not good news.

"It's been a very hard labor. The baby seems strong and vigorous but I fear for your wife." Mrs. O'Sullivan's apron had smears of blood and her hands looked none too clean either.

From her bed, Maggie screamed and the other woman turned to dash back inside. The sun went down and Sean came home to tend to the animals, ignoring convention and taking them to their indoor pens, then climbing to his own sleeping loft. John made beds for the children in his workshop, convincing them that it was a game called camping. He held up the new box he'd made and told a story about how an evil sheriff had once handled it and how the courageous wood carver took it away and saved the people of the town through his bravery. Their eyes grew sleepy and he pulled the blanket up to their chins as they began to slumber.

The moon was high and bright when he heard Mrs. O'Sullivan's soft voice call his name. He stepped outside. Maggie's cries had stopped.

"I'm sorry, Mr. Carver," the midwife said in a hushed tone. She held a tiny bundle of cloth. "The wee lad is so weak. I doubt he'll make it."

"And my wife—?"

The woman shook her head.

John felt the breath go out of him. Maggie, gone? How would he cope? His eyes prickled but he felt the midwife's eyes upon him. John reached for the bundle and opened the blanket. The newborn's face looked unearthly—although the woman had wiped him clean, the skin was pale and muddy rather than rosy. His eyes were closed, mouth absolutely still.

John remembered how his own afflictions had disappeared after he'd handled the wooden box, how quickly Ethan had responded. He laid a gentle hand along the side of the tiny infant's face. He stroked one side then the other, hoping to see the child's color improve, to see it trying to make suckling motions. Nothing happened.

"I'd best tend to your wife's body," Mrs. O'Sullivan said quietly. She walked away, leaving him in the yard with the unresponsive baby.

He carried the child to the open back of his cart and set the tiny boy gently there, opening the blanket and placing his hands carefully over the baby's chest, its stick-like arms and legs. When he leaned over it, his ear to its face, he could detect no breath. What had happened—why hadn't the magic worked this time?

* * *

Two days later, he thought of the two carved boxes again as he struck his shovel into the muddy earth, digging a grave for Maggie and the wee one who'd never even had a name. What the boxes had in common was the fact that the wood had come from the same tree, that and the work of the carver himself. One box had delivered a miracle; the other only heartbreak. He thought of the evil Sheriff Dunmoor, the fact that the man had touched the new box. Could he have tainted it with his negative powers?

He heard voices and looked up from the hole in the ground to see a procession of neighbors carrying the coffin John had spent all night making. Tyrel Smith, Gordy O'Sullivan, Tom O'Roark and Gerald Mulligan carried it. Ethan and the younger ones tagged along beside Mrs. O'Sullivan, their faces somber and unsure. John leaped from the long hole in the ground and dashed toward them.

"Tell the priest to wait a moment," he said to Tyrel. "I cannot say goodbye to Maggie in this state."

He ran home, tugging his shirt off, and plunged his hands and face into a pail of water outside his woodshop. Scrubbing quickly, he rid himself of the black earth coating his arms then dried his face with an old towel. He spotted the priest riding toward the village along the cart track, so he hurried to pull on the clean shirt he'd set out this morning and raked his hair back off his face.

As the man spoke at the graveside, John could only wonder—where would the next clean shirt come from? Who would feed and dress the children, if not himself? And while he had his hands full with the household, who would produce items and take them to market? He had a feeling little Ethan would act as caregiver to the little ones; the lad would quickly become an adult.

All too soon, the grave was covered, the religious promises made. John's skepticism surely showed on his face. The neighboring women had filled their larder with food, answering an immediate concern. While the children napped that afternoon, John turned to his shop and tried to decide what he would do with his life.

* * *

The two carved boxes sat on his work table, along with the remaining pieces from the tree. He picked up the first one and a rush of good feeling and energy ran through his hands and arms. Quickly, he set it down. Cautiously taking the second one, he felt the energy drain away. Almost instantly, a weight of depression settled upon him. Good and bad—the two boxes.

From far back in his memory came a story his old Norman grandmother used to tell when John was a tiny child. It had been the story of a gypsy, or perhaps it was a witch—he didn't remember for certain—a story where the evil spirit was called Facinor. He remembered being terrified when Grandmother spoke of this. He picked up a small blade and began to carve the name on the inner surface of the lid of the second box. He wanted to remember always that this one had been the cause of grief and pain, that if a wooden item had a spirit, this one was evil.

When he finished he took up the other box. This one created energy and joy and healing. To honor those attributes he thought of a word and began carving: Virtu. He stacked the boxes with the good one on top, looked at them carefully.

"I cannot keep either of you," he said quietly. "You both remind me of her." Not to mention how badly he needed the money from a sale. He tossed them into the cart, ready for the next trip to market.

Meanwhile, he picked up the last of the wood from the lightning-struck tree. *I cannot keep this either*, he thought. He carried the largest hunk of it outside and set to work with the axe. But as soon as he had split it into two pieces he realized that it was not in his nature to waste a good piece of wood. He drew out his small hatchet and, almost from memory, began hewing it to the same shape as the other two. Perhaps a set was the way to approach this; make a set of three boxes, which would appeal to someone of wealth.

The week's end would bring the Feast of Beltane, and with the celebrations in Galway would come wealthy merchants from other cities and loosen the money from the pockets of nearby farmers as well.

That would be his answer—to sell all three boxes at the festival market. He worked quickly, roughing out the shape and placing the pattern across the top. By the time the children woke, wanting food, he knew he could have the third box finished yet tonight.

Sean came in from the fields before dark; Maggie's brother had been quieter than usual since her death and

John feared he was thinking of a way to suggest that John and the children move elsewhere. Already, Sean had hinted that John would do well to look for another wife. John washed the children's faces and set the table neatly, the way Maggie used to do. Mrs. Mulligan had sent her grown daughter over this morning with a stewed chicken and some potatoes prepared with a seasoning unfamiliar to John. But it tasted good. He laid out the meal for Sean, as if he were now the wife waiting on the farmer.

"Feast of Beltane starts tomorrow," Sean said. "The baron sent word that we've two days off." He seemed in a good mood as he told John he planned to visit the marketplace and to watch the performers on the common.

"I'll be at my usual market spot, hoping for good sales of my wares. There are three boxes finished now—perhaps they will sell as a set. If that happens I can add to the food supply, even some delicacies."

Sean nodded and grunted approval at the quality of tonight's meal. He reached into his pocket. "Say, I found these out in the dirt. These past few days the plow has been turning them up. Maybe you can use them somehow." He dropped a handful of small stones on the table—they appeared to have some color to them but it was hard to tell under the crusty, dried dirt.

Eager to get back to his work, John cleared the table and put the children to bed. He dropped the handful of stones into a bowl of water, hoping to clean them without too much extra labor. He already had an idea for them.

The next morning he rose early and loaded the cart. He had completed the third box during the late hours last night and now he checked to be sure the finish had dried.

Mrs. Mulligan's daughter had offered—a bit too eagerly—to watch the children all day. Maybe Sean was right about a wife; a man couldn't very well manage four children and conduct business at the same time. Kate Mulligan was not an attractive girl but that wasn't the important point right now. He resolved to think about it later.

In town, the market square was bustling with activity earlier than usual. He parked his cart and gave a shout to Tyrel when he spotted his friend.

"I want to show you something," he said.

He pulled out a small cloth pouch and dumped out the stones. Clean, it turned out they did have a bit of color to them, mostly red, green and blue. He picked up one of the wooden boxes and held a stone to the top of it, letting it rest in the low center where the quilted design formed an X. He placed more stones, selecting colors randomly, placing them in the crisscrosses on the box.

"What do you think?" he asked Tyrel. "Is there a way to stick them on as decoration?"

"Oh sure. I've seen such things done with small metal prongs that grip the stone. First, you'll want the stones polished and shaped."

John thought about how that might be done, especially on such a small scale.

"I know a man," Tyrel said. "Let me take a few of them."

"Take them all. They're no use to me in this bag."

The morning started with good-sized crowds, but it seemed everyone was there for the entertainment, and although several people commented to John over the set of unusual boxes he had no buyers. Two different women had asked whether they could purchase only one box, but

John decided it was early yet—he would try to hold out for selling them as a set. Even to himself he didn't admit to the nagging thought that the good and evil needed to remain together, to balance one another. He had no idea whether the third box would have any such traits and, if so, which direction it might go.

Tyrel was waiting for John when he arrived at the market the next morning. He held out his hand. John couldn't believe these were the same stones. Each was nicely rounded now and the colors showed through much more vividly. Tyrel pulled a bit of metal wire from his pocket.

"This is how we'll attach them," he said. "Show me that box again."

With a few taps of his small hammer, he set four prongs into the wood and then gently bent them to grip the stone.

"I can do it more efficiently at my shop, where I can heat the metal to make it easier to work," he said. "If I may take the boxes? I will have them done this afternoon."

John felt a little trepidation. What if one of yesterday's potential buyers came back? He looked at the mounted stone, his eye drawn to the beauty of it, away from the less-than-ideal finish on the wood. He handed over all three boxes to Tyrel and turned his own attention to setting up an attractive display of his other wares.

Tyrel returned shortly after the midday dinner hour, carrying the three boxes in a stack, smiling broadly.

"There were only enough stones for two of them," he said. "But see—I've put them around the sides as well, not only on the top."

Before he had set them down a woman stopped to admire them.

John's moment of pride began to dim as the afternoon

wore on. Heavy clouds had gathered and many of the festival-goers were now out of sight, probably taking to indoor activities as the threatening rain began to fall in a drizzle. He adjusted the tarpaulin to protect his wares but the effect was that they did not display nearly so well. He debated about leaving as his formerly ebullient mood dimmed to irritability. Topping it off, he spotted the old woman known only as Moira, the one whom half the town believed to be a witch.

She approached and stooped to pick up one of the carved boxes. Her unkempt gray hair fell like a veil across her face. His temper flared.

"Out of here, witch!" he yelled. "You'll not be touchin' my work."

She looked up and gave him a steady stare, laying the spread fingers of both hands over the tops of the three boxes.

"Out!" he yelled again.

She stood slowly, looked straight into his eyes and began to speak. Her voice was low, a nearly musical tone. "Carver, you know not the depth of the power you hold here."

With that, she slowly turned and walked away, vanishing around a corner. John felt the hair rise on his neck. What had she done? How could she know about the powers of the boxes unless she somehow had access to it?

"That's an odd one, ain't she?" A man's voice startled John. "Moira. Some says she's a witch, but I don't believe it. Witch hunters has been to her place, ready to haul her out and put her to the stake more'n once. She's never there and they say she uses magic to get away."

The stranger lowered his voice. "My wife says it ain't so. She's cleaned the woman's house before. Says there's a false back in the cupboard. Whenever Moira knows they're comin' she jumps in there and hides. Laughs at 'em when they're gone."

The man laughed raucously and John forced a smile. What he said might be true, about Moira hiding, but it didn't explain how she knew that the boxes had special powers. John endured a friendly fist to his shoulder as the man walked away, cackling over his story.

The rain increased to a torrent and a violent crack of lightning sent horizontal fingers of light sizzling above the stone buildings surrounding the market square. Then—as suddenly—it stopped. John had the eerie feeling he had just received a message of some kind.

* * *

Torches illuminated the market stalls as night fell. Puddles from the afternoon rain had largely dissipated, the water soaking into the ground, what part of it hadn't been absorbed into people's shoes and clothing. Vendors threw straw on the muddy earth to encourage longer stays at their booths and John was no exception. Tomorrow being the final day of the celebration, people realized they had to make their purchases soon.

John prayed that no one other than the man who'd told the silly story about Moira had witnessed the witch's visit. No matter whether it was true or not, in the superstitious minds of the Irish an item being touched by a witch would forever carry bad luck. John could only hope the man had not spread the tale. Still, the incident had only further solidified his plan to be rid of all three boxes.

He polished the boxes with a cloth, stacking them to

suggest their attractiveness as a set. Many of the citizens paused and looked at them, but when he quoted the price for the three they walked on. He looked anxiously at the size of the crowd; it was dissipating now as the evening grew later and those with youngsters began to leave.

"How much for this one?" said a man with an English accent.

John had never held any fondness for the English, but a buyer was a buyer. The man wore common clothing but his garments were in neat repair and not unduly worn. His beard was trimmed and he had most of his teeth. John quoted a price one-third the amount he had been asking for the set, allowing just enough hesitation into his voice to let the man know he might bargain with him.

"Eight pence?"

"I could go to seven," John said, wishing he didn't sound so eager. It was Virtu, the box with the healing power, although it was the least attractive of the lot.

The Englishman set it down and touched the third box. "And this one?" The one of unknown power. He had carved the name Manichee, meaning the middle path, inside the lid of this one.

"Eight, as well."

The man debated and his show of interest attracted another man to stop. John recognized this one as the local bishop, known for his penny-pinching ways. He didn't want the bishop to witness as he sold one of the boxes cheaply or the churchman would insist upon getting an even better deal for himself—in the name of God, of course.

The Englishman had picked up the first box again. "Seven it is," he said, reaching into his sleeve and coming up with a small pouch. He counted out the coins and took the box called Virtu.

The bishop remained, examining the two remaining boxes closely, muttering something about a good size for storage of candles. While he debated, a man of obvious wealth approached. He wore clothes of fine cloth and an ornamental chain of gold across his vest. The merchant class, John thought, they always showed off a bit more than others.

"Ah, what interesting wood carvings," the wealthy merchant said heartily. "My wife loves this sort of thing and I'm in need of a gift when I return home. Although I think the stones make nice ornamentation, she prefers a plainer look. I'll take that one."

He pointed to the box called Manichee and asked John to wrap it in a piece of cloth for travel. Leaving his servant to handle the transaction, he sauntered on to the next vendor. When John finished the matter, he noticed that the bishop's interest had quickened.

"Last one," he told the man. "It won't be here long."

The bishop eyed a woman who was walking toward them at a clip. "All right. Seven pence?"

"Eight."

The woman was only a few feet away. The bishop grumbled and pulled out his purse. He counted out eight pence as if God were nearly out of money and the extra cost would starve some angel in heaven. John ignored the attitude and thanked the bishop for the purchase. Surely the Church would not be affected by the negative power of Facinor.

As the robed man walked away, John stared around the marketplace. The Englishman was strolling toward the narrow street that led to the docks; the wealthy merchant was browsing bolts of cloth across the way, his servant laden with his purchases; the bishop had tucked the remaining jeweled box into his robe and was making his way toward the high doors of the church.

What would become of the three boxes? John Carver wondered. Perhaps more importantly, what would happen to the people who came in contact with them? Would the pieces continue to have the power to heal or deny healing? Would they remain nearby or, as with the one in the hands of the merchant, end up in a foreign land?

The voice of a woman wanting to purchase some wooden spoons only drew his partial attention. His gaze grew distant as he contemplated the future.

Chapter 2

Flames Dance

Sophia Vermejo polished the surface of an ornate wood cabinet, keeping one ear toward the adjoining room, attuned to her father's work. Young Simón Borega squirmed in his chair during his sittings, so greatly that it was all Abran Vermejo could do to keep his subject posed in the stiff ruffled collar and small, scratchy suit, much less mix the paints and adjust for the changing light.

The rooms assigned to them at the large Borega home in Sevilla were not ideal for the task, but they were provided gratis in deference to the artist's reputation. In return, Sophia performed tasks of light housekeeping.

"All right," said the voice of Abran from the next room. "A respite for you, lad. Until tomorrow."

Sophia heard the door to the hallway close, followed by a long sigh from her father. She peered into the long room that had been converted to a temporary art studio. Abran had set aside his palette and was standing at the side table where dozens of small bottles contained the pigments and oils he used to mix his paints. She loved the smell of his work area.

"Children! Why did I ever agree to accept this commission?" he fumed, as he reached for the cadmium yellow.

"Because we needed the money," Sophia reminded gently. *And because living under the roof of one of the city's most reputable families offers some degree of protection.* The arch in her eyebrow as she met her father's stare conveyed the meaning; it was a subject of which they dared not speak.

"Don't worry, Papá. You've finished three of them already. Simón is only a normal little boy for his age."

She swore that a low growl came from her father's throat.

He picked up a palette knife and deposited a large swath of umber on the palette, smearing it with yellow and small touches of blue and red, blending until he had the shade he wanted. He set to work, filling the background around the outline of the child's feet and legs. The face was looking quite good and details of hands and clothing would come later, in the moments when he could get the squirmy eight-year-old to be still.

"I love your new style of painting, Papá." Sophia stood behind his left shoulder, watching the adept brush strokes. "The details in the face remind me of that Italian, Botticelli. Remember when we saw his work on display?"

"Ah, if only I were painting important pieces. They say Botticelli is currently working on depictions of the Graces and Venus. Instead … family portraits for me."

Sophia stretched an arm around his shoulder. "Your work is beautiful and I will not have you listen to anyone who says otherwise."

Abran winced. "I must stop for the day. My body aches. Perhaps tonight you could prepare one of your warm soups for our supper?"

"For you, Papá, of course." She kissed his cheek. "Put your things away and go up to your room. I've three more rooms to clean on this hall and I shall be along after your nap."

She watched as he began to pick up his brushes but realized that she must move along to her own duties. *La señora's* small sitting room looked tidy enough, Sophia decided, and she moved to the next. Señora Borega's bedchamber was cool and quiet this time of day with the family typically away from the house. Soon, however, they would return from their day's activities and the lady would be ready for a short rest before dressing for dinner. Sophia left the door to the corridor standing open as she set about neatening the items on the dressing table and wiping at near-invisible flecks of dust with her cloth. She'd never lived amid such cleanliness, always barely staying ahead of the clutter in a man's art studio.

Her father had cared for her the best he knew how and her mother was barely a memory. Girls her age had married and now had their own families. Sophia didn't suppose she would ever marry. None of the young men in their old *barrio* showed an interest in the girl whose time was spent trailing along in the wake of an artist. When commissions were scarce, they moved back to their Toledo neighborhood where moneylenders carried on as secretively as possible under the watchful eye of the Church, and rumors kept everyone running scared. Sophia had hinted to her father that he should work a bit slower here in Sevilla, extending their time under the roof of such an influential family where protection was implied more than actual. If Torquemada's men wanted to question you, they did—no matter where you lived.

She arranged *la señora's* perfumes on the dressing table and turned to the wide armoire which housed the collection of dresses that never failed to astound Sophia—fine linen chemises, over-gowns of fabrics such as silk with their hanging sleeves and bejeweled belts as ornamentation. Sophia opened the double doors on the cupboard and stared, more conscious than ever of her own brown homespun-cloth dress, apron and cap. If she were more adept at the household arts, she would probably have made a bit of lace or sewn a decorative design on her cap, but if she were more adept she would also probably have a husband by now. She sighed and flicked the exotic long feather duster across the shoulders of the garments.

An item on the shelf above the elaborate dresses caught her eye. A box, carved in a simple pattern of crisscrossing diagonal lines. Almost on its own, her hand reached for it.

The piece looked old and almost certainly had not originated in Spain. The style was nothing familiar to Sophia, even among the variety of artistic styles to which she'd been exposed in all her twenty years. The thought of an object that had come from another land excited her. An image came to her of the box inside a cabin on a ship, one with a round window and a table covered with intricate maps and unfamiliar instruments of brass. An odd, tingling feeling passed through her hands and up her arms.

"Sophia? What are you doing?"

The voice of Maria Borega startled her and Sophia almost dropped the box as she spun around.

"I am so sorry, señora. I meant no—"

"Let me see what you have there." The voice was not unkind.

Sophia held the box forth.

"Oh, this." Maria Borega handed it back and turned away, pulling the lace mantilla from her head.

"I was only dusting it—I shall put it exactly where I found it," Sophia said, reaching for the shelf.

"Would you like to have it, Sophia? As your own?" She crossed to the dresser and removed her earrings.

"Oh, señora, I ... I couldn't . . ."

"Certainly you may. If I wish to give it to you, it is my privilege."

"Oh! I didn't mean—"

"Sophia, it's all right." The mistress, who was probably only a few years older than Sophia herself, smiled indulgently. "I wish for you to have it. I think we have more in common than you would guess."

Sophia stumbled through a hasty *gracias*, practically bowing as she backed out of the room, leaving the lady alone. A maid gave her a hard look as she began the ascent to the third floor. Sophia met her gaze. She might only be the unmarried daughter of an artist, but she was still a step above an indentured maid.

She tapped very softly at her father's door, then opened it. Abran snored softly from his bed, and Sophia closed the door quietly. In her own room, adjacent to his, she set the box on her bed. Each of these windowless, cell-like rooms contained only a narrow bed, a small table, a candlestick and a row of rough nails upon which to hang clothing. Nothing was private or sacred here. She lit her candle and sat on the bed, pulling her shawl more snugly around her shoulders to ward off the persistent chill.

A tap sounded at her bedroom door. "Time for prayers," said a female voice. This happened often, whenever one of the local priests showed up to hear confessions and pray with the family in their home. And, Sophia suspected, to manage an invitation for dinner. Unfortunately, the religious ceremony was not optional.

On the other side of the wall she heard her father stir in response to the knock at his door. Ever since the decree by King Ferdinand and Queen Isabella, Abran had grumbled quietly about the enforcement of these customs which felt so foreign to them. Gone were their Seders and holy days such as Rosh Hashanah; the family menorah was buried beneath the floor of their home in far-off Toledo. For Jews in Spain, the choices nowadays were to leave, to convert or to be subject to the Inquisition, with the great likelihood of being put to death.

* * *

Father Benedict sensed something secretive about that young woman, the daughter of the current artist in residence at the Borega home. He took his duties at the cathedral quite seriously, and that included not only looking after the spiritual condition of his flock but also keeping a diligent eye out for those who would seek to blaspheme or denigrate the sanctity of the one true faith. The Holy Father was correct—and reinforced by the King himself—

Jews and Muslims had no place here.

He peered out through the lashes of his closed eyes, gauging the mood of the family and their staff while the words of prayer came out by rote. Did the girl seem restless and inattentive? And her father—was that a hint of derision on his face? They didn't *look* like Jews or Muslims, but one never knew.

Already Maria Borega had insisted that he stay after the prayers, to share some wine with the family and partake of the evening's repast. He would remain observant of these newcomers. It was, after all, his duty to report to the head Inquisitor if he noticed suspicious activity anywhere in the city. He gave the final blessing and the bowed heads looked up.

Señora Borega rose first, followed by the three children who were old enough to attend prayers. The baby must be off with its nursemaid, elsewhere in the house.

"Mamá, mamá . . ." Young Simón was tugging at his mother's sleeve.

Benedict waited to see what discipline might be inflicted for such rudeness, but the woman allowed their conversation to be interrupted as she turned to her son.

"Can Father Benedict see the painting?" the child begged.

"We should ask Señor Vermejo. Perhaps later." She turned her attention back to the priest.

From the corner of his eye, he could see that the boy had approached the artist, posing his question once again.

"The paint is wet," the artist responded, looking toward *la señora* to help him out of the predicament.

"Oh, we shall not move it," she replied with an indulgent

smile. "Let's take Father Benedict up to the studio—for a quick look before dinner."

"It isn't finish—" But Abran Vermejo's words were lost in the bustle as eight people took to the stairway.

A more famous artist would never stand for such disregard, the priest thought as he followed behind the mistress of the house and her exuberant child. He'd heard of the temperamental dispositions of the great ones, the stories of men who stormed from a room or slashed a canvas when their wishes were not followed. Clearly, this one was not a successful man.

The room set aside for the portraits was at the end of a second corridor, a former drawing room chosen, no doubt, for the fact that two large windows faced north. In the last of the daylight outside, the high spires of the cathedral glowed with golden light.

"See? It's me," the young lad was saying to his mother as he pointed to the canvas on the artist's easel.

Maria Borega patted his blond curls indulgently. The two daughters, ten-year-old twins, shared a quick glance. Señor Borega seemed distracted, no doubt by thoughts of the mistress he kept in another part of the city. Father Benedict prided himself on his keen observational skills.

He admired the half-done painting for an appropriate length of time. The details on the child's face were quite good, especially the way in which the curls of blond hair were depicted in exacting detail. No doubt the man would impart the same elements to the clothing and background. If Vermejo had been a young artist, beginning a career, he might become well known.

"We have already commissioned a frame for the portrait

of the girls," Maria was saying. "Once the individual portraits are finished, our maestro here has agreed to paint one of the family as a group."

"Ah, how nice." Benedict turned toward the thin old man to offer congratulations.

The artist, he noticed, seemed nervous, eyes darting between the painting on the easel and the clutter of materials on his nearby work table. The young woman—the artist's daughter—she also seemed particularly edgy this evening. Perhaps they were simply worried that one of the children might touch the paints.

Benedict's gaze fell to the tabletop. Bottles, brushes, a jar of liquid with two brush handles protruding from the top, a carved wooden box. His breath caught.

The box. He had seen a very similar one.

A year ago. Holy Week. Here in this city. As the pious gathered for the solemn procession depicting Christ's passion, a band of *gitanos* had begun loud singing, that discordant wail so horribly Muslim in its tone. The very thing that Pope and King and Church had worked so diligently to eradicate, the gypsy sounds and dances that were abhorrent to civilized life. Father Benedict had stood among the Church leaders on the steps of the cathedral, with a view over the heads of the parishioners.

There they had gathered, merely one street away. The women with their wild, loose hair which they refused to wear tucked inside a cap or wimple, the bright colors of their clothing, the unshaven men in peasant garb. They were rowdy at the best of times, but in that place—it was sacrilege to show up during those holiest of days! He had turned to Bishop Andreas and saw that his superior's face was livid, his jaw clenched tight.

No one in the crowd had moved yet, although a few heads had turned toward the source of the tribal sounds. Andreas nudged Benedict with his elbow and the two of them slipped into the quiet of the cathedral.

At the altar, candles cast a soft glow and incense gave the air a hint of saffron. In another hour, when four thousand people crowded inside, it would serve its true purpose, keeping the odor of that many humans under control.

Quickly, the two men hurried down the south aisle, slipped into the transept and made their way through the sacristy and chancel to a door which led outside. Out of sight of the gathering out front and the watchful eyes of the palace across the square, they followed an alleyway to the street where the gypsies' celebration had become no quieter.

At the center of the gypsy crowd a man and woman danced (together!) with suggestive looks in their eyes and much swishing of skirts that showed the woman's calves from time to time.

"Stop this!" Bishop Andreas ordered. "Stop this immediately! I hereby order each of you to appear before the Tribunal of the Holy Office of the Inquisition."

The male dancer did a final flourish with his arms and stepped forward insolently. "You have nothing to say to us, priest. We do not live by your laws."

"You live by the laws of the land, as decreed by King Ferdinand himself!"

An old woman with strands of white in her dark hair stepped forward, fixing the two clergymen with a steady scowl. In her hands was a wooden box, carved with diagonal lines. Small, colored stones blinked with an unnatural light as the woman gripped the box.

"I see a murky aura surrounding each of you." Her

voice was low and ominous.

The gypsies had gone dead silent.

"There is a cloud of deep red ... it obscures your face. You, sir, in the white robes of pretension. You have evil motives. The people shall *not* be bound by you and your ways!"

With that, she flung a hand toward the two holy men. Benedict felt as if her hand had actually touched him, had heaved him backward violently. He lost his balance and sat down hard on the cobbled street. The old woman, in a swirl of skirts, turned and vanished down a narrow pathway. In under a minute, the rest of them were gone.

His chest pounded, the sound of rushing air filled his ears.

He looked around to discover Bishop Andreas lying on the ground, as well, his face a gray-white contortion of pain, his hands clutching at the front of his robes.

"Eminence, what is it?" Benedict cried as he scrambled to the bishop's side.

"My chest—I cannot breathe," came the choked reply.

"Lie still. I will fetch help."

But the bishop's color began to improve and he was finally able to catch his breath. He stood and the two men made their way back to the cathedral in time for mass. By that same evening Andreas was pretending nothing had really happened.

Now, dimly aware of movement around him, Father Benedict reached out to touch the box on the artist's table. Could it be the same one the old gypsy woman had used to curse him? It had no colored stones on it.

The young woman's hand scooped the box from the table. "It's only—my father's valuable pigments—"

Benedict couldn't recall that he had ever heard the girl speak a single word until now.

"Where did you get that box?" he demanded.

Her face went a shade whiter. "It ... it was a gift—"

"I gave her the box." Maria Borega stood in the doorway, a firm expression on her face. "She may do anything with it that she wishes."

Benedict willed away his scowl.

"And now, dinner is served," Maria announced brightly.

Benedict gave the girl a hard stare before turning to his hostess with a frozen smile.

* * *

Sophia sat through the dinner, responding with gay laughter when Maria made a joke, managing to slide her gaze past the priest's chair with her lids lowered when someone at the other end of the table spoke. Papá seemed more tired than usual, after the interruption of his nap this afternoon, and she used that as an excuse to finally make their escape.

At the second-floor landing, she whispered to Abran that she wanted to check their studio, to be sure the children had touched nothing after the earlier visit. They parted at the narrow stairs to the third floor, he climbing that final flight, she taking a lighted candle from the hall table and walking the length of the corridor.

The north-facing windows were black squares of night against the whitewashed walls of the room. Shadows bounced from corner to corner, revealing elongated shapes from the standing easel, the jar of paintbrushes, the high wooden back of the chair where the portrait subjects sat. It occurred to her that someone walking the street below might find the movement of light odd this time of night, so she made her movements purposeful and quick.

The carved box sat among Abran's art supplies, exactly as she had left it—to her relief. She scooped it up and tucked it into the folds of her shawl, holding it to her side with an elbow so that she could maneuver the candle as naturally as possible with the other hand. She had no intention of stopping to talk with anyone but one never knew, in a household this size, who might be in the halls at any moment.

After checking to see that her father had a pitcher of water for washing and a fresh candle at his bedside, she closed the door to her own room. A lock would have made her feel more secure but there were none, as far as she knew, for any of the bedrooms. Certainly not the small cells here in the servant quarters. She sat on her bed, positioning the blanket so she could quickly flip an edge of it over the box if someone opened the door.

With the box on her lap, she raised the lid. It appeared that some letters had been carved along the edge of the lid, but they were old and worn now and she couldn't make them out. The first few letters might have been M-A-N-I but she realized futilely that had she recognized all the letters she could not read the word; girls were educated in cooking and sewing, not in useless skills they would never need. Boys who might enter the priesthood—they were the ones who might learn academic skills. A picture of the cold Father Benedict popped into her head. Asking him to take another look at the box was the last thing she would ever do. She'd seen his level of interest in the object.

Her hands had lost their chill, she realized, and she placed them on the carved top, spreading her fingers and closing her eyes to accept the welcome warmth. When she opened her eyes once more, a quick glimpse came to her, a vision of the box with small colored stones mounted within the pattern. She blinked. The surface was plain again.

Her hands were growing almost hot and the surface of the box now glowed with a brightness that had not been there before. Sophia raised the lid again and looked into the empty compartment. Light flashed, sudden and vivid, tentacles of lightning striking a tree. She gasped.

The lid closed with a small clatter. Had she cried out? Had anyone heard?

But no sound came from outside her room.

What *was* this strange artifact?

She stared nervously at the door. The one thing she understood instinctively was that she could tell no one of this experience. Not even Maria Borega, who might have, herself, seen these same things. For one thing was certain, in this city, in this time, anyone could report her to the Inquisition for any reason. Not fully embracing their new religion was one thing; being accused of witchcraft—that was even worse.

She blew out the single candle, curled her body around the box and pulled the blanket over her. Only after an eon of time, while sleep eluded her, did she remember that she had not even changed into her nightdress.

Sounds of the kitchen servants moving about the halls signaled the beginning of the new day. Sophia stretched, fretting over how to protect the box. She mouthed the words to a prayer from childhood; the action brought back the words of their old rabbi, now long gone. Worrying a problem does not solve it.

Exhausted, she pulled herself out of bed and dipped

frigid water from the bowl, washing her face, making herself more alert. The wise rabbi was right, of course. Her night thoughts had added only a little clarity. Surely Señora Borega had not experienced anything mystical about the box; she would not have so casually given it away if that were the case. In some way, however, the priest knew more about it than he had voiced the night before. The way he looked at the box—there on the art table—that was pure greed. If he concocted a reason to search Sophia's room, there was no safe hiding place.

Nor could she carry it with her at all times, awkwardly trying to tidy the rooms and dust the furniture with the object tucked under one arm.

In the end she decided the safest way might be to use it exactly as she had claimed, to store her father's most valuable pigments and keep the box with his art things. The Boregas would stand up to the priest if he tried to disrupt the artist at his work. She carried the box to the studio and picked up the chunks of lapis and cinnabar. During the day her father would let no one bother it; at night she would find ways to bring it to her room and keep it safe.

For three days the plan worked. Each evening Sophia carried the box to her room where she opened the lid to be sure no one had disturbed it. Each time, a new picture revealed itself to her. The first time it had been a porthole window in the cabin of a sailing vessel. Then she saw a man dressed in the quality robes of a wealthy merchant; he was handing the box to a beautiful woman who sat at a dressing table filled with trinkets and jewelry. The woman gazed at the box until the man left the room, then she set it aside and turned back to arranging combs in her light yellow hair.

The next night Sophia saw the box inside a palace formed of many buildings in concentric squares, a place with blue roofs that tilted upward at the corners. Women with pale, smooth skin and dark eyes that appeared half shut wore garments made of long pieces of brightly colored silk that they wrapped elaborately around themselves. Soft-spoken male servants lived among these quiet women who, it seemed, all belonged to one man. This emperor spent very little time with the young woman who held the box to her chest at night. In another scene this woman had apparently died, a male servant handed the carved box off to a trader and told him to take it far away from the forbidden city. Sophia tried to imagine where in the world that might be.

The next time, Sophia saw the box inside an elaborate white marble hall. The dark eyes of the women in this place were rimmed with black and each lady had a dot of red centered on her forehead. The carved box held spices of some sort. For a tiny moment Sophia caught the scent of them, foreign and exotic. Someone carried the box to a cooking area where an old woman in white took small pinches of the spice and sprinkled it into a flat pan that bubbled with some sort of sauce.

After that, Sophia observed a dusty city where camels roamed the streets, then a crowded bazaar with men in turbans arguing loudly over the prices of everything from cloth to vegetables. The box had become the object of one such discussion. After that, it sat in a tea shop in Venice. Sophia recognized the city from a description one of Abran's artist friends had given—a magical place of canals and palaces and narrow alleys and many bridges, and the boats! Oh, the boats! She came to treasure those few minutes before she fell asleep each night with the box resting snugly against her, a time when she felt as if she were in another world.

* * *

Abran was stroking tiny lines of nearly white paint onto the yellow curls of Simón Borega's youthful image when Sophia edged quietly into the studio.

"I'm out of linseed oil," her father said, not taking his eyes or his brush from the canvas. "Please stop in at Madrigo's shop this morning and get some."

Sophia thought of the four bedrooms in which the beds were still unmade, changes of clothing left lying about. Certainly Maria Borega would want those attended to before Sophia went out on errands. On the other hand, her father could not continue his work beyond a certain point without the linseed oil. She could dash to the shop quickly and return to her housework within the hour.

A stiff breeze fluttered her skirts as she stepped into the narrow street. The trees had begun to leaf out and a few blossoms showed tentatively on the large oleander bush at the corner. Spring. Nervous weather, to match the unsettled minds of the populace. Only last week she had overheard two women speaking in whispers in the market square. A neighbor had been called before the Inquisition, along with his entire family, and none had been seen at home since that day. When anyone spoke of it, images came to mind of dank, black prison cells somewhere. In other cities, rumor had it that people had been burned at the stake. Sophia turned her eyes downward now as she passed two priests who seemed deep in conversation.

Madrigo's shop was only three blocks farther. Her steps quickened.

The old man who ran the shop was nowhere in sight but his daughter came from an inner room at the sound of the small bell on the door. Although they were close in age, Sophia didn't know her and they transacted their business hastily and with a minimum of conversation. It was sad, Sophia reflected as she thanked the woman and walked out, that everyone was so wary these days. But to discuss anything other than the weather was fraught with danger. Even admiring the dress of a passing stranger might somehow be interpreted as sympathizing with one of the forbidden religions. You never knew who might pass along your comments and how they might be received. Best to stay uninvolved.

Just beyond the art store the air from a bake shop carried the heavenly scents of yeast and honey, pulling for Sophia's attention. She had brought two coins from home, for the linseed oil, but the woman reminded her that the Boregas had an account for the use of the artist. Sophia made a quick decision and stepped into the bakery.

"Two of the honey covered buns, please," she said to the old woman who was kneading dough on a work table.

With her purchases wrapped in a piece of cloth and placed into her bag, she felt suddenly lighter of heart. Instead of retracing her route home, she decided to take an alternate way back to the Borega home. A change of scene and a sweet treat to go along with their afternoon tea would cheer both herself and her father.

She turned into an unfamiliar lane, sensing that it would circle back in the right direction. Ahead, she could hear the cheerful shouts of children.

Rounding a curve, she saw four boys in colorful shirts running and shrieking in delight. *Roma*, she thought. Gypsies. The boy who appeared the eldest ran from the others then spun quickly, taunting them with something he held above his head. A smaller one, probably no more than three years of age, ran at him and at the moment the older boy turned, the little one crashed into him, lost his footing and fell hard. Sophia could nearly hear the crack of his little head against the cobbles.

The boy lay inert on the ground, like an old rag.

"Oh, no," she said, rushing toward them.

One of the other boys ran away. Two others stood transfixed at the sight.

Sophia dropped her bag and reached out to touch the small white face, pale against the black of his hair, but at that moment a woman came forward. Crying out, she gathered the child into her arms. She began to scream something in another language and adults of the community appeared, almost as if they were coming from nooks and crannies throughout the neighborhood.

"Magda! Magda!" Several of them took up the cry.

Sophia looked about in confusion. Within moments an elderly gypsy woman appeared. In her hands was a box. Sophia's eyes widened. It was a twin of the carved wooden box given to her by Maria Borega, except that this one had colored stones mounted in the crevices where each diagonal line formed an X shape. The stones were glowing brilliantly and the surface of the box—just as hers did—warmed to a golden glow.

Sophia stepped back. The mother of the unconscious boy looked up at the old one with a tenuous smile of hope.

"Magda, can you—?"

The white-haired woman pushed the black shawl off her head and gripped the box with both hands as she knelt beside the pair. Setting the box down, she rubbed her hands together quickly and then placed them on both sides of the child's head. She closed her eyes; her lips moved with silent words. The boy stirred and his eyes opened. He grew restless in his mother's arms and pushed against her to sit up.

The other gypsies gathered around, blocking Sophia's view. A couple of them cast suspicious glances toward her. She smiled encouragement to them and picked up her bag.

"I am happy that the boy feels better," she said as she passed.

The scene ran through her head all the way home. The Church taught that miracles were possible, usually performed by holy men or innocent children. Had she witnessed such a miracle?

* * *

Father Benedict stepped from the shadow of a cypress tree, facing the clan of heathens.

"Give me that box," he ordered holding out his hand.

Like roaches in the light, the *Romas* scattered and vanished into the labyrinth of alleys and doorways. Benedict started to give chase but the infidels were light and quick. Rather than admit that his lumbering size was a hindrance, he turned toward the cathedral as if that had been his intent all along. Bishop Andreas would want to hear about this.

He found the man alone in the cloisters.

"I must speak with you privately," Benedict said, fully aware that a normal tone of voice could carry in unimaginable ways through these stone passageways and arches.

Andreas tilted his head toward the door leading to his study. He closed the door behind them and indicated that Benedict should take the plain chair against the wall. The bishop circled the heavy table he used as a desk and sat in his own ornately carved chair.

"I witnessed an extraordinary event, only moments ago," the priest began. He detailed the story, relishing the look on the bishop's face as he spoke of the wooden box.

"They are practicing witchcraft, of course," Benedict said in conclusion.

"Yes ... yes, they must be questioned on that subject." The bishop's eyes met his. "But questions will not bring me what I desire."

The priest nodded. The two men had discussed the wooden box that he had discovered in the possession of the artist, Abran Vermejo. Stories circulated, and the rumors of a powerful artifact were not unknown to them.

"The woman was present, the daughter of the artist."

"And she performed this ... this deed?"

"I do not know if she had a hand in it. When I came to the place, she was standing at one side. An old gypsy woman had her hands on the box. She touched the child and uttered the words."

"So ... perhaps the two of them are in it together." The bishop ran a fingernail along the edge of his lower lip.

Benedict didn't believe this to be the case but there was no advantage to being right if it entailed an argument with a superior. He merely shrugged.

"I want that artifact." Andreas's eyes glittered at the

prospect of the miracles he could claim with all of that power at hand. Performing the royal edict would be done with effortless ease and he would take credit for ridding the kingdom of crypto-Jews and dirty, thieving *Romas*.

Andreas pulled a soft leather pouch from the deep pocket of his robe, loosed the thin leather strip that held it closed, and reached inside. Removing a dozen gold coins, he handed them to Benedict.

"Do whatever is required," he said. "Purchase the box or purchase the information, I care not. I want it before the end of this day."

The priest almost withdrew his hand before the coins could touch him. Suddenly, he felt much less sure of his knowledge.

Andreas had slipped the money pouch out of sight and he stood now.

"When the clock tower strikes midnight, that is when I shall expect to have the item."

Outside, the wind had become stronger, whipping around corners and sending a draft under his robe. Benedict gathered the coarse brown fabric closer and pulled the cowl over his head. The gold coins felt burdensome in the pocket. He turned a corner where the chill wind did not reach. On this side of the high stone walls the sun shone high in the afternoon sky. He paused a moment, fighting back the uneasy seed that the bishop's words had planted in his gut.

His eyes scanned the gardens and nearby streets. No sign of any gypsy anywhere. With a nervous glance over his shoulder at the clock tower he started walking.

At the small square where the children had earlier

played, where the old woman had healed the injured one, he paused. The area was eerily quiet. Not a face showed at a window, not an open door in sight. He could begin knocking on doors but these were wily people, able to sneak through small openings like mice. None would turn on a member of the tribe and they would offer assistance to each other in escaping. He glared at the surrounding buildings, wishing ill to any who harbored there.

Hours later, he had trudged every alleyway of the entire barrio; his head felt as if it would burst. Where would he find that box?

Wait a moment, he thought. Call it witchcraft or a miracle, no matter—the bishop had not witnessed the event. Only Benedict, among the Church hierarchy, had seen the old woman and the box. He had been charged with one mission—bring the box.

He set off in the direction of the Borega family home.

* * *

Sophia's thoughts ran in a tumble as she walked hastily home. There were *two* boxes, almost identical in appearance, both with mystical powers. So far, with hers, she had only seen visions that appeared to be scenes from other places and times—perhaps a minute peek into the history of the box itself. But what if it could perform miracles of the type she had now witnessed?

She had a brief glimpse of a life as a healer. No more would she spend her days uselessly brushing the dust off someone's furniture or cleaning messy paintbrushes while her father worked at his life's calling.

Perhaps I have found my own calling. The thought quickened her pulse as she turned onto Calle del Solano and made her way toward the Borega house.

From the dining room she could hear the lively sounds of a meal in progress, one that included visitors by the sound of it. She edged to the stairs and ascended quietly. In the studio her father seemed agitated.

"Where were you, girl?" He gestured toward the half-finished painting.

"A child was injured. I stopped to see if I could help." She reached into her bag and took out the linseed oil, setting it on the table. The carved box sat exactly where she had left it.

He made a scoffing sound and busied himself with his brushes.

"I brought you a treat." She unwrapped the cloth with the honey-coated bread inside. "Let me go to the kitchen and get some soup for you."

He eyed the bun but did not stop working turpentine into the delicate bristles.

"You've made good progress today, Papá. Stop for some food and a rest."

He sighed. "My shoulder aches. Worse each day, I am afraid."

Her gaze fell to the box.

"Go to your room, Papá. I shall ask the kitchen girl to bring the soup and then I will stop in and rub the painful area for you."

At last, a small smile. He set the brush down. Sophia guided him by the elbow, out of the studio and toward the stairs. After a quick trip to the kitchen, she came back to the studio.

She closed her eyes and remembered the old gypsy

woman, how she had held the other box. The woman had murmured some words, something Sophia could not understand. If that was a critical part of the treatment, her actions now might have no effect. But it was worth the attempt. She held the box with both hands, fingers splayed, concentrating on the sensation of warmth that traveled through them and upward along her arms. She carried it up the back stairs, her hands becoming almost fiery hot by the time she reached Abran's bedroom.

"Papá, show me where it hurts."

When she applied her hands to the muscles along his neck and shoulder, he moaned quietly. His eyes closed as she applied slight pressure and moved over the aching places.

"My Sophia," Abran said, "you are such a kind girl. I feel so much better I shall go back to my work."

She stared at her own hands. How could this be? No time at all and he felt well enough to go to work? She thought of the young boy who had been unconscious one minute and sitting up the next. She nearly laughed out loud. The things she could do with this power! The numerous people she could help!

A tap sounded at the door. "All right, Papá, but eat your soup first."

She admitted the kitchen maid. The girl placed her tray on Abran's bedside table.

"What's this?" Sophia asked, noticing a bandage on the girl's hand.

"Carelessness. I'm sorry ma'am."

"Don't be sorry. Tell me what happened."

"My hand touched the large kettle over the fire. Cook insisted that I put this cloth over it."

"Let me take a look."

As her father sipped the hot broth from the bowl, Sophia unwound the cloth, which looked none too clean, revealing an inflamed spot the size of a coin. The servant winced and turned her head away from the sight.

Sophia tentatively touched the area around the wound and saw the redness fade before her eyes. She laid the palm of her hand softly over the spot; when she raised it the circle was just faintly pink. Her breath caught and the maid looked at her.

"It doesn't seem too bad." Sophia forced the quiver out of her voice, afraid of showing her excitement.

The young maid stared at her hand, then looked up. Sophia smiled, like a mother who had kissed away her child's small scratch. All better. The girl's face was full of gratitude as she left the room.

"What did you do just then?" Abran whispered once the door had closed. His eyes were sharp.

"It was not so serious a wound as the girl thought."

"And my shoulder? Did I only *imagine* the pain that has wracked me for weeks?" He held up a hand. "I am only cautioning you, my dear. Do not speak of this, and be very careful as to who might observe. Your acts of kindness could easily be taken the wrong way in these treacherous times."

* * *

Father Benedict lifted the heavy metal knocker and dropped it for the third time. The sound echoed through the Borega house like a rock bouncing off the walls of a dry well. No response came. The sun was now low in the sky, throwing gray shadows over the streets and homes.

He needed to get inside and make a pretense to visit the studio of the artist. Bishop Andreas wanted the box that had performed the miraculous healing of the gypsy child, but the bishop had not seen the box. From the brief description he'd given, Benedict felt sure this other box would serve the purpose. When the bishop failed to perform a miracle with it, the explanation would simply be that the bishop was a holy man—he could never perform such an act of witchcraft. The box's very benign nature would be clarification enough.

Over the city, bells from the cathedral tower rang out, calling the faithful to vespers. There was the reason— the entire family, plus servants and guests, would be in attendance. Benedict turned away from the door. He made quick steps toward the high spires that rose above the other nearby buildings.

Inside the cool, dim interior sounds of the liturgy and the parishioners' responses echoed from the massive central pillars and surrounding stone walls. He took a place near the font of holy water, scanning the altar area for a sign of the bishop. He caught sight of white robes but at this distance could not be certain that it was Andreas. He would prefer not to cross the other man's path until he had implemented his plan. Fewer questions that way.

The final prayer ended and Benedict made his way to the tall, carved doors through which the parishioners would pass as they left. He smiled benignly at each family, taking note that Miguel and Maria Borega were walking slowly through the nave and would soon reach the doors. He edged slightly to the right, making sure that among the several clergy he would be the one to speak with them.

"Good evening Señor, Señora," he said, making eye

contact and giving his most practiced, benevolent smile.

"We've not seen you in our home in several days," Maria said. "A small supper will be prepared by the time we arrive. Would you care to join us?"

The conversation was almost an exact replica of the one they exchanged each fortnight. He filled his dialogue in the scene with a gracious acceptance. Miguel Borega gave a small salute as he donned his soft hat and Maria preened a little as others around them noticed the favorable attention bestowed upon their family.

An hour later, Benedict arrived once more at their front door and this time was escorted into the large hall and offered wine. He sipped it, surreptitiously eyeing the staircase and considering what pretense he might use to wander into the artist's studio on the second floor.

Outside, the tower clock chimed eleven.

The meal took far longer than he would have liked. He observed the various household members—the children who were sent to bed early, the artist who seemed distracted for some reason, the man's daughter who spooned up small pieces of fruit and studiously avoided talking to him. He kept up a lively discourse, telling stories on some of the parishioners who had participated in the recent *Semana Santa* observations, how the man charged with carrying the crucifix along the parade route had nearly dropped it. The tale drew polite laughter, nothing more.

Twice, someone else at the table had excused himself in the delicate manner that suggested he was visiting the outdoor privy. It seemed as good a reason as any to go away alone for a few minutes. He said the appropriate words and left the dining hall, turning in the direction he had seen others take. Once out of sight of the doorway, he slipped up the stairs and took quiet steps along the wooden floor. If he remembered correctly, the studio was the third door at the right. A cautious peek—yes. Moonlight streamed in through the windows where no one had closed the shutters yet. He let his eyes adjust to the gray-toned interior until he could make out objects on the man's work table. The box sat near some jars of ground pigments.

The clock struck once, a signal of the half hour. He visualized the bishop's face as he had ordered Benedict to meet him at midnight. He must hurry—carefully.

He picked up the box and something inside it rattled as it shifted. Lifting the lid, he saw small lumps of rock. Carrying those along would not do; the slightest sound would give away the fact that he'd hidden something inside his robe. He turned the box to its side, letting the rocks slide onto the table top.

Out in the corridor he heard footsteps. With the stealth of a cat he tucked the box into one of the inner folds of his robe. The steps passed by the studio and a door down the hall opened and closed.

He eased the studio door open and peered both directions into the corridor. No one in sight. He edged out and hurried toward the stairs. He had been gone too long already.

Voices rose from the large hall below and he had almost reached the stairs.

"Father Benedict?" It was Miguel Borega and the man obviously wondered how the priest had gone so far off the track to his stated goal.

"Ah, Señor, I so admired this tapestry at the top of the stairs. I had to come up to examine it more closely."

Maria Borega appeared at her husband's side. "It has been in our family for six generations," she said with a smile.

"It is lovely," Benedict said, descending the stairs and sending up a small prayer of hope that the shape of the box was not visible under his robe. He offered quick goodbyes, saying that he was needed at the monastery for midnight prayers. It wasn't until he stepped out into the fresh air and walked around a corner from the Borega home that he breathed slightly easier.

The cathedral came into sight as the bells chimed their first long, full note. Then came a second. Benedict gripped the box through the fabric of his robe and began to run. Two blocks to go.

Two more chimes.

He dashed into the nave, looked around for the bishop but saw only a handful of priests and novices in prayer near the front.

Another chime.

He quickly passed down the side aisle and exited by the door to the cloisters. Three more chimes had sounded.

The covered walkway had never seemed so long but soon he was within sight of the bishop's door. He tapped on it as the twelfth bell rang.

"I am glad you did not disappoint me," said Andreas as Benedict fumbled through the pouch of the robe and withdrew the box.

* * *

Sophia knew, the moment she walked into her father's studio, that the items on the table had been touched. The box—it was missing. A cry rose in her throat.

She lit two more candles and pawed through the items on the table. The lumps of pigment stone lay in a pile. All of Abran's other supplies seemed to be in place. Had her father taken it to one of their bedrooms? She extinguished the extra candles and rushed up the narrow steps to the third floor. A light showed under her father's door and she knocked before entering.

"No, *hija*, I have not seen it," he said, drying his face at the washbasin. "I did not return to the studio after dinner."

Dinner. The priest had excused himself shortly before everyone else left the table. Had he come upstairs? Sophia had passed through the great hall as the man was leaving and she distinctly remembered that his hands were empty as she bade goodnight to the Boregas. Tomorrow as she cleaned the rooms she would conduct a search, but she couldn't let go of the feeling that the priest had somehow stolen it.

She fell asleep against a pillow damp with tears of frustration, her dream of using the box's power to help others and to alleviate pain for them now dashed.

Gray dawn showed at the studio windows when Sophia made her way there after a restless night. She had clung to the half-hope that she had somehow been mistaken, but she could tell at a glance that the box was truly gone. The hours crawled as the household slowly rose and began to go about their day. By the time she began to tidy the rooms she found herself tired from the effort of staying awake.

Neither Miguel's nor Maria's bedchambers held any new items, as far as Sophia could tell, and although she looked especially carefully among the children's things she had not really expected to find it there either. She went downstairs, offering to organize the cupboards in the dining room and in the great hall. The señora had gone out but the housekeeper seemed happy enough to have help from an unexpected source. The woman was dressed in the cloak she always wore on market days and she disappeared almost immediately.

Sophia gave the furniture a cursory dusting, focusing instead on any cabinet with space where the box might have been hidden. It was a hopeless quest almost from the start. The items in the dining room were familiar to her—candlesticks, vases and serving dishes used on an almost daily basis. The great hall contained everyday items as well.

The Boregas, she realized, were successful but not wealthy to the point of owning a lot of silly fripperies. She shoved a heavy wool blanket toward its place in a tall armoire but it didn't seem to fit as it had before. She pulled the blanket out, deciding to refold it and try again. When her hand hit the rear of the cupboard, it resonated with a hollow sound. She stopped dead. Hidden compartments almost never meant anything good.

With a glance in each direction to be sure she was not being observed, she ran her fingertips around the back panel of the armoire. On the left edge of it, something loosened. The panel came away, revealing a space behind it, a place about four inches deep and the full width of the cabinet. But more startling than the fact the space existed was what it contained—a golden menorah, some candles and a parchment scroll.

Sophia knew she had discovered a very dangerous secret. She carefully slipped the wooden panel back in place and laid the refolded blanket on the shelf exactly as she had found it.

She found her father in the studio and suggested that

they take a walk. Young Simón Borega wiggled off the chair where he posed and gave a wide smile as Abran agreed to dismiss him for the day.

"A walk? We do not often do such together, you and I," he said as he cleaned his brushes. "Ah, it is market day. Perhaps you have something in mind you would like to purchase?"

"It's not that, papá." She picked up his cloak and draped it over his shoulders, steering him toward the door.

Outside, spring had returned giving them the perfect excuse for a walk along the river and away from the market crowds.

"Did you know the Boregas are Jewish?" she asked after telling him of the hidden items she had found.

He shook his head. "They are *conversos*, as are many in this land now."

"But their Spanish names . . ."

"As are ours," he reminded. "Changing my name from Abraham was not for my pleasure, *hija*, it was for my survival."

It was true. Since the banishment of all Jews and Muslims who did not convert to Catholicism, the stories had become more frightening. Raids and arrests in one's home, immediate imprisonment until trial, a trial that sometimes did not happen for many months. And after the trials—being burned at the stake was not an uncommon sentence.

Two young men walked toward them on the path and Abran squeezed Sophia's arm, warning her to silence until they passed.

"Do not speak of this," he hissed through clenched teeth. "Do not so much as entertain the thoughts. Anyone—

any person at all—can make an accusation and we will find ourselves before the Inquisitor. Perhaps even Torquemada himself."

"Surely we can trust the Boregas."

"No more than they can trust us. You have no idea what a person will say under torture. Husbands have been known to give up their wives, mothers their own children." He turned to look behind, in case someone might have come upon them. The pathway was clear. "Erase these thoughts from your head. Now!"

"But—"

"Once I finish the portraits, we shall find a way to leave. Perhaps get out of Spain to the north, over the mountains into France. But until then, I will not be paid except in small increments. We shall need all of our resources in order to make a journey of that length."

Sophia considered this. It was more important than ever, she believed, to get the box back. With its power they would have a much better chance of safe passage, and with its power she could enter a new land with a skill that could help people. At a large copse of fig trees they turned and walked back toward the city center. Sophia forced herself to amble at the pace her father set, although in her heart and mind she wanted to race back, to confront the priest and demand the return of the box.

Those thoughts turned to horror as they saw a cloud of smoke from the center of the city. Nearing the market square they caught the stench of burning flesh and she realized with revulsion that the flames danced around tall stakes set in the ground, consuming the clothing of some poor man and woman.

* * *

Father Benedict smelled the bishop before he saw the man. An odor of foul smoke wafted into the library where the priest was meticulously drawing illuminations for a new biblical codex. He looked up from his work when a shadow darkened the open doorway. His nose must have wrinkled because the bishop spoke before Benedict said anything.

"Crypto-Jews. They were caught secretly reading the Talmud. And after renouncing that blasphemy and being baptized!"

Andreas came close to the table. "This box?"

"Yes, eminence, I brought it back, as you asked."

The bishop eyed the object suspiciously. "Did you not describe it as having brilliant stones on it? This one is not the same."

Benedict felt his facial muscles freeze. He had not remembered mentioning the stones.

"Can this one perform miracles also?" Andreas snatched the box and held it up, examining all of its sides. He raised the lid and peered inside. "What are these traces of color?"

"I—I don't know—"

Before he could think of a response, the bishop had turned toward the open door. He gripped the box with both hands, raising it toward the sun.

"Those gypsies have tricked you, but I am not so easily fooled. I shall find them and they shall pay." He stepped out into the garden courtyard, lowered the box and looked inside it again. In a moment he spoke. "I can see them!"

Benedict had followed him outside. "What do you mean, 'see' them?"

The bishop's eyes glowed. "I see that clan, the lot of

them, living down in the *barrio negrito*. The women in their scandalous clothing, children running like wild creatures. Heathens!"

He held the box out before him and began walking, as if following a compass. Benedict trailed along.

The two men wound their way through twisting streets and narrow alleys, the neighborhoods changing as they left the church properties, then the upper-class merchants' homes, then the small *tiendas* of the working class, finally passing through a low gateway to what had previously been the Jewish quarter before that group had been driven out and the itinerant sorts had moved in.

Four women with long, wild hair were sitting on short stools beside a stone wall, peeling oranges into a bowl. Nearby, several children ran and whooped. Benedict recognized one dark-haired boy as the one who had been healed by the old woman. As if a silent whistle had sounded through the group, they all looked up at the two clergymen. One woman shouted a single word.

The fruit bowl went flying—a flash of skirts, mothers grabbing at the hands of their children—and the gypsies scattered.

Andreas shoved the wooden box into Benedict's hands and gave chase. Only one little boy was not quite so quick— the others got away. Andreas closed his fingers around the child's arm and yanked him to a halt.

"Where are your parents?" he demanded.

The boy's eyes were as wide as the full moon.

"Where! You must tell me!"

In a flash, the child's fear switched to defiance. His small mouth hardened.

The bishop spun the boy around, grabbing both arms

and lifting the lad from the ground. "Tell me! Where are they?"

The boy's bladder let go and a yellow stream hit the cobbles, splashing the bishop's soft leather shoes. He let out an invective and threw the child against the stone wall. The little one was stunned for only a moment before he scrambled to his feet and ducked into a tiny passageway, dragging one leg.

"Andreas! Did you need to injure him? Our Lord said—"

"Shut up!" The bishop stared at his ruined shoes, then spun and stomped back toward the cathedral.

Benedict trailed at a distance, a rushing sound in his ears, a sick feeling in his stomach. Had it really come to this? The effort to bring all citizens into the Church—and now people were being chased in the streets, forced to hide and to lie. Children being harmed by a man of God. He halted and stared down at the box in his hands. This was not right.

He began to formulate a plan. There were two boxes. He felt a new resolve as he resumed walking.

At the monastery, several people were gathered outside the bishop's office. Among them, Benedict recognized Rodrigo Garcia, a successful merchant who had been most generous in his gifts to the Church. The man was shouting, his face livid. It took only a moment to realize that Rodrigo and his wife had been nearby when the incident happened with the child. An archbishop was listening intently. Benedict veered toward the sleeping quarters, seeking the sanctuary of his own small room.

Inside, he dropped the box on his thin mattress and fell to his knees. *Help me*, he prayed. *Help me to right these wrongs.* When he opened his eyes his gaze fell to the box. He took it between his hands and thumbed the lid open. A scene appeared, a moving tableau that showed the barrio where he and the bishop had been a short time ago. A door, once painted blue but now faded and chipped ... a narrow set of stone steps inside ... a room with primitive cooking facilities and a single loaf of bread ... another wooden box. The one with the stones attached to it. The box sat on a shelf. He knew somehow that it was the one the gypsy woman had used to heal.

Could it be that one box bestowed powers for good, the other for evil? Benedict had witnessed the bishop perform an evil act after staring into this box, the one he held now, and yet he felt no malice in his heart as he looked at it. Perhaps each box took on the personality and intentions of the holder. The one thing he did know—they held too much power to be out there in the hands of people who could wield it unthinkingly. He needed to obtain the other box and then he needed to destroy them both.

Someone tapped at his door. Hastily, he threw a blanket over the box.

"I am leaving for Rome in the morning," Andreas said without preamble. He closed the door behind him and lowered his voice. "We will not speak of today's events, you and I. Where is that carved box?"

"I do not know." He shifted so that his robes blocked a view of the bed. *God forgive me for the lie.*

"What? Do you mean that you left it behind?"

"I suppose so. I do not remember." *And for the second one.*

The bishop seemed agitated but he went away. Benedict remained in his cell-like room through supper and evening prayers, into the dark hours of the night when the monastery and cathedral became silent. Then he made his way quietly through the streets.

* * *

Sophia stood in darkness at the top of the stairs, listening to the soft voices below. A caller had arrived minutes earlier and Miguel stood talking with him. It was Rodrigo Garcia, a friend whose family socialized with the Boregas. Without revealing her presence, she caught only scattered words. Enough to know that the danger was closer than ever to this home. Apparently Garcia had done something today which now had the Inquisitioners looking into his business contacts and friends. Miguel said something about planning a holiday with the family.

"Do not tell me where you are going," said the other man. "Go very quietly."

It was the first Sophia had heard of a vacation. The portraits were not finished. Everyone, it seemed, was running scared. She tiptoed back to the third floor.

"Papá, we must go," she whispered when they were alone in his bedroom. She explained the overheard conversation but did not mention her certainty that the priest had taken the carved box the previous day. The less said about the artifact, the better.

"I believe evidence is being gathered against us and against the Boregas. They will be unable to protect us."

"But we have no money," he protested. "I've not been paid for my work. How will we travel? Where will we live?"

"It will be all right. I am not sure how, but it will."

He nodded. An artist's livelihood was uncertain in the best of times.

"We can go back to Toledo," he suggested.

She shook her head. "Not yet. The Inquisition is as

active there, if not more so. It may be some time before we can return to our home."

He seemed befuddled.

"Papá, let us go quietly to your studio. On the pretense that we are cleaning and organizing your materials, choose only those things you must have. We can probably walk out with my shopping bag, but it cannot appear that we are moving away."

His eyes darted back and forth as he considered this, his forehead wrinkling and his chin quivering.

"Papá, be strong for me." Yet, somehow, she knew that it was she who would need to be strong for both of them. Wherever they stopped, perhaps in France, perhaps across the sea somewhere, she could find a midwife to apprentice herself to. She could learn the healing arts and find a way to support them.

The cathedral bells chimed midnight as they left the Borega house, keeping to the shadows as they made their way toward the edge of the city.

* * *

Father Benedict felt breathless as he closed his door and leaned against it. Two of the gypsy men had spotted him leaving their neighborhood. Attempting to outrun or outwit them in the maze of unfamiliar alleyways where they lived would have been foolhardy. He'd relied on his robes—both to conceal the stolen box and to bluster his way through with the voice of religious authority. They had trailed him nearly all the way to the cathedral.

He shoved the box with the colored stones on it under

his bed, next to the other one, and moved his small trunk of possessions in front of them. Now, to find an implement he could use.

A team of builders had been working for months on a new porch for the rectory. Surely there would be a heavy stone at the site. He wound his way through the cloisters, into the nave and out a side door near the narthex. As expected, a pile of cut stones waited for the crew to arrive at daylight. He bent to pick up one, only to discover that the blocks weighed far too much. He looked for a smaller one.

At last he found one he could lift—and it would certainly do a fine job of smashing the wooden boxes—but if anyone were to see him struggling with the burden or to hear him carrying out the task in his room, there would be no sensible explanation. He should have brought the boxes to this location.

Retracing his steps, he retrieved the boxes and returned. Side by side on the ground, they looked benign enough. One could never guess the power that came from them. He picked up his chosen chunk of stone and managed to raise it to the height of his chest.

"What are you doing?"

The shout made his heart thud.

Bishop Andreas rushed across the moonlit work area, his white robe making him appear like a frantic bird. He stubbed his toe and let out an oath.

"Where did you get those boxes?" he demanded as he came within a few yards.

Benedict's instinct was to set his stone down and answer politely, with proper deference. But the bishop's earlier action against the little dark-haired child came back to him, flashing in an ugly scene before him. He held the stone high, maintaining eye contact with the bishop.

"Do not do this!" Andreas was no more than three feet away now.

It was a direct order and yet Benedict knew in his heart that he could not obey it. He dropped the stone.

One wood splinter zipped by his cheek, opening a small gash. Andreas made an undignified dive at the boxes, one of which had apparently only been grazed along one edge by the heavy stone. The bishop scooped the object into his arms and rolled aside while Benedict stared in mute dismay.

The second box had survived intact. The priest reached for the stone once more. It was imperative that he strike another blow, that he destroy at least one of these repugnant objects.

Before his fingers touched the rough rock, something slammed into him. Andreas had cast aside the rescued box and was now out to save the second one. In a moment of clarity Benedict wondered what an observer would think; two holy men tussling on the ground like children fighting over a toy.

His head struck something hard on the ground. An incredible stab of pain went through him. His teeth ground together and his vision went black.

| *|* *|*

Beneath the solid walls of St. Peter's Basilica, winding under the various buildings of the Vatican, run a series of catacombs and tunnels. The man in white robes carried his parcel with the reverence he had been told it deserved.

Velvet wrappings cushioned the item and cords were tied in such a manner as to prevent tampering—sealed with wax in each place they came together, a holy seal pressed into the wax.

As explained to him, the unseen object had made its way across the south of Spain, through the waters of the Mediterranean, and into Rome under holy edict from Bishop Andreas himself. Two men had died in the course of its journey. This man did not want to become the third.

He and his two-person entourage located the designated storage place, set the rectangular object inside, and moved a stone in front of it, as prescribed. With a stick of charcoal he made a small symbolic mark on the stone. Only one more step, then his duty would be complete.

Chapter 3

OSM

The man in the brown robe paused at the corner of Via dei Corridori. Ahead lay the shapes of the clustered buildings of the Basilica di San Pietro, marked by the distinctive obelisk rising above them into the evening sky. A chill wind fluttered his robes and moved scraps of ragged cloud across the face of the waning gibbous moon.

He paused, looked around and, not seeing anyone, turned the corner quickly and entered a narrow stone building beside the piazza. Down a short set of steps he came to a small chamber lit by three candles. Four men waited there—a monsignor, two archbishops and a cardinal. No names were exchanged; all were familiar to each other by reputation and position.

In front of the cardinal, at the head of the table, sat

a cloth-wrapped parcel tied with cords which were sealed with wax. When Father Benedict took his seat their leader broke the wax seals, pulled back the velvet wrapping and revealed a carved wooden box with a dull brown finish and small colored stones mounted on it.

"I retrieved this from its hiding place. It is time for us to decide what to do."

"Only the one box?"

"It is all that remains."

"But I saw two—" The priest paused, the truth dawning. Andreas took this one, apparently making good on his oath to see that it came to a secure place. But the second box? God alone could know where it was now. Andreas may have kept it for himself. Benedict had never forgotten the glitter of raw greed in the older man's eyes.

For the benefit of the three younger men, the leader asked Father Benedict to repeat the story of the events of more than ten years ago.

"It was in Spain, Sevilla to be exact. A band of gypsies was seen practicing unholy acts of magic and witchcraft using this box. At the same time, I discovered another of very similar design. I feared that both boxes might be used in service of the devil's power. I meant to destroy both boxes but our Bishop Andreas convinced me otherwise." *By knocking me to the ground.* "This box survived a blow from a heavy stone building block."

The men around the table exchanged furtive glances.

"In hindsight, I believe his decision was correct. If shattered, small scraps of wood from these artifacts might have been used as talismen by those with evil in their hearts." He touched his cheek where the splinter that struck him had festered and left a scar. "It was best that the box come here to be locked away and protected by holy men of knowledge and purity."

"And the second box?" asked one of the archbishops.

Benedict shrugged. "I fell, losing consciousness. When I awoke it was gone."

More shuffling in their seats. Benedict briefly wondered who in this room, other than himself, knew more than he was saying.

The cardinal spoke up: "It is the opinion of those in high places within the Church that no good can come from the use of such artifacts. It is our mandate to gather and destroy them."

Benedict took a risk in speaking. "We must be cautious of the powers of the box. This one should have been smashed into a thousand pieces by the stone that I cast upon it, yet no harm came to it."

A rustle of robes, a flicker of the candles.

"Perhaps the boxes are linked in some way. The power of one cannot be destroyed because it is receiving help from the other?" suggested another of the men.

"That idea sounds dangerously pagan in itself," cautioned the leader.

"I only meant, Holiness, that somehow with *God's* help the boxes are linked. As twins, as two halves of a whole."

The leader pushed back the sleeves of his cloak, his expression thoughtful. "Perhaps."

"We must place this one back into its hiding place until we locate the other," suggested the monsignor at the opposite end of the table. "When we have both, we can bring them out and place a holy edict upon them declaring that their destruction is, in itself, the divine will of God."

The leader nodded. "A wise idea."

The man beside Benedict shifted in his chair. So far, he had not spoken. "And how are we to locate the others?"

"The *one* other," Benedict corrected.

"There are stories of a third box," the man insisted.

Startled silence. Even the leader had nothing to say. After a few moments' quiet the men became restive.

Their leader sensed he would lose control unless he proposed an idea. "We will begin with the mission of locating Bishop Andreas. Even though he has left Rome, Vatican records will show where he went. We shall locate the box which he last possessed. Andreas may have knowledge of the third."

"Andreas is dead. Whereabouts of the other two boxes are unknown," stated the quiet one.

"How do you know this?" Benedict demanded.

The quiet man fixed him with a hard stare that caused the priest's skin to itch. "Accept it as fact."

The leader cleared his throat. "In that case, we shall begin at the beginning. It is imperative that we control the power of these artifacts of mystery, that they not be allowed into the hands of the populace. Great destruction would ensue."

Devastation to the Church itself, Benedict thought. He kept his mouth shut.

"Begin at the beginning?" the man on the cardinal's left scoffed. "When there was only the heaven and the earth?"

The leader saw the meeting quickly spiraling out of his control. He slapped his hand against the table's polished top. "I mean—we must go about this with a plan. We shall, this night, form an organization with the sole purpose of locating and confiscating any article of a mystical nature, any item that might be used for the proliferation of ideas outside the beliefs of the one and true Church, as decreed by the Holy Father."

Heads nodded. This mission fell well within the undertaking of the Inquisition. There would be no question that their motives were the purest, their objective of the highest calling.

Their leader saw his advantage increase. "We shall call the organization the *Officii Studendi potest Mystici*, although we will not in fact *study* mystical objects but will keep them out of the hands of those who would practice any method of healing, conjuring, or seeing which does not conform to our teachings. We are saving these souls from condemnation," he added.

The outspoken monsignor brought up a point. "These artifacts are small—they could have been easily transported—perhaps out of the country, to some other nation."

"The reach of the Church knows no national boundaries. It is God's will that we pursue these abominations wherever they are. I would commission each of you to establish offices of our organization elsewhere. We must be capable of exerting a long reach."

"Since the time when Ferdinand and Isabella combined their two nations, there has been talk of Spain sending explorers to establish new trade routes. A man named Columbus is working to secure funding for such a voyage. We must accept the fact that Europe will no longer be the only place for God's work."

"Yes. I am aware of this," said the cardinal with an impatient wave of his hand. "Already, the Church is making great plans to spread the word of God to new lands. If—Lord help us—these boxes should be carried outside of Europe, then our offices must also extend to every corner of the world."

The holy man's words resonated, the mood lightened, and excited chatter erupted as ideas flowed. Bells from the nearby basilica began to chime, reminding them that the hour was very late.

As they rose from their chairs the leader cautioned, "Go one by one. It is best that no one, even in this holy part of the city, realize that we are meeting. I myself, shall secure the artifact in a new, safer location. Secrecy must be our watchword."

Benedict walked up the steps, the last to leave. At the end of the street he watched their leader turn a corner. On impulse he hurried forward and followed the one man who would know where the carved box was to be hidden.

Chapter 4

Ships Sail

Frigid rainwater poured from the edge of a parapet, striking Rodrigo del Fuentes on his head, trailing down the back of his neck and the inside of his shirt.

Damn this country, he thought, ducking away from the deluge. *Curses upon the rain and the wet and the mud.* A picture of his faraway homeland, with sunny dry hills and olive trees and clean white buildings flashed through his mind. None of this dull gray stone, the local rock which made up the structures and the roads and the roofs and the shoreline. Brightened only by endless green fields, in the rare moments when the sun came out, Rodrigo could see no reason why his king could possibly be so eager to conquer this soggy place. Spain was, by far, more warm and hospitable. He pressed his back against the rough stones of the city wall, edging along, his only wish to be warm and dry once more but knowing that was a faraway dream—at least until he accomplished his mission.

He'd been in Ireland a mere four days, dropped along the shoreline at the quarter moon by an unnamed sailor who rowed their small dinghy through the glassy sea with the silence of a sleek porpoise. They skirted Galway Bay at low tide and spoke not a word as the sailor indicated the point at which he expected Rodrigo to leap out and slog his way through the remaining few feet of water to the rocky point where he could make landfall without being seen from the nearby watchtowers along the city wall.

"I shall return at the half moon," the sailor had told Rodrigo earlier as they launched from the *Santa Teresa,* which lurked behind a ragged outcrop several miles down the coast. "You will be there, waiting. If not, we sail without you."

"*El Admiral* needs the information I will procure," Rodrigo said.

"He *wants* that information. But he *needs* for the mission to take place at the right time so that we join the armada in time for the invasion. If you fail, we simply go forward without it. Without you."

Rodrigo held his tongue as the dinghy bobbed gently on the waves. What the admiral wanted were maps and diagrams, something only a man who spent time ashore could obtain. Plans for the English fortress and schedules that would inform the Spanish Armada of the opportune time for their planned invasion in the autumn. Privately, he thought it the height of arrogance that the admiral would even consider moving forward with the invasion without the priceless information Rodrigo could deliver. But *el*

admiral was precisely such a man, conceited to the point of—
He stifled the thought. He knew better than to voice his opinion, especially on that particular night in that particular small boat. The sailor was a man who did no more than follow orders: drop this unknown man on the shore, pick him up six nights later. No questions, no opinions.

Now, after scurrying about the walled city for days, poking into corners, stealthily listening to conversations, Rodrigo had a plan. Admittedly, it was a loosely formed plan. He had ascertained the location of the English captain's office, a moderately sized room in one of the main halls of the government building. He'd heard two men discussing maneuvers that would send all but a small contingent of Irish troops away from the fort tomorrow. It would likely be his only chance to get inside; the dinghy was due to come for him on the following night.

He watched the steady splatter of rain on the ground at his feet. The boat's arrival was far from a certainty. There had been no clear night, no smooth sea since his arrival. It would require an act of God to change this weather pattern and no man alive could predict whether that would happen. He tamped down the thought and stared once again at the imposing stone building with its steeply pitched roof.

"Right ugly old thing, ain't it?" The female voice behind Rodrigo startled him.

He whipped around to find a short young woman with vivid blue eyes standing in the rain. Her rough peasant cloak was beaded with moisture and unruly strands of wavy yellow hair poked from beneath her heavy woolen hood. She might have been as young as twelve years, but the work-roughened hand that gripped the edges of her cloak suggested that she was nearer to twenty.

"You got anything to eat on you?" she queried. "A bit of bread?"

His mouth opened in surprise but he closed it and shook his head. He understood enough English to know what she'd asked, but any verbal response would give him away.

"Huh," the girl said. "I'd wager that them inside that fortress ain't goin' hungry."

He gave a sympathetic shrug and moved a few steps away.

She followed. "I'd wager that it's warm and dry in there, too. I'd be willin' to grant a favor or two to the gentleman who could get me a bit of supper and a dry indoor corner for the night." She pulled aside the top of her cloak and revealed a triangle of white flesh above the neckline of her brown homespun dress.

The temptation lasted no more than a moment. Rodrigo had greater concerns, although he had to admit that he was hungry as well, having last risked walking into a public house for a bowl of stew two days ago. But the last thing he needed was this young woman with the garrulous mouth trailing him through the township. He turned his back and walked away from the building.

"All right, then," the woman said, trotting along to match his strides. "Let's take ourselves somewhere else. I know an old woman what raises chickens. They got nests in a little coop. We could wait by until her lamp goes out and grab up a couple of eggs. Not so tasty as when they're cooked but they'll fill your belly."

He walked faster. She apparently took it as a sign that he was eager to go along with her plan. She was practically chasing him now and the speed of their movements would surely attract attention. He stopped and spun toward her.

"*¡Vete! No me molestes!*"

She stared at him, speechless at last. Rodrigo realized his critical error. Perhaps a fatal error. He faltered a moment to come up with the English words.

"Sorry. Sorry. We … we can eat."

He reached into a pocket and drew out the small pouch that still contained a few of the local coins. He held them out, hoping she would snatch them from his hand and disappear like a street urchin.

Her gaze slid up the street and back. No one else was in sight. She gave him a knowing look.

"What's your name?" she asked. "I'm Meggie."

He thrust the coins toward her again.

"C'mon, I'm not likely to turn you in now, am I? I saw you out here earlier. Yesterday too. If I wanted trouble for you, I'd of told them already. I'm thinkin' you need my help as much as I need yours." She studied his face, figuring out that he'd understood only a fraction of what she said.

Rodrigo's eyes flicked toward the fortress, for a mere moment.

"All right, then," said Meggie, pressing his hand closed around the coins and threading her arm through his. "We'll have a meal and talk about this."

To anyone who might have witnessed the exchange it seemed obvious what was going on: a man offered money, a woman took his arm and walked away with him. Rodrigo thought frantically for a way out of the situation but came up with no answers. For now, let the townspeople and the soldiers in that fort think what they may.

They walked around a corner, past a row of solid stone buildings, through an alley, until they were well away from the fortress. Meggie pointed out a wooden door and as they approached, Rodrigo caught the scent of richly stewed meat. His mouth watered.

Meggie handled the conversation, placing an order for two bowls of stew and two pints of stout. The tavern mistress brought their food to the dark corner table they'd located. Meggie had acted as if he were her brother or her friend, and now she picked up her spoon and dug into the food as though she had not eaten in a fortnight. Rodrigo felt himself relax as the stout coursed through him.

Her bowl was empty before Meggie set down her spoon. "So, as I see it, you want something inside that fort and you could use some help."

Her blue eyes were so direct that he couldn't look at them. He stared at his stew.

She reached toward him, touching his hand lightly, speaking so softly he barely heard. "You need something. I can help."

He shrugged, pretending he didn't know what she was talking about.

The direct blue gaze would not go away. Finally, he spoke.

"Why? Why you do this?"

The pub had grown noisy with the midday crowd and Meggie raised her voice slightly, without risk of being overheard.

"My father was shot down by the English." She gestured the firing of a gun. "My brother too. I've no love for them. You come from another country—I don't know where. I don't care. But you're here to take something from the English—am I right?"

He worked to follow her words but caught only the gist of it. He nodded.

Meggie looked down at his empty bowl. "C'mon. We'll figure it out."

She stood and he followed her out of the pub. As they walked he whispered of his goal, to get inside the fort and find the room where the generals planned their strategy. He needed to know where the English sailing fleet was.

"I know which one he is," Meggie said. "The general in charge of the fort."

Her expression hardened and Rodrigo understood. This was the man responsible for killing her father and brother.

* * *

The sky had cleared slightly by the time darkness fell. As the bell in the church tower struck eleven, a watery half moon began to peer through the clouds. Meggie led Rodrigo from the small, abandoned stone cottage where they had stayed away from the prying eyes of the populace and of the soldiers. Anyone seeing them come and go from the place might think it a lengthy tryst, but she did not care. In reality they had spent the afternoon scratching out diagrams with a stick on the dirt floor. The fortress, he told her, consisted of a rectangular stone building, with entrances on each side, guardhouses only on the two longer sides. After midnight, one of those was locked. All ingress and egress had to take place through the one guardhouse facing the main road. Now, they had a plan.

Two lanes away from the fortress they split up, Rodrigo planning to work his way to one of the side doors where, with luck, Meggie would come to let him in. First, however, she had a less-pleasant task ahead of her.

She peered around the corner of a woolen shop and studied the front gate of the fortress. As they'd hoped, two guards provided the extent of the contingent. According to Rodrigo's information the rest of the men, along with most of their leaders, were away on a series of military maneuvers near Dublin. She waited patiently until one of the guards said something to the other and walked away.

She lowered her cloak and let one side of her dress slip off her shoulder. With a sway to her gait she crossed the road and began singing quite loudly, a bawdy pub tune. The middle-aged, paunchy guard's attention became riveted on the young blonde woman who was obviously intoxicated. When she stumbled into him, neither was particularly surprised.

"Hello—where did you come from?" she said with a wink and a slur. She dipped to pick up the end of her fallen shawl, making sure that her breasts were easily visible to him.

He reached to assist with the shawl and she ran a finger down the length of his arm.

"Ooh, a right strong one you are," she said, prodding at his bicep.

He subtly flexed the muscle and sent a stupid grin her way. Men were so easy.

"Say, maybe we could find a little privacy?" she whispered when he leaned in close, ostensibly to drape the shawl over her shoulders.

The guard glanced both directions, but Meggie had already seen to it that the road was clear. There was still no sign of the second guard. The man squeezed her shoulder as he let go of the shawl.

"Sure, luv." He pulled her into the small enclosure that served as a guardhouse.

"Not here," she breathed urgently. "Your friend will come back."

The randy man seemed to at least have enough decorum to want the lady to himself. He lifted the latch on a door at the back of the enclosure and pushed a heavy door inward, into the fortress itself.

"Wait there," he said, pointing to another door across the corridor. "When the other bloke comes back I'll take my break. Ten minutes, no more, I promise."

He gave a final, longing gaze at her almost-exposed breast as he watched her walk into the second room. She backed across the space then blew a kiss across the corridor and smiled to herself as he tugged at his trousers.

The room in which she found herself was apparently the bunk room for the troops who were away. Rows of beds lined the walls. By the sliver of light from the corridor she rummaged through a couple of knapsacks, coming up with only a roughly bound soldier's diary and a few coins in addition to the articles of worn clothing she expected to find. She pocketed the coins, with the fleeting thought that she could run now and avoid more contact with the pudgy guard who had practically slobbered at the prospect of fondling her.

However, if he came back and she was gone he would have no choice but to go looking for her and raise the alarm about a stranger inside the fortress. That would not do. Before she could come up with an alternate plan she heard voices, the guard telling his comrade that he would take a turn at patrolling the corridor. She stepped outside the bunkroom the moment she heard the heavy wood door to the guardhouse close.

"Not here," she whispered. "It's … smelly. Like a hundred unwashed men slept there."

She grabbed his hand before he could protest and pulled him toward the better-lit end of the corridor.

"It'll be a lot more exciting in a nicer place," she said.

The guard seemed at a loss. Clearly, he should be ordering her to stop, threatening to kick her out, but libido had taken over and his stupid smile indicated that he would go along with nearly anything at this point.

"What's this? The general's quarters?" Meggie didn't read well, but she recognized a familiar name on the plaque at the door. "Ooh, I feel meself gettin' all steamy."

Before the guard could protest she pulled him into the room and closed the door behind them. Moonlight coming through two large windows revealed a large desk with a high-backed chair behind it.

"Sit in the chair," she ordered, lifting her skirt. "I love to ride a powerful man."

Where did that come from? She closed her mind to the act itself as the guard unbuttoned his trousers and she faced him. Over his shoulder she could see that the rest of the large office contained a worktable with maps spread out on it. In the dim light she couldn't make out what they were but they seemed something that would be of interest to the Spaniard.

On a shelf beyond the worktable she saw more papers. A carved wooden box sat there, probably too small to contain valuable documents, but Meggie felt attracted to the design. She might as well get something for herself out of this little adventure.

The guard pumped away, taking far longer than she would have expected, but at last he heaved a contented sigh and relaxed against the back of the chair. In an awkward attempt at after-play he mauled her breasts with his hands and planted wet kisses on them.

Meggie stood up and backed away. "Button up, now," she said. "Can't let you get caught in forbidden places."

He didn't catch her meaning until he noticed that she was looking around the important man's office. His eyes widened and he quickly put his clothing back in place.

"There must be a back way out," she whispered. "Quick! Show me!"

He peered out into the corridor before fully opening the door. Grabbing her hand, he pulled her out of the office and closed the door behind them. They headed away from the guardhouse and Meggie could see that the long corridor made a left turn shortly ahead. Immediately after the turn, an alcove revealed another heavy wooden door. The guard reached into his pocket and brought out a heavy key, which he inserted into an ornate metal lock. He gave a twist and pulled the door open.

"Here. Stay to the left and that path leads to another along the quay. Follow that one to the right and you'll be back in town with no one the wiser."

Meggie moved in close, placing her hands on his chest. "I could come back tomorrow."

The man beamed. Obviously he had pleased her. He nodded and moved to kiss her on the mouth.

She teased him with a smile just before he could land the kiss. "Tomorrow. Now go. Before you get in trouble."

She pressed against his shoulders, turning him back toward the corridor. The moment his back was turned she slipped the corner of her shawl into the lock in the doorframe. He pressed the door shut and she heard his footsteps move away. Dropping her shawl on the stone stoop, she hurried away to find Rodrigo.

"Psst!" came a sound from a large shrub at the corner. Meggie slowed, turning to be sure she hadn't been followed. At her low words, Rodrigo emerged.

"Come," she said. "I have the way."

They kept to the shadows and she hurried to the fort's side entrance where her shawl had disabled the locking mechanism.

"Quickly!" Any passerby could notice the garment and alert the soldiers.

Meggie pushed inward on the heavy door, retrieving the cloth, and Rodrigo ducked inside. With quiet steps and hand signals, she showed him to the general's office. While he snatched up the maps and folded them, she checked the contents of the shelves. A heavy bag clanked with the satisfying sound of coins and she peered inside to discover that they were gold. It was probably the payroll for the entire fortress. She wound the strong cloth tightly around them and shoved the bulky packet into the wooden box she had spied earlier. Two treasures!

"Is this box not beautiful?" she asked, holding it up.

Rodrigo had shoved the folded maps into the inner lining of his cloak and was shuffling through papers that littered the general's desk when Meggie heard a sound from the corridor. She hugged the wooden box to her chest and picked up a knife that the commanding officer probably used to remove sealing wax from his correspondence. A hand signal to Rodrigo sent him scurrying to conceal himself beside a large cupboard.

" … no rest for me tonight," a male voice was saying.

A second man responded with a formal, "Yes, Sir." Meggie recognized it as the guard's voice.

The door opened and a tall man with wide shoulders entered. He carried a glowing lantern and his gaze took in the entire room at one glance. He spotted Meggie with the wooden box in her arms.

"Thief! Put that down!" he shouted.

Meggie backed away a step but did not relinquish the box. The general came farther into the room, holding the lantern high for a good look at her. She thought fast but could come up with no options. She would surely be put to the gallows. At this point all she could do would be to help Rodrigo get away. In the corridor, she heard the guard call out to the general, asking if everything was all right.

"Put that down," the general said in a menacing tone. He took another step closer.

Meggie stepped toward the man who'd murdered her father, raised the short knife and brought it across his neck. "Run, Rodrigo! Go!"

Blood gushed from the military man's neck in horrid spurts. Meggie jumped aside and leaped over his fallen body.

"Go, go!" she said to Rodrigo, dropping the knife and reaching for his arm. He stared at her with wide, dark eyes.

She yanked at his sleeve and rushed to the corridor. At the far end, the guard she had seduced stared in their direction, not quite comprehending what he saw. There was not a moment to lose. Meggie, pulling Rodrigo with her, raced for the side door where they'd come in, hearing the guard call out to the other one. By the time they reached the turn, both guards were thundering down the hall toward them.

She fumbled the latch for a moment, forgetting exactly how it operated. Precious seconds flew by but eventually it gave way and Rodrigo yanked the heavy door open. He pinched at her sleeve and guided her to the left, away from the street. Behind them they heard the fortress door slam, a sound that would surely wake the city. Meggie hugged the wooden box to her chest with one hand and gathered her skirts with the other, racing after Rodrigo down toward the quay.

"Run faster!" he called over his shoulder.

She stumbled and dropped the box. In one move, he turned and scooped it up, then pulled her to her feet with his free hand.

"We must hurry. A boat is coming for me," he said, his breath coming in rasps now.

Behind them, a soldier's shout ordered them to stop. Meggie hesitated a fraction of a second, turning to look. The shot caught her in the chest, taking her breath, stopping her heart, throwing her to the cold, muddy ground.

* * *

Rodrigo stood at the rail as the sun appeared at the horizon. The Irish coast, only a pale dark line now, vanished as he stared toward it. The woman, Meggie. She'd given her life for something she didn't even understand, for the precious information needed by Phillip II for the planned invasion of England's kingdom. He remembered her upturned nose, the way she'd teased a hot meal from him, her later sacrifice to help him get into the fortress.

In Rodrigo's memory the events stood out clearly: the bleeding general, the sprint from the fortress, reaching to assist Meggie followed by his own hard-breathing dash down the quay to the spot where—blessedly—the dinghy bobbed at the coastline. He'd fallen, nearly unconscious, into the small boat while the Spanish sailor's powerful shoulders took them past the range of musket fire as the two guards must have rallied additional troops to the chase.

"We are safe now," said a voice at his side. "Go, *descansa.* My cabin is yours for the day."

Rodrigo knew he should rest but the captain's offer would have to wait.

"I hope the maps are useful," he said. "I had no time to look them over, to choose carefully."

The stocky sailing man nodded. "I have seen them— the king will be most pleased. We have only three months to prepare and it is vital that he know where the British reinforcements are stationed. We shall bring this intelligence to him with all haste."

True to his word, all sails on the *Santa Teresa* were fully raised, the wind filling them and moving the galleon at a clip through the waves. At last, Rodrigo allowed himself to go below decks to eat a meal and stretch out on the bunk assigned to him. Beside him, he wrapped the wooden box in his cloak and kept the bundle secure beside his body as sleep overtook him.

The nights ashore in Ireland had taken their toll, for the spy slept through two days and three nights before he awoke to realize that other crew members were snoring away in the bunks around him. He stretched, patted his blanket to be certain that the box of gold coins was safe, and discovered that he was starving. He could make his way quietly to the galley where there would surely be some scrap of bread or perhaps a joint of salted meat left from the evening meal before, but he came to understand that the heavy box would soon become a burden. Was he to carry it to the privy, to each meal, to have it at his side as he walked the decks? And there was no place—other than on his person—where it would not be discovered and preyed upon by the men. His head fell back to the thin mattress and he drifted to sleep thinking of it.

When he woke again, the other bunks were empty and the sounds of heavy footfalls overhead indicated that the crew was already at work. He distributed most of the gold coins throughout the pockets of his garments, placing them carefully so they would not jingle against each other, and went to seek out the captain.

"Ah, Señor del Fuentes, you slept well indeed," said the man when he saw Rodrigo approaching him.

"I did." On their port side, Rodrigo could see the hazy edge of a coastline.

"France," the captain explained. "We dock in Portugal in two days. The Armada is already assembling, I am given to understand. More than one hundred ships."

He gave a sigh and Rodrigo was unsure whether it meant this captain and the *Santa Teresa* were to be included among that number.

"Captain, I meant to ask a favor?" He explained about the wooden box, that he wanted it kept safely somewhere until he could present it to the king. "It contains twelve gold pieces, a contribution to the war effort."

In reality there were more than sixty gold coins but Rodrigo wanted no one other than himself and King Phillip to know this. Temptation ran too strongly among sailors; he dare not let the word get out.

"I shall be happy to secure it in the strong box in my quarters."

Rodrigo handed the box over and watched the other man walk toward his cabin at the stern. It was all he could do to assure the safety of the items he had taken in Ireland. His stomach growled, reminding him that he was long overdue for a meal.

The next two days went smoothly, Rodrigo spending most of the time at leisure as he had no crew duties and knew no one to speak to, other than the captain. Apparently, the story given to the crew was that his position was as an emissary who reported to the king. It was mostly true—a year ago he had been a supply master in Cadiz when the devastating raid by Sir Francis Drake took place and decimated their fleet and their stores. He'd taken the loss so personally that he had volunteered to do whatever it took to help his king defeat the English. Now, he hoped the box of gold coins would redeem him in the monarch's estimation.

The port of Lisbon teemed with life—galleons, galleys, and carracks anchoring out in the harbor, awaiting their supplies. Smaller ships ferried crates out to the massive ones. On shore, throngs of men moved in a hive of activity. Shouts overrode other shouts, commanders organizing their men and readying to sail.

"The fleet is due to leave within the week," said the captain when Rodrigo found him in his quarters, leaning over his table of charts. "I understand that thirty thousand soldiers will join them, to be picked up in The Netherlands."

He rolled two maps together into a tight cylinder and tied a piece of twine around them, then reached into his safe for Rodrigo's wooden box.

"Catch the next transport ashore and deliver these maps. You'll find the king in his temporary headquarters." The shorter man looked up into Rodrigo's eyes. "God be with you."

"And with you, sir." Rodrigo couldn't help wondering what the coming months would bring.

He descended the rope netting at the side of the *Santa Teresa*, took a spot in the bobbing transport boat and stared toward the city as they drew near the shoreline. To Rodrigo's experienced eye, the loading of supplies and munitions followed a logical pattern; he watched muscular men lift the massive wooden crates with rope nets and swing them into the holds of the warships. The chaotic part of the operation was the sheer number of young sailors who appeared somewhat bewildered at their surroundings. So many. During his months in the British Isles, gathering intelligence, Rodrigo had noticed the superior numbers of the English fleet, the readiness of their soldiers. Was this a lost cause for Spain?

He shoved those thoughts aside and spotted a man who appeared to be somewhat higher in rank.

"Headquarters is over there," he replied gruffly to Rodrigo's inquiry. He waved vaguely toward a couple of large stone buildings.

One was clearly a warehouse with large bays and stacks of materiel piled about. The other might house the port master's offices—he couldn't tell for certain. Rodrigo set off in that direction.

Searching out the most important-looking person at each crossroad and at each building led him eventually to a set of offices where uniformed men were bustling about with documents and maps. He clutched his own roll of maps and proceeded.

Raised voices caught his attention. Two men with the bearing of royal equerries stood outside a doorway with their hands clasped behind their backs.

"Farnesio, your concerns are noted but we shall proceed. The costs have been addressed through papal dispensation to levy taxes, the men have received indulgences and are free to sail. The matter is closed."

"But, your majesty, the new commander … with the loss of Álvaro de Bazán?"

"Medina Sedonia is most capable." The monarch's voice grew ominously quiet. "The matter is closed."

A dark-haired man stormed out of the room. Rodrigo recognized the long face and neatly trimmed beard of the Duke of Parma. His face was suffused with repressed rage, however, and the king's two servants, along with everyone else in the corridor, averted their eyes and cleared a pathway for him.

"Next!" came the voice of the king. "And do not bother me with those who wish to make a case in favor of that *woman*. I think not of any Protestant as a relative of my own."

He referred, of course, to Elizabeth, now the queen of England and formerly his own sister-in-law. She had supported the Dutch Revolt against his country, and only last year had sent Sir Francis Drake to decimate the fleet at Cadiz. Her open support of the Protestant cause went against everything the Spanish king believed and reinforced his own determination—at the urging of Pope Sixtus—to send crusades to assure that the entire earth be populated with believers in the Catholic faith. The current rearming of the Armada and planned invasion of English soil was pure retaliation.

Both servants outside the door quaked at the king's tone, and three men who had been waiting suddenly seemed to have other missions elsewhere. One of the servants looked at Rodrigo. "You have the privilege to enter, sir." He asked Rodrigo's name and announced him.

The king was pacing before a tapestry-covered wall when Rodrigo entered, and he came to a halt near a long table. Every portrait Rodrigo had ever seen showed the man in full dress regalia, complete with white hose and shoes, richly embroidered doublet, and stiffly starched ruff at the neck. Today, the king was more simply clad in a plain black jerkin over light grey doublet and black hose. His only ornamentation was a wide livery collar with the coat of arms of his royal order. His short, sand-colored hair and neatly trimmed beard bore threads of gray.

Rodrigo approached with lowered gaze and a respectful bow.

"Hurry up now—what have you here?" King Phillip demanded, holding out a hand.

Rodrigo raised his eyes only to the level of the monarch's chest and offered the rolled maps. "From the intelligence mission to Ireland, your majesty."

The king accepted the maps and placed them on the table beside him, without so much as a glance. "And what is that?" He pointed at the box cradled in Rodrigo's left arm.

"Money for the treasury, your majesty. I confess that I took it on a whim, because I had the opportunity, from the offices of the commandant of the Galway army contingent."

The admission brought a fleeting smile. "Well done."

The monarch reached for the box and Rodrigo held it forward. Brows knitted sharply over the arch of his nose, the king frowned and studied the box before raising the lid. The contents obviously pleased him. He pulled out the bag Meggie had taken, hefted the weight of it, and absently shoved the box back toward Rodrigo. Loosening the bag's drawstrings, he peered inside.

"Very good work, young man. On behalf of the kingdom I accept your gift to the war effort."

The box rested on Rodrigo's outstretched hands.

"I've no interest in that cheap object. Take it away."

Rodrigo felt a pang at the memory of Meggie's delight in the carved box. The simple Irish girl had thought the item beautiful. Obviously, the king already owned much finer things. He tucked it out of sight under his arm.

"That will be all." Phillip dismissed him without a glance and turned to carry the bag of gold to his desk.

Rodrigo backed out of the room and hastily left the building, only to be assaulted once again by the noise and bustle of the thousands of sailors milling about the docks. His liaison officer had promised a short leave of absence if he completed the mission to Ireland and returned alive, and Rodrigo intended to take advantage of that offer. He still had the written orders, carefully sewn into the lining of his shirt so that no matter what happened to him he would not lose the slip of paper.

He thought longingly of Cordoba, that small city where his family still lived a quiet life. Mamá would be baking bread on a morning like this and his little sister, Ermelinda, either playing with her friends or helping in the kitchen. Papá's work inside the new cathedral at the Mezquita would be taking shape as the Church converted the former Spanish center of Islam to a new and beautiful edifice to Christ. A wave of homesickness gripped him and he looked about for a way to get there. All he saw in any direction were miles of sailors and ships, huge piles of supplies standing in readiness to take to the sea.

In the end, he spoke with the driver of a mule cart who had just unloaded a wagonload of fresh oranges and was preparing to leave. The man could give Rodrigo a ride as far as Badajoz. From there he managed rides with an olive merchant, then with two friars from Monesterio, walking the final twenty miles south through green, hilly country where he followed goat trails much of the way until he saw the pillars of the old Roman bridge. His steps quickened as he followed familiar streets. The summer sun warmed him as he had not been warmed since Ireland and the long sea voyage—home!

Mamá shrieked with delight when she saw him from the side yard where she was draping wet clothing over a line. She dropped a white shawl and ran toward him, taking his face between her hands as tears ran down her face.

"Rigo, Rigo! *Mi hijo, Te echaba de menos.*"

"I missed you, too, Mamá." He glanced around. "Where is Ermelinda? And Papá?"

A young woman stepped out from the kitchen, lowering the shawl that covered her hair, revealing a pretty face with high cheekbones and full lips.

"Ermelinda?" He felt his mouth gape.

"Ay, si, our Ermelinda has become woman. You were gone many months, *hijo.*" Mamá gripped his arm as if he might escape before she could get him into the house.

"And I suppose you will eat all our food, now that you have traveled so far," the near-stranger piped up. She gave a petulant grin that he recognized. This was definitely the little sister who had teased him about his appetite since they were small.

"Come, come," Mamá said. "Bring that heavy bundle inside and I will find you some food. Wash your hands first."

Some things never changed.

He went to his old bedroom and dropped the bag that contained only one change of clothing and the wooden box onto his bed. His favorite bow and quiver of arrows stood in the corner still, but there were signs that the family had needed the space for other things as well. His mother's sewing basket rested near the door, along with a bolt of cloth which looked newly woven.

In the kitchen he caught undertones of unease in the conversation between his mother and sister.

"What is it?" he asked, dipping his hands into the water bucket that had stood near the door for as long as he could remember.

Mamá's eyes grew sad.

"It's Papá," Ermelinda said. "There was an accident at the work site in the Mezquita ... a large stone ..." She turned away.

"One of the carved lintels," Mamá said. "It fell and he was pinned."

Rodrigo felt his world fall away. "Papá is dead?"

"Nearly a year ago. *Lo siento*, we had no way to get word to you."

The aroma of the beans and fresh bread suddenly held no appeal. He pushed his way out the door, through the small side yard where the clean laundry flapped much too cheerfully on the line. His head buzzed and his eyes would not focus.

Papá, gone. It was unbelievable. He stumbled down the narrow street, stubbing his toe on a stone that jutted up, reaching out to touch the white walls of nearby shops. Papá. Gone.

In the next lane he caught sight of the spire of the great cathedral above the smaller rooflines. It became his beacon and he headed that direction instinctively. At the steps leading to the wide entry doors he stopped cold. How could God let this happen? He should go inside, light a candle, say prayers for his father's soul, but he could not summon the will to walk through those doors. He turned his back on the building and sank to the steps, sitting with his head in his hands.

Dimly aware of people around him, including a priest who paused briefly to lay a hand on his shoulder, Rodrigo stared across the square. A fountain bubbled and women came to fill jugs with the water; two young boys crossed in front of him and ran down one of the lanes that branched away from this central part of the city; the bell in the church tower chimed, several times; the midday sun beat on his back then passed behind the cathedral. When the priest came outside again and spoke to him, Rodrigo realized he had been there for hours. He should go home and check on Mamá.

Practicality set in as he slowly made his way back over the same streets. How had Mamá and Ermelinda supported themselves all these months? Where did they get food? Who made repairs to the house for them? It hit him that he was now the man of the family.

The kitchen felt stifling when he walked in. A long row

of bread loaves sat on the table and Ermelinda was pulling two more from the oven using a wide wooden paddle. At one end, mama sat with a length of the white cloth he had noticed in his room, stitching two edges of it together.

"Rodrigo," she said. "*Siéntate, debemos hablar.*"

He sat, as instructed. Yes, they should talk.

"We are doing all right," she said. "When you stayed away all afternoon, I knew you would be thinking of Ermelinda and me, but we are all right."

"We sell our bread," his sister said. "I bake enough each day to supply the monastery and that new hostelry on the road to Alameda. Mamá, she sews for the nuns and sometimes for the rich woman whose husband owns the big winery."

"We eat simply and put aside all the coins we can. My son, do not worry about us. You have your duties to the king."

For a moment the image of Phillip II standing in that command center, planning to invade the British Isles, popped into his head. Then he realized that Mamá knew nothing of this conversation, she meant simply that he was still under obligation to his naval commander, at least until he was released from duty. Tomorrow, he would visit the local commandant and request his discharge based on family need.

Ermelinda covered the new loaves with a cloth. "Now, surely you are hungry," she said with an impish grin. "Your beans are still here for you.

This time, when he smelled the food on the plate, he remembered how hungry he'd been earlier. Despite the heavy stone of grief that pressed on his heart, he wolfed down the meal his sister set before him. Darkness was setting in when he stepped out to see his mother taking down the laundry from the line. He noticed one of the hinges on the door seemed loose; he would repair it in the morning. He was glad the women had figured out ways to feed themselves but it was still apparent that they could use a man's touch.

Back in his room he set his bag of belongings on the floor, stripped off his travel-dusty clothing and fell into bed. His body ached with the days of travel but his joy at being home felt dim in comparison to his grief. He fell asleep to the sound of the church bells in the distance.

A shaft of sunlight crossed Rodrigo's bed, waking him to the realization that he'd slept well beyond his usual hour.

He sat up and saw that his dirty clothing was gone and a basin of fresh water waited on the table near the door. He washed then reached into his bag for something to wear. He brought out the carved wooden box wrapped in his light summer cloak. He set it on the bed, wondering why he had bothered to bring the thing along over all these miles. A vision of Meggie's face came to him when he looked at the object. Again, a stab of regret that she had become involved in his mission.

He sat down beside the box, suddenly feeling the weight of his dual grief sapping his energy. He picked up the box and opened the lid, half hoping the king had missed a gold coin or two. Foolish wish—the coins had been in a sack inside the box and the monarch would certainly have noticed any extra.

Inside the lid he noticed, for the first time, some light carving. Letters. V-I-R-T-U. Goodness. Virtue. Why would that be written on the box? He shrugged—*no es importante,* he thought. He tipped the box upside down and shook a few grains of sand onto the floor. Cleaned up a little, it would be a nice gift for Mamá, a place for her to keep her additional sewing supplies. He ran a finger around the inner edges of the box—perhaps with a little sanding …

As his finger traversed the fourth side, completing the circuit, a jolt shocked him. He screamed and dropped the box, jumping away from the bed. What on earth—?

His door opened slightly. "Rigo? Everything is all right?"

"Si, mamá. Sorry—I am not dressed."

The door closed again and he stared at the box on the bed. Edging toward it, almost sneaking up on it, he reached out and gave a tentative touch. Nothing happened. He laid the palm of his right hand on the lid. The wood warmed slightly and the ugly dark brown finish lightened a little. Rodrigo's breath came in quick gasps.

He glanced at the door but it remained firmly closed.

The box sat benignly on the bed.

Rodrigo never took his eyes off the strange object as he picked up his fresh clothing. He slipped his shirt over his head and pulled on workaday pants and jerkin. Running his fingers through his damp hair he neatened it and smoothed his narrow beard. A deep breath.

He sat again on the bed and picked up the box. Carefully raising the lid he saw nothing out of the ordinary. The letters carved into the top were its only inner ornamentation. Taking a look carefully for the first time at the outside of the box, he saw that it had been crudely carved in a pattern of diagonal lines in two directions. At some of the intersections where the design formed an X someone had added small polished stones, held in place by metal prongs. As his hands traced the design, the wood turned lighter in color, and after a few minutes the stones began to brighten as well. He felt his forehead wrinkle as he puzzled over it.

Certainly in artistic objects, mostly held by the Church, he had seen much finer workmanship. But there was something special about this one, something that caused it to react to his touch. He needed to learn more. He could not give this item to his mother until he understood what had just happened. He slipped the box back into his travel bag and finished dressing.

In the kitchen Ermelinda was already at work, kneading a huge mound of dough. A plate with two boiled eggs and fresh fruit waited for him.

"Lazy, as always, *mi hermano*," she teased. "While the women slave away."

He tried for a casual tone as he responded, but his thoughts were already on the day ahead. Finishing his breakfast quickly he walked to the main room of the house, the salon, where he found his mother sewing another garment. At his inquiry she pointed out his father's tool box.

Done with the repair of the kitchen door hinge in a short time, he asked what other little items needed fixing. Both women were happy to supply lists.

Before the sun reached its midday point he had made a new broom handle and replaced a broken one, repaired a leaky bucket, cleaned and moved the outdoor privy, and carried a day's supply of water from the city well at the fountain near the cathedral. Even Ermelinda had to apologize for calling him lazy that morning. His excess energy was becoming noticeable and he took a moment alone in the side yard to wonder at the cause.

Last night he had been so tired he could do no more than drop into bed; now he was buzzing about the place like a half-crazed animal, and still he felt as if he could go all day at this pace. He had to get out, away from the inquisitive eyes of his family.

"*Hijo*, you have been so helpful," his mother said, eyeing the full barrel of water when she walked outside.

He kissed her cheek. "You work too hard, Mamá. I should be here all the time."

Her smile warmed his heart.

"In fact, I am going to my commandant's office today, to request my discharge from service. Our family has need of me, more so than the king does." He didn't wait for her response but set off in the direction of the city center.

The central administration building, built of fine tan stone more than two hundred years earlier, sat adjacent to the cathedral. The affairs of Church and State were closely entwined and the proximity of these seats of power only reinforced the fact. Rodrigo walked down the same corridor and into the same office he had visited four years earlier when he enlisted. As before, a man sat at a bulky desk in the anteroom. He barely looked up from writing notations in a large book of thick, bound pages.

Rodrigo asked to speak with the military commandant and received a nod toward an open door on the right. He started to introduce himself to the commandant inside, a man who obviously ate well and dressed in fine embroidery from foreign lands.

"I know who you are, Señor del Fuentes. Word of your mission in Ireland and your contribution directly to the king has reached my ears. His Majesty was most impressed."

Truly? Rodrigo had assumed that the king barely noticed his presence.

"The armada is sailing very soon for the British Isles …"

For a moment Rodrigo had a horrible feeling that he

was about to be asked to dash back to the coast and report for duty, to go along and fight.

"Meanwhile, once they go, the king has other needs. We shall be outfitting another treasure fleet to travel to the New World, carrying supplies to the Church missions there and returning with the, shall we say, items we need here in Spain. Your experience as a supply officer and your proven honesty will be needed for the mission. Rich veins of silver in Mexico are feeding our economy now, and the man I choose will supervise the loading of the silver bars, keep careful logs down to the ounce, and see that the convoy returns safely."

"But, my father—"

"I want you for this duty, del Fuentes. You will be gone fewer than six months. I'm sure your family will understand. Especially when you come home with the large bonus which is given each year for the autumn delivery of these riches to your homeland."

Patriotism, God, duty, financial gain. The man had hit upon all the points that could convince Rodrigo to accept the assignment.

"See to your family's needs for the next two months—then report to Sevilla, prepared to sail." The commandant picked up a quill and dipped it into his inkwell. "That is all."

Dismissed, Rodrigo left the building in a daze. Mexico! For twenty years now, Spain had been reaping the rewards of having established a trade route to the New World. He'd heard men in Cordoba brag about the vast amounts of gold and silver that were routinely being mined by Indian slaves and carried back to his own country. Now, it seemed, he was to be a part of it.

His steps slowed as he approached his mother's home.

He'd gone this morning with a promise that he would be there to fill his father's shoes, to watch out for the women and make their lives easier. Now he was to be gone again. He did not relish telling her the news.

By the time he walked into the salon at home he had decided upon his approach to the subject. He was man of the house now; he would inform the women rather than apologize.

* * *

Sevilla's central district teemed with life like nothing Rodrigo had ever experienced. Merchants and bankers attired in fashionable clothing strolled along with women of unimaginable beauty. Shops displayed piles of food, fine gold jewelry and rich cloth. He walked until his feet burned and the bag slung over his shoulder grew wearisome, unable to take in all that glory. That the port city received shipments directly from the New World and was connected to the major ports on the Mediterranean was obvious. When he returned from the voyage he would buy some of these fineries for himself, he decided.

Gradually, he made his way to the docks along the Rio Guadalquivir where he had been assigned to one of the galleons in the *Flota de India,* the Indies Fleet. The captain of the *Niña Linda* (an auspicious sign, Rodrigo thought, that the ship bore a version of his sister's name) greeted him almost as an equal. Being supply officer aboard one of the treasure ships was a prestigious position.

He was shown to his quarters, a cabin shared with no one since he would keep the logs and private records of the shipment's contents there. The cabin contained a bed nearly as large as his at home, a desk, oil lamp, a large supply of quills and paper, and a strongbox in which he was to store the sensitive information whenever he was not physically present. He dropped his bag on the bunk, taking out only the carved box and locking it into the strongbox before he headed above decks again.

At the gangway, the captain handed him a sheaf of pages tied at the top with a leather thong.

"The manifest. Check off each item as it arrives and order the crew to properly stow everything in the hold."

The man walked away, leaving Rodrigo to familiarize himself with the list: Food, cloth, nails and other construction implements, weapons and ammunition, canvas, rope and tar for ship repairs, even paper. Apparently, nothing was manufactured in the untamed place across the sea. His new job had begun.

He quickly realized that many of the ordinary sailors were far more experienced at making this journey so he began shamelessly listening to their conversation.

"Enjoy the ham and bread," one commented to another as they handed crates down to the hold. "Coming home, the only thing they send back with us is corn, maybe some potatoes. Once, I got a taste of that Indian drink—chocolate, they call it. But mostly they save that because they can sell it to rich people."

Rodrigo checked off the items on his sheets.

"It's stupid to fill the hold with food on the return trip," a tall, thin sailor added. "The whole ship will be full of silver and gold!" A lascivious look crossed his face before he caught sight of Rodrigo.

"Stop and open that crate," Rodrigo ordered. "I want to count the contents." Impossible that he would let the men think they could pilfer, not when it would brand him as an easy mark. His bonus was on the line when it came to arriving at each end of the trip with everything the manifest called for.

The skinny man frowned but pried the lid off a wooden crate of candles and another of rosaries for the mission priests. Rodrigo made a show of counting them and watching as the man nailed down the lids once more. He ordered them to open several more crates and a few barrels, randomly. It slowed progress but showed that he was diligent in his work.

As the hold filled and the day wore on, Rodrigo realized they had several more days ahead of them before the entire shipment would be aboard. This was a far bigger undertaking than he'd ever imagined. When cook called time for supper, Rodrigo turned to the crew who'd been under his supervision all day.

"There's a cup of wine for each of us. Let's relax now."

The tall, thin sailor stayed aloof but the others soon warmed up, seeing their superior officer was not above dining with them.

"Wait until we come back," said a stocky man with muscles of iron. "Sevilla calls a public holiday, there's fireworks and wine—a lot better than this—" he held his cup high. "And we all go home to our wives for a bit of a good time!"

"Until the next ship sails," muttered another.

"I didn't say I don't take my good times elsewhere too," said the first one with a chuckle.

Rodrigo left them to their banter and went up to the deck for fresh air and a view of the city while he had the chance. Soon, there would be nothing but water to look at in any direction. Not that he couldn't handle it, but endless days at sea were not his idea of a good time. Again, he mentally counted on his bonus from this trip to get him established in something more enjoyable back at home.

Down at the dock level he saw a boy of twelve years or so, running through the crowd and making his way toward the gangway. The lad was flushed and breathing hard as he said something to the guard at the lower end. Whatever it was, he convinced the guard to escort him aboard the *Niña Linda.*

"Where's the captain?" the guard demanded of Rodrigo.

"Probably dining in his quarters—I don't know."

The two started to rush off but the captain appeared just then in the doorway to his cabin.

"The Armada went down," the young boy said before the guard could steal his thunder in making the announcement.

"What? Niño, what did you say?"

"Off the coast of Ireland. The invasion failed and our ships got off course. Most all of them went down and our sailors were captured or killed."

The captain's face went pale but he thanked the boy and ordered the guard to go down to the galley and get him some food.

"Do not speak of this. I must make the announcement myself. Muster the crew as quickly as possible."

Within minutes he had sent the messenger away with a piece of bread and some ham. Rodrigo watched silently as their leader disappeared into his cabin and reappeared wearing his dress coat and medals, taking his place at the railing of the forecastle and gathering his thoughts. The ship's bell rang and men began pouring up to the assembly.

* * *

The port of Veracruz boasted nothing similar to the comforts they had left behind in Sevilla. The *Niña Linda* had anchored beside the island of San Juán de Ulúa and a host of small boats waited to transport their cargo and men across the stretch of water to the Mexican shore. A stone warehouse was the largest building in sight on the mainland. Beyond it, a cluster of small wooden buildings formed the city which Hernán Cortés had named *Villa Rica de la Vera Cruz*, the Rich Village of the True Cross, because of the discovery of gold in the area and to make certain that the Church's influence would not be forgotten. Otherwise, there seemed nothing rich about the sad village where palm trees hung limply in the stifling heat and dark-skinned workers rolled barrels along a series of makeshift ramps that seemed flimsy for the burden they had to bear. Rodrigo stumbled from his cabin when he heard the shouts of his jubilant sailors.

Rough seas and days on end of rain had left every man queasy and disoriented, and in the distance he could see the first to disembark as they wove unsteadily on their feet, working to regain their land legs. For his own part, Rodrigo knew that his malaise went beyond unsteadiness. A fever had wracked his body for most of the voyage and when he emerged from the darkness to stand on deck, the tropical heat hit him in the face like a hot, wet blanket.

A shout from the captain drew his attention. "All hands make ready to offload the cargo!"

Rodrigo wove his way back to his cabin to retrieve the manifest pages. In his strongbox he spotted the carved box from Ireland and picked it up. Clutching it to his chest with both hands he felt its warmth travel up his arms and into his body. Within minutes he felt better, with some of his old energy returning. He carefully set the box back in its safe place and gathered the papers to complete his duties.

Above decks, the crew had already begun bringing crates and barrels up from the cargo hold. A small mountain of them were stacked near the gangway and Rodrigo quickly made his way there.

Item by item, he confirmed the delivery of each barrel, box and crate they had loaded aboard back in Sevilla, all these necessities brought with them that could not be obtained here. He felt a sense of otherworldliness, the fact that he was on a new continent, in a place where few of his countrymen had ever, or would ever, set foot.

"Señor del Fuentes." The captain's voice caught his attention. "Are you well? You look very pale."

Rodrigo realized that he was clutching the manifest pages to his chest and that he was leaning against the ship's rail. "Um, I believe so. Yes, sir, *muy bien.*"

The captain gave him a hard stare. "Go to the galley and get something to eat. I will see to this until you return." He took the pages from Rodrigo and gave his shoulder a gentle push.

The minute Rodrigo took a step he realized the captain was correct. His legs barely held him as he crept down the ladder into the belly of the ship. A piece of cheese and a hunk of hard bread did nothing to revive his energy, but he knew what would help. He struggled up the ladder and made his way to his own cabin. A short time later he emerged and took his place at the gangway.

"Ah, I thought some food would set you right," said the captain.

If only you knew, Rodrigo thought, as the man gave

a quick salute and descended to one of the ferry boats to ensure that the offloaded supplies were being properly handled within the large warehouse.

The midday sun became intolerable and several times Rodrigo thought he might have to excuse himself to revisit his private source of energy or risk collapsing right there on deck. At one point he noticed that even the natives had disappeared. He spied two of them sneaking off into the thick growth of leafy plants, and another man was openly sleeping with his back against the base of a palm tree and his wide-brimmed hat pulled over his face.

"I do not see why we cannot rest also," grumbled one of the Spaniards who had paused for Rodrigo to check the contents of his crate.

Rodrigo shrugged. He was barely staying upright but as an officer he could not admit as much to a crewman.

"The captain wants this work completed quickly," was all he could say. They all had their orders.

The man hefted the crate once again and placed it in the net to be lowered to the transport boat. Another sailor, this one with a barrel of wine, approached and Rodrigo flipped to another page. They were less than halfway through the cargo list.

At last a blessed darkness fell, cooling the temperature only a little but at least the blazing sun was gone. The mood among the men lightened and became jubilant.

"We have leave to go ashore," said one of the crewmen, part of a group who had washed their faces and put on clean shirts. "Come with us, Señor del Fuentes?"

"Go ahead. I shall catch the next ferry." Rodrigo felt torn. All he really wanted was to go to bed for a week. But he wondered if part of his malaise was due to the close, airless quarters and nonstop motion of the ship. Perhaps he would indeed feel better if he were to walk on solid ground again and partake of food that was not dried or salted. Surely there would be fruit and fresh fish in a place like this.

An hour later, with his first steps on dry land, he realized that it would take some practice to remain steady on his feet. He slowly walked past the customs warehouse where guards stood at every door of the dark, hulking building. The fortress-like place probably already held quantities of the precious metals the *Niña Linda* would take back across the Atlantic. In two weeks' time, most of it spent unloading the European commodities they had brought with them and refilling the ship with the king's treasure, the galleon would once again be eastbound. Rodrigo closed his mind to the prospect of being underway again. Beyond the coming hours he could only focus on Cordoba and a vision of his lovely mother's face. Home.

Sounds of revelry interrupted his thoughts. He followed the noises toward a lighted area where, in an open square, small fires blazed and the smells of food wafted on the night air. A black woman wearing brightly colored loose clothing was frying something in fat, stirring and turning the little packets with two wooden sticks. Next to her was a man with rounded, indigenous features who called out to the sailors in a curious mixture of Spanish and some other tongue. Several of the *Niña Linda*'s crew held out cups to the man and he filled them with clear liquid from a barrel.

"Best Caribbean rum," the man said, turning to Rodrigo. "Will make you feel very happy."

Judging by the level of raucous laughter from the rest of the men, that was seemingly true. But Rodrigo's stomach was not yet ready. He declined when he spotted another little stand where the meat and vegetables simmering in a savory sauce caught his attention.

The man cooking the meat concoction spooned a portion of it onto a piece of flat, soft bread and handed it to Rodrigo in exchange for a couple of *reales*. He found a seat on a rough-hewn bench and sat down with his meal.

"There's more fun to be had for your money than that!" called out one of the sailors who had clearly partaken of the rum already and was now hanging onto the hand of a flamboyantly dressed woman.

Rodrigo watched the two disappear into a narrow alleyway between blocks of the low wooden houses. He didn't envy his captain trying to keep order among this crew and assure that all reported back to the ship for the return voyage. Three sailors stumbled by, clearly having been at the rum for some hours now, and another had his face buried in a woman's cleavage in a dark corner at the edge of the small plaza. For all Rodrigo knew, no one checked on their whereabouts. Maybe it was every man for himself when it came to returning home safely. He finished the burrito and sat for another half hour, observing.

The following night he followed the same ritual, coming ashore for a meal after a day during which he felt nearly overcome with exhaustion. He'd handled the wooden box several times, but its powers were becoming less effective. He knew he wasn't well and, from his seat on the bench, he debated whether he should seek out a doctor. If this city had doctors.

The *Niña Linda* was due to sail in a week's time and he could not fathom the misery of being aboard for several more weeks feeling this way. He scanned the area, his vision not quite right, but did not see any sign of a medical facility.

When he returned to the ship he would ask the captain for advice. The burrito in his hands had lost its appeal; he set it aside and wiped his hands on a corner of his cloak.

When he stood, sparks appeared before his eyes. He blinked. Then his vision narrowed and the world went dark.

* * *

An angel's face appeared above him—so young, so beautiful with her halo of white. He smiled and drifted into a pleasant sleep.

Voices entered his consciousness. A man saying, "… cannot wait …" A woman, "condition is grave …" Another long, dark period.

"… better today, padre. See for yourself." It was the voice of the angel this time.

He smiled and slept again.

The next time he heard the voices he struggled to open his eyes. A small sound came from him but he could not form words—it was more of a moan. His eyes felt crusty and stuck shut; he saw light and shadow through the fringe of his lashes.

"Señor del Fuentes? You are waking up?" Her Spanish was soft and welcome to his ears.

A gentle hand with a cool, wet cloth dabbed at his eyelids. He wondered how the angel knew his name. Of course, God had told her. How silly of him not to realize that. He smiled again and this time managed one word. "*Agua.*"

A trickle of tepid water ran over his tongue. Little of it touched his throat.

"*Más agua, por favor.*" His words came a little easier now. Another trickle. This time he swallowed.

His eyes opened, only a slit; the light was too bright, although he could tell that it came from a single candle. "*¿Dónde estoy?*"

This time a male voice responded. "My son, you are at the clinic in Vera Cruz. You have been very ill." A priest in brown robes stepped into his field of view.

Rodrigo puzzled over that for awhile. He remembered nothing beyond a very hot day where he stood at the rail of a ship with a handful of papers. He looked at the priest's kindly face. Movement on the other side of him drew his attention to the white-clad angel. She patted his hand and agreed with the priest. Rodrigo closed his eyes again.

When he woke the room was very light—a new day. He heard more sounds than before, the moans of others followed by reassuring words from the nurse. He lay very still and flat, staring toward the wood-beamed ceiling. Other noises intruded. Wind, howling through tight spaces. A patter of rain, silence, more rain, heavier this time. He groaned and rolled to his side.

Less than a meter away was another bed where a man lay with a terrible wound to his head. A white strip of bandage was wrapped around his matted hair and blood had soaked through it in a circle the size of a saucer. He let out a continuous moan but no one came to attend him. Rodrigo raised his head and saw that the entire room was filled with beds, probably twenty of them, all occupied. Was this the extent of the town's medical facility?

The nurse turned quickly away from another patient, a wad of bloody cloth clutched in one hand. She dropped the messy bandages into a pail and went to the next bed where it appeared that she applied an ointment to a woman's forehead. Clearly, she was too busy to come to the side of a man who was not presently in pain. Rodrigo let his eyes close once more.

His mind became too active for sleep. When had all these other sick people arrived? Had they been here all along but he was so deeply unconscious that he never heard them. The noise of their cries and pleas was nearly intolerable. He raised his hands, looked at them (the thin bones showed quite clearly now), and placed them over his ears.

A touch to his forehead startled him and he opened his eyes again.

"Your fever is gone, Señor del Fuentes," said the nurse, with a gentle look on her face. "If you lived here in the city we would be ready to send you home."

"The city?"

"You are still in Vera Cruz, but I am sorry to say that your ship sailed away without you."

He raised up on his elbows. "What?"

"The captain was here, asking about you, worried at your condition. But he informed us that he could not delay on account of one crew member. The ship had to go, to meet its schedule."

Rodrigo remembered the sailors talking, before they left Sevilla, about the huge celebrations upon their return, the fireworks, the fine wine and the fiestas all over the city. He would now miss it all.

"How long—?"

"They sailed four days ago."

"I—"

"You have been here in the clinic for ten days, *señor*. You were unconscious when they brought you."

His head fell back to the thin pillow as he absorbed this information. Ten days!

"My things?" If they were to discharge him from the clinic he had no money, no clothing … and the carved box. What happened to it?

"Your captain brought them. But do not worry yourself—we will not send you away yet. There is a storm, *más terrible*. No one can be outdoors now. Roofs are blowing off buildings, trees are flying through the air. Too dangerous to go out."

To punctuate her declaration, the wind howled through the rafters again and a drizzle of rainwater poured through a space in the ceiling, dripping into a bowl that had been strategically placed on the floor beside his bed.

The nurse patted his hand and pulled the sheet up to his chest. "Rest. Gather your strength. A hurricane such as this usually passes in a day. Tomorrow you may go home."

Home. Unfortunately, home was a lot farther away than this godforsaken place in the tropics. As the nurse turned to check on the man with the head wound, an involuntary tear ran down the side of Rodrigo's face. He thought of his mother. When would he see her again? How would she manage the house without his bonus silver from the voyage?

* * *

He walked out of the clinic in the early afternoon of the following day, wearing simple Mexican peasant clothing provided by the priest who had visited his bedside and, he now knew, had once administered the last rites for him. In the bag over his shoulder were his useless, overdone clothes from Spain—minus the money he'd carried in a small purse within his cloak—and the carved wooden box. Perhaps the priest had felt it his due that the clinic receive the money in exchange for the care they had given, or maybe one of the sailors had come across his sea bag before the captain delivered it ashore—no matter. The first thing he needed to do now was to find work.

Meanwhile, to feed himself for a few days, he could sell the box. It was no treasure, certainly not worth much but perhaps he could find a ready buyer or negotiate a trade for food. He walked the narrow lane from the clinic toward the shore, alert to any possibility for a job. The priest had informed him that the next Spanish galleon was not due for another three months, due to the hurricane season, and that ship would be his first opportunity to find passage back to Europe.

As he walked toward the turquoise sea, he began to see signs of the hurricane damage. Broken tree limbs and shredded leaves from plants littered the streets, some of the homes were missing their roofs and farther along, evidence of a surge wave where entire wooden structures had been swept out to sea. In the distance, he caught sight of the water. It was oddly calm, deep blue-green and beautiful now.

The stone edifices of the customs warehouse and the stone docks on the *Isla* were intact, but the beach was littered with a million pieces of debris—palm fronds, boards, even cooking pots and clothing that had once been inside those shattered homes. People were staring—most of them in shock—at the carnage. Some were picking through the detritus to recover lost possessions or salvage what they could to start over. Rodrigo's feet carried him to the shoreline, drawing him to join the others. Perhaps he could help someone with even less than he.

Gentle, foamy waves lapped at the beach, each new one carrying some additional thing to add to the clutter at the water line. He saw a large piece of wood drifting toward him. As he stared, it moved closer, like a raft cast loose and traveling on its own. Nearer, he could tell that it consisted of several planks, broken now but clinging together by some impossible means.

Blue paint. Yellow flashes. A few letters … NDA. It was from the hull of the *Niña Linda*.

He thought of the captain, a man who had been kind to him. The cook, who always saved him a bit of the best meat. The manifest, which had been his responsibility, the document that detailed the tons of silver and gold aboard that ship. All of them gone now. He began to shake. If not for the tropical fever and his grave condition, he would have been among those who went down, never to be seen again.

He fell to his knees on the sand and raised his eyes toward heaven, vowing to be never again ungrateful for the fact that he still had the opportunity, one day in the future, to get home.

Chapter 5

Traders Go South

The city of Durango appeared as a cluster of tan buildings, nestled in a low place in the land, when Carlos Martinez first saw it. The convoy had reached the halfway point of the journey now and he only had one wish—that the traveling party locate an inn where they might find a hearty meal and a hot bath.

"Papá! Is it Mexico City?" Carlito asked, tugging at his father's sleeve.

If only that could be so. "No, *hijo*. Did I not instruct you to count the days? We have been away from home only sixty-five days." Carlos scanned the horizon, aware that too strong a focus on the town ahead might lessen his awareness of other dangers.

He had nearly canceled this year's trip. Stories were

everywhere in early 1680, rumors that the pueblo Indians all along the Rio Grande valley and into the province of Nueva Vizcaya were on the verge of rebellion. Indeed, his traveling party of five wagons and twenty men had caught the tension as they made their way south along the well-used Camino Real.

In Santa Fe, the Spanish garrison was on high alert. South of Isleta Pueblo no one accosted them, but as they neared El Paso they spotted an Apache raiding party watching from the edge of a mesa. Carlos and the others kept a close eye on the Indians, their weapons ready, but no trouble had ensued.

The unrest was nothing new. Ever since his ancestors had come, fanning expansion of European beliefs and ways northward where only indigenous peoples had previously lived in solitude, there had been uprisings. Even among the tribes who'd always inhabited this land there were wars. So far, in their ten years of making the annual trek from northern New Mexico to Mexico City, trading their corn, potatoes and dried chiles for finely manufactured goods of silver and leather, Carlos and his brothers had remained unharmed. He raised his eyes and sent a quick prayer to the Holy Father that this year would be no different. Josephina would have his neck if anything were to happen to Carlito.

The boy's request to come along had created strife where previously there was none, although at twelve he was certainly competent with both horses and weapons. Josephina was a devoted mother who wanted all of her eight children nearby, under her own watchful eye. Carlos was still uncertain which of the many arguments in favor of the boy coming along on the trip had won her over. At any rate, it would not do to become complacent yet—they would not be safely back at their hacienda north of Santa Fe for another four or five months.

He slapped the reins against the sturdy back of the donkey pulling the small wagon and envisioned a bathtub as they moved toward tonight's destination.

The rich smell of meat cooking over a fire drew the men's attention to a neat, whitewashed home at the northern outskirts of the city. A gray-haired woman in a bright skirt and shawl bent near the outdoor *horno*, pulling two loaves of bread from the squat, rounded oven as they watched. When the wagons came to a stop a man appeared, walking out of the orchard to their right.

Carlos called out, "*Buenas tardes, como esta?*"

The man replied in kind and came closer, shaking hands with Carlos and with each of the other men in turn. He gave Carlito an indulgent smile when the boy extended his hand in the same manner.

"*Por favor*, may we camp here on your land for tonight? And, if it is possible, may we purchase a meal and a bath?"

Clearly, the elderly couple were accustomed to such requests. Traders on El Camino Real must be a frequent sight to them. It was no coincidence that a large kettle of hot water was one of the vessels on their cook fire. The man introduced himself as Ernesto Aragon and his wife as Gloria. As the men climbed down from wagons and horses, Gloria began dipping hot water from the kettle and carrying it to a side room of their home, where she poured it into a large tub and tempered it with cool water from a nearby pump.

"Carlito, help the lady," Carlos ordered. His son hurried to take over filling the tub.

The sun dropped behind the surrounding hills while

Carlos and his brother Hernando tended to the animals and secured the wagons. The men would sleep on the ground beside their cargo, as they had every night since leaving home. They drew straws and Carlos won the right for the first bath. Carlito found himself drawn to Gloria's side, as he would to his mother's, helping to finish the meal.

"Come, eat," she called to the men, dishing out plates of beans and the thick stew of pork and red chiles to go with thick slices of her freshly baked bread.

They took turns eating while the next one bathed and soon they began to relax. Carlito followed Gloria into the kitchen, carrying plates to a waiting pan of water. He accepted the towel she handed him, drying the utensils after she washed them.

"What is this?" he asked, pointing to a carved wooden object on the shelf where she had directed that he stack the plates.

"Ah, that old thing. A box that has been in my husband's family for a long time. I put my spoons in it, but it smells funny. Someone must have stored herbs in it once. You will have to ask Ernesto."

Carlito ran his fingers over the lumpy shapes carved into the box, feeling an attraction to its very ugliness and the small, dusty stones mounted with tiny metal prongs. The fact that it was not a beautifully polished item captured his attention.

When he went back outside, the men were gathered around the fire, smoking hand-rolled cigarettes and taking nips from a bottle that was being passed around.

"Señora Aragon said I should ask you about this," Carlito said to Ernesto, holding up the box.

"Ah, that is a very interesting story," Ernesto said,

settling onto the ground and patting a spot next to himself for Carlito to sit.

He took the box into his hands and stroked it with his thumbs. Carlito swore that the wood looked much prettier in the firelight. Ernesto raised the lid, revealing traces of carved lettering. Carlito ran his finger over the letters.

"It says Virtu," Ernesto told him. "That is a good thing. My great-grandfather lived in the port city of Vera Cruz when he was a very young man. He came from Spain on a galleon, they say, and he stayed behind to work in the king's service at the customs house. All this I know only because my own grandfather told me of it. He said that great-grandfather was there, keeping records and collecting taxes for the king in 1588, the year of a very bad epidemic. A fever gripped many of the townspeople after some sailors from one particular ship brought the disease ashore. Some survived but many died."

He stood up, handed the box to Carlito, and added a log to the fire. Resuming his story, he sat once more.

"One sailor was so ill that he missed the departure of his ship for Spain. It was his good fortune that he did—the ship went down in a hurricane. That young sailor had this box in his possession."

"Was it the box that brought him good luck?" Carlito asked.

"Maybe. Maybe so. Anyway, the sailor had no money for food and no place to stay until the next ship could come, so my great-grandfather took this box in trade for a few weeks of room and board."

"What happened to the sailor? Did he go back to Spain?"

"That part of the story is lost to me—I do not know."

Ernesto glanced at the box in Carlito's lap. "I do believe, though, that the box has had a lucky life. In 1618 the whole city of Vera Cruz was nearly reduced to ashes after a large fire. It was almost the biggest city in all of Mexico at that time. Can you imagine? My grandfather was a tiny child then. The family barely escaped, but they made their way to Mexico City. Lucky that they did—Vera Cruz became a rough city, overrun by pirates. Eventually, the king of Spain had to station the Barlovento Armada there for protection."

"Did your grandfather fight the pirates?" Carlito's eyes were large.

"No, I am afraid not. By then our family had moved west."

Once the part about the pirates was done, the boy's attention waned. Carlos saw that his son was getting sleepy.

"Give the box back to Señor Aragon," Carlos said, placing a hand on Carlito's shoulder.

Carlito held the box a moment longer, hoping that its good luck would rub off on him. He said goodnight to their hosts, followed his father to their encampment, and in the morning they rose early to hitch the animals and get on the trail once more.

The capital city enthralled Carlito—endless stalls in the bazaar with amazing items such as he had never seen. Leather saddles trimmed in silver, made locally; heavy, carved furniture from Guadalajara; fabrics and shoes and oranges from Spain; cocoa beans from the rain forests of Guatemala. He escaped his father's watch one afternoon after they had unloaded their own products and spent a joyful hour exploring and tasting foods that he had never seen before. Until his uncle Hernando found him at the woodcarver's stand.

"Your father is worried, niño," the tall man said. "You'd better come back."

They had found a place to stay, two rooms in a boarding house about a quarter mile from the central market square. They would rest here in the city two weeks, choosing the items on Josephina's shopping list, before they loaded the wagons for the trip back to *nuevo méxico* and home. Carlito could not stop thinking about the wooden box Señor Aragon had shown him, the one that had saved its owner's life from certain disaster. At each vendor that sold wood carvings he looked for one like it.

"Can we stay again with the Aragons when we go back through Durango?" he asked his father after meeting with disappointment in his quest.

"You liked that wonderful supper, did you? *La Señora* is as good a cook as your mamá, no?

"Si. That is the reason." How could he explain his fascination with the box? He wanted to have contact once more, if only to see it. Perhaps to touch it and see if it would bring him luck.

"All right. We leave in two more days. Remember, though, it will be at least a month before we get to their place."

Carlito vowed to be patient but his feet felt itchy to be on the road again.

At last, on a Tuesday morning, Carlos declared the band of travelers ready to leave. The wagons had been carefully packed with a table and benches, two new saddles (sadly, only the plain ones), a bag of oranges from Valencia, several thick bolts of cloth from which Josephina would make curtains and clothing, and a heavy ceramic jar containing the wonderful chocolate powder. Carlito and his father had both become very fond of the hot beverage each morning.

The days crawled by but Carlito's thoughts were so lively that he did not mind the slow pace. His head was filled with images of Mexico City, the market and the many things he'd seen for the first time in his life. He would have so many stories for the younger ones when he returned home. By the time they reached the southern outskirts of Durango, his uncles were eager to stop and enjoy town comforts for a night but Carlito reminded his father of the promise to stay with Ernesto and Gloria Aragon. They pushed onward to the end of the day to reach the northern ranches before stopping.

From the moment their small caravan slowed in front of the *casa*, Carlito had a bad feeling. A strange burro stood in the yard near the *horno*. Where the fire had been blazing last time with pots of savory stew, there was only a pile of cold ashes. No chickens pecked at the ground. None of the animals were in sight.

"Maybe they went into the city," Carlos said to his son. "Let's check."

They had no sooner descended from the wagon than a priest stepped out the kitchen doorway. He held up a hand, partly in greeting, partly to stop them.

"Do not come inside," he cautioned. "I am sorry to say that there has been a very unfortunate ..."

Carlito cried out and started to run to the house but the priest stopped him with hands on both shoulders.

"My son, do not."

"What has happened here?" Carlos demanded. "Where are the Aragons?"

The priest shook his head. "Indians, from the mesa. They came last night to several of our neighboring ranches.

I have checked at the Mascarenas place, the Chavez's, at Diego Sanchez's ranch. All are *muerte*, all those good people. The animals were stolen, the houses raided. Two of our friars have taken the bodies to the church for burial tomorrow but I am afraid there is no food left for you to even make your own supper."

Carlos stood, stunned at the turn of events. Although they had been told of the dangers of this journey they had never yet encountered the brutal reality. He scanned the surrounding hills and mesa tops. All was quiet.

"They will not return soon," the priest said. "They took what they wanted. For now, it was food and horses. Next time it may be a direct attack on the church or the fort. They take out their anger on Spaniards, I am afraid, wanting us to all go back to Spain and leave the land as it was. They do not understand that after almost two hundred years in this place, we will not be going away."

Carlito observed the adult conversation, comprehending only that the elderly couple who had been so kind to them were gone now, forever.

The priest gathered his robes and mounted the sad little burro. "I must go now, return to my church to say the evening Mass. Feel free to stay here if you like, but I would recommend that you stand guard."

He nudged the burro and started toward the city.

"What do you think?" Uncle Hernando asked Carlos. "Is it safe to stay here or do we go back to the city also?"

Carlos stared at the hills around them. "It is at least five miles back and darkness is coming fast." His face took on a determined look. "Build up the fire. Gather the wagons and animals close together. We will take watches during the night. Two sleep and two remain on guard. It is dangerous, I know. We would be overpowered. But, as the holy man said, the Indians already took what they wanted from this home. They have moved on."

Carlito gathered sticks and small branches for the fire and watched as his uncles pulled food from their packs. They ate a simple supper of bread, beans and jerky. The night was quiet and the animals settled peacefully at their tethers. A half moon lit the landscape and the men realized they would see anyone who approached, as long as they stayed diligent. Hernando and Carlos agreed to take the first watch, and soon the others were asleep on their blankets on the ground.

Carlito said a prayer for Señor and Señora Aragon, remembering what his mother had told him about souls going to heaven. He remembered their evening together a few weeks ago, wishing that tonight had been the same. Then he thought of the carved box and the stories Señor Aragon had told about it. Where was the box now? He crawled out of his nest of blankets.

Carlos saw him as he approached the fire. "Why are you up?" he whispered, joining his son at the edge of the low embers.

"I need to check something." Carlito stuck a twig into the fire, setting the end of it aglow.

"*Hijo*, you need to—"

But Carlito had already taken his small torch and was running toward Gloria's kitchen door. The priest had barely closed it; at the boy's touch it swung inward. Moonlight from the one window showed the big items—Gloria's worktable lying on its side, a wooden bucket of water where she had left it near her dishpan, the corner fireplace where she prepared meals in winter. His flaming stick illuminated the details—broken dishes fallen from the shelves, jars that had contained corn and beans but were empty now, a pool of something dark on the floor. His breath caught but he refused to dwell on what that might be.

"Carlito! Come back outside—now!" His father's harsh whisper cut the absolute stillness in the room.

"*Uno momento*," Carlito said, his eyes darting back and forth.

On the floor, in a corner beneath the shelves where Gloria's dishes had once been stacked, he spotted the familiar lumpy shape. He rushed toward it, feeling a stab as a shard pierced his foot. It did not stop him. He limped on, being more mindful of the broken pottery, and picked up the wooden object. Someone had opened it and, discovering that it contained nothing of real value, had thrown it to the earthen floor. One of the hinges was broken; the lid hung by the remaining bent one. He fitted the top back in place and stroked it gently, as he might have done with an injured kitten.

"Carlito!" This time the whisper was more commanding.

"Coming, papá." He cradled the box and picked up his little torch again. The flame had burned nearly to his fingers and he tossed it to the ground the moment he reached the outside air.

"What have you taken?" Carlos asked.

Carlito showed him. "Señor Aragon told such good stories about it. I think he would not mind me having it now."

There was certainly no one else who wanted the ugly, broken object; both the Indians and the priest had left it behind. And the old couple had no children to inherit it.

"Fine. You must watch out for it yourself. Now go to sleep—we have many long days ahead of us."

* * *

The newlyweds placed the last of their things into the cart which had been his parents' gift to them, along with the droopy-eared burro who pulled it. Ramona turned to her mother, Carlito to his father, to say goodbye.

Beside her husband, Josephina Martinez wept softly. Her eldest son was leaving and who knew when they might see each other again. Of all the children, Carlito was the hardest to hold down. Josephina put on a smile for her new daughter-in-law—did the girl truly know what she was getting into? Probably so. The couple had known each other since childhood and Ramona had watched Carlito leave on the yearly Camino Real journey six times already.

"Did we pack my paints?" Carlito asked his new wife, a concerned frown crossing his face.

"Yes, my darling. All your supplies are safe in the wagon."

He poked under the oiled cloth covering the cargo anyway until he felt the reassuring bumps on the lid of the old box in which he stored his precious pigments. Relieved, he offered Ramona a hand up to the cart's seat and then followed, taking up the reins and giving the old burro a slap while all seventeen members of their families waved frantically.

Their goal before nightfall was to follow the old Camino northward for a few miles beyond San Juan Pueblo to an area of natural hot springs, a place Carlito had explored a few years ago. As an inquisitive fifteen-year-old he had come upon the place, with its steaming pools of mineral-laden water and tall, shady trees, thinking that he would one day paint pictures of this astounding scenery and would make love to a woman on the soft ground under the cottonwoods. At the time, he had not known this would be Ramona but thinking about it now, as the cart carried them along, it could not have been otherwise. He had loved her ever since the day his father's caravan of traders had returned from Mexico, the first of several times Carlito had made that journey. Ramona's raw emotion, her absolute joy at his safe return, had captured his heart. It took him only eight more years to find the courage to propose marriage. It took her only a moment to accept.

"So … Carlito, my dearest … do you still plan to paint my portrait one day?"

He turned his eyes from the road and looked deeply into hers, dark chocolate irises that matched his own. They would make beautiful babies together, he realized.

"Yes. I absolutely will paint your portrait. I want to paint you in every light, in every setting." He raised his eyebrows. "Perhaps in the morning, on our blanket under the trees, when your skin is flush with love and the warm air caresses you."

A pink tinge rose under her pale brown skin and her eyes immediately shifted toward her lap. Her mother had told her good girls do not have such thoughts as she was having right now, good girls do not discuss intimate details with men, not even their husbands. But Mamá did not consider that Ramona and Carlito had been best of friends since they were twelve; she did not know that they had already experimented with tentative touches and many kisses. Tonight would only be the beginning of so many more delicious experiences.

Ramona looked back up into his face, meeting his gaze straight on. "My wonderful, beautiful artist husband. How soon will we be there?"

He slapped the reins against the burro's back again but the creature was not to be hurried. One day he would receive a commission lucrative enough to purchase them a fine carriage and a pair of strong horses and then they would travel in style. And *much* faster.

"Patience, my love," Ramona said, sensing his haste. She ran the tips of her fingers over the light cloth covering his thigh. "Patience."

The setting sun lit the western clouds with shades of orange and mauve and brilliant pink as they turned toward the small enclave of trees where he knew the hot pools were. While Ramona gathered wood for a fire, he quickly staked the burro near a grassy patch and pulled out the straw-filled mattress and blankets she and her mother had made as part of their household goods. The clouds faded and dispersed and soon the Milky Way made a brilliant swath across the black sky.

"There will be no rain tonight," he said. "We shall sleep under the stars." He was practically trembling as he loosened the tie that secured her blouse.

Her hands were quick and eager, and in moments their clothing had fallen to the ground. The straw mattress crackled as they sank into its depth and Ramona giggled. He stilled the sound by covering her mouth with his and the giggle turned to a moan as he ran his hands from her shoulders to her buttocks. Holding her gently he positioned himself and discovered that her body eagerly awaited him.

She let out a tiny cry and he was finished, his pent-up energy released in a moment's time. She lay beneath him, breathing hard and kissing his face all at once.

"Is it always so quick?" she asked, a trace of disappointment on her face.

"The next time, I promise you …"

She kissed him again.

He made good on the promise, twice more before the moon reached its zenith and again at dawn's first light.

"My mother never explained it *this* way." Ramona laughed as Carlito rolled to one elbow and brushed the hair back from her face. "Thank goodness Graciela was willing to talk freely."

The older sister who had married only a year earlier. Graciela was already nursing her first child and the thought crossed Ramona's mind that the same situation could be a very distinct possibility for her. She tucked that idea away. For now, she wanted Carlito to herself.

He had risen from their outdoor bed and wrapped her shawl around his waist, reaching for his box of charcoal and a sheet of sketch paper.

"Do not move," he said, pulling lines down the length of the page. "I want to catch you exactly like this—your smile and that lazy look you have in your eyes."

She laughed with delight, holding her position, knowing her mother would be scandalized if she knew how wantonly her daughter could behave.

"As long as this drawing is for your eyes only," she said. "This is our own very private moment together."

"Moment? My darling, I want us to have a lifetime of these private moments, exactly like this one."

* * *

"Carlito—we are moving *again*?" Ramona felt the sway of uncertainty. The baby in her arms sensed her anxiety and began to squall. A tug at her skirt told her that little Miguel was hanging on tight, most likely with his thumb in his mouth. And she'd missed her monthly cycle again, although there had been no chance to inform Carlito of this.

"There is work in *Tejas*, a group of missionaries and explorers have branched away from the Rio Grande Valley and are discovering new places. There will be construction work and they will want art to beautify the hundreds of churches they plan to build."

It was always this way. Three years of marriage, soon to be three babies, always somewhere new to explore. She was happy for him, truly, that he had such a love of life and a thirst to learn more. But did he realize the difficulties? Packing their belongings, leaving half of their household goods behind each time and having to start over. The daily problems associated with keeping the children fed, their clothing washed, treating their injuries along the trail and praying every single night that no one became ill because there was rarely a doctor in any of the tiny settlements and pueblos where they ended up. She opened her mouth, intending to tell him.

The baby let out another long shriek and Carlito came to her side. "Here, I will take him for a walk down to the stream. He always likes to watch the water rush by."

That had been Miguel, their water-watcher. Little Lorenzo always seemed to have a stomach ailment.

"He's hungry," she said. "Take Miguel and I will get this one fed."

Like a dog after a rabbit, her husband's focus changed

in a second and he did as she suggested. She sank into the chair where she usually nursed the baby, thankful that this landlord had provided a few simple furnishings. On an easel near the window sat Carlito's most recent painting, a view of the Taos Indian Pueblo done from memory since he had only been there once, right after their wedding. It was the week she had told him she was pregnant for the first time. He'd been so overjoyed that he'd immediately stopped sketching the pueblo and moved the family to a rented room in the nearby settlement that passed for a town.

Before the birth of Miguel, however, he had received word that another mission settlement needed wood workers and they moved south, six days over a road that was barely a track through the high-desert terrain. They had stayed there long enough to welcome Miguel, conceive Lorenzo, and finish a beautiful altar piece. It only made sense now that Lorenzo was ready for solid food they would pick up and move again. She sighed.

"They are calling the new place San Antonio," Carlito said as he spooned portions of beans into bowls for the two of them. The boys were already asleep on their pallets in the corner. "There will be a mission church, so I can use my woodworking skills. And this time I want to convince the priests to allow me to paint a mural. I can see it in my head, a series of pictures depicting the life of Christ, one leading to the other so that it spans a long wall. Maybe even two walls. Such a project would give me work for a very long time."

"Do you think we might stay there, then? Long enough for the children to settle down, perhaps even to learn a little reading and writing from the priests?"

He shrugged and chewed a large mouthful. "Maybe so.

San Antonio might be the place."

She didn't think he said it with much conviction and she was beginning to remember the little comments from her mother-in-law. Josephina had hinted at Carlito's need for adventure and change.

She made up her mind to accept it—what choice was there anyway?—and then she informed him she was once again pregnant.

* * *

Carlito reached for the carved box on the high shelf of his studio, lifting it down and regarding it closely for the first time in years. How differently he saw it now than he had at twelve. The workmanship was not good—his own skill at woodworking had far surpassed that of whoever made the box—but still, it held a place in his heart. He remembered his fascination with it as old Señor Aragon had told of its history, his boyish enthusiasm when his father gave permission for him to own it. He cradled it in his arms the way he did as a boy then set it back on the shelf.

"What is that, Papá?" came the small voice of Enrique, his four-year-old.

"Ah. Well, *hijo*, I used to keep my paints in it when I was a young man, when Mamá and I first married." Since those early days he had accumulated more art supplies than the small box could hold so he had fashioned a larger one with compartments and a tight-fitting top.

He took the old box down again and placed it on his worktable where brushes and paints were strewn in disarray. Sitting on the stool where he often worked, he took the child on his lap and picked up the box.

"It is very old," he said, "and the man who owned it told of how it came from Spain and then went to a town on the coast of Mexico, a place where there were pirates!"

Enrique's eyes went wide, more from the tone of his father's storytelling voice than from any knowledge of what a pirate was.

Miguel walked into the room just then. "There are pirates on the coast still," he said. "Father Dominique told us that they are evil Englishmen who come to cut the wood and kill Spaniards. They steal logwood from the forests and take it away in their ships. Father says the English will be doomed to hell because they don't belong to the Church."

"They have their own church," Carlito responded absently. "Maybe they think the same thing about us."

Sometimes he wondered whether Ramona's idea of educating the children at the Catholic mission school was a good one, although he had to admit that the three who were old enough to attend impressed him with their reading and writing, despite the strong ideas they brought home. He had heard the stories of battles between the English and Spanish along the Caribbean coastal areas—battles for territory and natural resources. He supposed they would sort it out somehow. Meanwhile, he wondered whether he might find work in that area, might have access to some of those beautiful hardwoods.

Little Enrique had stroked the box in his father's hand and Carlito suddenly felt the wood growing warm. He stared at the object and quickly set it back on the table, out of the youngster's reach. Enrique began to whine.

"Come, boys, let's see what Mamá has made for lunch."

Fights among nations, artifacts that demonstrated strange tendencies ... he wanted to ignore it all and simply get back to his art. He had never seen the sea but an artist he had worked with on the church at San Antonio a few years ago had described it—vivid turquoise water with waves that broke over the reefs. The man had showed Carlito two paintings he'd done when he journeyed there, breathtaking scenes of a land Carlito could barely imagine from his experiences in dusty desert lands. He would talk to his wife later about the idea of moving, just one more time.

"No! No, no!" Ramona screamed. "We have five children, three of them in school. I do not want to uproot the family again, only to go to a place we know nothing about. I am tired of starting over."

By this time tears were pouring from her eyes and the four children who were able ran from the room. The baby squalled on Ramona's lap and she stood abruptly and carried her to the bedroom. A moment later she came back, wiping her cheeks with her apron. Taking up a towel, she protected her hand and lifted the metal coffeepot from the cook fire in the corner of the kitchen. She poured the black brew into two cups and took her seat across from him. She seemed much calmer and Carlito took hope.

"Neither I nor my children will leave this place," she announced in a voice that was quiet and far more frightening to him than her earlier hysterical shouts. "Not until the children have received proper schooling. When they are older and can make their own choices about staying or going, then we might discuss this again. Until then, my answer is still no."

It was the first time he'd ever struck her and the violence of his reaction shocked them both. The cup she had lifted to her mouth flew across the room, shattering against the adobe wall.

"You, woman, have no say in the matter," he said through clenched teeth.

And with that, he stomped out the door. The chilly air in the yard cooled his emotion immediately. Overhead, stars sparkled brilliantly in the clear desert sky. Their small rented house stood a hundred yards from the home of their landlord, separated from the larger one by a chicken coop and a pen of wooden stakes that held three goats. At this time of year, with the doors and windows closed, no one had likely overheard the altercation. With his fingers, he raked his hair back from his face. Exhaled deeply.

They fought, certainly, as all married people did. But the fire in their arguments almost always sparked the flames between them in the bedroom and a disagreement nearly always ended in passion of the other sort. He feared it would not be so this time.

He set out walking, trying to reconcile his deep inner desire to move along, to be in a different place, with his wife's practical ideas about raising a family with stability. Up the road, toward the center of town he trudged. His heart ached with the yearning to leave, to explain again to her how important this was to his very soul. He came to the church, pressed his palms against the still-warm adobe, laid his forehead there for a moment. He could not bring himself to go inside and share his anguish with the priest.

A sob escaped. He quelled it, turned and started the half-mile walk back home. With each step he felt his spirit drain away. The artist inside had become dulled with the lack of inspiration in this tiny Mexican town in south *Tejas*, the same disincentive that inevitably fell over him once he had completed the project for which he'd chosen the locale. He could only paint bright flowers on so many plates and cups, make one or two murals in the home of the town's one wealthy man, talk the priests into a certain number of Biblical scenes to adorn the walls of the predictably small local mission church. And then each town lost its allure and he was ready to move on. Perhaps his mother had been right when she cautioned him about taking a wife. A family was not for the man with wanderlust.

Chill bumps rose on his arms as he walked the two-track road; he'd not thought to grab his serape or a hat. His pace quickened although he dreaded to see Ramona again. Had his slap raised a welt on her beautiful face? And what harm would it do to stay awhile longer? San Ignacio, the next town down the road, could be new territory for his wares. He could force himself to paint plates and cups for a few more years.

Years. The thought depressed him. But he walked on.

In the kitchen, the fire was banked for the night, the dishes cleared and cleaned, the broken cup nowhere to be seen. Ramona stood with her back to the door, placing clean plates in a stack on the narrow storage shelf. On the floor the children's pallets were neatly laid out and four sets of large dark eyes watched, waiting, it seemed, to pull their blankets over their heads if his foul mood had followed him home. Ramona turned, ready to protect her babies if that were the case. Carlito gave each of them—Miguel, Lorenzo, Francesca and Enrique—a smile and a wish for good dreams.

To Ramona he said only one thing: "We will stay."

He went into the bedroom where tiny Aurelia lay asleep in the center of the marital bed. Normally he would gently pick her up and deposit her in the wooden cradle beside them—one of the few pieces of furniture that had followed all the moves of their lives together—and he would snuggle into the warmth of his wife and they would laugh together, to touch, to kiss. Tonight, he left the baby in the center of the bed, crawled under the quilt on his side, and turned to face the wall.

*　*　*

Carlito coughed and his paintbrush wavered, making a crooked black line across the bright yellow sunflower before him. He stifled the cough with the crook of his arm and then sipped of the honey and water mixture Ramona had left in a cup for him. A damp cloth removed most of the black smear on the current plate, part of a large set he hoped to sell to a shop in San Geraldo. He was nearly finished with the big job and the end could not come soon enough. He swore that if he ever saw another sunflower design he would kill himself.

"Ready for your haircut?" Ramona asked, peering through the open door from the yard. "I've finished the boys."

"Papá! Papá! Look at my work from school," Francesca shouted, brushing past her mother and holding up a small slate. "I can write all my letters now."

He set down his brush, more than willing to take a break from the tedious work. "That's beautiful, *hija*," he said to his seven-year-old. "You are making your papá very proud."

"Me too!" Little Aurelia could not hold still. She danced around the back stoop as he walked outside and showed him a collection of squiggles she had made with a stick in the dirt. "My letters!"

He laughed and patted her head. "Very good. You will soon write a book!"

Ramona pointed at the stool sitting near the door. Around the base of it were piles of hair clippings. In the winter she allowed the males of the family to let their hair grow, mainly for warmth but also because she did not relish doing the job inside the house and having to sweep for days to clean up the hairs. So this was a spring ritual—everyone got a haircut at once. She brandished the straight razor and then draped a towel around her husband's shoulders.

"Ah, Carlito, look at this gray in your hair since last autumn!" She cut off several inches and held out the strand for him to see. "Are you becoming an old man, my darling?"

"No more than you are becoming an old woman."

She laughed. Lucky for him she had not taken it as an insult. She took another strand of hair between her fingers, aiming with the razor to shorten it. Carlito held up a hand.

"*Momentito*," he gasped, a second before he erupted in another fit of coughing.

Ramona stepped around to look at his face. "This is becoming worse."

"*Es nada*," he insisted, working to hold another cough inside.

"It is not nothing. Have you talked to the doctor?"

"That gringo in San Geraldo? He wants to take my blood. The man is *un idiota*." He cleared his throat loudly and forced himself to sit still.

Ramona worked quietly for a moment before speaking again. "I have been thinking about this, Carlito. I worry for your health. I worry for your spirit. You are not a happy man."

He breathed very cautiously. Where was she going with this?

"The son of Isabella Contarde came through town last week. He has been living in Belize, on the coast, for five years now and he says things have improved there and the country is becoming much more prosperous. British settlers have gone there, wealthy men and their families, to oversee the log cutting and to keep peace." Her words tumbled out quickly now. "He says there are still problems at times but that the settlements of these wealthy men are providing work for many. I think we should go there."

He turned to look at her. Was this a joke?

"Don't move! I just cut too much from one place." She placed her hands on each side of his head and forced him to face the goat pen.

"Ramona, please do not joke about this." He would not become hopeful again, only to have his dreams thwarted.

She combed through his hair with quick strokes and then stepped around to stand in front of him.

"I am serious, *amor*. It is time."

Obviously, she had been thinking of this for some days. He felt a flutter of joy in his chest. To leave the desert where the winters were cold and the summers blistering hot. He remembered the paintings he had seen, all those years ago, of tropical beaches and turquoise water.

"Miguel and Lorenzo are old enough now to provide help," Ramona said as she began cutting again. "Even Francesca and Enrique will be far less of a burden than they were at a younger age. Aurelia is still small. But she is strong and willful. She can be entertained by the others teaching her what they have learned from school."

Somehow he knew that was at the heart of Ramona's decision. Finally, her children had the basics of their education. They would not grow up to be ignorant peasants in a dusty Mexican pueblo.

"I am almost finished with the sunflower plates," he said. "We can begin packing soon?"

"Immediately. In fact, if the plates are not already promised, pack them. We can sell or trade some along the way for food."

He reached over his shoulder and took her hand, clearing his throat to cover the emotion that welled up. "Thank you," he said simply.

By the end of the day the children had picked up the excitement and were racing around underfoot. Ramona decided that they must be given tasks or they would make her crazy.

"Enrique, stop running in and out the door! Help your father pack his art supplies. Francesca and Lorenzo, help me in the kitchen. Miguel, put my washtub in the wagon and then you can begin carrying out the items as we pack them."

Carlito watched with a certain admiration. His lovely wife had done this so often that she knew how to organize everything perfectly. He set to work making wooden crates for the pottery and instructed Enrique on packing everything safely in straw.

Three days later, their accumulated household items were aboard the wagon, except for the most important cooking pots, a supply of food, and their bedding—the items that would be pulled out each night to make camp along the journey.

"What about this, papá?" Enrique asked, handing Carlito the last few boxes they had filled together. He was pointing to a high shelf and the carved wooden box old señor Aragon had given to Carlito as a child.

"Hmm … I don't think I need it," Carlito said, thinking of the wagon that was now crammed with their things.

"Papá! It is special. If you don't want it, I do!"

Carlito reached for the ugly old box. He'd been equally insistent as a boy; he remembered his father saying that he would have to hold it on his lap since their carts were so full. He smiled indulgently and gave his own son the same advice. Enrique clasped the box to his chest and ran from the room.

The journey took months but every step was worth it, Carlito decided when he caught his first glimpse of the sea. His Mexican artist friend had not begun to capture the fantastic shades of the blue-green water and white sand, or the curl of the waves as they rolled toward shore and gently broke in foamy trails. He walked to the water's edge, let the swells break over his bare feet.

A bubble of happiness welled up inside him and burst in a glorious outpouring of joy.

* * *

Enrique watched in fascination as his father exchanged words and gestures with the Englishman who wore multiple layers of outrageous clothing, garments that must surely feel like an oppressive mantle of death in the humid heat of midday. Neither man understood the other's words—that much was obvious as they signaled what they were trying to convey. But at the end of an hour, the Martinez family had a small wooden house to live in and the Englishman with the improbable name of Mr. Clarence Smythe-Brookington (Enrique could not even pronounce this) had extracted a promise from Carlito to paint portraits of the man's beautiful wife and two children.

Enrique ran back to the wagon, excited to tell his siblings that he had learned two English words—*house* and *slave*. The latter referred to the great number of people he saw with skin even darker than that of the Indians of Mexico's interior. These slaves moved with a frightened demeanor and they all had jobs moving the heavy logs being cut from the surrounding jungle. As for the house, it had a wooden floor and the family was specifically instructed to use only the designated fireplace for cooking indoors. There were two bedrooms, which meant the children no longer slept in the kitchen. He wondered how they would keep warm at night but discovered, after sundown, that the tropical heat never quite went away. Luckily, the windows in this new place could be opened to the coastal breeze which kept them from roasting in their beds—unfortunately, they also let in the mosquitos.

Ramona and the children spent the first day unpacking and setting up the house, while Carlito was shown to the special room inside Brookington's big house where he would work. Enrique caught glimpses of two children with extremely white faces and pale hair, both dressed in white clothing head to toe and trailing behind a stern-looking older woman like little ghosts. He smiled at them and received tentative smiles in return, although the woman quickly shooed them back inside from the wide porch of that huge house.

Miguel and Lorenzo had piled their clothing on the big

bed that the three boys would share, disappearing toward the shore, and Enrique found himself snagged by his mother who was setting dishes and cooking pots in place in the kitchen.

"Put away all the clothing," she instructed, " and help Francesca tidy your bedroom. Francesca can watch the baby while I make lunch and you will go find your brothers."

He started to protest the unfairness of having to stay inside and work while the other two boys escaped, but it was simpler to do as she asked rather than fight about it. Plus, this way he could have control over the bedroom arrangement. He found Aurelia sitting up, a trick she had recently learned, in the middle of the narrow bed that would belong to the girls. Francesca had brought in the wooden crates their father made for the journey and she was folding her own skirts and shawl and placing them in one. Two more of the boxes sat on the floor.

Well, if his brothers could not be bothered with work, then they would not reap the benefits either. He picked up Miguel's extra pair of pants and the two shirts cast off by their father that nearly fit the oldest boy now; into the larger box they went, followed by Lorenzo's things. He shoved it under the edge of the bed. In the other crate he set the carved wooden box that was now his prized possession then began folding his shirts. He'd told no one about his experience under the stars one night during their travels.

It had been the darkest night of the new moon, with only the glow of the Milky Way and the planets above, when Enrique woke suddenly. All the others were asleep on their pallets under the wagon but he swore a voice had spoken to him. He listened, the hairs on his arms rising. No sound but the soft breathing of his family and a heavy sigh from the horse that was hobbled a few yards away. It came again—like a whisper. He lifted his head from the roll of clothing he used as a pillow. Cradled beside his stomach, the carved box felt warm. He saw that the colored stones on it sparkled faintly in the starlight.

He slid out from under his blanket and edged away from the wagon, keeping the box with him. Barefoot, he padded through the dust to the fire pit his father had made the night before, where his mother had cooked their supper. The embers gave off a faint glow, visible only because the night itself was so dark. He sat cross-legged on the ground and opened the box's lid. He imagined that the interior glowed slightly too, but that was impossible. The stars were simply giving out more light than one would imagine … it was because the desert all around was utterly black in the depth of the night.

Enrique brushed a dusting from his father's charcoal stick out of a corner of the box. The glow intensified. Hmm. His interest perked up. He ran two fingers around the interior edge of the thing. At the instant the fingers completed the circuit a jolt of energy shot up his arm and into his shoulder. His last thought was to keep the box away from the remains of the fire.

He remembered how he had awakened, sprawled on the ground by the fire pit, as the sky was turning pale gray. The family was asleep still; no one had moved. He rubbed his aching arm and shook out the soreness. The box lay about two feet away, the lid open, and he picked it up. Immediately, the wood began to warm in his hands; it glowed with a golden color he had never seen and the stones sparkled red, green and blue. His breath caught.

All trace of pain was gone from his arm. His mind raced with the possibilities—what was this thing? Did it possess some kind of magic?

The moment his thoughts settled on that word he knew he must keep silent about it. The priests were free with talk of God and His miracles, but they also spoke of witches and evil humans who would be caught and burn in hell for the sin of practicing magic. He set the box on the ground and its color quieted. Perhaps he should destroy it before it had the chance to destroy him.

He watched it as the minutes went by. The color became quite dull and plain, the beauty of that glowing wood and the sparkling stones only a memory. He felt sure his father had never experienced anything like this with the box. He would have said so. Or he would never have given the item to his young son. Somehow, in that moment, Enrique knew he alone was meant to have the box, that he and this artifact would have a special relationship. He carried it back to his sleeping pallet and wrapped a blanket around it. Suddenly, he was shivering in the early morning air.

Now, in a new house in a new land, he folded the last of his clothing and arranged the items to cover the carved box. He would have to decide what, if anything, he should do about it. His mother saved him the trouble of making a decision by calling out that lunch was ready. "Enrique, go find your brothers."

Francesca carried the baby into the kitchen. Enrique raced out the door and found the other boys near the water. Lorenzo was poking with a stick at some creature that had washed up on the shore, a slimy-looking thing with short horns coming out of its head. Enrique backed away from it. Miguel stood staring toward the big house, where a girl about his age stared back. Her skin was very black and her simple dress suggested that she was a maid at the house. He nudged Miguel and laughed when his brother jumped. Girls! Was this what it would be like to be fifteen years old?

Everyone had settled at the table when their father arrived, flush with excitement.

"I have an actual studio inside the house," he said, as he washed his hands in the bowl by the door. "There is a work table where I can mix my paints, and Señor Smythe … oh, I cannot say his entire name yet … he says to call him Brookie. What a silly name. Anyway, he says he will order the finest *canvas* from *Europe* for the portraits. See? I have learned two more English words! Meanwhile, until they come, I think I am free to use the space to paint other things. This afternoon I will walk along the *playa* and look for suitable subjects."

"Is he a nice man?" Ramona asked. "This Mr. Brookie?"

"He seems like a very devoted father, very kind to his children. But he also has a stern way with the slaves. I heard him bellow orders to the foreman and then when Mr. Brookie turned his back the other man lashed out with a whip at two of the dark men who were not moving fast enough."

Enrique had seen incidents of cruelty between people—there were nice ones and mean ones everywhere, he supposed—but never one who was allowed to use a whip on someone else without punishment for doing so. He would stay clear of these Europeans.

* * *

Brookie sat on a chair on the wide veranda of his shady home, rocking slowly when Enrique mounted the steps.

"What seems to be the problem today?" Enrique asked the man whose hair had grown pure white over the years.

"Probably the damned lumbago," Brookie growled. He shifted in his seat and grinned as he indicated the other chair. "Can you believe us? I remember you as a skinny little Mexican kid when you were eleven years old. Now you're my doctor, speaking perfect English, and our families have blended so thoroughly that I can't see the edges anymore. Where's the old man?"

It took Enrique a moment to realize he meant Carlito. Among the extended Martinez family, Brookie himself was often called the old man.

"Ah, Papá is resting. He finished a new painting yesterday and decided to take a day off."

"I'm not sure I like his new style," Brookie commented.

Enrique laughed. "That's actually his old style. When we were kids in Mexico he always painted the popular primitive way. He switched to realism when he came here because it was what Europeans wanted." He turned to the older man. "Stand up. Let's see about that back of yours."

He'd handled the mysterious box before coming over and wanted to apply his healing touch before the effects wore off. From the moment he'd held his direly ill little sister—was that really almost forty years ago?—he realized that he had great power with that box. Aurelia's deadly fever had subsided within minutes, and since that day he had used his gift to heal hundreds of people.

Of course he had studied the Western medical books and often used those medicines that he found useful, but in his experience modern medicine was still a mixture of experimentation and quackery. Just because men could now name the organs inside the body, it did not mean that all was understood or that all cures recommended in 1790s medical practice were effective. In the local community, many people referred to Enrique as a *curandero* while others like Brookie actually used the word doctor.

He asked Brookie to lift the back of his shirt and Enrique rested both of his hands on the skin over the muscles at the lower spine.

"Ah, that feels good," the old man said.

Slight pressure, gentle movement of the hands. He massaged the area for five minutes or so, mainly to make it seem as if he was actually doing something medically.

"Do you still have that salve I gave you?" he asked as Brookie tucked in his shirt.

The older man nodded.

"Use it, every morning and every night. The herbs in it will help keep those muscles flexible."

"And stop trying to kick logs around on my own?"

They both chuckled.

"Papá! Mr. Brookie!" Shrill voices rang through the morning air and the men turned to see Enrique's two young sons racing toward the Smythe-Brookington house as fast as their short legs could carry them.

"Boys! Decorum." Both boys came to a halt and then approached with small steps. He agreed with Catherine, his wife and Brookie's daughter, who tried valiantly to instill a bit of English manners in their children. Given a choice, the boys would run wild on the beaches like natives.

"That's better," Brookie said. "You know that good little lads get a story."

George and Jonathan responded by walking slowly onto

the porch and sitting at Brookie's feet. "May we hear about the pirates again, sir?"

Brookie and Enrique exchanged a smile at the small triumph.

"Certainly, lads." He leaned forward in his chair, hands clasped, elbows on his knees. All part of the anticipation. "Well, when I came here to Belize with my family, oh, this was many years ago when your father was hardly bigger than you are now, it had not been that many years since pirates roamed these beaches at will …"

Enrique stood quietly and tiptoed away to visit his next patient, just up the dirt road in the town that had grown steadily. How many times he had heard Brookie's tales—how British pirates would raid the Spanish settlements for gold and silver, how the Spaniards would build forts along the coast and fight back, how ships were hijacked and the two empires battled. Things had certainly quieted down since then although rivalries were not unknown even now. Word of a Spanish attack on the settlement of St. George's Caye had only reached them two weeks ago.

His father-in-law's voice rose with the excitement of the story, as Enrique walked on. Life had changed drastically in that man's lifetime. The American colonies had won their freedom, the Caribbean islands were being sorted out—some attaining nationhood, others remaining under control of their European discoverers, be they English, Spanish, Dutch or French. People, too, moved on. He knew of ancestors back in the New Mexico territory but had never met any of them. Perhaps one day there would be a means more effective than a horse-drawn cart to travel inland. For now, transportation to other parts of the world remained best navigated by the hundreds of ships that dominated the seas.

He put all that rumination aside when he reached the cottage of Alphonse Mbaba, a patient wracked with such a cough that Enrique suspected some sort of virulent cancer eating away at the poor man's insides. This one, he knew, was beyond his help for a recovery. Sometimes all he could do was offer consolation.

From Alphonse's bedside he made his way through the village, stopping to check on three additional patients and responding to a frantic shout for help when a young mother discovered her son had fallen from a banyan tree. The lad had the breath knocked out of him but responded quickly to Enrique's touch. Luckily, he had landed on soft sand and there were no broken bones.

At home Catherine's cook had kept his dinner warm in the miraculous new six-plate cast-iron stove her father had imported from Germany as their wedding gift. He pecked a kiss on his wife's cheek as she set his plate on the table.

"Where are the boys?" he asked. "I hope they've not overstayed their welcome with your father. He was in the middle of his famed pirate stories when I last saw them."

She laughed, the light musical sound which had drawn his attention when he was fifteen. "That was long ago. They came home and would have eaten everything in sight, including your own dinner, I'm afraid, had I not stopped them. George has gone to study his lessons with the Galbraith children and I believe Jonathan is reading in the parlor."

He smiled at the way she clung to the British words, such as parlor. In his childhood homes there had usually been one common room, sometimes a separate bedroom or kitchen, sometimes not. His parents would have never conceived of having different rooms for each purpose and certainly would not have imagined a thing called a parlor.

Since Ramona's death five years ago, his father had spread out in the small wooden house which he had bought from Brookie at some point, now using the children's former bedroom as his studio. He lived a solitary life, painting in the mornings, the better time for his failing eyes to take advantage of the light. Catherine normally took him some dinner in the early afternoon but Carlito ate little these days. Enrique recognized the signs—his father would not live much longer.

He handed his empty plate to his wife and gave her another kiss. His youngest son sat on the couch, another addition courtesy of Brookie, the softest piece of furniture in the house, with its padded seat. The wooden arms and back had been carved to match the room's other chairs and Catherine took great pride in seeing that their slave girl dusted and polished them until they gleamed.

"Not outside playing?" Enrique teased.

Jonathan looked up with copies of his own dark, serious eyes. He pointed to the book on his lap. "It's the history of ancient Rome. Did you know that the Romans held nearly all of Europe and built roads that are still in use today?"

Enrique actually had not known that last part. "You are an excellent scholar. Mr. Billingham says so."

"I like his classes. He loaned me this book but it isn't part of our course work."

"Good. I'm glad you get along with your teacher and that you are learning so much."

"Papá? Can I ask you something?"

Enrique nodded and took a seat nearby. While George's questions always followed the lines of, "may I take some more pudding?" or "can I sail with one of the galleons when I'm sixteen?", Jonathan's questions were likely to come from the inner reaches of his intelligent mind and could concern anything. It was often a challenge to provide answers.

"Papá, that box you keep on the shelf … would you teach me how to use it one day?"

A knot formed in Enrique's stomach. "To use it?"

"Yes. I have noticed that you take it down and hold it nearly every day. Always on the days when you visit your patients." The boy closed his book and looked at his lap. "I have a confession, Papá. I touched it once."

The knot went tighter. His thoughts flashed through a half-dozen scenes—events where he had cured sickness, times when he found himself with such unlimited energy that he had to leave the house for fear of the destruction he might do, and one time when someone else had touched it, an old woman whose eyes then glowed with the frightening power of the devil itself. He watched his young son's expression carefully. "And what happened?"

"I … I am not sure I should say."

"You will not be in trouble. But you need to tell me."

"You know how the box is normally somewhat dark and dull? This day, you had not put it on the shelf. It was on that table by the window. I thought it looked more attractive, much handsomer in some way. That's when I touched it."

"And?"

"The wood was warm. I thought the sunlight had been

on it, but that window was in the shade at the time. I put my hand on it like this ..." He laid his palm flat on the book. "... and the box became even warmer. I think the color of it grew brighter. The little stones ... they were most definitely brighter."

"Did you open the lid? Put your hands inside?"

The boy's eyes went wide. "No. Only the lid, I promise. I'm sorry, Papá, if I should not have done it."

"But the box has aroused your curiosity and you want to know what makes it react."

Jonathan nodded vigorously.

"I will tell you. I promise. But you are not yet twelve and it's an important responsibility, an adult responsibility, to use that box. A time will come in the next few years when I can show it to you, teach you what to do with it. For now, though, I need your promise that you will not touch it again."

"I promise."

Their eyes met, two dark pairs. They understood each other. At least Enrique hoped they did, for the futures of many people could depend upon his finding exactly the right person to hand the box to one day.

* * *

Carlito's time came on the eve of his eightieth birthday, although dates that far back in time, births that were never officially recorded in the small pueblo towns of northern New Mexico, were rarely remembered and in Carlito's case he had long since lost track of his age. He was unsure even of his children's ages. Ramona had once remembered them but she had left this earth many years ago. They gathered here now, those remaining.

Miguel must be close to sixty—his hair was completely gray—and his own children were adults. His wife, the freedwoman Adana who had changed her name to Edna, had died giving birth to their third.

Lorenzo had long since sailed to make his fortune in Spain. The family had never heard another word, and his fate was unknown. Many ships went down in those years. He never would know, Carlito realized as his final breaths wheezed in his lungs.

Francesca went away with a Cuban who came to Belize on a ship that delivered rum. Once in a great while, during the years her mother was alive, she had written. That man had beaten her but she met another, a good man. As far as Carlito knew, she still lived there with him.

His eyes moved to Enrique, the son who had stayed closest, who had helped his parents through the years. His wife, Catherine, stood at his side with tears in her eyes. He wanted to tell her not to be sad, that he had finally reached life's ultimate goal. Beside the couple were their two boys. Something in that younger one was special. Carlito knew it but was too tired at the moment to figure out what that special quality was.

Then he thought of baby Aurelia. Prone to fevers and tropical diseases, she had fought a brave fight but one day an especially bad bout came. Her brother cried over her, wanting so badly to save her, but despite the fact that he was able to cure many people of many troubles he had not been able to keep her alive. She'd lain in the graveyard beside her mother for several years now.

A tear slipped from Carlito's eye and ran down the side of his face. Although his eyes were closed now he heard

Catherine sob loudly.

"Do not worry about me. I have lived a good life, a satisfying life," he said, wishing his voice did not sound so garbled. Then he exhaled for the last time.

* * *

"Jonathan, come with me," Enrique said, motioning his son toward Brookie's old study in the house he and Catherine and the boys had moved into after the old man's death a decade earlier. He closed the solid door behind them.

The paneled walls and sturdy furnishings had always felt reassuring and comfortable to Enrique, here in this place where he had established his medical office so patients could come at any time to see him. Many had come to the house during the past two days of visitation, for everyone in town knew the Martinez family, most had been treated by Enrique and all were respectful of his father. Now that the burial in the plot next to beloved Ramona was done, nothing was left but the empty hours until everyone left.

"The subject we talked about, years ago, when I told you the right day would come," he said, reaching for the shelf which held the carved wooden box.

"I am ready now?" asked the young man whose deep brown eyes were now magnified by a studious-looking pair of spectacles.

"I believe so."

Enrique set the box on his ornately carved desk. He stepped back. "Open it."

Jonathan took a deep breath and moved forward. Both hands steady, he raised the lid on its hinges. Enrique watched, practically holding his breath, waiting for any sign of trouble. None came. He breathed again.

"Your grandfather repaired those hinges once, I had forgotten the incident until this very minute."

Not taking his eyes from the box, the young man tilted the lid fully open. Enrique remained watchful but said nothing. Jonathan touched the inner lid where a few letters had been carved in some unknown long-ago time. They were faint but in bright light he had once been able to make out a few V-I- something-T. The rest was unreadable. He ran his index finger along the inside edges of the box, following the perimeter. Enrique remembered the exact moment when he had done the same, and the box's reaction. The very same thing happened this time.

Jonathan's hand shot away from the box, his arm flailing in the air, his legs buckling. Enrique grabbed a chair and steered his son's limp body toward it. He checked the pulse and found it racing. Gently, he stroked his son's hair until—more than one hundred counts later—Jonathan's dark eyes fluttered open.

"What happened?" he murmured.

"I will tell you everything I know." Enrique pulled another chair close, sat facing his son and began to talk.

Chapter 6

Scientific Minds Converge

Phineas Dailey pressed his horse to move more quickly now that the road was smooth and dry. How nice to be away from the streets of the new District of Columbia where construction continued non-stop and the plethora of workers, slaves and conveyances kept the muddy roads continually churned and boggy. Alexandria was a refreshingly quiet, charming town by comparison.

His two-wheeled trap approached the address he'd been given, rolling to a stop beside a massive brick building. At the side, two other carriages waited—a fine landau which he felt sure belonged to Walter Brannigan and a nice little tillbury cart he recognized as that of his tobacco-farming friend George Randall. During his drive he had wondered if Mr. Benjamin Franklin might also be present but he did not see evidence of the great man yet.

It was at Randall's suggestion that today's meeting should take place here. Phineas stepped down from his buggy and handed off the reins to a slave who stood by tending the other vehicles as well.

George stood at the top of three steps leading to a wide front door.

"Greetings! So good that you could come, Phineas." He descended to street level and extended his hand. "Come in, see what you think."

As a scientist Phineas supposed he would always be the quiet one of the group, the man who lived inside his own head. George Randall, with his plantations and multitude of slaves, was an outgoing man with large hands and full-blown facial features including bushy side whiskers that were not quite in fashion. He followed his host through the white-painted double doors.

Inside, the space was large and hollow, echoing their footsteps and voices. A table that would have over-filled his own dining room in the city seemed quite small in the cavernous room. Three men stood around the table, where a decanter of golden liquid sat in the midst of a set of cut-glass aperitif glasses.

"Come, come. Let me introduce you."

George quickly presented the businessman Walter Brannigan, of whose reputation for success Phineas was well aware, along with Roderick Smith and Isaak Templeton. Smith's British accent revealed that he was a recent immigrant, but with the fight for independence now finished the colonists were becoming more accustomed to having Londoners as neighbors. Smith was apparently another source of financing for their little venture, while

Templeton and Phineas himself were included as the scientific side of the equation.

"We shall partition off various rooms," George was saying. "It was originally a warehouse but with the newer ones being built closer to the river's edge, I've begun storing my own crops there and this building has stood empty for nearly two years now."

He picked up a roll of white paper that Phineas had not previously noticed and unrolled it on the table.

"Now, here," said George, pointing at the largest room on the drawing, "I would envision the laboratory. If it meets with our scientists' approval, of course. Two small rooms serve as offices for the financial accounting and a secretary or two. I am certain there will be additional uses, but this is a start. What do you think, gentlemen?"

Brannigan suggested the addition of a large vault for safe storage of items of value which, in turn, expanded the size of one of the offices. Phineas felt his pulse quicken as Templeton pulled out a pencil and sketched a layout for work tables and storage for the burners and beakers they would use to conduct experiments.

"What level of financing will be required to get the project started?" George asked rather bluntly.

"At a bare minimum …" Templeton began.

"Let's not talk of minimal in anything we do," Brannigan interrupted. "If we plan to do this we should do it correctly and without frugality."

Templeton asked to have a moment and drew Phineas aside. They talked quietly and Isaak wrote a list. When he handed it over, he sounded apologetic. "It will run into the thousands of dollars, I'm afraid."

Brannigan and Smith turned to George Randall now.

"Do you plan to donate the use of the building?" Brannigan asked George. Phineas was learning that these two did not mince words or stand on niceties. "If so, I believe that Smith and I can put together the funds for the renovation and equipment."

Smith had not actually said much up to this point, but he nodded agreement. Phineas could only surmise that the two men knew each other fairly well and had already discussed the matter.

"Before we move forward, I think we should clarify our goals and set forth a mission statement," George said. "Privately, each of us has discussed our interest in science and in unexplained phenomena. May I state it now for the group, that this is our intention: We are here to study occurrences and items that may come to our attention, those which are purported to or have a reputation of demonstrating a power beyond our knowledge. We will use any and all scientific techniques available to us, as well as any new techniques that shall become available in the future. Our own fortunes and those that might be offered by others with a similar interest shall be used to fund our research, but we shall never accept money from any entity with a vested interest in the outcome of any finding."

"Hear, hear! The science speaks for itself and shall be conducted diligently and without prejudice." Brannigan's sentiment was echoed by the others.

"And what shall we call our new scientific institution?" Smith asked.

George Randall had clearly considered this question as well. "I would propose that we name it for the man who first piqued the interest of several of us here today, the scientist who, although his name will never be known by most of the world, is the man who set the standard for the sort of research we hold in esteem, Helmut Vongraf."

"The Vongraf Foundation." The words slipped from Phineas without a second thought.

Brannigan had reached for the decanter. "To The Vongraf Foundation!" he said, filling each of the five small glasses.

Phineas sipped the sherry. He had met Helmut Vongraf once when his father financed a trip to Europe during which Phineas was to finish his studies and open his mind to the wider world beyond the small American colonies. The Austrian had been a visitor to Paris, along with his lovely wife Kirsten, who had also studied science and acted as the great man's laboratory assistant. Phineas suspected that Kirsten may have contributed significantly to her husband's discoveries. His enchantment with the lady, however, might have been based on the fact that he developed a glorious youthful crush on her that summer.

He tamped down those thoughts. The truth was that the Austrian pair had brought scientific interest in the unexplained into the modern age. They disputed tarot, magic and alchemy even though those topics were still popular in parlors across the continent. He suspected he knew what they would think of superstitious American colonists who believed that the devil and his minions lived in the heavily wooded areas of New England. Such legends as the Jersey Devil would surely draw their scorn, as it did his own.

"One more item for discussion," George said, holding his half-empty glass. "For the present time I believe that we need to keep our activities quiet. We are not a so-called 'secret society' such as the Masons, Illuminati or Rosicrucians. We know that. We know ourselves. But others may become suspicious as they learn of the types of artifacts we want to investigate. Prosecution for the practice of witchcraft is not supposed to exist anymore but there are yet those who would think of us in that way."

All heads nodded.

"Until we prove ourselves as diligent seekers of scientific knowledge, I say we do not discuss our work or our beliefs. As long as we are experimenting in the unknown, the unexplained, we run the risk of being seen as heretics. And *that*, gentlemen, could be very dangerous indeed."

Chapter 7

A Balloon Drifts

Elizabeth Cox stood within the wicker enclosure looking out over faces in the crowd. Her husband, handsome in his top hat and tails, gave her a hearty smile then turned back to the crowd. Their two little girls, Nancy and Constance, were in the front row where their father could keep watch over them. Nancy, in particular, would fidget through the entire ceremony, Elizabeth knew, but at this moment the enormous balloon held the girls' attention.

"Friends! Fellow Texians! This is a momentous day indeed," shouted James Cox. "For we have declared our independence from all other powers and have become a sovereign nation unto ourselves. March 2, 1836, will be forever marked as a day to remember!"

A roar rose from the crowd.

Beside her in the balloon's gondola, Elizabeth felt Rory Duncan move about. The pilot—her husband's acquaintance from the newly formed legislature—checked the dozens of ropes that secured the inflated bag of gas to the basket, yanked a few times for good measure at the sacks of sand that hung around the edges, and looked up critically at the valve where the gas had been pumped in.

"All is perfectly well," Rory said under his breath. "We shall launch the minute James's speech is finished."

The excitement among the people became palpable; to see a balloon floating over Galveston was a first-time event, and to have the mayor's wife aboard—well, Elizabeth knew she was the envy of all her friends. Virginia McDermott had been unable to quell her snide remarks at the Ladies Aid meeting on Tuesday, a sure sign of her jealousy over the fact that Elizabeth had been chosen to stand here in front of the gathering in her new spring finery and to experience the upcoming excitement of the aerial view.

James talked on … the bravery of Stephen Austin and Sam Houston, the treaties with Mexico which had finalized the breaking away of the new republic. He glossed over the squabbles between Mirabeau Lamar and Mr. Houston, each of whom had different ideas about the direction the newly formed country should take. Elizabeth had heard all of this discussed in her own parlor until she was sick of all subjects political. Now she merely wanted the balloon to launch and to float over her city. What would it be like? Would she be able to pick out her own house? Surely so, it was the largest at the north end. They planned to land as close as possible to the park, where a luncheon spread was being prepared. A crowd would greet them and bear them back in triumph to the celebration. It would be the perfect way to cap the afternoon and to rub her little achievement in the face of Virginia McDermott.

Rory's voice caught her attention as he instructed the four men holding handling lines attached to the corners of the basket to release them. James had finished talking and was looking over his shoulder at them. Rory pulled the tie string on one of the sandbags and as the sand poured to the ground the basket became buoyant and she felt the floor of it wobble under her feet. Oh, my!

Her daughters waved the white handkerchiefs she had insisted they carry. Everyone else in the crowd waved small paper flags with the Lone Star. The red, white and blue bunting around the dais fluttered in a light breeze. A cheer rose. Elizabeth found herself looking at the upturned faces of the entire citizenry. Her stomach fluttered and for one tiny moment she wondered what on earth she was doing. Then a smile spread over her face.

They rose to treetop level. None of her friends had ever viewed a fully grown elm tree from its crown. And the houses! The peaks and gables of the Cox home stood high and beautiful, just as she had known they would. Only the church was larger and she realized with a start that they were drifting right toward the steeple tower. She turned to tug at Rory's sleeve but he had already spotted the danger.

"Not to worry," he said, reaching for another of the sandbags. "We drop more sand, we rise a little higher."

But the string seemed to have knotted and he had to resort to another tactic. Pulling a deadly-looking knife from its leather holster at his belt, he bent over to slice the canvas bag. The steeple was coming at them with alarming speed and Elizabeth edged back, not wanting to see it, trying to leave Rory extra space to work. He bent at the waist, over the edge of the wicker basket.

Too far. With flailing arms he went over the edge, a frantic shout escaping him as he went. Incongruously, she noticed a hole in the bottom of his right shoe just before he disappeared completely from sight. Elizabeth Cox did something she ordinarily thought crass and stupid—she screamed. And screamed, and screamed.

A quick peek over the edge of the basket showed that Rory had hit the steep roof of the church and was sliding swiftly toward the ground. The balloon, on the other hand, now shot upward at a frightening rate. Her heart threatened to burst from her chest and her breakfast rose in her throat. She looked around, without a clue about what to do.

Her house seemed much smaller now, the trees merely a fuzz of green and the people mere dots. Had anyone witnessed what had happened? Would someone figure out a way to rescue her? She felt frozen at the edge of the basket, watching everything on the ground grow more distant, wanting to reach for the sandbags. She had a dreadful feeling that rescue was impossible. She was on her own.

She pressed her hands to the sides of her head and forced herself to think. What had the pilot told her? Dropping sand made the balloon go up. She stepped away from the temptation to touch those bags. Venting gas made the balloon go down, but she had no idea how he had intended to perform that feat. None of the equipment or the rubberized cloth bag made a bit of sense to her. She risked another glance over the edge and her eyes widened in horror.

Instead of moving inland over the city, the craft had now changed direction. She had just crossed over the narrow strip of beach. In no more than a moment there would be nothing below her but the blue-gray waters of the Gulf of Mexico. She felt her legs give way as she fainted to the wooden floor of the gondola.

* * *

James Cox watched the red and yellow balloon drift lazily over the city; he sported a smile at his successful planning of this day of celebration. He stepped off the dais and stood next to his daughters as he shook hands with well-wishers. The plan was to make his way slowly by open carriage toward the city park where, with luck, Stephen Austin planned to join the Galveston citizens for the midday meal. The important man was very busy, so there had been no promises, but still—a local politician could hope.

"What's happened?" someone in the crowd called out.

James followed the fingers pointing at the sky. Why was the balloon going so high? This did not fit with Rory's plan to skirt the treetops, make his way to the north end of town, and then tether the balloon so he could give rides to the populace during the picnic.

"I'm sure it's fine. The pilot knows what he's doing," he assured the people nearest him. "He's very experienced."

James hoped to God that was true; he'd only known Rory Duncan for a few weeks.

"Let's continue to the park," he said with his best political smile. "Refreshments await!"

He steered Nancy and Constance toward the road and the open carriage with his finest trotter hitched to it. It was all he could do not to betray his concern over this unplanned turn. James Cox was a man who made plans and expected them to go perfectly.

He'd no sooner released the brake on the carriage and given the horse a gentle smack with the reins than he heard shouts of alarm. A man on a chestnut quarter-horse rode toward him full-out, yanking his mount to a stop only a foot from Cox's carriage.

"Mayor—" his breath came in gasps. "There's been—" He glanced at the two little girls next to James. "I need to speak—"

James set the brake again and told the girls to sit absolutely still. He climbed down, wishing that bad knee would quit acting up, and walked to the back of the rig. The other man had dismounted, leading his horse and standing very close.

All around them, concern turned to shock on the faces of the crowd as some kind of news rippled through the gathering.

"It's the balloonist, Mr. Mayor, that Rory fellow. He's fallen. By the church. We saw him fall off the roof and— I'm afraid he's dead, sir."

"Dead?" James repeated the word as if he'd never heard it before. Comprehension dawned. "But then, where's my wife? Was she thrown out too?"

"I don't think so, sir. Well, no one's seen her."

James stared skyward. The balloon was a small spot in the sky now, and it was much too far south. Over the water.

* * *

Elizabeth stirred. The air around her felt cold, so cold. She sat up, her fuzzy mind trying to recall … the situation coming back to her at once when she saw the wicker basket all around. Her light, spring shawl offered little protection and she hugged herself, scrubbing her hands along her upper arms for warmth. Her skirt and petticoats were tangled around her legs, and she gathered some of the material around her upper body. But the muslin dress was of little help.

She looked up. The fabric of the balloon seemed a bit more slack than before. Had some of the gas leaked out? She got to her knees, briefly considered praying but decided God had already abandoned her. Gripping a piece of rope tied to the inside of the gondola she pulled herself to her feet and risked a glance over the side. Nothing but blue, far below.

She sank to the floor again, placed her forehead against her bent knees. James was a man of action and he would do anything in his power, she felt sure, but what could he really *do*? Nancy and Constance—her sweet little ones. Their faces appeared, clean and neat in their best dresses and the bonnets she'd chosen for them that morning, exactly as she'd last seen them waving from the ground. A physical pain stabbed her heart at the thought of them.

Her situation was hopeless and she could only wonder how long the balloon could possibly stay airborne before either it crashed or she simply died from exposure. Her spirit felt crushed. She curled into a small ball and cried.

When next she opened her eyes the air had changed. The sun was low in the sky and it was, if possible, even colder. She shivered until her muscles ached. Her mouth was so dry. She looked about for a canteen of water—anything to eat or drink—but there was none. They'd only planned to traverse the city and then partake of a sumptuous barbeque luncheon at the park. All of that would be long finished, she realized, watching the sun hit the far horizon.

Where were James and the girls now? Had anyone gone by the church and discovered Rory? Did he live to tell the story, to tell them what to do now? Probably not. If hitting the tin roof had not killed him, surely the fall to the ground did. That church roof was high. She remembered when it was built—the stone edifice, the wood beams inside, the pounded metal for the roof that would keep the structure safe and dry for generations to come. James had been in on the planning and Elizabeth had watched men sit around her dining table, discussing and revising the plans.

And what did that have to do with her plight now? Nothing, she realized, but it was something to think about other than the bleak prospect of what lay ahead.

She saw the last scrap of sun disappear and could not face the dark sky. She wrapped every bit of her clothing around her and closed her eyes.

* * *

Sammy Avila started the day early. Living with three women sometimes made him feel crazy and he liked to get outdoors, to walk along the beach, to see if he could scare up something to eat. Once in awhile a nice grouper or eel would wash up on the shore; other times there were mollusks or clams caught in the little tide pools down by the big rocks. If they were still alive or only recently dead, he would catch them and take them home for breakfast.

His mother would be awake by now, perhaps stirring up a batter for plantains. He loved the way she fried them and served them hot with a little agave syrup on them. But if mama was awake, so too would be his sisters. Cornelia had a boyfriend in the village and he hoped the *hombre* would hurry up and marry the little witch so she would move out. She did nothing but criticize and torture him.

Yolanda was a confirmed spinster at thirty—she had already promised (threatened!) to live at home and care for Mamá until her last breath. Sammy had thought that duty would fall to him as the only son, after the summer before last when his father's fishing boat had gone out to sea and never returned. Well, pieces of it had returned, smashed to bits on the rocks. Hurricanes in the tropics posed a constant danger, even though the resulting waves sometimes washed interesting things ashore.

Now that Yolanda's position in the home was confirmed—never to change—Sammy supposed he could consider finding a wife and a place of his own. But the village had few choices and he found none of the young women appealing. Plus, a wife would insist that he take up some type of work to support her, and then she would get grand ideas of living in a nice house like those on the banana plantations, and Sammy knew he could never go to work for one of those big companies. He loved the sea and would have followed his father's trade except that, if he had to confess the truth, facing the same fate as his father terrified him. He'd not been out in a boat in nearly two years.

The tide was on the rise. Each successive wave splashed a little harder and came a little nearer to his bare feet. He counted to ten with his eyes shut and, surely enough, the very next wave lapped at his toes. He opened his eyes and scanned the foamy edges for signs of a fish that might come within his reach. He carried a small net made of fine rope and a long spear of flexible wood.

A dark shape bobbed on the water, just inside the reef,

farther than he wanted to venture just yet. As he watched, the waves brought it closer. It was large—maybe even a young porpoise. His eyes remained fixed on the spot. It was not swimming away, so it had probably been injured. When it came close enough he would snare it in his net and drag it in. But he had to be careful—if it had much life left in it, the creature would fight him. He could swim, but not strongly. He could not chance that it would drag him far out to sea, and he could not afford for it to get away with his only net.

Closer it came. He caught flashes of white, along with the dark parts. It looked like no other fish he'd ever seen. He stealthily took one step after another until he was in the water nearly to his waist. When he got a clear look, his breath caught.

It was a person.

Long, dark hair floated away from the head and that was what had first caught his attention. A woman, he saw, with very light skin. Her eyes were closed against the morning sun. She floated on her back and one hand held fast to something else that was dark—a piece of driftwood maybe? He waded out another two steps, nearly chest-deep now, the buoyant salt water trying to lift him off his feet. He touched the woman's arm and she jerked. She was alive!

Her feet kicked and she sputtered for a moment.

"*Tranquilo, te tengo a ti*," he said gently.

She stared at him with blue eyes such as he had never seen before, but she seemed to understand that he only wanted her to be still and let him help. She gripped the small wooden object more tightly with her right hand but allowed him to take her left arm and pull.

"You can probably stand now," he said gently in Spanish.

The woman struggled to place her feet on the sandy bottom of the sea but she wobbled and fell backward, nearly taking Sammy with her.

"*Está bien.* Do not worry. I will help you."

She weighed practically nothing in the water, so he pulled until the sea came barely above his knees and he was having to lean over too far to keep hold of her.

"Try again to stand," he said.

Again, she fluttered a bit but this time she was able to get her feet under her. He draped an arm around her waist and took much of her weight as, together, they struggled ashore. The woman immediately sat down hard when she reached dry sand. Sammy's net had become tangled around his arm and shoulder; luckily, he had left his spear ashore and it had only floated a short distance away. He retrieved it, unwound the net, and set them down.

The white woman sat with her legs bent slightly, the chunk of wood on her lap. She had not let go of her tight grip on it. No wonder—hanging on to the one thing that would float may have saved her life.

"Who are you?" he asked, kneeling beside her.

She gave him a blank stare.

"*¿Hablas español?*"

She nodded vaguely but did not answer. Sammy stared out at the endless sea. "*¿Dónde vienes?*"

She opened her mouth but only a small croak came out. She tried to swallow, to moisten her throat to speak, but no words came. He tried to think quickly. Water. She was thirsty.

"Can you walk? Come to my house and my mother will give you water."

The blue eyes rolled upward and the woman fell

sideways onto the sand.

Sammy stared for a moment. What to do? He bent over her, tried to lift her but she was as large as he and with the wet clothing was far too heavy for him to manage. He looped his hands under her armpits and dragged her, but quickly saw how impossible it would be to get her all the way home. He had walked well over a mile from the house.

A banyan tree cast its large shade over the sand, twenty yards away. A few steps at a time, Sammy got her to the cooler spot, then he headed for home at a run.

"Mamá! Mamá! I found a woman on—"

"Finally," teased Cornelia. "Sammy, ready to marry!"

"No, you stupid fool," he said. Could she not simply let him finish? "She was floating in the sea. She almost died, but she is alive. I need water—and help. I cannot carry her."

Bless her, Mamá responded by drawing water from their drinking cistern into a small jug. "Take this. Cornelia, get Manuelito."

The tide had risen even farther by the time Sammy and Cornelia's muscular boyfriend arrived at the banyan tree. The woman was exactly as he'd left her and Sammy rushed to her side, afraid she might have succumbed. Her shallow breathing told him she was alive—barely.

"What's this?" Manuelito asked, kicking at something with his toe.

The chunk of wood, to which the woman had been clinging, lay near her feet. Sammy felt drawn to it, this object that had probably helped save the lady's life.

"I'll get it if you can lift the woman," he said.

Manuelito caught the hint of doubt Sammy had put into the question and he bent to pick up the woman as if it were no effort at all. Sammy reached for the wooden thing and discovered that it was a box, carved in a pattern like quilting, with small stones mounted on it. He fell in behind the other man as they walked back to the house, pondering this odd item. Although the wood was fairly well saturated with seawater, it should dry out nicely.

The box might have washed out to sea during the hurricane that ravaged the entire area a couple of weeks ago, but where had the woman come from? Not from around here; he knew everyone in their tiny village. Maybe she belonged with the Americans who had recently begun to move to the nearby plantation to cultivate bananas. It was the only logical explanation, he decided. She was one of them and had foolishly gone out in yesterday's high waves in a small boat.

At the house, Mamá had already prepared a bed with a clean blanket and both sisters were standing by.

"Put her there," she instructed.

Manuelito seemed happy to deposit his burden, although he made a point of preening in front of Cornelia, acting as if it were no difficulty at all. Sammy set the wooden box on a table near the bedside and they all watched as the unconscious woman stirred. Her eyes did not open.

"I wonder how she came to be in the water," Yolanda said as she dipped a cloth into a basin of cool water and began wiping the soft white face.

Sammy gave his theory but Manuelito quickly shot it down. "She's not from the plantation. Only two of the Americans have brought women with them. She is not one of those."

"Well, she must have left home with more clothing than she's wearing now," offered Cornelia, eyeing the fine cotton chemise. "These are only her undergarments." She glanced at her fiancé. "And I think you men should leave the room now."

"Very true," said Mamá, giving Sammy a stare.

As he walked toward the back door he heard Yolanda say, "She must have realized that heavy skirts would pull her under the water so she took them off."

"*Sí.* Can you imagine her fear?"

Sammy thought of his father. This poor woman had nearly met the same fate. He walked away from the house, remembering that he'd set out this morning to catch some fish. Now, most likely, his net had washed away on the tide.

The day passed. Yolanda watched the white woman on the bed. She and her mother had managed to get the poor thing out of her sodden undergarments, had washed the salt from her skin and dressed her in a clean nightgown. Still, the woman had not awakened. She tossed in her sleep, at times crying out. Once she said something that sounded like *nanci*. None of them knew what this word meant.

If the woman was not from the plantation her sudden appearance here was entirely a mystery.

* * *

James Cox extended a hand to the black-clad man who approached, accepting condolences on the front steps of the church. At his side, Nancy and Constance picked at each other. For the first two days they had continually asked when mommy would come home. James had tried to stay cheerful, to let them think she was away on a grand adventure and would ride up in a carriage with whatever kindly soul had followed the balloon and brought her back to them. But the balloon had last been seen over the open sea and he knew, down inside, that if it did not change direction and drift back inland within the first hour it probably never would. Despite the lookouts posted up and down the beaches, the small aircraft had never been seen again. The funeral served as hard evidence of the facts.

The line of mourners moved forward, each stopping to shake his hand and to purse their lips at the sad sight of those motherless little girls.

"Now, James, if there is anything …" Virginia McDermott laid a gloved hand on his arm. "Of course, I will continue to bring your supper by each evening. You have much more important things on your mind than preparing meals."

He knew the woman had been Elizabeth's best friend, but ever since Bill McDermott went away to the Congress of the Republic, James had found Virginia to be just a little too cloying.

"It's all right," he said. "I have Elvira and she's doing a beautiful job with the house and the meals."

"Still … no one makes a chocolate layer cake like mine." She actually batted her eyelashes. "I'm bringing one over this afternoon and I will accept no argument."

What could he say? He sighed and put on a brave smile.

The brother of Rory Duncan stepped up next in line. He mouthed nearly the same words James had said to him yesterday in almost this exact spot. James had spent four days wanting to hate the balloon pilot but somehow simply could not work up the energy to do so. The man was dead. Elizabeth was gone. He had to accept that.

Eventually, the whole sad procession moved to his house where it seemed every woman in town had brought dishes. For one man, two children and a maid, it was an obscene amount of food. He began insisting that people take some of it home with them, and he was pleased when he overheard Elvira getting a little firm with Virginia McDermott, telling her not to show up with one more thing to eat.

He had telegraphed Elizabeth's family back in Maryland to let them know of the tragedy. Her mother became bedridden at the news and her father was a somewhat frail man, a banker who'd never traveled west of the state line. It was no surprise that they had not attempted the journey to Texas.

"Mommy missed having this delicious chocolate cake," little Nancy said as Elvira used a damp cloth to wipe smears of icing from the child's face. "Be sure to save her a piece for later."

The colored maid turned quickly away, stifling a sob, and James tried once more to explain to his youngest that mommy would not be here for cake. Or for anything. As much as it pained him to think of it, once the prescribed year of mourning was over he really should look for a wife, a mother for these babies. They needed a woman's care.

By the time the month was out, James was beginning to think more frequently of his own needs. He missed Elizabeth in their bed at night; her reticent manner in public did not extend to the bedroom and he'd never lacked for satisfaction of that sort, until now. He invented a *meeting* to attend each Tuesday night and left the girls in Elvira's care.

In reality he strolled down to the waterfront, wearing simpler clothing than the top hat he usually sported when performing his official mayoral duties, deceiving himself into believing that no one would notice his presence at one of the smaller saloons or see that he often walked up the stairs with a young woman who went by the name of Fancy.

Fancy delighted him in ways that even Elizabeth had never dreamed of. For one thing, the oil lamp in the room was never turned off. And he had never seen a woman wearing red satin undergarments before. Her blond hair and the perfume she wore enchanted him, although sometimes afterward he realized that only a few months ago he would have thought them tawdry. And if a spot of her lip rouge stained his collar now and then, at least Elvira had the good sense not to mention it.

He continued to sit at his desk in the mayor's office five days a week, to make speeches as needed, and to attend church on Sundays with his daughters. Two months passed and he had *almost* become accustomed to the fact that Elizabeth was not waiting in the parlor to greet him when he came home. The sight of her clothes in the cupboard startled him less often—he should gather them for charity, along with her hairbrush and mirror.

Yes, he had almost grown used to his widower status but still, it did not suit him. Then one Sunday as he took his little girls' hands after church, he noticed Mary Conway. The young Sunday School teacher had stooped down to tie Nancy's bonnet ribbon and the interaction between them was so sweet, so loving. Mary would be a natural mother someday, young and energetic and very attuned to the activities of children. He decided to call upon Mary soon.

* * *

The day the strange woman woke up, Sammy happened to be alone in the room with her, pouring water from a pail that he filled at the rain barrel into the little cistern his mother used in the kitchen. He heard a moan, which was not unusual, but then the woman said something he did not understand. She was sitting up in bed with the blanket drawn up to her chin and a worried look in her eyes.

"*Usted está despierto. ¿Cómo te sientes?*"

"I feel well, thank you," she said. "Where am I?"

He did not understand a word of that; he thought she was speaking English.

"Wait here," he said in Spanish. "I will get help."

He motioned with his hands for her to stay in place, then he rushed from the house. Manuelito would know what to do. Despite the fact that Sammy did not care for the man's bragging ways or the way he took pride in demonstrating superior strength, his sister's fiancé worked for the Americanos and could find someone to translate their guest's words. He ran toward the plantation office.

When he returned an hour later, Mamá was sitting at the woman's side, applying an herbal compress to her forehead.

"She was sitting up when I came in, but she fell back to her pillow a few minutes later."

The lady must have heard the voices because her eyelids fluttered and she stared at the strange faces surrounding her. The American man, Manuelito's supervisor, spoke to her.

"I am an American," he said. "Do you speak English?"

"Yes! I understand you."

"What is your name, ma'am? Where did you come from?"

"I—" A blank look came over her face. "I don't know."

She clutched at her blanket again. "Where am I? How long have I been here?"

Sammy started to explain how he had found her in the

water. "*Estabas en el mar. Te trajo a nosotros.*"

The plantation man started to explain but the woman interrupted.

"The sea brought me here? When did this happen?" It seemed she understood some Spanish but only spoke English.

The American translated.

"Two months you have been here. You had a very high fever and were delirious at times."

She accepted this news with a gentle nod but when they asked her name she became agitated again.

"I don't know! I can't remember anything. Not about my life or how I got into the sea."

"There is a doctor at the plantation," the American said. "I will fetch him. Maybe he can provide answers."

But the bespectacled old man seemed stymied as well. "She's got no injuries to her head. Perhaps the fever harmed her brain," he said as he packed away the few instruments he'd brought along. He turned to Sammy's mother. "Did she have any personal items with her?"

"No, *Señor*, only her undergarments."

Sammy, who had waited outside while the doctor performed his exam, came back into the common room just then. "There was one thing. A box."

He located it on the shelf above the cook stove where it had been drying, picked it up and held it out. "You had this in your arms when I found you in the water."

"Do you recognize it?" the doctor asked, watching her face closely.

She shook her head. No sign of familiarity showed on her face.

"Only time will tell," said the doctor as he picked up his bag. "Send for me if she gets worse. Otherwise, I'm afraid there is nothing I can do for her."

"Let me get you some clothing," Mamá said. "You will stay with us. Meanwhile, we need to call you by a name. Sirena—she is a maid from the sea."

"Find a skirt and blouse," she directed Yolanda, who did not look pleased. "She is close to your size."

"I can help with the housework," Sirena said, "and I can make some clothing for myself later."

What will become of her? Sammy wondered. Perhaps he should consider applying for work at the plantation. The house had been too full of women before this one woke up and began adding her own ideas. Mamá would welcome the help, but Yolanda had a deep crease between her eyebrows.

* * *

Mary Conway opened the picnic basket that James had carried from her buggy. Sunday dinners after church had become their routine, the four of them sitting on a big quilt under the shade of the tall elm beside the church along with other families on their own blankets.

Families. James realized he and his daughters were increasingly thinking of Mary as part of theirs. She uncovered a bowl of potato salad and set it beside the plate of fried chicken before handing plates and cutlery to each of the girls.

"Hold still and let me tuck a napkin here at your neck," she said gently to Constance. "We don't want to mess up your pretty dress."

"Mrs. Johnson says there's ice cream for dessert," James said with a wink at each of the children. "Her boys began cranking the freezer right after Sunday School."

Nancy let out a cheer and nearly upset her plate.

"All right, one thing at a time," Mary said. "Hold that chicken leg tight until you've finished it. Then we'll think about ice cream."

Those thoughtful words and touches, so like Elizabeth would have done. He turned slightly and stared off across the open field to the north of the church. Five months and he still missed her so badly that his heart literally hurt at times. The grief would hit at the oddest moments—as he tied his own tie instead of her doing it for him; when Nancy stared at him with Elizabeth's eyes; when Elvira complained that she couldn't seem to get the pancake batter just right, the way Miss Elizabeth always did. His eyes would water and a strange prickle would start on his upper lip, and the only way to get past the moment was to bite his lip and blink and make himself very busy with some inconsequential task.

And then there were Sundays like this one. Mary bringing a homemade dinner, serving it under the tree and the four of them sitting together and conversing, acting like a real family. She would be a wonderful mother. A wonderful wife, too, he suspected.

Convention said it was too soon. Mourning should last a full year. A year, he knew, was far too short a time in which to forget the person you had loved with all your heart, the mother of your children, the sweetheart you had known since the fourth grade and had traveled with from the east coast to the wild land of the Texas territory. But then his heart ached in a different way at the sight of his daughters and the way they sometimes wandered the house with lonely expressions on their faces.

James had to admit that he was lonely too, and that his Tuesday night visits to Fancy were no substitute for what he really needed.

"One more bite of your green beans," Mary was saying, "and then you may run off and play with the others."

Nancy seemed itchy to move but she complied. Constance had cleaned her own plate and was picking the fried crumbles from her sister's.

"Now when Mrs. Johnson announces the ice cream, I expect you both to act like ladies and await your turn with manners and decorum."

Yes, James thought. He definitely needed a wife. He took a generous bite from the chicken breast Mary had served and watched as she gathered the children's plates and stacked things neatly back in the basket.

"Can we take a walk, out to the grove?" he asked. "There's something I want to ask you."

* * *

Sirena carried the heavy water bucket toward the house, her blue cotton skirt dragging against her legs in the heat of the day. Something told her that September weather should not be this hot, this sticky. Wherever she had come from, she suspected, it was not a tropical climate like this one. She was, it seemed, the mystery of the Yucatan.

As happened more frequently in the month since she had regained her health, she found herself thinking of the future, more so than the past. The Avila family had been extraordinarily kind to take her in and she hoped that her contribution was helping—fetching water, pitching in with the cooking and cleaning. But it didn't change the fact that she was not a daughter of the household and had no real right to be there. She considered getting a job to support herself and finding a small home of her own.

Perhaps she could teach English to the village children, although most of them had no real use for it. Those who got jobs at the plantation were hired as labor to tend the banana plants and the yards around the company housing built for the supervisors and scientists who were here to study how to grow varieties hardy enough for shipment to other parts of the world. Female workers generally were hired only for cooking and cleaning. So far, few of the Americans had brought their families down here, but when they did maybe Sirena could suggest starting a small school. She seemed to remember enough of her language and mathematics skills certainly to teach at an elementary level.

Meanwhile, she would help the Avilas prepare for Cornelia's upcoming wedding and do her best not to cross Yolanda.

In the kitchen she poured some of the water into a dishpan and began to scrub the breakfast dishes. The rest of the common room had simple furnishings: a shelf beside the stove where dishes and pans were stored, a built-in *banco* for sitting, chairs around a table, and the bed where she had convalesced which she later learned was Sammy's. The dear boy had slept on one of the *bancos* for weeks until Sirena insisted that she exchange places. It was another reason she felt the need to find herself a separate home.

She set the dishes to drain on a towel while she tidied the rest of the room. Sammy tended to leave shoes in the middle of the earthen floor and whichever of his three shirts he had dirtied would be draped over the back of a dining chair. She gathered the things and put them in their correct places.

A layer of dust coated nearly everything, stirred by their walking about, so she found a rag and began going over the surfaces. Beside the longest of the *bancos*, a small table held the lantern they usually lit at night and beside it sat the wooden box Sammy once told her she had brought with her from the sea. It was not an attractive piece, certainly more crude than the *rustico* style of furniture found so prevalently here. The carved lines on it were fairly straight and the rounded areas of the quilted pattern were burnished smooth with age. The color was, frankly, ugly—a stain that had been unevenly applied and then darkened to a murky brown. Of course, the discoloration might be blamed on its time in the sea; it might have been beautiful once in its life. Funny, she felt no connection to it. Why had she clutched it in her arms as he described?

Most likely it was simply something floating in the water and she had gripped it in a moment of desperation. Surely it was impossible that the small object had kept her afloat. She picked it up, dusted the table beneath, then decided to sit and have a closer look. Previously, she had not noticed the hinged lid. It came open with a squeal of swollen wood and a shower of rust flakes from the metal. Faint markings showed on the inside of the lid but they were nearly worn down. The first stroke could be part of the letter V. She worked it back and forth a little until the hinges loosened. A bit of oil could help, but it would be better to have the hinges replaced. She supposed the box belonged to her, but did she really care?

She started to set it back in place on the table but noticed that the box seemed more attractive now. The wood had taken on a golden glow and it felt warm to the touch. She raised the lid once more and looked inside, touched the inner surfaces tentatively with her fingertips.

Almost immediately, pain stabbed at her temples. She dropped the box to the floor and grabbed at her head.

"Sirena— *¿Qué pasa?*" Sammy crossed the room and rushed to her side.

"My head. It—"

"*Iré a el doctor.*" He was gone before she could respond.

By the time Sammy, Manuelito, Señora Avila and the doctor came back, Sirena felt much better. The pain had come and gone with a jolt, leaving only a disoriented feeling.

The American doctor knelt beside her. "Can you tell me where it hurts?"

"The pain is gone. But I have the oddest feeling. I remember things."

"The boat wreck at sea?" Sammy asked.

"My name is Elizabeth, Elizabeth Cox. I lived in Galveston, in Texas."

Four sets of eyes stared at her. The doctor spoke first.

"My dear Miss Cox, how on earth did you arrive in this part of Mexico?"

She sat very still, memories returning in bits and scraps, like wisps of cloud that formed and vanished.

"I think—" She shook her head with a jerk. "I think there was a balloon."

The doctor sent her a look of disbelief. The Mexicans clearly had no concept of what on earth she was talking about.

"I think I had better lie down for a moment."

When she awoke, dinner was on the table and her first conscious thought was another memory: a man with a loving look on his face, a man who called her Elizabeth. Two little girls. Their sweet faces broke her heart. She wiped at the tears that streamed down her face, rose and offered to help Mamá Avila serve the tortillas. Before they had finished their meal, a knock came at the door. The American doctor was back.

"I have some good news for you, my dear. Our next shipment of bananas leaves day after tomorrow and the destination is the port of Galveston. I have secured you a cabin."

She stared at him.

"You're going home."

* * *

Mary Conway stared into the mirror, past her own shoulder. Her mother was moving fussily about the room, holding one glove and apparently looking for its mate.

"Your glove is probably right there with mine," she said, "beside my bouquet. Now stop worrying and let's get into that sanctuary. James is waiting."

Wasn't the bride supposed to be the nervous one, the mother offering reassurance? She imagined it had to do with the unconventionally quick marriage, barely six months after James's being widowed. Or the fact that he was older and Mary was becoming the mother of two? She handed her mother the second glove and took her by the elbow.

"Go on now, take your seat. Daddy and I will be right along."

Mary watched her mother bustle through the church's

small vestibule, say something to Dad, then go inside. She took a final glance in the mirror, tucked in a stray wisp of hair, and went to join her father. She had dreamed of this day, as she supposed most girls did, all her life. Had dreamed of being with James since those first tentative days of courtship with the Sunday picnics under the big elm tree.

Her father smiled as she approached. "You look radiant, my dear."

She took his elbow and faced the double doors leading to the sanctuary. Behind them, the outer door opened, casting a shaft of light into the dim space. They paused. A last-minute guest. Mary turned and saw the silhouette of a lone woman against the sunlit doorway. Then the door closed and the woman spoke.

"I … Sorry to interrupt. No one was home and I saw all the carriages here …"

Elizabeth Cox.

Mary felt her face go pale. Her dream shattered into a million tiny bits.

* * *

Sammy Avila whacked with his machete at the tall grass beside one of the plantation houses. Robert Smith always wanted the grass trimmed short, a silly custom he thought. It always grew back. The grass had grown back every few weeks for the ten years he had held this job. Sammy's wife worked inside—cooking, cleaning, washing the clothes of the Americano family. Each week they accepted their pay and laughed together at these people and their funny habits.

This week Sammy made sure the boss did not catch

them laughing. He needed a favor, an advance on his salary. He had fallen into the habit of playing cards with some of the younger *jardineros* and last week he'd gone beyond his usual limit. He'd lost the money they needed for his little granddaughter's surgery. He spotted Robert Smith, who was walking toward his office in the main building. Sammy dropped the machete and caught up with him.

"Sammy, you asked me the same thing two months ago. What are you doing with all this money?"

Sammy looked down and kicked at the ground. "Okay, Mister Robert, how about it's not a loan, instead I sell you something?"

Smith looked at him skeptically. "What would you sell?"

"Avocados."

"Which you picked from my trees."

"A dinner *especial* prepare by Dora and me, you invite all you guests."

"Dora does that anyway. It's part of her job. Look, I'm late for a meeting with my boss. Let me think about this."

Robert Smith walked away and Sammy went back to the grass, thinking of another way to solve his problem. Leaving his machete behind, he walked to the tiny casita where he and Dora lived behind the Smith's house. One thing came to mind.

He went to a cabinet and pulled out the wooden box that the strange lady they had called Sirena had left behind. Sammy hardly remembered her after all these years but had always found a certain fascination with the odd artifact. And what use did he have for it, really? He remembered showing it once to Robert Smith's young son and the boy's eyes lit up when he saw the dark wood and the little colored stones.

Perhaps this could be his bargaining chip. He carried the box outside, set it near the base of a palm tree and resumed cutting the grass.

When Robert Smith emerged from the supervisor's office near lunch time, he seemed in a good mood. Sammy seized the opportunity.

"Señor Robert! I have something," he said, a little breathless from dashing across the yard. "This box—very old, very special. It has been in my family a long time. Your little boy would like it very much."

"But your family—"

Sammy made a serious face. "My grandbaby's operation is more important. We want to part with the box."

Smith reached into the pocket of his trousers and drew out some paper money. "You are sure? You want to sell the box, not simply have a loan?"

Sammy nodded vigorously. His eyes were on the cash as he handed the box over without a second glance.

"Thank you, señor. *Muchas gracias, muchas gracias.*"

Smith smiled and tucked the box under his arm before walking the rest of the way to his house. Sammy thought of the next card game. Tonight he could probably double this money.

* * *

Robert Smith walked into the kitchen where the maid, Dora, was preparing lunch. Some kind of fish with chopped hot peppers and tomatoes, her homemade tortillas, and plantains for dessert. Always some form of banana in the meals here.

"Smells good," he said, setting the wooden box on the table.

He noticed her eyeing the box.

"Sammy sold it to me," he said. "I felt badly taking it, being a family heirloom and all." He realized she probably understood half of what he'd said. He slowed down. "If you want it back …?"

She got that. She shook her head. "I do not want."

"The money for your granddaughter, for her operation … You may keep it anyway, even if you want the box."

Dora looked out the window to where Sammy was again cutting the grass. A knowing look came over her face. She shook her head and went back to the melon she was cutting.

"Darling, I'm so glad you are home for lunch!" Susan Smith came into the kitchen and gave her husband a kiss on the cheek. "What a busy morning I've had. The wives club—"

Robert was bursting with news and Susan saw it on his face.

"What's going on?"

"I'll tell you over lunch. Warren too." He called out to the boy who came running at the sound of his father's voice.

Little Warren lurched to a stop when he spied the wooden box on the table.

"Later," Robert said, setting the box aside. "I've got big news. Take your seats."

"So, what is it?" Susan placed a small serving of the fish on Warren's plate and passed the platter to her husband. "A new banana variety got the office in a twitter?"

"Panama." He said simply. "They're going to build a canal through the isthmus, a great feat that will allow ships to pass between the oceans. It's the biggest thing to happen for world trade, ever! Shipping companies will save months of time and thousands of dollars. Initial surveys have been done and I've been offered an engineering position, in consultation with the French."

Susan blinked a few times, processing the information. When Robert had accepted the position with The Caribbean Fruit Company he'd promised they would move back to America after his five-year contract was finished. She'd imagined going back to life in Chicago, richer for the experience of living abroad, her children able to obtain a first-rate education. After Warren's unplanned birth she'd taken precautions against having more babies until she could have them at home.

"The pay is fantastic, dearest, and the engineering work should be completed in a year, two at the most." His eyes glowed with the prospect of the enticing job, the boost to his résumé.

What were her choices? An unthinkable divorce and a return to living under her father's roof? She swallowed hard and would not meet his eyes.

"That sounds like a wonderful opportunity for you, dear." Her next bite of food stuck in her throat and she excused herself from the table, clutching her skirts and coughing as she ran to the bedroom.

Robert turned to Dora. "Don't worry. The company will bring in another man for my position. You and Sammy will always have work here."

Dora merely gave her usual enigmatic smile.

* * *

The Smiths arrived at the port of Colón in December, with rain pounding at the deck of their ship and runoff water from the inland mountains forcing the vessel to anchor offshore for three days until the rush of mud subsided. Susan's stomach revolted and she found herself bent over a bucket, losing her breakfast, four mornings in a row. An awful suspicion began to nag at her.

Robert left his wife and son in the cabin and ran up to the bridge to consult with the captain, pleading for a quick landing as he was already late to report for his duties.

"That canal job, she ain't going nowhere," the captain replied.

Truer words were never spoken. When they docked a week later, Robert became caught up in the task of engineering a cut through the mountains. After his first horseback ride over the forty-eight mile distance and back, he had a sinking feeling the French plan to cut straight through would never work.

"De Lesseps built the Suez Canal," Robert's boss repeated. "The man knows what he's doing."

"But—" He stopped. Months had passed and all arguments had failed already. The financiers still stood behind the original plan.

For the next three years, during the day he revised plans according to the hierarchy of *La Société internationale du Canal interocéanique,* his employer. By night he worked at home, secretly working out the equations and measurements for a different system, one with locks, which he felt would be necessary to raise ships to the elevation needed to cross the spiny mountainous interior of the country. When the French plan failed, as it inevitably would, perhaps his drawings would be useful. He stared at the drafting paper in front of him. There were still so many details to work out.

Susan approached his desk. "I'm going to bed. The children are already asleep. I think Simone's fever is better."

"That's good, darling." Robert gave her a quick glance.

"Do you even hear me these days?" Her voice sounded weary. "We lost one child to malaria already. I'm afraid that's what the baby has now."

He looked up finally. His wife had dark circles under her eyes. "Has the doctor seen her?"

"Yes, but he doesn't know what to do other than give quinine and cool baths to keep the fever down. What if Warren should become ill as well?"

"He's a sturdy boy. He will—"

"There is no guarantee for any of us, Robert! Strong, grown men are succumbing to this disease every day. This horrid tropical climate is killing us and I want to go home."

"My work here is important—"

"And your family is not? Your own safety is not? May I remind you of your original promise—this job was to last a year or two. That time is over and I am at the end of my wits." Her skirt swiped at the edge of his desk, scattering his pages as she fled the room.

Their bedroom door slammed. Robert planted his elbows on the desk and held his head with both hands. Susan had barely accommodated his wish to come to Panama in the first place. And she was correct; he'd already kept them here a year beyond the agreed-upon deadline. His eyes fell to the papers that lay scattered on the floor.

Completion of the canal was vitally important. Anyone with a wider world vision could see that. But there were rumors of financial problems within the company. The project was millions over budget and the vast excavations already made were only a fraction of what was needed. The workers knew nothing of this, of course, nor did the families but among the engineers there was talk of a possible bankruptcy and the ousting of de Lesseps. No one knew what might happen after that. Perhaps they would all be sent home. Maybe Susan was right; he should pack up his family and get out now.

He gathered the spilled sheets of paper and tamped them into a neat pile on the desk. In the bedroom his wife lay on top of the bed in the muggy heat, wearing her chemise but eschewing a sheet as cover. On the bedside table sat a brown bottle with the cork beside it. Laudanum. He sighed. So this was the reason for the dark circles under her eyes and the gaunt look on her face.

He walked to the open window and poured the contents of the bottle on the ground outside. The bottle and cork went into the waste can. There would be a fight over this.

He shuffled to the other bedroom and looked in on the children. Warren, at seven, was indeed a sturdy lad. He performed well in school and loved to read. Simone's forehead felt hot to the touch again and he replaced the cloth on her forehead with a fresh one dipped into water from the nearby basin. Between these two, another boy had been born, seven months after their arrival by ship. Poor little Alexander had not lived to his first birthday.

A mosquito buzzed through the room; Robert swatted it but heard the ominous buzz of another. Tomorrow he would enquire about getting some netting for their beds.

But in the morning, little Simone had become unconscious. The doctor came and pronounced a coma without much hope of recovery; Susan retreated to her room where she could be heard her rummaging about; Robert fed Warren his breakfast and sent him out to play while he sat with his infant daughter until she took her last breath.

* * *

Three graves on a hillside, rain pouring down and turning the freshly-moved earth into a mire. Robert Smith stared at the two small mounds and the larger one. Numb.

Perhaps Susan had been right—they should have left Panama and taken up a normal American life in a normal place. She would have never been happy here and he'd been too blinded by his own satisfaction with his work to notice until it was too late. On the night Simone succumbed to her disease, Susan had located her secret extra bottle of laudanum and downed the entire contents. Where she'd kept it hidden, Robert did not know but he suspected the carved wooden box on the top shelf of the clothes cupboard, the box he had bought from old Sammy Avila.

He walked back to the house, a mile in the driving rain, uncaring that his only suit was soaked through as he tried to calm his mind and make a plan for the future. Only two things mattered to him now—his son and his work. An unhappy wife had only added to the number of burdens a man had to bear. Two of those encumbrances were now gone. In a peculiar, probably sick, way he found this comforting. He felt freer, lighter.

At home, Warren sat in the living room bay window with a book. The neighbor who had brought the boy home after the funeral was in the kitchen, filling a kettle with water.

"He's said nothing to me, Mr. Smith," she said. "Just picked up his book and went to that seat."

"It's his way," Robert said. "I wouldn't worry."

"You'll get chilled in those wet clothes. Change out of them and I'll have the tea on in a jiffy. Don't want you catching the fever as well."

No, we wouldn't want that.

He dried his skin and put on fresh clothing. Drank the tea, responded to the woman's conversational attempts until she left. The boy had not moved from his window seat but Robert watched long enough to assure himself that his son was not upset; he did seem genuinely engrossed in the book. Robert wondered how much attention Susan had really given the little ones. Her unhappiness had run so very deep. Their son had found engagement and enthusiasm from another source.

Robert stood beside his desk. "Reading anything good?" he asked as a way to let Warren know he cared.

"An adventure story," the boy answered with only a quick glance up. "And you, Dad? Are you all right?"

Robert's eyes welled up for the first time in days. He and his son were so much alike; emotions stayed inside both of them.

"I'll be all right. One day."

Warren nodded and went back to his story. Robert sat behind the desk and paged through his design sketches.

* * *

Warren Smith shrugged into his jacket, rolled up his set of blueprints and headed for the kitchen. Rosa was pouring coffee—that deep Panama roast he loved to savor—into his favorite cup.

"Off to work early, *mi amor*," she said, pecking a kiss on his cheek.

"As always." He grinned. "I don't think Roberto is awake yet."

"Ah, the way of the teenage boy. They sleep all day and want to be up all night."

"Fine with me," Warren said, wrapping an arm around his wife's waist and pulling her close.

"There is no time," she teased as he nuzzled her neck. "You have meetings."

"It's hard to believe the Canal is nearly done. It's taken my lifetime, do you realize? My father started after the initial surveys were done, and still … It has *still* been so many years."

"Will your father be at the meeting today?"

"Oh yes, they cannot hold the man down even though he should probably be retiring. He wants to see it through. I understand."

She set a plate of toast on the table. "You and your father—very much alike."

"I don't know what either of us will do once the Canal opens and our jobs are finished. Stay on, I suppose. Well, I know you and I will. All of your family is here and I have no one at all in America. Roberto—well, who can say? He's American by birth but aside from those few years at Windlyn, he's lived the Panamanian life. He may decide to stay too. The Canal will provide jobs of some sort … forever, I suppose."

"Our son did not seem to care much for boarding school in America," she said with a regretful expression.

"He never confided whether the boys shunned him or picked on him. I suppose his decisions about his adult life will tell us something."

"It won't be that long." Warren brushed the toast crumbs from his hands and picked up the roll of blueprints. "Anyway, I'm off for Gatun. See you later."

His father joined him, along with three Army engineers, for the short train ride to the Gatun Dam. By noon they had reviewed the blueprints and inspected the latest work to be certain that it met their specifications. The other three set off for the nearby canteen where lunch was served each day for the workers, while Warren and Robert held back to recheck one last item.

"An amazing feat, I have to say." Robert Smith stared over the man-made lake where ships would wait after negotiating the first set of locks that raised them a hundred meters above sea level, before sailing to the western set that would lower them to the Pacific. "I do swear, son, there were times it looked as if it would never happen. The French scandal, the opposing viewpoints about straight-cut versus the locks ..." He paused—his son knew he'd been on the side of installing locks right from the start. "... the endless bureaucracy. Theodore Roosevelt had vision for this, but the Congress and the Army could not keep their fingers out of it. I thought they would never get it sorted out."

Warren followed his father's gaze, imagining a day when dozens of ships would use the Canal. "So sad about all the losses along the way."

"Tens of thousands to malaria alone, until they figured out that the mosquitos were behind it all." He had long since accepted the sad fact that two of his children had succumbed to the disease and that it may have been a factor in Susan's death as well. As there was no way to undo those tragic events, Robert had taken the practical stance: move on.

"Not to mention the construction accidents. We've learned a great deal, haven't we?"

Robert nodded, his gaze still far away.

"We'd better get inside before the food is all gone," Warren finally said. "I'm starving."

"Yes, and tell me what Roberto is up to these days. I haven't seen the boy in a few weeks." They began walking.

"I have a hard time reading him. His friends consist of the other Canal families' sons. The other day two of them were at the house, listening to something on the wireless. I heard Johnny Jamison say something about enlisting in the Army. There's a bit of tension going on in Europe, as I understand it."

Robert held the door to the mess hall open for his son. "I don't like what I'm hearing."

"I don't either. I don't want to think of America becoming tangled up in all that. I doubt it will happen—I hope it won't." Warren accepted a metal tray of meat and potatoes from the server, distracted by his thoughts. It was the significant difference between himself and his son— while Warren had always kept to himself and studied, Roberto was a follow-the-crowd sort. He was likely to do whatever his friends did.

"Our boy is nearing that age," Robert said as they took seats at the end of a long table. "He'll be old enough to enlist if he chooses."

Warren thought of the rumblings about that German Kaiser in Europe. Suddenly his hunger vanished.

Chapter 8

A Field Trip

Aurora Potts walked away from the post office staring at the envelope she'd just received. *Smith?* she thought. *What Smith is this?* The paper carried a faint musty smell, explained by the foreign stamps and Panama return address. *There is one way to find out,* she chided herself. *Simply open the thing.*

She lifted the hem of her skirt as she ascended the steps to her office building. The red brick structure had changed little on the outside, with **The Vongraf Foundation** neatly lettered on a white sign near the door, but Aurora was proud of the changes she had wrought within these walls since accepting the directorship five years ago. Science was a man's world, by and large, but she was one of the few with a background in both science and in business, not to mention connections in academia. She could study specimens under a microscope with the best of them, but she could also track the Foundation's financial progress and knew whom to tap for donations, whose trust fund was well enough endowed to spare the money to support Vongraf's work.

Her secretary handed her a stack of correspondence. "For your signature, Miss Potts," Charles said.

She thanked him and walked through the laboratory, taking quick stock of the projects currently underway, before stepping into her private office. Through the large windows she had installed the previous year—no more sitting behind a closed door wondering what was happening in the lab— she admired the new equipment, the finest microscopes with German lenses and the small centrifuge that was the pride of the lab. Along the walls, neat racks of bottles held the chemical compounds they needed for testing. Of course, many of the requests involved more detective work than chemistry, and The Vongraf handled them all. Three scientists (besides herself) and two lab assistants kept the place in top form.

She removed her jacket and hat, placing them on the rack near the door, then took her seat behind the simple wooden desk. Charles had neatly organized the letters for her signature, but the piece that drew her attention was the letter from her personal mailbox. She picked up her pearl-handled letter opener and slit the envelope.

A single page of quality cream paper came out, along with a photograph printed on stiff paperboard.

Dear Miss Potts,

We have never met, but I believe you may remember my son, Roberto, from Windlyn. He mentioned you as one of his favorite teachers. We recently saw the news of your leaving the academic world (sorry, news reaches us slowly here in Panama), and taking a position in which you study unexplained phenomena. It is in this regard that I am writing to you today.

My family is in possession of an artifact that puzzles me and I hope it might be of interest to you. This wooden box came into my grandfather's possession more than fifty years ago and the story that went along with it was that the box had performed several miracles. This would have been in the Yucatan region of Mexico. In one event, it is said that a woman stranded at sea was saved by holding to the box and that it guided her ashore. I know this sounds vaguely plausible, but if you saw the box, a mere twelve inches in length, you would question this claim, as I have over the years.

In later times there were other stories—of people being healed when it was thought there was no hope, of the box changing its appearance seemingly at the mere touch of someone's hand. I can tell you of these events in greater detail, although I must admit that I have never experienced it myself.

If a study of the box would be of interest to you and your Foundation's work, please let me know and inform me of the best manner in which to get it to you. Thank you for indulging the whims of an old man.

I remain, Yours truly,
Warren Smith

Aurora set the letter aside and stared at the photograph. A wooden box sat on a table and the contrast and lighting were not good, the sepia tones blending too much for great clarity. She carried the photograph to the one exterior window where sunshine warmed the room. In the stronger light she studied the picture and felt her heart quicken. She had heard rumors of a box like this.

She dropped the photograph on her desk and picked up Mr. Smith's letter, bustling past the work tables in the lab and heading toward her secretary's desk.

"Charles, respond to this gentleman's request in the affirmative. Tell him to securely pack the item for mailing and give him our address."

"Certainly, Miss Potts." He pulled a sheet of the Foundation's letterhead from his drawer and inserted it into his typewriting machine.

"We shall hope this is not just another bendable spoon," she said.

He smiled at that. Their work was filled with investigations into cheap parlor tricks and hucksters whose games bilked people out of their money while trying to make them believe in the magical. Whenever that was the case—a shyster taking money for performing his or her feats—The Vongraf Foundation was honor bound to turn their findings over to the police.

Aurora's thoughts churned as she walked back to her office. Somehow, Smith's story did not have that feel to it. A wooden box with healing powers. Stories of such a thing had floated about during her years in college and she had begun taking notes even that far back. Somewhere, here … She opened a drawer in the tall wooden filing cabinet behind her desk. Yes. She had kept the notes.

A sketch sat at the top of the pages. Someone had described such a box, had made this drawing. As she recalled, it was a young man whose ancestors from Ireland had spoken of it. At the time, Aurora had marked it up as just one of those Irish folktales, along with leprechauns and pots of gold. The boy, who had been somewhat sweet on her, offering to buy her a coffee now and then, might have simply been telling tales to keep her attention. But something about the story he told or the fact that the sketch was so detailed, something had told her to keep it. And now she had photographic evidence of a box that looked very similar.

She paged through the papers in the folder, a collection of notes made over time, refreshing her memory. One handwritten note stood out. At the top were three simple letters: OSM. She was familiar with them in name only, a highly secretive organization, a rival to The Vongraf, really. She had written this note the first time she heard of them and her notations reminded her that OSM had shown an inordinate interest in another artifact, some sort of religious icon. She had jotted her thoughts at the time, that this organization investigated religious miracles, although now she could not recall where she'd gotten that idea. The note was brief, without enough information to form any sort of conclusion. It must have related to the Irish box, though. Why else would she have filed it in this particular folder?

She stared at the photograph once more. How had such a box traveled from Ireland to Mexico to Panama? She read the other notes in the folder. One account told of the existence of other boxes, including one whose characteristics could change—good or bad—according to the person holding it. That seemed even more farfetched than Smith's claims. Of course, anything was possible and her scientific side told her to make no judgments, to form no opinion, until the facts were in evidence.

The day the package from Panama arrived, Aurora was

out at a fundraising luncheon in nearby Washington. It had been a long day and she'd been tempted to go straight home, but aside from her cat, Mittens, no one waited for her there. The lab was always an exciting place. Plus, there might be messages, telephone calls to return.

Charles had gone home to his young wife and most of the staff had left, as well. One of the senior scientists stood at the worktable, a dour older man named William whose opposition to having a woman as his boss was well known. Aurora greeted him politely but did not linger to chat.

On her desk sat a package wrapped in brown paper and tied with many rounds of twine. The sight of Panamanian postage stamps made her heart quicken. She pulled scissors from her drawer and quickly cut loose the secure wrappings.

The box sat there, a benign little object of carved wood, small stones and drab, dark stain. It was certainly not an example of fine art. An educated guess was that it had been made by a tradesman of European descent and was probably quite old. It was a bit smaller than she had expected. Now she saw what Warren Smith meant in his skepticism over this item having the mass to keep a grown woman afloat in water and to direct her safely to the shore. She took measurements of its dimensions, reminding herself not to form an opinion at this early stage.

William put on his street coat and left without a word, which was just as well. Aurora was eager to work on the box but didn't especially want his observations. She carried the item to one of the lab tables and studied it carefully. Inside the lid there were faint traces of some sort of lettering or characters, unreadable now. She used onionskin paper and did a light rubbing but only scattered marks revealed themselves, no words. The piece had obviously been used and handled a great deal during its history.

She wanted to examine the molecular structure under the microscope but would have to take a sample of the wood first. Preparation involved using several chemicals and a stain, and if the box truly was ancient, it would not do to ruin it; she sliced a few centimeters of wood from one of the inner edges then pulled several bottles from the supply on the shelves above.

An hour later she had the tiny sample under her lens. She had seen this condition before, although not in a long time. To be certain that her conclusion was valid she located a book among the reference texts in their small library and consulted.

The molecular structure indicated that the wood had, indeed, been subjected to a massive jolt of electricity—most likely, the tree from which it was carved had been struck by lightning. Interesting, but certainly not proof that any supernatural powers were conveyed by it. Warren Smith had said that the box changed color when handled by certain people; however, obviously not every person got this reaction from it or Aurora herself would have immediately seen the result. He told her it held certain healing properties; she thought of a simple way to test for this. She held the box closely in both hands for ten minutes, then touched her index finger to a small cut on her left hand. She saw no reaction at all.

She raised the microscope's lens and began a detailed study of the surfaces, inside and out. She discovered that the box had once held paper made from high quality cotton; it also bore traces of sea sand, wax crayons and a type of clay found in the deserts of the Southwest. Minuscule granules of salt verified Smith's story that the box had once floated in the ocean. If only she could find someone whose handling would bring about the reaction he had described.

She stood up and stretched her aching neck and shoulders. The clock on the wall beside her office door chimed and Aurora was shocked to see that the hour was three-thirty in the morning. Mittens would be anxious and hungry, although this certainly was not the first time Aurora had worked nearly through the night. How fortunate that the old building had been wired for electric lights a few years ago. She gathered the bottles and tools, leaving her work area neat, and carried the box to her desk where she locked it safely away in a drawer.

Expecting to sleep until midmorning, Aurora was surprised to find herself wide awake at eight o'clock. A quick toilette then she pulled on one of her simple work dresses and walked the four blocks to the Foundation. She had awakened with an idea.

Rather than making an announcement, she made her way quietly among the staff, asking each person in turn to hold the wooden box for a few minutes and offer an opinion as to its age and origin. The box showed no reaction, nor did its handlers, until she brought it to Charles. Within moments after he took the item she noticed that the wood began to lighten and take on a prettier, golden appearance.

Her secretary stared at it. "It's becoming warm!"

So Smith's story did have some validity.

"Do you feel any differently?" she asked.

"Not especially."

"Thank you. What you have noticed is very helpful."

She took the box back to her office and began to write down her findings for a report to Warren Smith. When she left for lunch she handed the notes to Charles, whose desk looked remarkably clear for so early in the day. He already had fresh paper in his typewriter. He began to strike the keys and Aurora paused, startled at how quickly he was typing the words.

"I plan to return in an hour or so," she told him.

"I will have your letter ready."

Out on the street, she was more determined than ever to conduct one final test with the box. She stepped in front of a woman who was pushing a baby in a pram and introduced herself.

"I wonder if you would mind holding this box for a moment or two. It's in the name of science."

The woman gave her an odd look but complied. Aurora asked about the baby and commented on the lovely weather, edging a glance toward the box every few seconds; it changed not one bit. The same dull finish, the same dark wood stain. She thanked the woman and went on to her favorite coffee house.

During her meal she found excuses to ask several other people to touch the box. No one elicited a reaction from it; Charles was the only one. Was it possible that the box's enhanced molecular structure made it react only to people whose own bodies contained more electricity than others? Or was there some sort of destiny involved?

She shook off that idea—she was not a big believer in fate unless there was a scientific explanation. Perhaps this morning's event was a one-time occurrence. She paid for her sandwich and walked back to the lab.

At Charles's desk the finished letter to Warren Smith waited. She picked it up and asked Charles to hold the box again. Once more, it began to warm and to lighten in color.

"Miss Potts? May I set it down now?" He dropped his

voice to a whisper. "It gave me so much energy this morning that I worry I won't sleep all night."

She covered her desire to laugh with a businesslike answer. "Of course. I shall take it. Perhaps you could put that energy to good use in sorting files and neatening the drawers."

In the quiet of her office she closed the door and set the box on her desk. The fact that the occurrence had now happened twice filled her with elation. It was extremely rare that their investigations into the paranormal were validated. She wanted to leap and shout, to tell the world. But that went against the principles of the Foundation's code. They were to investigate and document, not to sensationalize or create a public stir. In fact, of all the verified mystical artifacts and events they had researched none had been put on display. Each artifact went back to its owner. The Vongraf Foundation's mission was about science, not vulgar publicity.

Still, she would see to it that their documentation was flawless. She called Charles and another man, the one most proficient with the camera, into her office. If at all possible she wanted to capture the box's glow on a photographic plate and see how well it might print on paper.

The telephone rang as the men were setting up the camera on a tripod. Aurora reached for it herself.

"Aurora Potts, please," said a male voice with a slight accent.

"Speaking." She waved the two men out of her office.

"I represent an organization much like your own," he said. "We are known by the initials OSM. I am in the Washington office."

She waited, working to place the accent. European. Italian, perhaps.

"We understand you are currently investigating a very unusual item, something far different from the mundane artifacts we see regularly. Our group requests that we be able to examine it as well."

Something in his tone and his words caused the hairs on her neck to rise.

"I'm not familiar with OSM," she said, hoping the lie sounded convincing. "Who do you represent?"

"Only ourselves. We are an independent research facility."

Her mind tried to go back to her old college notes which she had reviewed weeks ago. The letters OSM, handwritten at the top of a page, and the vague notion that they had something to do with religion … but none of that made sense. This man could be behind any number of schemes.

"And exactly what item do you believe we have?"

"A box. An oddly carved wooden box. It has colored stones on it and is carved in a symmetrical pattern similar to the letter X."

His voice made her skin crawl. His exact description of the box … she knew she could never admit to him that she was staring at it this very moment.

"I'm afraid I don't—"

"Excuse me, but you do know. You know exactly what item I refer to."

Something hardened inside her. "I was about to say that I do not have the item anymore. It was shipped back to its owner this afternoon."

"Oh, that is too bad. Please, who is it? We would like to contact him."

But Aurora refused to say. She was breathing hard when she replaced the receiver. How had this man, this organization if he did represent one, found out about the artifact?

Her street foray during the luncheon hour came back to her. Someone had seen her passing the box around, asking others to touch it. Among those who had spoken with her or someone observing at a distance, someone had reported it to this OSM. Her hands shook as she picked up the telephone directory and thumbed through the pages. There was no listing using those initials and as she perused the lines of type she saw nothing that could conceivably use the initials as its abbreviation. Of course, the entity could exist anywhere in the world other than Alexandria, Virginia. She considered the possibilities.

The telephone connection had been very clear, so the man's assertion that he was in a Washington office could very well be true. Of course the organization could be farther away but with a local representative who tracked the activities of The Vongraf Foundation.

Charles and the photographer came back in when Aurora signaled them. As they set up the camera and took several images she found herself thinking furiously. The box would go into the evening mail by Special Delivery to Warren Smith. She penned a note to him, to go along with the typed report.

Dear Mr. Smith,

It has been our pleasure to examine the artifact you submitted. Enclosed is the scientific data forming our conclusions. On a personal note, I would like to caution you about sharing this information with anyone you do not know. We received a call from an organization called OSM. I am not familiar with

She stopped with her pen aimed toward the inkwell on her desk. What could she say, really? The man gave me an uneasy feeling? I don't know this organization so you should not trust them either? She balled up the sheet of paper and tossed it into the waste basket.

"Make those prints for me as quickly as possible," she said. They would go into a folder with a copy of her data and the letter to Mr. Smith. The folder would go into the innermost depth of the Foundation's vault. She would ask two of their men to accompany her to the post office and see the box safely on its way.

Tomorrow she would see to the implementation of security measures for the building.

Chapter 9

The Great War Rages

The stink of a thousand male bodies—jammed shoulder to shoulder where they sat on wooden decking, anticipation and fear wafting off them—sent Patricio Sanchez's stomach lurching. He looked down at his olive drab wool uniform, would have taken a whiff at his own armpit had he been able to lift the arm. No point in that. He knew he smelled as awful as the rest of them.

They had been marched aboard the former cruise liner six days ago and no one had benefit of more than a damp sponge bath in all that time. At night they removed their hats, boots, puttees, and tunics so they could stretch out on narrow bunks, five high, but sleep did not come easily. For days on end the greatest fear was of a fate like the *RMS*

Lusitania three years ago. To the Germans, the fact that the passenger liner was filled with families, women and children had made no difference. No one today was under any illusion about his own destiny should they be spotted by one of the dreaded underwater boats. Patricio could only hope and pray that they had already reached safe waters—the transport ship was due to dock within the hour. Otherwise, all he knew was that they were to be taken to various war fronts in the French and Italian countryside.

A few weeks of training and he hardly knew any of the men in his company, much less any of the others comprising the regiment. The one man he had to keep in his sights was his sergeant, a bulky man named Calloway. The ship bumped something and faces went a little greener. If a loss of breakfast felt inevitable you were expected to snatch the hat from your head and make use of it. He swallowed hard and thought of home, of sweet-faced Emelia who had given him her lace handkerchief and agreed to wait for him. Nothing of his former life in the high-desert climate of northern New Mexico had prepared him for this.

"Caramba! Una mala," growled the man next to him who looked Latino but had the English surname of Smith. The poor fellow looked clammy.

Patricio glanced up to see if Calloway was nearby. The two of them had already been chastised for 'jabbering away' when their superior officer couldn't understand the few words they exchanged.

"Yeah, that was a bad one," he agreed in English, perhaps a trifle too loudly.

"All right, men! To your feet," the familiar voice shouted from the other end of the hold. "On deck you'll go to the gangway. On shore, assemble by companies and wait for your commanding officer. Transport trains are waiting."

"Yes, sir!" arose the appropriate response.

Patricio sent the other doughboy a half-smile which he hoped conveyed encouragement. He didn't like the idea of the trains. Having his feet on solid ground for a few days would have been far more welcome. He strapped his canteen to his belt, picked up his blanket roll and the standard-issue .30-06 Springfield bolt action rifle that practically felt like a third arm now. A groan escaped him as he stood for the first time in five hours.

Beside him, Roberto Smith, the one man he'd begun to think of as a buddy, also rose. They exchanged a look that said *here we go*. But the going was extremely slow as men and gear moved single file up the narrow ladder to the upper deck.

"Drape it over your shoulder!" shouted a man at the top who handed him a white canvas bag as Patricio emerged into daylight.

He blinked and looked around, feeling a little like a prairie dog on the first day of spring.

"Keep moving!"

He shuffled forward as best he could among the throng of men on deck. Places along the ship's rail were already crowded and men stood in clumps or stood slack-jawed, realizing for the first time that they were far, far from home. Thirty yards away he found a less-crowded spot on the rail and edged his way toward it.

From the shore he could hear shouts as sailors handled massive ropes and the ship edged against the pier. A gangway wide enough for two was being trundled into place. Beyond the dock, men with smiling faces gathered in masses and paced about, getting a feel for the earth beneath them once again. A general air of jubilation floated toward him on the light spring breeze. A row of buildings led from the dock area then spread out to form a small town. Only a few curious civilians showed their faces.

"See any of the others from our company?" asked Roberto Smith, coming closer and fiddling with the strap of the white canvas bag he'd been given.

Patricio looked around and noticed that most of the men had draped the strap around their necks, diagonally across their chests. He did the same.

"What is this thing?" Roberto muttered, still having problems untangling the strap.

"Gas mask." The gruff voice came from a man neither of them knew. "It's gonna be your best friend this time next week."

Patricio felt a new wave of fear. News of the German gas attacks had even made it as far as New Mexico, and shell-shocked soldiers were already convalescing in the sanitarium at Albuquerque. The excitement of landing in Europe dimmed.

The sound of leather boots on wood decking became more organized and he realized men were moving toward the gangway. Two by two they trooped ashore and a corporal at the bottom shouted and pointed them in various directions. He and Roberto joined the tide of movement, slowly making their way. No sense in rushing; this ship wasn't leaving until every last man was off.

At the bottom of the slanting gangway the corporal took one look at the insignia on their tunic collars. "Infantry C, over there." He vaguely aimed his arm toward a warehouse where Patricio recognized Sergeant Calloway who appeared to be checking names off a list.

"Over here! Look sharp!" Calloway said, fierce yet somewhat bored at the same time. He marked his list and pointed for them to join the others.

Eventually all two hundred fifty men stood in front of the warehouse which, by the smell of it, once contained damp bales of wool. Calloway ordered them to stand in rows and a photographer set up his tripod and made fussy little motions to get everyone in the picture. The men shuffled into place accordingly and the photographer draped a black cloth over his head and told them to stand perfectly still. Patricio wondered if his parents would see that photograph someday. He hoped his hat was straight and his tunic neat.

An hour later they were marching through the streets of some tiny Belgian town, filling the railroad depot, being herded into train cars with hard wooden benches.

"At Cantigny, we join the French Army," Calloway announced. "There's been German action in the area so stay together and be alert!" The sergeant moved on to repeat the information in the next car.

"Any luck, maybe the Froggers will already have the trenches dug," said a man next to Roberto and Patricio. "My brother wrote home, said that was the messiest part of the work."

Patricio tried to imagine digging trenches in the soft sand near home. He couldn't see it holding together well enough for a group of men to fight from such a position. The train started to move and gather speed. He saw Roberto become drowsy with the rhythmic movement. As for himself, he felt hungry. He rummaged into the pack at his feet where he had stashed the last of the empanadas his mother had mailed to him at training camp. The little sweet packets of fruit filling baked into a delicate crust didn't always make the transit intact but even when he had to pinch the crumbs in his fingers to eat them, they were still his favorite treat from home. These two had survived and he lifted out the cloth napkin containing them.

Roberto stirred and opened his eyes. "Your mama bakes those too? In Panama, mine did the same."

"Have one," Patricio said. "They're good."

Roberto did not have to be asked twice. The crust practically dissolved in their mouths, and the apple filling was both sweet and tart.

"At home, mama often made them with pineapple," Roberto said. "Did you have that?"

"Once. My mother got some tins of it. My first taste—kind of exotic."

"And plantains—mama made a sweet batter and fried them." His eyes rolled upward. "Her family were all local and she really can cook."

"You grew up in Panama? How come you're in the US Army?"

"American by birth. My father and grandfather were both with the Corps of Engineers on the Canal project. It was expected of me, to do part of my schooling in the States and to enlist."

Patricio nodded. "It's a little strange for me. New Mexico wasn't even a state until 1912, barely six years ago. We were a territory the whole time I was growing up. But my *abuelo*, he tells stories of traveling *el camino real*, walking beside a donkey cart all the way to Mexico City and back. It's open desert country. Parts of it, they call it the *jornada del muerto* where it weaves away from the Rio Grande … he remembers Apache attacks being a real danger."

He reached into his pocket and extracted a flat piece of silver, nearly an inch long, stamped with an old-fashioned symbol.

"A Spanish *real* that's been in my family since the 1680s. Someone brought a few of them back then and mama insisted I carry it with me for luck."

Roberto examined the coin and handed it back. "Mine made me carry her personal crucifix." He pulled back the high collar of his tunic to reveal a silver chain. "I suppose all mothers are alike."

"I heard there are ten thousand men arriving in France every day," Patricio said after awhile. "Hard to imagine, isn't it? There probably aren't that many living in my home state."

"What's it like?"

"New Mexico? Well, not like here," he said as they chugged through a countryside of green farm fields and entered a town where an ornate cathedral dominated the surrounding one-story stone houses with thatched roofs. "Up around Taos a lot of buildings are made of adobe— you know, mud with grass mixed in and dried in the sun. Our house has an *horno* out in the back where my mother bakes the bread and the empanadas. Up at the pueblo, just outside town, the Indians always did it that way too. There's a few Anglos, but everyone is just now starting to get along. The Indians didn't want the Spanish governor telling them what to do. Pretty much the same with the American governor, too."

"Panama changed a lot with the Canal," Roberto said. "They put in theaters and clubs and things to keep the workers occupied. Otherwise, all they did was drink—

at least in my grandfather's day. It's better now. Lots of families. Pretty good schools."

They watched as the French village disappeared behind them. Neither one commented when they passed through miles of burned forest. The sight of towns with crumbling buildings and people picking through rubble became more frequent as the hours passed. With every mile, their buttocks increasingly felt the unforgiving surface of the wooden bench, and they knew they were coming closer to the war.

* * *

Mud, everywhere, mud! A rat scurried into the trench, not pausing as it ran over Patricio's shoulder and down his leg, poking its nose among papers on the ground but finding only inches of water that had turned the muddy bottom into a bog. The rat ran on.

Patricio undid the top twelve laces on his knee-high right boot, getting down close to his foot, poking the fork from his mess kit inside to scratch at the itch that never went away. He wiped the tines on his tunic and put the fork away. But the itch was still there.

"Don't scratch if you can help it," Roberto said, lowering himself to sit on the wooden crate beside his friend. "My sores have started bleeding. Maxwell says he's got pus coming out of his."

Patricio stared at the narrow strip of sky, wishing for a scrap of sun to dry the intolerable, never-ending wetness. He smiled at his naïve comment about France being different from New Mexico—if only he'd realized just how very different. Dark clouds scudded by. Four days since they'd seen a shred of blue above.

"Think these sandbags will hold?" he asked.

Roberto patted one of the fat, once-white bags. "Seems solid enough. If these walls give way, we're cooked. In more ways than one."

The good news about the constant rain was that the Germans had slacked off the shelling. Patricio hoped they were every bit as miserable in their own set of trenches less than a mile away. The rat had come across a candy wrapper that someone had carelessly forgotten to stow inside a container. Its happy squeal was barely audible to the men but five more rats ran down the reinforced wall and skittered across the wooden crates the men were using as seats, joining their lucky pal. Within moments, another dozen joined the fray.

"Quick! They'll overrun us!" Four men grabbed their shovels and began whacking at the rodents. Blood splattered Patricio's boot.

"Get the candy—that's what they want!" he yelled.

No one got the message so he snatched his own shovel and scooped up the paper wrapper, flinging it over the top of the trench. Two of the rats figured it out and scrabbled up the wall after it. A minute later, the other live ones had followed.

Sergeant Calloway's voice boomed. "What the hell! Get those things out of here!"

At least shoveling up the dead rats and throwing them out of the trench gave them something to do, Patricio thought as he joined the effort.

"Nasty, disease breeders," muttered Calloway as he walked down the line.

"Once the rain lets up I'm getting a haircut," Roberto said, making conversation as the last of the dead rats went over the top. "There's some Italian guy from New Jersey brought his gear with him, says he ran a barbershop back home. A real haircut by a guy who knows what he's doing would be nice."

"Better than the sloppy one the Army gives you. Maybe I'll have him do mine too." Any activity was better than none; the weeks of inaction showed in the blank eyes and slack jaws of the men. No wonder they'd leapt to the task when the rats came.

The patter of rain on their helmets (those things the men joked about looking like inverted soup bowls) lessened, and as if the clouds had overheard their conversation a large patch of blue appeared. And, in answer, a volley of mortar fire began to land heavy rounds nearby. From boredom to terror—it was the story of their lives these past three months.

They took two days and nights under siege, returning rounds from their own mortars to push back and retake the slight advantage the Germans had gained. Eventually, there came the reassuring roar of tanks and Colonel Dugan, in charge of the battalion, redoubled the offensive, sending infantry to aid in taking the village only two miles away. Patricio lost track of Roberto in the mad cacophony of sound and flying dirt, only to find him again when they mustered outside a tiny patisserie.

"We lost about two hundred," he overheard Calloway reporting to the colonel. "Close to a thousand injured."

"Dig graves," Calloway was told. "The medical corps is coming along to treat the wounded."

Calloway began shouting orders. Patricio and Roberto were sent down the narrow lane between buildings to find a group of well over two hundred Germans sitting on the ground with their hands on their helmets guarded by a dozen or so armed Americans. Prisoners.

"We're marching them to Bois de Folie where the train will take them to a POW camp," a Sergeant O'Malley informed them. "Then we're off to Belleau Wood where we'll join up with the Marines."

Patricio had heard rumor, trench talk, that Belleau Wood was the real objective; it would probably be one of the larger battles of the campaign with two full U.S. divisions plus British and French troops. It looked as if he wouldn't get his haircut for some time.

* * *

Twenty-six days. Patricio's company joined the battle after the Germans had already broken through the French lines to the left of the Marine division, which had then force-marched ten kilometers through the night, trampling grain fields and negotiating through patches of forest. By the time his division assembled and joined the fierce fighting for Hill 142, the carnage included a significant number of officers as well as enlisted men. Some of the French began to retreat but the cry often repeated through the American troops were the words of Marine Captain Lloyd Williams who said, "Retreat? Hell, we just got here!"

The sentiment got them through as waves of soldiers were cut down when they advanced on the German positions, as attacks and counter-attacks went on with little progress in either direction for days, then weeks. When the Woods were finally declared to be definitively in American hands, the men spent the following days digging graves. Patricio and Roberto had lost a number of comrades—but at least not each other.

Calloway had been killed and the new sergeant in charge granted the men a brief leave to go in small groups to the nearest town on the Paris-Metz road. A command center had been set up there, and Sergeant promised them a place to get a hot bath and to receive mail from home. The six mile walk felt like nothing, not after the torture they'd been through.

"All I want—after the hot bath—is a letter from Emelia," Patricio said, his step remarkably light.

"I'll just be happy to have the bath," Roberto said, with a little pang of envy. There was no girl waiting for him, either in Panama or America.

It turned out that the bath would be a shower, since the first tub of water filled for one of the soldiers had turned to a muddy mess and water was too limited to allow each man a full tub of his own. But the water coming from the spigots in the tiled room was hot and there was plenty of soap. No one complained.

Patricio waited his turn, pulling off his nearly rotten boots and socks, massaging his aching feet. He would need to ask for salve for the blisters, but at least they had not become infected from the endless damp during their month in the trenches.

His tunic came off next and he poked his fingers into the inside pocket for the reassuring feel of his lucky Spanish *real*. His finger went through a hole in the material and he realized with a sinking feeling that the ancient coin was gone. Lost somewhere on the battlefield. All the terror of being shot at, all the blood, burying hundreds of his fellow soldiers—he'd held himself together through it all. But now he felt tears spill over his eyelids. A piece of home, of his family heritage, was gone forever.

"Next up," said a man with a towel around his waist who had just stepped out of the shower.

Patricio picked up a towel for himself and stumbled blindly toward the tiled enclosure. *You've been through worse,* he told himself. *Surely papa has more of the coins at home. He can send another one.* But as he scrubbed his hair with the bar of homemade French soap he had to wonder—had his luck already run out?

An hour later he stood in front of the dark green command center tent. The mail truck had apparently been delayed but was due soon. Roberto came limping toward him, a dour look on his face.

"What's wrong?" At least Patricio's mind had something to focus on other than his own loss.

"Doc says my foot's pretty bad. I have to stay here, get admitted to the hospital tent."

"Don't joke around."

"Not joking. It's the stupid infection I got out there in the trench."

"I told you not to scrat—"

"I know, I know." Roberto looked down at his feet which were, Patricio noticed for the first time, clad in soft slippers instead of his regular boots.

Patricio's thoughts bounced around. He would go back to the front without his best friend, the one who had kept him sane out there with his silly jokes and his comments about haircuts and stories of his sweet little mama from Panama.

"My toes are turning black," Roberto said quietly. "Doc has to cut two of them off. If it gets worse, I could lose my whole foot."

"What!"

"Shh—don't say anything in front of the others."

A dozen men from their company approached, jostling each other, big smiles all around, relief at having survived the past month's horrendous battle, happy to be clean and anticipating mail from home. In answer to that prayer, a large truck lumbered around the bend in the road, a big transport with canvas cover and squealing brakes.

"Got mail for Companies A, C and G," shouted the man who had bounded from the passenger side. "Give us a minute."

No one wanted to give them even two seconds, but one thing you learned in the Army was to wait for things; wait weeks in a trench in the rain and mud until your day came to be shot at, followed by your few hours of freedom so you could be told your foot might have to be cut off. Patricio slid a glance toward Roberto. His friend looked grimly determined to enjoy the possibility of a letter from home. Any bit of joy in the face of the unthinkable.

"Packages first!" shouted the PFC. "Santini!"

He handed down a small box to the dark-haired man who ran forward with a whoop.

"Atkins!" A happy shout from the back of the crowd. "Foster! Smith, Robert-o!"

Patricio smiled at the mispronunciation while Roberto pushed to the open tailgate of the truck. Inevitably, most of the fellows in their unit had taken to calling the two of them Patrick and Robert. They'd discovered there were only so many times you could correct someone's mangling of your language before you decided to give up and go along with it.

Roberto came back with a box about twelve inches long

and five inches tall, wrapped in heavy brown paper and pasted with unfamiliar postage stamps. His grin stretched the full width of his face. "From my *mamacita*—it has to be something good!"

The PFC had opened a big canvas bag and was pulling out fistfuls of letters. He called out names and tossed the envelopes, like flat paper airplanes, into the crowd. Patricio focused, aware of the ache inside him for news—any news—of home.

"Sanchez!"

The envelope was not one of the flimsies with a red and blue border which many families used for military mail. This one was of quality paper, heavy. The soldier who passed it along to him sniffed it and grinned knowingly. "Sanchez has a girl back home," he taunted.

Patricio grabbed the envelope and shot the guy a look. *So what, you don't have someone?*

He wanted to rip open the flap and devour the letter on the spot but names were still being called and there was the chance that he might get something else, a letter from his parents or his little sister. He tucked the precious envelope inside his tunic. Emelia's words should be saved for a private moment anyway.

Beside him, Roberto had torn through the brown paper on his package. Inside, Patricio could see that it contained something carved of wood, a box with a lumpy surface.

"Ah, cookies from mama!" Roberto said sniffing the lid. He cradled the box closely. "We will get into these right away."

Just then the mail guy called Roberto's name again, holding up a letter.

"Here!" he shouted, and others passed the letter over

their shoulders.

A second letter for Patricio, this addressed in his mother's hand.

"That's all," the PFC said with a shrug toward those who had not received anything. The disappointed ones shuffled away listlessly.

"Over here," Roberto said, nodding toward a quiet spot near a clothing boutique that didn't look as if it had been open in months. They slid to the ground, their backs against the stone wall, and tore into their letters.

Emelia's delicate handwriting filled the single sheet of her personal stationery. *My dear Patricio …*

My *dear.* She still loved him! He read the words, which told of everyday events—the church bazaar, her younger sister making her first skirt on the new sewing machine their father had purchased, a calf getting out of its pen and coming into the kitchen—but the image he clung to was of Emelia the last time he'd seen her. Wearing a blue dress with some kind of small flowers printed on it, a darker blue hat with a brim that dipped in front and shaded her delicate skin. Her face … somehow he remembered her dark eyes and arching brows, but he could not quite make her smile come into focus. He stared at the letter more intently, as if it would make her face appear clearly to him. His eyes dimmed a little. What if he forgot her before he could go home? What if she forgot him?

A quiver of panic raced through his gut, the urge to run down the street and leap aboard one of the trucks and demand that it take him to the coast, to an outbound ship, to his home. He glanced at Roberto, who was reading his own letter with a little smile on his face. The anxiety passed.

He reached into his pocket to touch his lucky *real* but it

was not there and he remembered that it had disappeared somewhere on the battlefield. The panic threatened to return and he forced himself not to think of it.

He folded Emelia's letter back into its envelope and opened the one from his mother. Three lines down, her words stood out. *I do not want to worry you, but thought you should know this. It's your father. The doctor says it was a mild heart attack. He will be fine, my dear son, please do not worry. We have arranged extra help with this year's crops and everything will be fine. The corn is already growing tall ...*

Patricio blew out a long breath and reread the passage. Papá? His heart? Heart attacks were for old men and his papa had only turned forty; was he an old man already? He stared at a spot somewhere in the middle of the road, thinking frantically. Could he obtain a leave of absence, plead a family emergency? But the commander would want to see the letter and Mamá had made it sound as though everything would be all right. More than ever he wanted his lucky *real.*

"Where are you?" Roberto asked. "You seem a million miles away."

Patricio shrugged and put his letter away. "A little incident at home. Mamá says it is fine."

Roberto had torn the remaining brown paper from his parcel.

"This funny old box," he said, holding it with both hands. "My mamá kept it on a shelf in the living room. It's been around forever, maybe from my grandfather's side? Oh well, it's full of cookies now and that's what has *my* interest."

He raised the lid and held the open box out to his friend. "Have a couple. *Bizcochitos con canela.*"

The first bite filled Patricio's mouth with the warm,

familiar cinnamon flavor of home. His mother often baked a similar recipe and he found that the memory was nearly enough to bring tears. He cleared his throat noisily and thanked Roberto for the cookies.

"Remember the day we met, on the train? You had empanadas from home and you shared with me. So, this is my way of sharing back."

So much they had endured together. Patricio had heard men talk of the bonds of wartime, lifelong friendships that formed because of the trauma. No one mentioned that simply sharing cookies was a part of that. In the distance, the heavy thuds of shelling punctuated his thoughts.

Rowdy voices caught his attention, a half-dozen soldiers laughing together, light roughhousing as they walked along the street. No doubt they had already located the bars, or the women. Patricio bent his knees, drawing his legs in close. Roberto had the wooden box on his lap and was balling up the paper in which it had been wrapped. One of the soldiers came to a dead stop in front of them.

"Hey, *amico*! Where did you get that?" He was staring hard at the wooden box.

Roberto placed a hand protectively over the lid. "A gift from home."

The dark-haired soldier knelt a few feet away, while his buddies staggered on down the road.

"My uncle had one just like it," he said. "Back in the old country. Torino."

He held out a hand. "Marco Santini. Company A. I'm from Jersey—New Jersey—but my family, they come from Italy. I was just there, stationed on the Italian Front. Crappy job but I get sent there cause I can speak enough Italian to issue orders at those *stupidos*. Man, talk about cold! Snowy mountains, terrible clothing … Italy not at all ready to be in a war, I kept telling my Uncle Giuseppe. But, you know, he's nothing to do with the government. He's a bishop, doesn't get to make those decisions."

Marco shook his head. "Bad place to be all last winter. Belleau Wood was … well, awful … but I'll take a summer battle over a winter one any day."

Roberto looked confused.

Patricio spoke up. "So your Uncle Giuseppe—he had a box like this one?"

"Oh. No, that was Uncle Marco. I was named for him. He's the one in Torino. Giuseppe was in Rome, actually kind of high up in the church, emissary to the Holy Father, I think. Something like that."

He touched the box with his index finger. "So, yeah, the uncles came to see us once and that's when Uncle Marco had the box with him. He'd packed his socks in it. I was pretty little then, so I was fascinated. Giuseppe was telling us how he'd found this old thing down in some vault at the Vatican, locked away in this big room full of stuff, like treasures. Except all the other treasures were gold and silver and shit like that. The box was really ugly and plain compared to everything else so I guess he used his 'power of office' or some such and he took it. Laughed about how it was the cheapest birthday gift he'd ever given Uncle Marco. Marco just stayed quiet. I got the feeling he really loved the thing. He seemed pretty attached to it."

"It couldn't have been this one," Roberto said. "It's been with my family in Panama for a long time."

"Yeah, yeah, I'm sure it was. I mean, the one my uncle has couldn't have left Italy for a hundred years or more, not until he brought it with him on that trip. It's just funny, you know, to see two of them. Who'd be dumb enough to make two boxes alike, when neither one of them's exactly a work of art—know what I mean?"

Santini stood up and gave a little salute before dashing off to join his friends who were now two blocks away.

"Quite a talker," Roberto observed.

"Yeah." Their eyes met and they laughed. Then Patricio remembered their earlier conversation. "So … your leg. What's going to happen?"

"Oh, not much. They'll take me to the hospital up the road, docs will take off those two bad toes and I'll rest up awhile. Probably be back at the front with you in no time. A few weeks." He shrugged it off as though he believed that was all there was to it. "They told me a transport leaves at three o'clock. I suppose I better get back there."

He started to rise and Patricio saw his friend's face go white when he put weight on the bad foot.

"I can't believe you walked those six miles this morning."

"Hey, they promised a hot bath." Roberto found his balance, forcing the heel to take the weight. "And mail— don't forget the treats."

He nearly tipped over when he waved the box of cookies toward Patricio.

"Let me carry that for you. I'll walk you back to the truck." Once again he wished for his lucky Spanish *real*. Right now he would give it to Roberto to ward off a bad outcome from the foot surgery.

He tucked the letters into his tunic and the wooden box under his right arm, offering his left as support for Roberto's increasingly bad limp.

"Nearly there," Patricio said. "Lucky you, getting a ride *and* going farther from the front." The sounds of gunfire had grown progressively louder from the south. The rest of them had better get back to their company soon.

The troop transport vehicle sat in the middle of the Paris-Metz road, facing the opposite direction from the way Patricio would need to hike back to their bivouac area. Two other vehicles, one an escort and the other carrying a general, were idling in front of it. A corporal waved Roberto forward.

"We're rolling in five minutes. Good thing you got here when you—" His final words vanished in an explosion of fire, dirt and hot gas.

Patricio found himself lying twenty feet away, face down with Roberto's wooden box pressing into his chest. A high-pitched whine screamed in his ears, but no other sounds came through. He shook his head and rubbed to get granules of dirt out of his eyes.

When he could see through the rolling dust, the general's vehicle was a mass of tangled metal and the escort truck lay on its side a dozen yards farther along what was left of the road. Men were running, their mouths working but Patricio heard none of it. The truck Roberto had just climbed into was nothing but a charred mass at the bottom of a crater.

* * *

"Patrick Sanchez?" The faint voice came from very far away. "Patrick? Can you hear me?"

Patricio became dimly aware of a young woman's face near his. Her lips moved but the sound was unclear and seemed distant. He felt his eyelids flutter and then he went back to sleep. A gentle touch on his arm wakened him at some later time.

The same female face smiled at him. "Patrick?" This time he registered enough to know that she had Anglicized his name.

"Pa—" The word caught in his dry throat and he coughed. Pain ripped through his body. "Patricio. It's a ... Spanish ... name."

"Well, Patricio, it's good to have you with us again," she said. He caught about three words of the sentence but her smile told him what she meant.

"My ears ... I can't hear too well."

She nodded. "The doctor said that might be the case. It's a miracle you're alive. You were standing right next to the place where the shell hit."

He worked up a smile, still unsure what she was talking about. A bandage on his face itched and blocked part of his right eye but he couldn't seem to move his hand to scratch it. Soon it was too much effort to decipher her words. He slept again.

The light in the room was different when he woke this time. Three shafts of golden sun came from behind him, hitting a pale gray wall somewhere beyond his feet. As he watched, the light grew more intense, then quickly faded. Sundown.

His eyes traveled the expanse above his head. Angels floated on fragile wings above him; a white-bearded man in flowing red robes pointed toward some people who stared upward at him in awe. Then Patricio knew. He had died. This was heaven.

But if that were the case, why did his body hurt so badly?

He dragged his gaze away from the beautiful scene. Elaborately carved stone molding decorated the junction where the painted ceiling met a wall. It registered someplace inside him that he was in a building. He couldn't remember the last time he was in a building, and never inside one like this. He heard himself moan.

A man in a white coat immediately appeared at his side. "Well, Corporal Sanchez, you seem to be feeling a little better today. I'm Doctor Mitchell."

"Corporal?"

"You received a promotion and, I believe, a couple of medals for bravery."

Patricio turned his head aside. Roberto was dead—he remembered that much. What good were medals?

"Once the leg has mended you'll be given light office duty for a few months."

Leg. Patricio looked toward the foot of the bed. A thick white cast encased his right leg, which hung suspended from a contraption of metal and wires.

He fumbled through the information, working to make sense of it while the doctor talked quietly with a nurse who had appeared at his bedside and was making notes on a clipboard full of pages.

"A box—" Patricio said. "I was holding a box."

The doctor had a blank look but the nurse's expression brightened. "Yes, they found it. The medic said it was under your body and it looked like something of a keepsake. It was on your stretcher with you when you arrived."

She tucked her pencil behind her ear and set the clipboard near Patricio's uninjured leg. A metal-frame table sat beside the bed and she knelt to pull something from its lower shelf.

"The box is right here," she said. "A little scuffed but basically it's just fine."

He reached for the box, laying it beside his hip, keeping one hand on it. The ringing in his ears made him want to scream. Sensing his distress the nurse injected something into his arm with a large hypodermic needle. She pulled the sheet up to his chest and he began to drift away once more.

The next time he opened his eyes, the ward lay in darkness but for the soft glow of a few small lamps. Patricio turned his head to the left—saw a long row of white-sheeted beds filled with wounded men. The same to his right. Had they been here all along? Some of them tossed in their sleep, some groaned with the pain of their injuries. Aside from the patients, the ward was empty and quiet.

He drew a hand from under the blanket and took inventory: A bandage wound around his forehead, one very tender area beneath it; scabbed-over abrasions on his nose and right cheek; wads of cotton in both ears—he pulled them out; the right leg in its cast—he remembered that—and a length of gauze around his right forearm. His hand touched something hard on the mattress beside him. Roberto's wooden box.

He pulled himself up against his pillow, awkward with the leg in its harness, scooping the box onto his lap. *Roberto, my friend*— Images filled his head—scraps of that mangled vehicle. *Your poor infected foot. You thought an amputation was the worst that would happen.* Patricio's tears began to flow. The horror of the trenches came pouring back, all the times he had been certain he would die, then the shock of the completely unexpected shelling. He allowed himself the moment to mourn all that had happened to them.

Tears dripped from his chin, landing in the dust that coated the box. Absently, he picked up a corner of his sheet and began to wipe it clean. The dark wood became more attractive the more he rubbed at it. It felt warm against his thighs. He laid both hands flat against the carved surface and a rush of comfort traveled up his arms. He could hear a man three beds away whispering a woman's name, the swishing of sheets as the man rolled over in delirious half-sleep. He paused and listened, picking up tiny sounds from all over the ward.

The box now appeared to be golden brown, not the uneven, blotchy dark color as before. For the first time he noticed small stones of red, blue and green, and they sparkled now as if lit by some inner source. He ran his hands across the lid and down the sides. The colors intensified.

"You saved my life, didn't you?" he whispered to the box. "There is something magical about you."

He slid back down, flat on the mattress once again, his hands resting on the wooden box on his belly. He felt his eyes drifting shut.

* * *

Patricio woke to the sounds of efficiency. Nurses bustled through the ward, delivering breakfast to those who could eat, bowls of some sort of porridge. Some of the men sat upright, feeding themselves; others relied upon an attendant to spoon the food for them. Plenty were still incoherent in their misery and he saw that the nurses were doing their best to attend to everyone.

The wooden box still rested on his belly. He must have slept very quietly after his wakeful period in the night. Staring at the box he wondered what had happened—it looked perfectly ordinary now, no special colors, no glowing stones. The dust was gone. He remembered that he had cried, had wiped off the dirt. He lifted the lid. Only crumbs remained of the cookies Roberto's mother had sent.

Roberto's parents. Had they received word yet? He supposed so, with the miracle of the telegraph. Still, he should write to them, find some words of comfort if he could.

"Good morning, Patrick," the cheery nurse from yesterday said. "You look much better this morning."

She set a bowl of the porridge on the small table beside his bed and suddenly he felt hungry.

"Can I take that for you? Put it out of the way?" She reached for the box.

"Don't take it away. I want it close."

"It will just be right here," she said, showing him that she would place it on the shelf of his table.

Patricio watched the box, still dark in color; it showed no reaction to the woman's touch. "I had a strange dream last night. That box—" He couldn't put it into words; the experience had been too peculiar.

She waited with a little smile. "It's fairly common. The drugs we give you to sleep. Some men have very outlandish experiences—all in their sleep."

That must be it, the reason for his perception of the glow and the colors. Easily explainable. He picked up the spoon beside the porridge bowl. He had nearly finished his breakfast when the doctor approached his bedside. The man studied Patricio's face more intently than before.

"Your injuries are healing quite nicely," he commented, gently removing the forehead bandage. "Very good."

"The one on my arm itches, much more than yesterday."

"Don't scratch it. That was a fairly deep gash and we don't want to see it reopen." He signaled for the nurse to return. "Check and redress this wound. Let me know if there is any sign of infection."

The doctor moved on to the next man's bedside and the nurse went to work quickly. Unwinding the cotton wrapping, then lifting a strip of padding she revealed a four-inch line on his forearm, with a track of black stitches tied in somewhat bulky knots.

"This doesn't seem normal." Her voice was very soft.

Patricio stared at the wound. "Is it bad?"

"No … no, it's actually quite good. I've never seen one heal this quickly."

He felt a little rush of pride, as if he'd accomplished it through his own efforts. His eyes drifted toward the wooden box. No. Impossible. That had been a dream, just a dream.

The nurse glanced toward the doctor, as if debating whether to call him back. He seemed busy with another patient three beds down. She shrugged and placed clean padding over Patricio's wound and rewrapped it.

"I'd like to write a letter," he said.

"I can send an orderly with paper and pen," she said cheerfully. "It's good to let the family know you are all right."

He had not even thought of his own family, but the woman was right. They might have received a telegram saying he was wounded and would not know his condition.

"Bring enough for three letters."

By the time the orderly arrived much of Patricio's earlier energy seemed to have drained away.

"I can write them for you," the young man offered, setting down a black pen, a bottle of ink and a few sheets of paper. "I do it for many of the soldiers."

"I'd rather do them myself, but thanks." The letter to his own family would be the easy one, the reassuring one. For

Roberto's parents … he was not yet sure what or how much he should say. "You may leave the paper here. And could you hand me that box from the shelf?"

He uncapped the pen and placed a sheet of the flimsy paper on the lapboard the orderly had left. What to say? *Dear Mr. and Mrs. Smith, Roberto died just before he was about to have his foot amputated because of the nasty conditions we endured in the trenches together …?* The truth would be too brutal and far too soon after receipt of the dreaded telegram. *Dear Mr. and Mrs. Smith, your son and I had become extremely close …?* It would sound too much as if they were queer for each other. Impossible to explain to anyone who wasn't there that the bonds formed in wartime were nothing like that. It had been more like having a brother, perhaps even a twin brother, a relationship gestated together in the womb of that section of trench where one's blood practically flowed interchangeably with the other's.

He capped the pen and put the top back on the ink bottle, staring at the blank page. Let out a deep sigh. Losing his best friend was still far too fresh.

He opened the pen again and began: *Dear Mamá and Papá, I am well. By now you have probably received word that I was wounded …*

The words filled a page and a half and he sealed them into an envelope and wrote the address on it without rereading. He would be tempted to edit away half of it, and they deserved to know as much as he could bring himself to tell. He'd skimmed over the reality of trench life, gone into detail about the joy of that hot shower after the battle, mentioned the death of Roberto as only one of many comrades he'd lost in the past month, ended with a wish for a quick end to the Great War and the hope of seeing them soon. He drafted a similar message to Emelia, making light of his wounds, assuring her that none of them were life-threatening. It, too, went into an envelope without a second reading; he had a feeling it was too impersonal but he did not have it in him to write words of love and devotion right now.

He rested for a few minutes then tried again to write a letter to the Smiths. It came out sounding too much like the one he'd written home—too centered on himself, too general. Roberto's parents would want news of their own son, something profound about his final hours. Patricio wadded up the page. He would try again later.

* * *

Patricio limped to his desk. A month in the hospital outside Paris, another month in a convalescent home, and the damn leg still ached with the chill of autumn weather. Worse at some times than others; the doctors said he would have to live with it and made him feel somewhat guilty that he *had* a leg—many didn't. His current post was an office job in Bapaume, a little town somewhere in France—he did not quite recall how he'd arrived there, except that it was by train and he'd carried a duffle with his few possessions on his lap during the grueling hours of the trip.

Now, his duties included writing up supply orders for the commanders of troops still in the field. He thanked God every single day that he'd not been sent back to the front lines; as a relatively mobile soldier it was a possibility. He was quartered in a converted warehouse that housed fifty men in bunks. It was damp in the evenings and cold by morning but, unlike the trenches, it provided a roof and walls and since the German occupation had been overcome more than a month ago he did not have to listen to the sounds of shelling and gunfire. He actually slept, every fourth night or so, when exhaustion overtook him.

He sat, keeping his sore leg outstretched under the desk. A stack of forms awaited his attention but his thoughts went to the other task on his mind, the unwritten letter to Roberto's parents. While he rubberstamped and signed requisitions words ran through his head. Tonight he would write the letter and post it tomorrow. Be done with the obligation.

"There's rumor of an armistice," the fellow at the next desk said to another corporal who sat at an identical desk facing him.

"Can't happen too soon for me," replied the corporal.

"Nice if it happened before another winter sets in, especially for those poor chaps in the mountains."

Patricio remembered the Italian he and Roberto had met on that fateful day in early July, how the guy told them of the misery of serving on that particular front.

Yes, he would write to the Smiths tonight. Finish out his tour here, go home, put the whole sordid, bloody, smelly experience behind him and find happiness hoeing a row of corn on his father's little plot of land in Taos County, with warm sunshine to bake away his aches.

Later, he plodded back to the barracks, leaning heavily on the cane provided by the Army, his leg throbbing with each step. The pain constantly increased as each day went on, and falling into bed at night was always a welcome relief. One end of their warehouse-barracks served as a mess hall but Patricio bypassed it. Might have gone there if he'd remembered to take the bottle of aspirin to work with him this morning, but he hadn't and now all he wanted was a bit of relief from those little white pills.

He rummaged in his duffle for them and came across recent letters from home. His mother wrote regularly, each communication expressing her relief at his recovery and gratitude that he was no longer caught up in the fighting. Emelia's letters had become less frequent. Perhaps she was wary, wondering whether he would be the same or if his war injuries had caused irreparable damage. He had no idea how to answer that. Below the letters he found his writing supplies. He swallowed three of the bitter pain pills and lay back with his leg propped on a pillow.

Dear Mr. and Mrs. Smith, I apologize for the lateness of this letter. I should have contacted you weeks ago ...

He went on to let them know what a good friend Roberto had been, embellishing a couple of amusing episodes, omitting any reference to the rampant infection of trench foot and the fact that their son would have returned home minus part of a limb. At this point they probably would have welcomed that, as opposed to his not returning at all.

His gaze traveled to the wooden box; a corner of it showed down inside his duffle bag. Should he mention it to the mother who had sent it to her son filled with his favorite cookies? By rights he should offer to return it to the family. But perhaps it would serve only as a painful reminder of the events, of the fact that Roberto had died on the very day he received the gift. He ended the letter with *Very sincerely yours* and tucked it into an envelope. He stared at the envelope flap before sealing it.

Was his true reason for not offering to return the wooden box because of the pain it would cause the Smiths? He suspected a more selfish motivation. The box had saved his life. And he still faced surviving this god-awful war for some unknown period of time. He could always contact them again once he was safely at home in New Mexico.

* * *

Dockside in New York Harbor thousands of people milled about—sailors, soldiers, weeping women and shrieking children. Jubilation rode at the surface of the greater anguish over all the war had cost, like the very thin skin over the pulp of an apple. A smile on a grieving face barely masked what was going on inside, and he saw those expressions everywhere. Patricio stood still in the middle of the moving human tide, staring at his surroundings, unsure what to do next. It wasn't home but it sure felt American and better to him than anything he had encountered in the past seven months.

With discharge papers in hand, he had no orders, no plan. Somehow he would get from the dock to a train station—he knew nothing about where to find it in the city. From there, west. A few days and he could be arriving near Santa Fe. All the logistics were attainable but at the moment his head swam with the prospect of putting it together, of finding his way around in the throng.

A chant arose at one edge of the crowd, female voices shouting and waving placards on sticks that said "The Saloon Must Go!" above the heads of the crowd. A uniformed man nearby muttered something about 'the damn temperance league' and asked Patricio if he knew where the nearest bar was.

"I don't," Patricio admitted, "but I think I would join you if you led the way."

He needed a few minutes respite from the unending noise. Maybe a glass of beer would settle his nerves. The man turned and extended his hand.

"Franklin Hastings. Last duty station, Paris. Believe me, I can find us a bar."

Patricio followed as quickly as he was able, half wondering what he was getting himself into, the other half thankful that Hastings was leading him away from the thickest part of the huge crowd. One beer, he told himself, then directions to the train station and he would be on his way.

"Ah, don't settle for a beer," Hastings said once they had settled themselves on stools inside a little neighborhood place that called itself, simply, O'Ryan's. "Those preachy temperance women get their way we'll soon be out of anything decent to drink. Have a whiskey."

He ordered from the bartender before Patricio could say a word. At the back of the bar a piano player launched into the song that summarized the ending of the war, 'Pack Up Your Troubles in Your Old Kit Bag and Smile, Smile, Smile.'

"Fifteen states have ratified the stupid prohibition idea already," Hastings was saying. "The rest have it coming up for a vote in the next few months."

Heavy glasses with golden brown liquid appeared before them.

"Here's to the rest of 'em seeing the light and defeating the damn thing," Hastings said, raising his glass. A half-dozen others in the bar joined in.

Patricio let the tepid liquid burn a path down his throat. He'd never had anything quite like it.

"Where you from?" Hastings asked.

"New Mexico. You?"

"New Mexico—is that a state? Me, I come from Chicago. My family's on the north shore there, father in real estate. Mother spends his money. One sister, my little dollface. I haven't seen her in two years and she's probably turned out to be a real beauty by now. Deborah is her name."

"I have a sister, too—"

"Yeah, my father's got a spot for me in the family business already. Can't wait to get back and start raking in some of those post-war profits." He raised his refilled glass and gave Patricio a stare that seemed intended to mean something.

A light rain was falling when they left O'Ryan's. Patricio turned up his collar, the overwhelming crowds and noise assaulting his senses once more.

"Hey, you staying somewhere in town?" Franklin asked as they huddled under the bar's narrow awning.

"I had planned to catch the first train to Santa Fe."

"Well, there's nothing direct from here. You want the Santa Fe DeLuxe out of Chicago. It's a weekly and they treat you right. Tell you what—let's catch the overnighter out of Grand Central, you stay over with me until Thursday and then we'll have you on your way."

"That's too much imposition—"

"Nonsense! You're a fellow doughboy. My parents are gonna love you. Nothing too good for my comrades. Besides, you'll be going that way anyhow. Like I said, really no better way to do it."

Franklin Hastings obviously knew his way around and it seemed so much easier than trying to figure out all the logistics on his own. Patricio felt himself acquiescing.

Franklin was scanning the traffic on the street, ignoring

the horse-drawn hansoms, spotting a bright yellow motorcar. He stepped off the sidewalk and hailed it, swinging the door open; Patricio tried not to be obvious about the fact that this was his first experience with a taxi cab. Before he knew it, Franklin had whipped out some cash and paid for both the taxi and the train tickets at the ornate Grand Central Terminal. People stepped aside when they saw the two uniformed men and the railroad clerk upgraded their tickets to the first class coach at no extra cost. Patricio wanted to protest that he was no one special but Franklin reminded him of the time spent in the trenches and how he had sustained an injury.

"Never sell yourself short," he said as they took their seats. "Someone wants to do something nice for you, you accept it."

Patricio leaned into the padded seat, exhaustion suddenly enveloping him.

* * *

Chicago. Big. Dirty. Notorious. Patricio caught the bold headlines on the city's three newspapers as he and Franklin Hastings exited the train station. Four murders overnight. The papers almost glorified them.

"This way," said Franklin. "We'll grab a cab and surprise the family."

The building where they stopped towered above the crowded sidewalk with an ornate face of cool gray stone, polished marble floors in the lobby.

"Hey, Harry!" Franklin greeted the elevator operator.

"Mr. Hastings, sir. So good to see you home safe and sound." The elderly man stood respectfully still, but Franklin wrapped his arms around him in a boisterous hug.

At the sixteenth floor the polished brass door opened to a small lobby with a heavy, paneled door beyond.

"This is us," said Franklin. "Don't have my keys so I guess we'll ring."

A uniformed Negro maid opened the door, her large dark eyes rolling upward as she took in their uniforms.

"My lord! Mr. Franklin!"

Her shriek drew attention. A man, a forty-year-old version of Franklin, stepped into the foyer from a side room. His eyes widened as he rushed forward to clasp his son's hand. The woman who followed him burst into tears when she saw them. Patricio took a step backward, feeling a little awkward; this should have been a private family moment. But Franklin turned toward him.

"My new friend, Patricio Sanchez. He served at Belleau Wood."

"Oh, my," said Mrs. Hastings. "We read about that one in the papers. Are you all right? You seem to be limping. Now come right inside and sit down. We were just having our morning coffee. Mattie—get more cups and saucers, please. You boys just drop your bags here for now."

The maid rushed away and Patricio realized that Mrs. Hastings wanted to take his arm so he extended his elbow. She subtly guided him to a room with high ceilings, large windows and velvet draperies that hung to the floor. A rug covered the marble floor, a richly patterned thing in shades of red and blue. A brisk fire in the marble-faced fireplace took the chill away and tall bookcases flanked both sides of it. Two sofas with richly embroidered red fabric faced each other and a silver coffee service sat on a table between them. He had never seen anyplace like it.

Movement caught his attention and he stopped cold. Rising from the end of one sofa was the most beautiful woman he'd ever seen and she was regarding him quite frankly. Blonde hair that must have been borrowed from an angel, blue eyes whose irises were rimmed just faintly in a deep gray. He blushed when she stood. A woman's ankles and clinging, filmy material were unfamiliar sights—how fashions had changed!

"Frankie!" she shouted, racing toward them with outstretched arms. "Oh, you're home, you're home!"

"I am, Deb. Finally." He lifted her off the floor and twirled around with his arms wrapped around her waist.

When he came to a stop he set her down and turned toward Patricio.

"Meet my sister—Deborah. Sis, this is Patricio."

"Patricio? Oh, come on … you need an American name now. I'll call you Patrick."

Patricio didn't even think to object. He was lost in those blue eyes. She reached for his hand and pulled him toward the sofas as the maid returned with a small tray containing cups, saucers and another silver pot of fresh coffee.

"Patrick comes from New Mexico," Franklin was saying. "He'll stay with us until the next Santa Fe DeLuxe leaves."

"Oh, dear, the DeLuxe stopped service last year." Mrs. Hastings turned toward Patricio. "I'm afraid they've only first-class service to offer now. I do hope that will be all right."

"Too bad, old man. The DeLuxe always greeted the ladies with an orchid corsage and the gents with a tooled leather wallet." Franklin had already reverted away from Army talk, had become more formal, Patricio noticed.

"But it's wonderful that you'll be in Chicago a few extra

days," Deborah sat across from him now and the blue eyes were constantly on him. "And do you know—since you wouldn't be able to make it home before Thanksgiving, I think you should stay and have it with us. Wouldn't that be perfect, Mummy? A war hero as our guest."

Although nothing had been said, she must have noticed the medals on his uniform. He started to protest, to talk about how he had really not earned the medals. But these people didn't want to hear of death and bombs and hospitals full of damaged men. The ladies were already talking about decorations for the holiday table. He accepted a cup of coffee that smelled like heaven and leaned back against the sofa's puffy cushion.

"We heard that the great pandemic flu had come to Chicago," Franklin said to his father. "You never said, was the household affected?"

"Oh, no. We were fine—went to the country place for a few weeks, even the servants. I'm sure your mother wrote you … must be a letter that never caught up with you."

Deborah spoke up. "It was deadly dull, I'll tell you. But then the city was deadly dull as well. They closed the theaters, cancelled concerts, even some of the shops shut down for awhile. There was absolutely nothing to do, and one didn't dare even ride the trains out of fear—the germs were simply everywhere."

"I suppose that's pretty much over with now," said Franklin.

"Oh, yes. We're all back up to our usual tricks." The blue eyes twinkled and her smile revealed one eyetooth just a tiny bit crooked. Patricio felt his heart flutter.

"Well, I am certain that you boys would love a hot bath and the chance to unpack before luncheon. Use the afternoon to rest, after that long train trip, then we'll meet for drinks at seven and dinner at eight." Mrs. Hastings stood to signal that she had other things to do.

They all rose.

Patricio and Franklin retrieved their Army duffle bags from the foyer and headed for the stairs.

"I'm not sure about this," Patricio said. "I don't have any suitable clothes for dinners and such. And I can't really afford to go shopping."

"Oh, nonsense. We'll rummage up something of Father's. You're very close to his size." He said it as if this were no problem at all.

Patricio trailed one stair behind. He could wear borrowed clothing for a few days until the train left. Unless he really did accept Deborah's suggestion that he stay for Thanksgiving. He found himself attracted to the idea.

"You'll be in here and I'm right up the hall, two doors away." Franklin interrupted his thoughts. "Bathroom is right through that connecting door … plenty of blankets on the beds but if you want a fire just say so. Normally they're lit first thing in the morning before we all go out. Otherwise, it's just the central heat here in the radiators but sometimes it's a little spotty."

Patricio walked into the room, decorated in shades of green with a high bed piled with luxurious-looking linens. Central heat? He wasn't even sure what that was. He thought of his family's cozy adobe with its one fireplace and the thick walls, which kept the place warm in winter and cool in summer. He dropped his duffle bag on the bed and peered into the bathroom. A flushing toilet, a deep, claw-footed tub, a handsome basin with both hot and cold water taps.

He had just pulled everything from his bag, finding a

hanger in the tall armoire for his spare uniform and stuffing used underclothes back into the duffle, when a tap came at the door. Without waiting for a response, Franklin opened it and peered around the edge.

"Brought you a few things. Try them on. If they don't fit properly we can have them altered. Father's put on a few pounds …" he patted his stomach "… but these did fit him a few years ago. I do believe you are exactly the same height, though." He handed over the garments and left without another word.

The items consisted of a tweed suit with shirt and vest, a simple tuxedo (apparently dressing for dinner was expected), and a good quality overcoat. Patricio looked down at his scuffed Army boots, his only footwear. Equally shabby-looking was Roberto's carved wooden box. He ran his sleeve over it to give it a little shine. So many months, so many events since he and Roberto had walked the streets of that little French village, eaten cookies from this box, read mail from home together. He thought of Emelia but could hardly remember her face anymore. Too much had intervened.

"Meant to suggest," said Franklin—he had not closed the door behind him. "You're welcome to browse through my closet for shoes. Come along now, if you'd like."

Fifteen minutes later, Patricio found himself completely outfitted for going out in public (although he could have certainly worn his Army uniform on the streets) and for the nightly dinner ritual. He closed himself away in his assigned room and sat on the edge of the bed, nervous about getting through it all.

A chime rang at seven o'clock, signaling the gathering for cocktails. Patricio had fallen into a deep sleep shortly after Franklin left the borrowed clothes, apparently missed lunch with the family, and had awakened only when his new friend tapped at the door an hour ago to make sure he was all right and would be joining them for dinner. He'd spent the hour figuring out all the parts to the tuxedo. A manservant who introduced himself as Hughes came by and righted the few bits he'd gotten wrong.

He followed the sound of voices and came into the same room where coffee had been served that morning, to discover another addition to the group. A female guest named Catherine ('the family calls me Cat') Bates; he quickly figured out she was an old girlfriend of Franklin's. The two of them drifted toward the windows, apparently to take in the city lights along the shoreline of the lake, leaving Patricio to make conversation with the elder Hastings and Deborah. It didn't prove to be a problem as she took the lead.

"Mother needs to see to some committee business for a charity ball and has had to cancel our plans to go shopping." She raised her eyes to gaze at him in a way that brought out the fine line of her nose and accentuated a dimple that he had not noticed before. "I was so hoping that you might go along, to act as my escort for a few hours."

He reasoned that there were certainly worse ways a newly discharged soldier could spend a day. He agreed, just as her father handed him a heavy crystal glass with an inch of imported Scotch whiskey in it.

"From our most recent shipment," Hastings said, "forty-year stock. I'm afraid we'll not be seeing much of that in the near future."

"Because of the new prohibition laws?"

"The good stuff will go first but there will always be something to wet a man's whistle." He took a long sip. "One thing you have to understand about basic human nature, son. The more strongly you forbid something, the more determined people are to have it. Ask the mother of any ten-year-old child!" He chuckled and made eye contact with his wife.

"I can speak from experience in raising this one," Mrs. Hastings said, staring at her daughter. "Remember that little girl you wanted to befriend, the Irish one? No matter how much I forbade you to play with her you always found a way."

"Maggie O'Hare? I hardly remember her now."

"I should have given you free rein—you would have discovered how little you had in common, years earlier."

Franklin and Cat had joined them now.

"Am I right, Frank? Prohibit the sale of liquor and even those who don't care much for hard drink will suddenly develop a craving. There are men who will make their fortunes from this ill-conceived whim of the nation."

An inside joke seemed to pass through the group, with Patricio never quite catching its meaning. Mrs. Hastings caught a glimpse of Mattie at the doorway, stood and subtly herded everyone. Deborah caught Patricio's arm and they entered a formal dining room with more plates and silverware than he had ever seen in one place. *Stay alert,* he told himself. *You can learn a lot from these people.*

He was seated with Deborah on his right, her mother on his left. At the head of the table, Mr. Hastings talked with Frank about his newest, very lucrative, real estate deal. Patricio found himself perfectly situated to pay attention to the men's conversation while observing which fork Deborah used with each course and when she sipped the wine and how she cut the meat into small bites. By the end of the meal he came away with a feeling this might be a lifestyle to which he could become accustomed.

The following morning Patricio put on his borrowed suit and rode the elevator down to the lobby with Deborah. Her errands seemed trivial to him—a packet of hairpins at the druggist's shop, a small loaf cake to be served with tea later in the day. As she paid for this last item she added a small wrapper of chocolates to the order and tucked them into her bag.

"Let's sit in the park for awhile," she suggested, "enjoy the sunshine of an Indian summer day and have a chocolate."

She asked about Europe but didn't want to hear the sordid parts. "No," she said, "tell me about the architecture, the paintings."

He described the ceiling in the former museum that had been converted to a hospital, the place where he'd awakened in the belief that he had died and gone to heaven. She laughed with delight at the way he told it. He found himself speculating at the amount of work that had gone into creating the ceiling fresco, embellishing the details and describing the biblical characters very specifically. She hung on his every word and his words trailed off when he focused on her face.

"I want to go to Europe, so very much," she said. "Mother had planned to take me when I finished school. It's just that by the time I might have experienced a debutant season, the war had started and my parents did not feel it safe to travel. I suppose now I shall have to wait until I'm married."

Did he imagine some kind of suggestion in her tone? He reached for the packet of chocolates, to take a second one, and his hand brushed hers.

* * *

The wedding was scheduled for Christmas week. A small ceremony at nearby St. Anthony's Chapel, followed by a reception at the Hastings apartment. As a gift Deborah's parents gave them an apartment in the same building, albeit on a lower floor and far less grand than their own. Patrick would be employed in the family business, managing two of the nightclubs which had begun to flourish under the prospect of full passage of the Constitution's eighteenth amendment.

He had never made the train trip back to New Mexico. By Thanksgiving in Chicago he and Deborah were spending a great deal of their time together; December first she began tiptoeing to his bedroom nearly every night. Once he discovered the joys of her uninhibited nature, he could not seem to remember much about his home state. These lavish walls and this vibrant city had become his domain. He wrote to Emelia to inform her that he would not be returning. He told his parents he would come after the first of the new year, when he could introduce them to his new wife.

Two important things happened in the spring of 1920. He booked tickets for the two of them to take the train to Santa Fe where his mother and father would meet them and they would all make the drive to Taos. And Deborah informed him that she was pregnant.

The journey went smoothly until his wife set foot in his parents' home. The disdain was clear on her face. Perhaps she had expected them to be wealthy landowners; perhaps she saw the accommodations at the La Fonda Hotel as bare minimum. Either way, she was openly condescending to both mama and papa and could not get out of there quickly enough. He tried to chalk it up to morning sickness and other things women went through during pregnancy; he really did not understand those things. The thing he did understand was that his wife wanted nothing to do with his parents.

"*Hijo*," his mother said, "you are a man now and your duty is to your wife and children. There is no other way. Write to us often and tell us of your new life. We will always love you."

She cleared her throat and turned away, but not before Patrick saw the tears coursing down her face.

Back in Chicago, Deborah decided to redecorate their new apartment. It had come furnished with perfectly nice things but she wanted to 'make it my own' she said. This entailed bringing in crews of plasterers and painters and an odious woman who gave advice on what colors each of the rooms should be.

"And I want to be rid of this piece of junk," Deborah said. She held up Patrick's wooden box.

"You will not!" he shouted.

She drew back, staring at him. He had never raised his voice to her. She dropped the box on a sofa and placed her hands protectively over her growing belly. He immediately felt contrite.

"This box saved my life. During the war. It will not be discarded like so much junk." He picked it up and cradled it against his new, expensive suit.

She glared at the box but obviously knew how to choose her battles. "It's only that it doesn't go along with the new décor. Keep it somewhere else, darling?"

She blew him a kiss and flounced out of the room. He

carried the box to his study and placed it on a high shelf, moving some books to conceal it. Emelia would have found the box rustic and enchanting. How had he come so far from his true roots?

* * *

Deborah turned toward him in bed, running a fingertip over his bare arm. "Darling? Do you still plan to take us to the park today?"

He rolled to face her, hoping that the playful tone meant something good. Their intimate relationship had been practically nonexistent since the birth of little Frankie, and that was nearly two years ago now. Between the demands of his work and the moodiness of his wife, he felt lucky if his needs were met every few months. Of course other men visited the brothels or took mistresses—he knew they did—including the men in this very family.

"The park?"

"Well, yes, Frankie loves it so much and I thought we could make it special, take a picnic along and ride the carousel the way we did when we met."

He eyed her cautiously. He couldn't remember the last time she'd demonstrated a playful or sentimental streak.

"If you will organize the food, I can meet you and Frankie there. Your father has called a meeting this morn—" Suddenly, he remembered the last time she had been in such good spirits. The day she informed him that she was carrying their baby.

She had already turned the opposite direction and was sitting on the edge of the bed.

"How far along—when is it due?" he asked.

She sent him her most earnest, dimpled smile. "Oh, darling, I had hoped to surprise you with the news, over lunch."

"When?"

"Six more months. Please tell me you are happy, please, Patrick?"

He thought of little Frankie and smiled. Maybe another baby would repair the strife between them. Surely *every* subject in a marriage couldn't lead to an argument. Surely there would come a point when they settled into their roles and felt the same happiness inside they portrayed to the rest of Chicago society.

Deborah pulled a satin robe over her peignoir. "I'm glad to see your smile, dear. So we'll be at McCormick Park at noon then? I've started to do a little rearranging, making space for the baby. I'll decorate the room in pink this time."

So much for the possibility of sex, he thought as she left the bedroom. He washed and dressed in one of his office suits for this morning's meeting. Some papers, contracts he was to discuss with his father-in-law, were in his study and he went to collect them. The moment he opened the door he knew what was going on.

His desk had been shoved to one side, the rug rolled up, the shelves emptied. Swatches of pink fabrics lay on his chair. He stared at the shelf where he had stored Roberto's wooden box a long time ago. It was missing.

His gaze darted about the room, landing finally on a waste basket that stood ready for emptying near the door. The box had been carelessly tossed there. Without a word, he picked up his prized item, tucked it under his arm and walked out the door.

He walked the streets for more than an hour. In the

back of his mind, the meeting over the liquor contracts loomed. He was late already and for the first time he didn't care. His mind churned. Responsibilities. Wife, child—soon two children—business, in-laws. He had been married in the church and took those vows seriously. There could be no divorce. But did he really want one? For the first time he faced the fact that the money had ensnared him.

He thought of the tiny adobe house where his parents lived. As enticing as the farming life might sound to some, he had been there, had known the backbreaking work his father performed, year after year, simply to feed the family. He'd lived without money, and he'd lived with it. He had to admit that having the means to own anything he wanted was the easier way.

Hating himself with every step, he approached a trash receptacle on the street.

No. He couldn't do it.

He turned and walked to the nearest post office.

"I need this item wrapped for shipping," he told the clerk. "And postage enough to mail it to New Mexico."

While the clerk wrapped the box, Patrick scribbled a note to his mother. *Please keep this safe. It's very important to me.*

Chapter 10

Magic Goes Missing

Cardinal Luca Pancetti gathered his red robe tightly about him as he followed the young priest who led the way and switched on lights in the dim and dusty catacombs. Pancetti knew of this area of hidden Vatican tunnels and alcoves. He had once visited here as a much younger man at the time of his assignment to serve in Rome—the day he had learned that this would be one of his life's responsibilities.

They rounded a corner, moving deeper into the maze of corridors. Glass light sconces gave way to a string of bare bulbs running along the center of the low ceiling. Dark smudges along the walls attested to the fact that illumination here had once consisted of burning torches.

"It should be just through here," said the priest in a hushed voice. He consulted a note his superior had scribbled on onionskin paper.

The young priest aimed a battery-powered flashlight toward a dark alcove to reveal a heavy wooden door. A key, produced from inside the cardinal's robe, worked smoothly in the ornate metal lock and the door swung open as smoothly as if it had been oiled yesterday. Perhaps it had. Pancetti knew nothing of the daily operations of this section of the massive underground archives, nothing other than his personal mandate. To check the contents of Chamber 13, the place allocated to storage of those items deemed heretical.

The study of so-called magical objects, of the Church's long battle against the intrusion of Satan himself into the world, had become Pancetti's life's work. As a youngster he'd been fascinated with tales of an old woman in his village who claimed to foretell the future. Young Luca lingered outside her cottage, hoping to learn exactly how she did this, until the day his mother discovered him there and with an incredibly strong grip on his left ear hauled him home. The next day he was enrolled in a program for troublesome boys under the tutelage of a rather strict order of monks. At their severe hand, he'd learned discipline and that it was wise to keep one's opinions to oneself. His fascination with things of a supernatural nature had never waned, but he kept his collection of reading material well hidden and his views were shared with no one.

Twenty years ago, Luca Pancetti had been called into a meeting in a narrow, backstreet building. The group called themselves OSM. How they ferreted out his secret was unclear; he suspected the orderly who cleaned his rooms may have discovered the false drawer in his bookcase. No matter—the organization had a mission for Pancetti and it was on this errand he came now.

He knew little of their history, only that once during the reign of each pope it was required that OSM's special emissary come to this secret chamber to inventory the artifacts and assure there had been no tampering. Although none of those influential men publicly acknowledged that a mere relic could contain power, it would not do for any such item to leave their control. Pancetti carried with him a list of some fifty objects which had been gathered during the past five centuries.

As the door to the chamber swung open he privately wondered why the organization's leader had called upon him now. The man gave no indication, other than to thrust this list into his hands and give the written instructions which had brought him here. It was no secret that Pius XI's health was precarious—a heart condition, they said—and the fact that his physician was the father of Mussolini's mistress probably did not bode well for the pope who had publicly denounced both Fascism and Nazism. Luca put this line of thinking aside; Vatican politics did not interest him.

He dismissed the young priest, who took his flashlight and closed the door. Pancetti switched on his own battery-powered lantern in the absolute darkness. What interested him were the artifacts in this room. His previous visit to the catacombs had taken him only to the outer door; now he stared in fascination at the niches built into these sacred walls. Illuminated only by the lantern, and therefore limited in the amount of time he could spend on this visit, he began. A less-enthused man would start at the first compartment and tick off the first item on his list, but Pancetti found himself walking past a bowl of small amulets, some books, a metal cask reputed to expand in size until a grown man could climb inside and travel to another universe. He focused, instead, on a gemstone that sparkled in the dim light. Even the coating of dust on its glass case did not dull the fact that this was an extraordinary item. Luca reached out to touch it.

No, he reminded himself, pulling his hand back. He'd been given a few short hours in which to conduct the inventory. If he moved quickly to check the items on the list, perhaps there would be time to actually handle a few of the most interesting ones later. He hastily checked off five amulets, a dozen books purported to contain magic spells, and the glowing gemstone. The next item on the list must be special indeed. Not on display in one of the niches, a description was provided for the means to reach this one: a stone one meter from the southwest wall would have small crosses etched on two of its rough-hewn corners. Press gently on the left edge of it and a compartment would be revealed. His heart beat faster. This, surely, must be a very important object to deserve such special treatment.

Already, his light was growing dimmer. He scanned the walls, unsure of direction here in this place more than twenty meters below ground. Southwest. Which way was it? His eyes were drawn to a section of wall that contained no other niches; he began his examination there. Finally, nearly a foot above his head he spotted the two small etched crosses. Standing on tiptoe he reached for the left edge and pressed. The stone released without a sound and slid outward, providing an easy edge to grip. He pulled it out of its place. Fascinating. It must be spring-loaded in some fashion. How had men of the thirteenth century concocted these mechanisms, he wondered. But there was no time to ponder it now. The lantern flickered.

Luca cursed the fact that he had been a slight child and had not grown taller as a man. He could not see into the empty space revealed by the missing stone. Glancing around the room he found nothing to stand upon other than the stone he had just removed. He placed it on the floor and found that it was precisely the size of his two feet if he stood carefully on it. The lantern flickered again and he raised it to the black hole in front of him. He could not see anything.

The space was supposed to contain a box of some sort. By the code markings on his list this was considered one of the collection's most important items. He jammed the lantern closer to the opening. Nothing. He ran his hand inside as far as he could reach but the space was empty.

His heart thudded now with a sound that must surely be echoing from the walls. An artifact was missing, and on his vigil! He'd been told a month ago to conduct the inventory count and be ready in time for tonight's meeting. Why had he waited until the last moment? Had the box disappeared within the past few weeks? It did not matter, he realized. The box was lost while under his care and now he had to report it to the powerful men of the OSM.

The lantern faded, like a candle guttering its last few moments. He stepped down and quickly replaced the stone in its slot. Before he'd turned the key in the lock, the light went out.

* * *

"It was there at the last inventory!" shouted the leader, a sharp-jawed businessman from Zurich named Humboldt.

"With all due respect, sir, that was nearly twenty-five years ago."

Luca Pancetti silently thanked the priest who had spoken up. Had he uttered the same words, his protestation would have sounded much too defensive.

Humboldt drummed his fingertips on the written list of artifacts. Luca had returned to the chamber with a fresh light, finished counting all the other items and thoroughly examined the compartment of the missing box. He'd used every remaining minute until he absolutely had to leave for this meeting to check the walls for other possible hidden spaces. There were none. He told the men this, feeling like a complete failure.

Faces around the table were grim. A bishop spoke up. "It's the one we could least afford to lose, the box called Facinor."

"And I would remind the gentlemen," said an American industrialist who had been appointed to the executive committee only four years earlier, "that this is the second of these boxes to disappear in OSM history."

Those representing the church bristled. Pancetti could almost hear them growling over the fact that non-clergy had been admitted to the organization. But politics and business were becoming ever more powerful in today's world; somewhere along the line it had been decided to include the secular.

The industrialist was still giving a pointed stare toward Humboldt.

"Way before my time," the Swiss man answered. "But yes, you are quite correct. I've read the history. The disappearance of the box called Manichee during the Inquisition was what prompted the formation of this organization. Our entire directive is to protect these artifacts and to keep them locked away where their powers cannot be misdirected by the average commoner who might possess one."

And the missing one now was Facinor, the box whose powers were purported to be evil.

"I suppose we should launch an investigation," suggested a priest whose reluctant tone said that the mere idea of investigating anything within the Vatican was practically sacrilege.

A man at the other end of the table cleared his throat. He was a politician from America and the fact that he had not yet spoken was unusual. "We are fairly certain that The Vongraf Foundation has examined one of the boxes."

He reached into an inner pocket of his jacket and brought out a sheaf of vertically folded pages. "In 1910, according to a spy we placed at the time, the piece definitely had paranormal powers. Jimmy himself witnessed a secretary to the director handling the box and the wooden material undergoing changes in appearance."

"It must have been the missing box, Manichee," someone speculated. "Facinor was in our possession when our own 1915 inventory was taken."

"There have been tales—call them rumors or speculation, if you will—about the existence of *three* boxes," Humboldt reminded them. "We cannot possibly know which one The Vongraf has."

"Had. They don't keep any artifacts that pass through their hands," said the politician, waving the sheaf of pages. "I verified that myself. The box the foundation examined was returned to its owner. Unfortunately, I could not find out who that was."

A dark quiet settled over the group. Luca Pancetti thought furiously. His name had been whispered in the halls of the basilica as a possible replacement for Pius XI when the ailing pontiff's time came. He would be swiftly withdrawn from consideration if it ever became known beyond these walls that an important artifact had been lost under his care. Not that the official church bureaucracy would acknowledge interest in such items, but the stain of having been placed in charge of something and having failed so miserably … that sort of thing would linger on his record forever.

"Let me lead the investigation," he said. "I have the previous inventory sheet. I shall begin by tracing backward in time to find out who had access to that room."

Glances flicked around the table. Clearly, some did not want to trust the man who had lost the box in the first place but most of them were looking for excuses to dodge the work. It was difficult to turn down a volunteer. The priest offered a motion to accept Pancetti's offer and it was quickly approved.

Two hours later, in his room in Vatican City, Cardinal Pancetti scanned the list he had composed. Everyone stationed within the archives, most everyone who could have handled the key to the special chamber, all members of the OSM directorship during the ensuing twenty-plus years. It was a daunting list. His head was pounding and he reached for the aspirin for the second time since he'd begun the task. How was he to narrow this down and find the thief?

* * *

A month later, the pontiff's condition had worsened and whispered speculation ran rampant in the halls. Pancetti had asked so many pointed questions in his quest for the missing box that his name was less frequently mentioned for the inevitable papal election. The stern-faced Eugenio Maria Giuseppe Giovanni Pacelli seemed to be the front-runner at the moment. But Luca had more pressing concerns. OSM would meet this evening and if he could not present the box itself he was at least expected to come up with a short list of suspects and some viable possibilities as to the item's whereabouts.

He could, at least, provide this. After eliminating all of the previous OSM directors and most of the archivists from his list, he felt fairly confident that his quarry was one of three men: a young novitiate whose uncle's position in the Basilica might have given him access (although unauthorized) to the keys; the uncle himself who was head keymaster for the entire complex, except that the man had an exemplary record for forthrightness and honesty; Giuseppe Santini, a bishop who was overseer of the archives for the two decades before his death.

He folded the list and tucked it into the concealed pocket within the folds of his red robe as he walked toward the Basilica. Once midday mass was over he would pursue his leads.

Before nightfall, Luca should have an answer from his source who could testify as to the actions of the youngest of these, the novitiate. He could either report the now-middle-aged man to the directors or cross him off the suspect list. The uncle who had been keymaster, unfortunately, had become rather demented in his old age and currently resided in the Vatican's rest home, unable on many days to remember his own name. He would be of no help in matters that took place decades ago. Giuseppe Santini, alas, had died nearly ten years ago but Luca had feelers out in the man's home village to see what his family members might know.

The Latin words of the service came out by rote, and soon enough Luca joined the procession of clergy as they walked the long center aisle when it was done. He had just crossed the nave when he felt a tap on his arm. Expecting to see a parishioner, he was startled that a black-clad young priest simply placed a folded piece of paper in his hand and walked away. Pancetti switched course and found his way to a quiet garden of roses before he opened it. Written on the small sheet was a name, Marco Santini, and an address in Torino. Luca's interest quickened. A visit to a relative of the deceased Giuseppe Santini, plus a chance to visit the site where the famed shroud of Turin had been discovered—the week might be both productive and interesting, after all. He stopped at the office of the priest who was an OSM member and said he would not be attending tonight's meeting. He would be on a train to Torino.

His mission was accomplished far more easily than he could have imagined. Marco Santini turned out to be a busy man, supervisor of an automotive plant subsidized by Mussolini and one of the few businesses in the city to offer employment in these troubled economic times. Santini met the cardinal in the vestibule of his office building and suggested that they walk together toward the huge manufacturing facility. Luca pulled his traveling cloak tighter around himself as a frigid wind off the Alps whipped past the buildings.

"It's a carved box, you say?" Santini asked as they hurried along a sidewalk with missing chunks of concrete. "I remember it, something my brother brought home once."

"Do you know where it is now?"

Santini's eyes rolled skyward for a moment. "If it isn't on the shelf in my closet, my wife has probably put it to some use in her sewing room or somewhere. How would I know what the woman does with things?"

Luca went into his explanation that the box was Church property and must be returned.

"Take it," Santini said. "It's not exactly a beautiful item."

They reached the floor of the assembly line and Marco guided the cardinal to a small, windowed foreman's office. He jotted a note, folded it and wrote an address on the outside. "Go here. If my wife gives you any argument, show her the note. I doubt she will. She's religious. She won't want to antagonize the Church."

And, just like that, within the hour Luca Pancetti held the carved box in his hands. Where the original woodcarver had lightly chiseled a name onto the rim of the box's lid, the letters had been worn nearly smooth. Not much of the name remained, but the first and last letters were clear enough that he knew he had the box called Facinor.

From the train station he telephoned his office in the Vatican and directed his secretary to phone the men he wished to attend a special meeting the following night.

* * *

Cardinal Pancetti walked into the meeting, his cloth-wrapped bundle held close to his chest, expecting a hero's welcome. After all, the box had disappeared prior to his taking over the job and he alone had retrieved it. He set the parcel on the table that was surrounded by these dozen important men and gently peeled back the square of black velvet.

"That's it?" said the American politician with a sneer. He started to pick it up but Pancetti stopped him.

"It may seem harmless but there is more to this item than would appear."

Humboldt, the leader, openly let out a derisive 'pah' and picked up the box. Almost immediately, the wood began to grow ominously dark. He quickly set it back on the cloth, brushing his hands together as if to rid them of dust.

"Wrap it up, get it back into safe storage immediately," he ordered.

Humboldt pushed his chair back, ready to end the meeting and go back to Zurich, but one of the quieter men spoke up.

"While you were away, Cardinal, there came another lead. I thought it might be of value … in case the trip to Torino proved unfruitful …"

"Yes, what is it?" Luca worked to keep the impatience out of his voice. Tensions were already running high in the room.

The priest handed him a piece of paper.

"Tell all of us," said Humboldt with more than a trace of impatience.

"A telegram came from Romania," the priest said, watching as Luca read it to himself.

"It's a reported sighting of a box fitting this description," Luca said, scanning the message once again.

"Would it be the same box The Vongraf Foundation examined?" pondered the American industrialist.

Luca shook his head. "I don't know. The person who sent this did so anonymously. They've given the name of a city and of a woman purported to be a witch."

He looked around the table. Did they really want to bring back the days of the Inquisition? To track and prosecute what were probably silly acts of fortune telling? In these times of political unrest, with the Germans on the march into other sovereign nations, was it wise to travel outside their own little realm?

The other men looked back at him with solemn faces. OSM's mission was to gather artifacts, not to pass judgment on people. Luca felt his pulse quicken. He knew he would volunteer to find this other box.

Chapter 11

Treasures Are Hidden

Helga Schantz turned down the bedcovers on one of the small beds then the other. "Boys, are you brushing your teeth?" she called out.

Hans and Fritz, her two small dynamos, zoomed into the bedroom.

"Geschichte, Mama, Über die verlorenen Kinder!"

Helga smiled and shooed them toward the beds. "Yes, you shall have your story. Are you not tired of that one, though?"

"Nein! Dass man!"

She pulled the woolen blanket up to Hans's chin, then did the same for Fritz. She sat at the foot of his bed.

"Once upon a time," she began. Two sets of blue eyes stared at her. "There was a poor young mother with two little boys."

She supposed if their next child was a girl she would

alter the story so that the woman had three children. It was the way her own mother had told it.

"They were *so* very hungry. They had to go out each day and look for food but there was none to be had because times were hard. The people of the town loved the woman and admired her for the way she cared for her children but most of them simply had nothing to give."

She stretched out this part of the story to emphasize how fortunate Germany was these days, coming through the Great Depression and now enjoying somewhat better times.

"So, one day the woman and her two little boys ventured into the woods, searching for berries, but they found nothing and it began to grow dark. And then a cold fog came in."

The boys burrowed deeper into their covers. She remembered the time little Fritzie had asked what a fog was and his older brother explained, with the identical description Helga had used in telling him about it.

"The fog rolled over them, they were freezing and they could see nothing, and they had no idea which way was home. They held hands tightly, afraid to move lest they go farther into the forest and become lost forever. They were staring in all directions, searching for something familiar, when they heard a roar—very close by."

The boys' eyes grew even wider.

"It was …"

"A bear," they both whispered.

"And not just one bear," Helga said. "Two bears came out of the woods, a mother and her cub. And as anyone knows, a mother bear is very protective of her cub and will attack any person who approaches the baby. So this poor woman and her little boys were very frightened. They shook in their boots.

"And then what happened? The mother bear coaxed her baby to come near the children, to lie down at their feet. And the mother bear circled the little family, gathering them together. The woman and her children huddled together and soon the large bear lay down near them and the bear's big body kept them warm all night long.

"In the morning the townspeople began to be concerned, asking each other, have you seen that poor lady and her children?

"*Nein*, no one had seen them. So the mayor was about to organize a search, when, out of the woods … out came the woman, the two boys and … two bears! The people were overjoyed to see everyone safe and the mayor declared, 'We shall build a tribute to these heroic bears and we shall call the town's name after them!' And he immediately commissioned a fine artist to make the statue."

"The one near the Marktplatz!" Hans said, unable to contain himself.

"*Ja*, the very one we see when we do our shopping." She stood up, straightened their blankets and reached for the lamp. Who knew if the fairytale was true? It had pleased children for hundreds of years. "And on that note, it is time for sleep."

She pulled the bedroom door nearly closed and moved quietly to the parlor where she saw that Johann had added a log to the fire.

"You're home!" She rushed to his arms, taking in the scent from his wool uniform, the damp of the night and something unfamiliar—a combination of crowded railcar with woods-like undertones of a foreign land. "How was Romania?"

"Helga, *liebling*, you know never to speak of what I do now. Things are changing and I should not have told you."

"*Ja, ja*. I have said nothing." If only he knew the depth of the secrets she kept. "Are you hungry? I can warm the soup we had earlier."

He shook his head, removing his tunic and loosening the top button of the shirt beneath it.

"What's this?" She noticed a carved wooden box on the small table near the door.

It was obviously quite old, with a plain quilted pattern carved into the top and sides. The wood had been stained a dark brown but there was something else, a powdery feel to it. She rubbed the surface and something black came off onto her fingers.

"I pulled it from a fire," he said, sinking into his favorite chair. "I will clean it before I present it."

"To whom?"

"The Führer is to be in Nuremburg again tomorrow night for another rally at the parade ground. I've a private audience with Himmler shortly before and I want to present the box as a gift."

"This thing? It's hardly worthy—"

"It's not of interest because it's beautiful art, *liebste*. You know of the Führer's interest in the occult—this belonged to a witch in Transylvania. I pulled it from the fire as they executed her."

"*Johann!* You watched a poor woman burn!" Helga felt her dinner rise.

He had the good grace to look regretful. "No, *liebste*, I was not there for her sentencing, I merely walked onto that *platz* as the flames were dying down. It was over for her. The *Polizei* were tossing her possessions onto the embers.

The box landed at the edge; I took it when no one was watching."

"But Johann, collecting souvenirs! It's so—"

"I'll not have you questioning me," he warned.

A good German wife cooked and cleaned and raised beautiful children but she did not second-guess her husband, especially when he was a member of the regiment. She kept a neat home, trusted whatever he read in *Mein Kampf* to be accurate and ignored the trains filled with Jews that left for some unknown destination nearly every week. And she stayed utterly quiet about the houses where two Jewish families who had not managed to get out early enough were hiding. Helga had once been a friend to Ruth Goldstein and her husband who had operated a fine jewelry store until it was smashed to bits on *Kristallnacht* along with the destruction of the synagogue.

"I'll have some of that soup now." He signaled for her to bring him the box. "And afterward …" He raised one eyebrow.

Helga went into the kitchen and picked up her apron. She had been wanting a third child for some time now. She forced aside her opinion about the wooden box and put on a smile. He was gone so frequently these days. If she wanted a baby she must make use of any opportunity.

Later, cuddling together under the warm quilts, Johann drew upon his cigarette, a rare indulgence. Good Aryans were not to defile their bodies; therefore, smoking rarely happened outside private moments.

"I miss you when I am away," he said.

Helga ran her palm over his smooth chest. "And I miss you."

"But I long for the excitement of Berlin when I am here

in Bernkastel too long. Great things are happening in our nation. Order is being restored."

"We are better off now that the Great Depression has ended."

"Outside Germany, there is no comparison. Our railroads and trains, our highways, our manufacturing facilities are far superior—der Führer's plans for expansion and improvement will make the entire world a better place. Being around the men who plan these things—I find it exhilarating."

The world—unless you were Jewish or Polish, thought Helga. Well, what did she know? Perhaps those displaced people were actually, as the newspapers and film reels told it, going to even better places. The only thing she did know was that she was at the correct day in her cycle and very possibly the seed for a new baby was beginning to grow within her right now.

* * *

Johann Schantz stepped off the train at Nuremburg's *Hauptbahnhof,* one of three officers being met by a Nazi Party car, a black Mercedes, rather than the standard open Army field vehicle. The man on his right slid his gaze toward Johann, barely suppressing his delight at the special treatment. Johann straightened his shoulders and acted as if he were always accorded such amenities. The big car whisked them directly to the Chancellery where Hitler's personal standard flew—the black swastika surrounded by red and embellished with gold trim and golden eagles.

A captain met them at the curb and escorted the visitors through a series of hallways to a large meeting room.

Outside the closed door, a general from the inner circle stepped forward and they responded with sharp salutes.

"What have you there?" the general asked of the package Johann carried.

"A gift. For *der Führer.*"

The man wiggled his fingers and Johann handed it over. Inside the cloth wrapping, the newly cleaned box presented itself as well as it could.

The general's forehead wrinkled. "What is this thing?"

"If I may ...?" Another man who had been standing by took one step forward. "I have seen a similar item. In Italy." He murmured something quietly to the man in charge.

"And this one?" The general gave Johann a hard look.

"From Romania. It is rumored to have certain—powers. I know of *der Führer's* interest in such matters, in things of the occult. I offer it as something of a curiosity, an item he might enjoy."

The general seemed skeptical but stuck the box back into its cloth wrapping and handed it back to Johann. "Go ahead." It's your neck, he seemed to imply.

Inside the room, Hitler sat at a large, ornate desk. Around him, Johann recognized the faces of Goebbels and Himmler along with two Field Marshals. All eyes turned toward the newcomers. Heels clicked, arms shot out in salute.

The national leader eyed each of them in turn, unsmiling.

"The soldiers from the ranks," one of the field marshals said. "You requested them, *mein Führer*, to stand at the podium behind. A show of solidarity for the infantry and for the people. I present Johann Schantz of the Operations Section, Wilmer Friedrich of Naval Command, and Joseph Milbach representing the Army."

Hitler nodded.

Johann noted that none of the others were below the rank equivalent of Oberst, a colonel in other armies, hardly the average soldier being asked to trudge through the mud. Still, he was not there to point out discrepancies.

"And what is that?" The Führer turned his direct attention on Johann for the first time, tilting his head toward the wrapped parcel.

Johann set it gently on the desk and their leader reached for it. "A little something for your collection of occult memorabilia. If it pleases."

The hand trembled slightly as Hitler pulled the cloth wrapping aside. He lifted the box, turning it to view all sides. Setting it flat on the desk he lifted the lid then closed it. A small smile formed. His hands stayed on the box, although he turned his attention to someone else and asked a question of Herr Himmler. Johann held his breath.

What does the Führer truly think of the gift? He seems pleased. Doesn't the smile indicate approval?

The stubby fingers tapped at the lid of the box all the while.

He is still touching it. Surely he likes it.

The finish on the box grew darker, richer in color. Johann's heart raced. What was happening? Would anyone else notice the change?

The other men were talking of the logistics for the evening's speech, who would enter first and who would follow, at which precise minute the Führer would begin his speech. No one was looking toward the box, noticing its bizarre reaction to the leader's touch.

The box was now nearly black, gleaming like the glossy finish on a Mercedes. The raised portions of the carving had begun to glitter, like scheming eyes. Johann knew everyone in the room could surely hear his heart pounding in his chest. All eyes at the moment were on the Führer, however. He had to create a diversion.

Each of the new men had removed his hat upon entering the room; Johann's was tucked under his left arm. He lifted his elbow slightly, letting the hat fall to the marble floor. The stiff bill clattered and everyone in the room started.

Johann gave a sharp intake of breath and took a step. "Sorry," he said, bending to retrieve the cap.

When he stood once more, he saw that his misdirection had worked. Hitler's hand no longer had contact with the box and the color had already begun to normalize. Had he just made a fatal mistake, calling attention to himself? If, later in private, the box changed so dramatically again, the Führer would certainly notice. And he would remember the man who had brought it. A trickle of sweat ran down Johann's spine.

* * *

The rally grounds of the Nazi party in Nuremberg stretched two-hundred-forty meters in front of the podium. Tall standards bearing red and black banners ringed the perimeter and lights glowed to show the way for the ranks of soldiers who marched in precision before their leaders, snapping crisp salutes before taking their places to stand below in strict, straight lines.

Behind Johann and the rest of the entourage the high pillars of the Ehrenhalle rose, flying banners of the Party colors. Two rows of pedestals held fire bowls, flaming high now that the Führer was in attendance. The moment he took the podium, cheers and chants erupted.

Johann and the others stood erect and unmoving while their leader began his speech, starting with reminders of the greatness of Germany and the important strides the country had made since the days of poverty following the last war. As he went on to pound home the new ideals for cleansing the population and building the nation into an empire unlike any the world had ever seen, Johann believed he had never heard such fervent words, such unabashed zeal. Even to followers and loyal Nazis tonight's speech had to rank among the most emotional of all time. National pride swelled—he could see it on the face of every man in the crowd.

He was a supreme orator, Johann thought, watching the way Hitler managed the crowd—shouting his words of patriotism, giving himself credit for everything good in the nation, saying all of it in such a way that no one questioned a word. Then the charismatic man left the podium at the moment when the maximum outpouring of love came from his listeners.

As the final cheers died away, the officers at the front of the Ehrenhalle turned and made their way behind the impressive colonnade to their waiting cars. In his own vehicle, the Führer appeared drained of energy. He had given his all for the soldiers tonight. The black car pulled away and the others began taking places in the other vehicles. Johann, Friedrich and Milbach would ride together to the *Hauptbahnhof* to catch trains to their respective duty stations. In Johann's case he would go to Frankfurt, but as he was not due to report for duty until Monday he could perhaps manage another quick visit home. He'd hardly spent any time with his sons on the last stop.

The other two men had stepped into the car when Johann felt a tug at his sleeve.

"Hauptmann Schantz?" said a voice. Generalmajor Kaster was standing beside him, a packet in hand. Johann saw that it was the wrapped wooden box, the gift.

"I am sorry … der Führer is interested only in collecting fine works of art, the work of the masters. You will understand." He shoved the box into Johann's hands and placed a hand on the car door, an unsubtle hint that the subject would bear no discussion and it was time to leave.

Johann slid into the backseat beside Friedrich of the Navy. A furious blush came over his face and the other man had the good grace to look away. Neither the driver nor the Army man seemed to have noticed the exchange. Johann set the parcel on the seat beside him, draping his coat over it, keeping his eyes directly ahead. Was this decision truly that of the Führer or had the generals decided for him? At whatever level, someone of high rank had decided that his gift was not nice enough for the leader's collection.

At Frankfurt he debated staying the night. As a ranking Party official he could easily get a room even at this late hour, but his thoughts were churning like a rushing whitewater river and he could not imagine being able to settle down for a long while. The train to Bernkastel would be along in another hour. He went into the station and plopped on a wooden bench to wait, the parcel still tucked under his arm. Although important men within the Party did not appreciate the box, it would make a good story to say that it had been in the hands of the Führer himself on the night he spoke to the troops at the rally grounds.

He continued to hold that thought until he actually arrived in his hometown. Then he recalled Helga's revulsion when he admitted that the item had come from a witch who had been burned. There would be no chance of her allowing the children to own such a thing, even if it had passed through the hands of their famous leader. He stepped off the train in the cold gray of early dawn and looked around.

A waste receptacle stood outside the *bahnhof.* He peered one last time inside the cloth. Perhaps Hitler was right— this piece was not beautiful enough to belong in a good collection. Not even good enough for his wife's humble home. He held it over the trash basket and let it go.

Striding away, thinking of a hearty breakfast, he didn't look back.

* * *

Nikolaus Schenke watched the soldier walk away from the train station, paying no attention to the huge stone building with its high plaster and half-timbered walls, its sloping gabled slate roof. Two other passengers had already hurried down Friedrichstrasse, drawing their coats closely about them for warmth in the chilly morning air. His eyes darted to the parcel the man had dropped into the waste bin. The train chugged onward and a quick check told him no one was watching. Quick as a fox (which his mother often called him), Nik dashed to the bin and leaned in to pull out the object. It felt solid—something made of wood— wrapped in a covering of fine cloth.

To examine it here was to invite trouble. Someone may have seen him take the item. He tucked it close to his body and ran up Bahnhofstrasse, staying to the right on the curve and bolting across the bridge. The Mosel flowed slowly and peacefully, a silver ribbon rounding a bend between hillsides of vineyards. Nik barely took it in as he paused at the stone gate beside the church. A glance over his shoulder told him that no one had followed.

Ahead in the Market Square farmers were already setting up their tables, bringing out crates of vegetables and tall buckets of flowers. Nikolaus bypassed them, and the famed Doktor Fountain, tucking into the narrow street that flanked the right side of tiny "Pointed House," all those sights which, in happier times, drew visitors to the village.

Now, few people traveled and no one spent money unless absolutely necessary. Although the political speakers talked in glowing terms of the new prosperity brought by *der Führer*, Nik's parents spoke in hushed voices about the rising cost of goods and lower wages. It seemed everyone had a job now but most of them did not pay a lot. His father and grandfather were bricklayers; aside from some government projects designed by the Chancellor, they had difficulty finding work and were more likely to be found helping with the grape harvest and then hanging about their favorite *weinkeller* for a glass or two.

Nik ran through the streets, happy to be free for a little while. He would soon need to get ready for school. Beyond the Ratskeller he made a few more turns and came to a stop at the narrow stairs that led to his family's apartment above the now-closed jewelry shop. The windows had all been broken out and the place looted a few years ago; now there were boards over them to keep mice out.

"Where have you been, Nikolaus?" *Mutter* called out from the kitchen alcove. "Your breakfast is ready."

She stepped to the table and leaned outward to see into the hall.

"What's that you have in your hands?"

He quickly shoved the packet behind his back. "It's a surprise. For your birthday."

She gave a patient sigh and waved him on. "That isn't for another week." She knew very well that none of her boys would plan so far ahead. "Put it away and wash your hands. You'll be late for school."

In their attic room on the third floor Nik could hear his two older brothers stomping about—a boot dropped, then a raucous laugh. He held back, tucking himself into the tiny space below the stairs until the others thundered down and into the kitchen. Behind him, he caught the sound of his father, clearing his throat noisily. A loud fart issued from the bedroom at the back of the apartment and Nik repressed a giggle. He slid around the corner and tried to be quiet as he climbed the stairs.

He couldn't resist taking a minute to examine his newfound prize. The cloth around the wooden box was of fine quality and it would actually make a nice gift for his mother. She could use it as a headscarf or place it on the table. He had no idea how women chose their adornments— she might do anything with it. It was the box that fascinated him.

Dark-stained wood, carved in a crisscross pattern, a nice texture. He raised the lid and held the box toward the lamp. Letters carved into the lid spelled M-A-N-I-C-H-E-E. He had no idea what that meant. As he held the box it seemed to grow warmer, the wood becoming a lighter color and taking on a glow. His breath caught. What was happening?

"Nikolaus! Breakfast—now!"

Oh, if only he could catch a fever or something so he would have an excuse to stay home from school. He wanted to play with the box, to learn more about it. His gaze darted about the small room, searching out a hiding place. Under his small bed was the only somewhat private place for his things. He pulled out the trunk that held his winter clothing and shoved the box in behind it, against the wall, then slid the trunk back in place.

"What are you doing up there?" his father shouted. "Get to the table—you will be late!"

Nik brushed the dust off his hands and raced down the steps, remembering at the last moment that he'd been sent to comb his hair and wash his hands. He smoothed the persistent cowlick and swiped his hands twice against his pant legs.

At the table, his father grumbled before turning his attention back to his cereal. Across from him, Grandfather toyed with a crusty roll and read the newspaper. His brothers had apparently already left.

"*Der Führer* is building a collection of fine art, it says here in the news. 'With the success of the Summer Olympics four years ago, Germany is rising to the forefront of European culture. Our beloved Chancellor wants to fill the museums in Berlin with the best examples of art so that the rest of the world will know how great a nation we are. Citizens are encouraged to donate or loan paintings and sculpture from their personal collections.'"

Nikolaus caught the glances between the adults.

"Puh! We are at war," said his father. "Who will come from the rest of the world to visit our museums? That newspaper is a rag."

Mother hushed him.

"What? There is no one around. Half the old shops are closed."

"There are other apartments ..." she said through her

teeth. "It is impossible to be too careful these days."

She gave a little tilt of the head toward Nik.

"I can keep secrets, *mutter*," he insisted.

"Well, see that you do, boy," his grandfather said. "She is right. These are uncertain times and everyone must be careful."

Nikolaus already knew this. In school his teachers now taught only from the state-issued books. No stories were told, no discussion other than the official curriculum. And in the market last week, his mother had asked after the health of one farmer's wife and got only a small shake of the head. People were keeping all sorts of secrets.

* * *

Martin Helgberg turned off the wireless, astonishment reverberating through his body. It started with Hitler's men making casual 'visits' to homes and public buildings in a search for artworks to enhance the displays in the national museums and galleries—all in the name of preserving national treasures. Now the latest news held that *der Führer* considered fine wines and good liqueurs to be among these treasures and a new law allowed the Nazis to commandeer almost anything they desired. Martin knew these items were going into the Führer's personal collection or were being hidden away, perhaps to be sold off to pay for the war effort. He thought of his livelihood, the vineyards and wine cellar, particularly his prized 1921 vintage *Bernkasteler Kabinett*.

Twenty years he had held that wine—a full case of it— knowing that its value increased each year. And that was but one of the expensive wines in his cellar. And in the aging room—forty casks of five hundred liters each, ten seasons of backbreaking work on precipitous slopes in the adjacent vineyard, ten years of nurturing and loving his grapes to make them the best in the region. And now the Mosel wine region had become a target.

Helmut looked up as Martin rushed from the office. "What is it? What's going on?"

"Son, they have reached Cochem and Zell, on their way by river!"

"They?"

"Nazis! They'll take whatever pleases them."

"The nineteen-twenty-one?"

"And more! I have a plan. Hurry and get Herr Schenke. His father, his son … As large a crew as possible." Martin was out the door, headed for their cellar on Grabenstrasse.

He rushed inside, pulling the heavy, carved door closed behind him. In the dark he reached for the electric light switch, knowing from habit exactly where it was on the wall. A string of small lights showed the way down the tunnel and into the main room containing the huge casks. He stopped when he reached them, heartsick. There would be no way to hide them all.

He sank to a wooden bench where he often sat while labeling bottles. What to do?

"Do *something!*" His shout echoed back at him through the damp and chilly chamber ten feet below ground level.

He got up and walked down the center aisle between the casks which, on their sides, stood nearly as tall as he did. The small room at the back—it was their only hope. He flipped another switch, illuminating the five- by five-meter space. It held rows of bottles, their older vintages, chosen bottles from the best years. If nothing else, he could save these. He heard voices and quickly shut off the light.

"*Vater*, it's me. I have our friends." Helmut and the two bricklayers were coming down the long tunnel toward him.

He showed them what he had in mind—bricking over the doorway into the special room. "We must use bricks that match."

"*Ja*, we can come close to a match," said Herr Schenke.

"And cover the light switch. We can leave no clue that this room exists. Once they are gone, once the war is over, then I will trust again and we can break it open."

Schenke was nodding, eyeing the job, taking some measurements.

"Be sure we bring the bricks here late at night—quietly. If anyone sees, they will figure out what we are doing and the secret might get out."

The older bricklayer agreed. "People are being very careful these days. We are slowly learning our lesson about trusting the Party."

It was true. Having a normal conversation in these times was becoming more difficult. There was so little that could be said, what with Nazis everywhere.

"You will be paid well," Martin said, "and in return I require your absolute honor in this matter."

"How soon do we need to finish? Keeping in mind that the mortar will take some time to dry in this dampness."

It was true. The walls of the tunnel dripped with moisture, so much so that mineral deposits formed, and the floor was constantly wet.

"According to the wireless, they have already raided Zell. They are coming by river so it will not be many more days."

Schenke spoke: "We will deliver the first load of bricks tonight and begin work in the morning. It will not be a problem to work down here in the daytime?"

"It is best. Traffic and other sounds out on the street will cover any sound you make."

"I can use some help. My youngest son is good at mixing mortar and my wife's brother is quick with a trowel. With them, I think we can finish this in two days. As long as no one pushes against the wall for a week, it should be all right."

Would they have a week before the troops began streaming through town? There was no way to know for sure. They could only make the attempt.

Martin Helgberg agreed to the plan and sent the others on their way. Then he went to the bank to draw out some money.

* * *

Nikolaus thought his father was acting funny. Uncle Remy had come over and the three men sat in the parlor with coffee and drawing paper. When grownups talked plans it was a good time for him to get outdoors, knowing he could roam the village without much supervision. He wandered to the *Marktplatz* to look around. It was late in the day so a lot of the merchandise would be gone—the best pastries and breads especially—but sometimes a sympathetic seller would see a child alone and give away their last strudel or *blachindla*. He meandered between the tables, trailing his hand along the edges, hoping he looked as hungry as he felt.

Ahead, a uniform caught his attention. It was usually best to duck into an alley if one could do so unseen. But this one appeared to be off duty, strolling along with an obviously pregnant woman and two young, blonde boys. Nik paused, his breath catching. It was the same soldier who had thrown away the wooden box last autumn, the one Nik now had hidden under the clothing in the trunk under his bed. He had given his mother the scarf, discovering that the fabric was nice quality but not unusual. But the box was. If this soldier happened to be one who searched houses, as he'd heard the adults saying, he would surely recognize the box immediately. Nik's heart beat very fast.

What would he do? Surely he would be accused as a thief and the penalty would be horrible. There were twelve-year-old children in prison, he felt sure of it. Soon, he would be one of them. Or he would be conscripted into the Army. The Hitler Youth were recruiting boys his age and soon it would become mandatory. His palms grew sweaty. The vendor selling wooden toys asked if he wanted to look at something.

Nikolaus turned, without a word, and dashed down the nearest narrow street. He raced straight home, trying to think, but thinking and running were hard to do at once.

"Nik! Did you not hear me?" His father's voice came from the parlor.

He slid to a stop in the hall and looked inside, straightening his shoulders and standing as still as possible.

"Tomorrow we have a rush job and I will need your help to mix the mortar."

Nikolaus nodded.

"*Mutter* will make you an early supper and then it's bedtime. We will start before daybreak in the morning."

"Do I miss school then?"

"Just for a couple of days. You are to tell your brothers you have a fever. *Mutter* can send a note to school."

A lie? A parent-sanctioned lie?

"Nikolaus, stop smiling. This is quite serious and you

are under an oath of secrecy to never mention it. Not to anyone."

He nodded again. The box upstairs under the bed was proof that he could keep a secret.

In the kitchen, his mother had a bowl of soup ready for him. Although she said nothing he sensed that she already knew about whatever was happening.

"I suppose that if you were to feel feverish during the night or early in the morning," she said, "it would be allowed for you to come and get into bed with your parents."

He spooned up the soup, watching her face, not saying anything. When he finished he followed instructions, washing his face and hands, cleaning his teeth and putting on his nightshirt. His mother draped his clothes over the foot of his bed and showed him that she had put a sandwich into his rucksack. He crawled beneath the blankets and thought about how he could pretend to have a fever.

The rucksack lay under the edge of his bed and it gave him an idea. He could remove the box from the house and find someplace to dispose of it, a place where the soldier, if he came upon it, could never connect it to Nik or his family. He crawled quietly from the bed as he heard the rest of the family gather downstairs for supper. The box went into his pack and he placed it gently back exactly as his mother had left it.

As things turned out, neither of his brothers spoke to him when they came upstairs later. Apparently their mother had simply told them Nik was not feeling well and had gone to bed early. He fell asleep without any coaxing.

The room lay in darkness when Nikolaus felt a hand on his shoulder. His father knelt at his bedside with a candle that cast a soft glow over the blankets.

"Gather your things. We need to go to work." He had already picked up Nik's clothes and boots. "Quickly. You can dress in the kitchen."

The picture became clear. In order to fool the other boys into thinking he really was sick, his father would take him downstairs and his mother would pretend he had come into her bedroom. What an exciting way to skip school! He pulled the rucksack from under his bed and followed his father down the stairs.

A cat ran down Grabenstrasse and jumped without effort to a window sill as they passed. Not a single person was out and only a few lights showed from windows. Nikolaus had no idea what time it was, only that he had never seen the streets of Bernkastel empty like this.

They came to an arched door set into the side of a wall, with a narrow lintel above and a carved sign advertising the name of a winery. Someone inside had heard their steps; the door swung open only a few inches and then enough to allow them inside.

His grandfather was the man who had opened the door and Nik nearly cried out when recognition dawned. The gray-haired man placed a finger to his lips. Together, by lamplight, the three of them walked down a very long, very frightening tunnel with water oozing from the walls and green moss growing like the hair of some ancient troll. Nik reached for his father's hand.

They entered a large room filled with rows of huge wooden barrels. At the far end, a brighter light filled the area, showing a substantial stack of bricks.

"We worked until midnight, bringing them here," Grandfather said, "then we were afraid of making too much noise. "Four wheelbarrows so far. I think four more will do it. I can bring another now, before many villagers are out."

"Fine. But hurry. It will be daylight within the hour and we dare not risk any more visible activity. We can get the remainder tonight. For now, this will keep us busy. Remy, set up a stack for me. Quietly. Once there is activity on the street we can work at a faster pace. Nik, you will mix mortar. I shall show you the first batch so you remember how to measure the sand, the cement and the water."

Nikolaus nodded. He had done this before—it would come back quickly. He set his rucksack aside and rolled up his sleeves. As his father laid out the first row of bricks, Nik spotted the perfect place to hide the wooden box. When the other men turned to assist Grandfather with the new load, he drew the box out of his rucksack and set it at the base of a wine rack in the room that would soon cease to exist. Once the Nazi threat was gone he knew the winery owner would come for his prized wines and this wall would come down.

That is when—Nik promised silently to the box—*I will come and get you.*

* * *

Nearly a month passed without incident. Nikolaus went to school each day, returned to take up his normal activities. His parents talked of politics, silently worrying in the privacy of their own home about the all-reaching powers of the Party. On the streets, Nik saw the same lines of anxiety on the faces of the townspeople, the invisible burden of keeping quiet.

Yet no one talked about it; conversations were about the weather or how beautiful the flowers had been last summer. No topic of consequence was ever discussed openly although the whispered rumors in the dark of the night spoke of camps and confiscation of property. It was on a Friday that the Nazi Party train pulled into the *bahnhof* and a great cloud of steam puffed from its engine as nearly fifty men in uniform streamed from the cars.

They spread out systematically, covering both the Bernkastel side of the river and the Kues side, quickly taking stock of the few valuables in the shops (most merchandise of any worth had long since been sold out of the country or secreted away in the owner's home), then they began door-to-door searches. The questions began innocuously enough: "What do you have to contribute to the war effort?" Within a household that gave up nothing there would then come a search of every room.

They had apparently found fine art, gold and silver jewelry, valuable collections in other cities along the river—larger, more prosperous places. But Bernkastel and Kues held little of that. They were small villages—historic and charming, to be sure, but not the homes of the wealthy. Nikolaus huddled beside the statue of the bears as the men spread through the marketplace and into the residential streets.

He edged his way along in their wake, hovering a block or two behind, until they came to the boarded-up former jewelry store. One man kicked the door in and three others rushed inside. Nikolaus could have told them there was nothing left. The Jewish family who once owned it had been taken away more than two years ago and the contents of the shop packed up in Nazi sacks. Nik and his brothers had ventured in the following day to find nothing but broken glass and shattered display cases. Other shops suffered the same fate and the mayor formed a committee to board them up so the village would be less unsightly. The men plunderers came back outside now showing empty palms.

"What about up there?" said the one who had kicked in the door. He stared at the apartment on the second floor and two of them pushed their way up the stairs.

Nik held his breath. When his mother opened the door she gave a friendly smile such as he had never seen when her parents discussed the government. Behind her stood Grandfather, seeming older and more stooped in the face of the danger. She opened the door wider and stood aside. Nik's stomach knotted. He thought of his parents' conversations about this. "We have nothing of value. They will see that. They will look around and leave."

He prayed fervently that it was true—the men would leave without harming anyone. He waited until the men came back down the stairs, fifteen long minutes later. They must have poked through cabinets and under beds to take that long in the small place. He was glad he had removed his only treasure.

Once the men moved along to the next house, Nik raced to the next block and cut through a tiny lane to *Grabenstrasse* where he tucked himself into a small nook beside a rather dusty clothing shop and watched. From the carved doors of the wine cellar, uniformed soldiers were wrestling with the huge wine casks that had lined the winery's main storage vault. Curses split the air as they fought the slippery wet, inclined floor trying to maintain control over the barrels which wanted to roll back inside. Nik hid a smile behind his sleeve as he watched their frustration.

Someone called for a truck and the big, lumbering vehicle arrived a few minutes later. Eventually, the men grappled and tugged one of the barrels aboard. A second and third waited. Nik saw that they had no individual bottles or cases of wine, only the barrels. Afraid of being spotted and nabbed as a spy, he ducked around the corner and made his way home.

His mother seemed shaken but there was a muted joviality at the fact that the Nazis had come and gone and the family was no worse off. Nik tugged at his father's sleeve and reported what he had seen at the wine cellar.

"I checked my work with my most critical eye. They will see nothing unusual," his father answered.

The Party train pulled away from the station after ten o'clock that night and the sigh of relief was palpable throughout the village. Lights remained on in the homes until well after midnight, with quiet toasts and cautious words of congratulation. The looters would move down the line, on to the next place. Bernkastel had passed the test.

However, the news grew worse in the coming months. America had joined the war effort against them—everyone knew that already—and the bombings escalated. Many of the larger cities were ravaged and people fled when they could to the small towns and the countryside. Most, though, had no option. It was a matter of holding onto their sanity while pretending to carry on with daily life—work, school, meals, trying to stay healthy enough to simply make it through another week, another month.

The reports came of Nazi victories throughout Europe and Nik's father muttered at the dinner table about how he suspected they were hearing a highly edited version of the events. The few people who had escaped Trier and Koblenz and made their way along the river hinted at far worse things than the newspapers reported. Hitler had an entire department of propaganda, Grandfather said. Don't trust a word they say. Yet the photos of the massive rallies were impressive and the Führer seemed a kindly man who patted the heads of little children and gave out sweets.

"I am tired of the whole thing," Nik's mother said one Sunday morning. "We cringe in our homes, waiting for events that do not happen, afraid of what—that another trainload of soldiers will come and search us again? We have nothing they want."

She had made Nik's favorite pancakes and set a plate before him.

"I suggest we have an outing. I will make us a picnic lunch and we can walk along the river path toward Andel. A change of scenery will be good for us all."

The boys immediately cheered the idea, even though their grandfather seemed less than enthusiastic.

"Come along. All of us shall put on our best boots and make the walk."

Their best boots were hardly good ones, but something about a new activity brought all their spirits up. The sweet-smelling spring morning gave them a clear sky, and the budding greens and unfurling leaves on the Riesling vines cheered them. The boys raced ahead on the footpath.

"What's this, father?" shouted Fritz. He pointed to something in the water.

Nikolaus had trailed behind, caught up in watching a small red squirrel. He saw his two brothers hovering at the edge of the riverbank, his parents catching up to them and Grandfather bending over, as eager as any child to see the odd thing sticking half out of the water. Fritz reached out to touch it and the thing shifted in the water.

Then it exploded.

Nik felt himself flying through the air and for one moment a thrill rushed through him. Flying! Then everything went black.

* * *

"Tell us about your hometown, Dad," Krystle begged. She crossed one bell-bottom-clad leg over the other and leaned back in her seat. Johann was driving, taking the exit to the E42.

Nikolaus ran a hand through his hair. When had it become so sparse? And gray—he refused to think about it. When he began to speak he was ten years old once more.

"I used to run about all over the village," he said. "My favorite thing was the statue of the bears. I hope it is still there …"

Forty years since he had visited Bernkastel or Kues. The days in hospital came back only as dim memories, flashes of scenes really, no more. Nurses in white, sympathetic glances. Poor little boy, lost his entire family … Where shall he go? A blond woman coming to visit. Swiss-German. He didn't want to see her. Wanted *mutter* and *vater*. Tears from the nurses when he asked about them. The Swiss lady came back, this time with a husband. "We will be your new parents," she said, but the concept was unreal. He was sent with them anyway, sent to live in Lucerne, and eventually he came to enjoy their home, and almost to actually love them.

And now, now these two sitting beside him in the train were his own. Modern children—young adults, he reminded himself—who hopped trains all over Europe, stayed in hostels with other kids like themselves and spoke four languages. Thirty years of marriage to their mother and yet he had never brought any of them to Bernkastel. Not until Christina died—four months ago. He could not believe it—and Krystal and Johann whispered behind his back far too often, conspiring to get him out of the house, back to pleasanter memories. So, here they were, slowing as the highway became Gestade and then Schanzstrasse.

"Watch for the old stone gate. It will take us directly into the Marktplatz. Go slowly now."

"Right, Dad, I have it," Johann said, taking the turn. A café with umbrellas at outdoor tables sat where the church rectory used to be.

"There! See to the right. That's the Doktor Fountain, in honor of the famous doctor whose medicinal wine saved the prince!"

Nikolaus could hear the excitement in his own voice and he caught the satisfied glance between his son and daughter. Coming here had been the right thing to do, they were thinking. He sat back grumpily for a moment, until another sight caught his eye—the statue of the bears.

"Find a place to park. We'll walk now. I shall tell you the story my mother always told me at bedtime."

Johann stopped the small blue BMW at a spot along the curb and they got out. Nikolaus stretched, feeling the creak in his joints. His career as an accountant, a desk job in Zurich, had not exactly kept him in shape for running through the cobbled streets of his childhood home. *Ach*, no one would expect him to run about these days anyway. With the hip that had never healed quite correctly and a weak heart, he had been suited for nothing more strenuous than a desk job, and his damaged hearing bothered no one as he worked in his narrow world of numbers and balances. He had become quite content with his life.

They paused at the bear statue and he recounted the story of the lost woman and her children and how the bears had saved their lives. Down a tiny side street he showed off the place they called the Pointed House and Krystal snapped a picture of it. Only ten feet wide at the street level, the funny little place had two additional floors above, each a little wider than the other.

"It's like a wedding cake upside down," his daughter commented with a laugh.

"Except for the very pointed roof, yes you are right."

His eyes followed the lane he had traveled hundreds of times. The shops were different now, with fashions that focused on blue jeans and vividly colored blouses, others featuring electronic things he would have never imagined as a boy. He began to follow the familiar way, taking in the structures which had not changed much, the little details that had—flower baskets now, electric street lamps, clusters of tourists. He allowed his feet to take him to his old memories, to ignore his analytical side.

The lane widened into an intersection now constricted by cars. Across the way a sight made his breath catch.

"It is still a jewelry shop," he marveled. "And above …" His eyes rose to the apartment.

The building was painted a different color now and there was a new iron gate at the bottom of the stairs, with a mailbox and a name—Werner. No Schenkes had lived here in a very long time. The jewelry shop was, of course, not the same one. That one had been owned by Jews—the Goldsteins, he seemed to remember. As a child he wondered why they went away so suddenly. As an adult, unfortunately, he was fairly certain that he knew. It was the national shame now, learning what had been happening right under their noses, and most of the citizens having no idea of it—being clueless, his children would say.

An image of a Nazi soldier came to him, a man who lived here in Bernkastel surely not far from his own home, although as he recalled he'd only seen the man around town a few times and never knew where he lived. There was once, in the Marktplatz, the soldier with a wife and children. He was a man, like any other, not a monster. Nikolaus believed that now, although he had experienced mixed feelings about it over the years. Some of them truly had been monsters.

That same soldier, Nikolaus remembered, had been the one who dropped a cloth-wrapped parcel into the waste bin at the old train station. Trains had not stopped in Bernkastel for more than twenty years now but the big old, grand dame of a building was still there—he'd spotted the distinctive roofline just before they made the turn— He digressed.

He'd been thinking about the soldier and the package. Little Nik had grabbed that package and run for home with his treasure. The heart-pounding excitement of discovery, the thrill of owning something all his own, a treasure not to be shared with his brothers. Hiding it in his clothing trunk under the bed … *gut Gott,* he had not thought of that in decades. That carved box—a few times it had warmed and changed appearance when he handled it. Fascinating to a small boy, magical. It had been his most prized possession. And yet, what had happened to it?

"Dad? What are you thinking?" Krystal asked.

"*Ach,* just old memories." His voice sounded faraway, even to him.

"Let's get some lunch. I smell bratwurst." She took his arm and he allowed himself to be steered away.

In the café, he speared the sausage with his fork, savored

the flavors of that and the sauerkraut together. Each town and each region in Germany had its own specialties when it came to sausages, beer and, here in the Mosel valley, the wines; these evoked the pangs of childhood even more vividly than had their walk through the streets. There was truly nothing like the food from one's home village. He took a sip of his wine and a vision popped into his head.

That wine cellar. He saw himself, aged ten, mixing mortar, his father and grandfather handling the bricks. The anxious owner hovering about in fear that the Nazis would catch them as they created a hidden chamber.

"We have to go. There is one more place in town I must see." He tossed his napkin on top of his half-finished plate.

"Almost done," Johann said, quickly downing his last two bites of the bratwurst.

Nikolaus tapped his foot, then reminded himself this was silly. If that wall was still there, it had been standing more than forty years and would be there in another fifteen minutes. The wine cellar and tunnel might not be there at all.

As it turned out, they were. The arched doorway with the carvings was the same, although he suspected the wood had been sanded and refinished a few times over the years. The tunnel walls still dripped with water.

"My grandfather bought the winery after the war," the new owner explained. "Unfortunately, the sons of the previous owner were killed in the war and he could no longer manage it on his own. Our family has cared for it, going on three generations now. We are quite proud of our Riesling, especially this year's vintage." He led them into a large room where chairs sat before a long table. "Here, have a taste."

Nikolaus looked around. The tasting room sat beside the aging-chamber he remembered, the dimly lit place where gigantic casks had towered over him. Now they were not quite as tall as he, but two rows of them lay on their sides, as always.

"What of the hidden room at the back?" he asked. "There were some very old wines stored there."

The young man who had escorted them seemed puzzled.

"May I?" Without waiting for an answer Nikolaus started walking the aisle between the casks, making his way in the gloom. The others followed.

The chamber came to an end at a bricked wall. Nikolaus placed his hands on it.

"There is a room beyond this wall," he said. "My father and grandfather closed it in when the Nazis were on their way. The room was used to store the most valuable of the wines and the owner knew they would be looted."

He turned toward the vintner with tears in his eyes. "I, myself, helped with the job and I placed something of great importance to me inside, just before the wall went up. A small wooden box."

The man appeared to hear nothing beyond 'valuable wines.' He rushed to the tasting room and picked up a telephone. Within minutes two men arrived with sledge hammers and pry bars; they were introduced as cousins of their host. Nikolaus and his family stood aside as the smashing began. A small hole opened; bricks were pried away, a light shone inside. Exclamations of excitement at the racks of bottles inside.

"Is the wooden box—?" Nik felt a childlike thrill.

A person-sized hole was made and the host went in with his flashlight. He returned with two wine bottles tucked under his arms, a carved wooden box in his hands. The box looked darker than Nikolaus remembered, nearly black.

Nikolaus reached out for his treasure, marveling that it had been there. He carried it to the tasting room, noting that the stain on the wood now appeared brown. While his attention was on the box, the other men were examining the labels on their wine.

"We must open one bottle," said the man who had brought Nikolaus's family here. "To celebrate our luck that you came here today." He reached for his corkscrew.

One taste told them that the wine had turned. Disappointment showed on every face.

"I am sorry," Nikolaus said. "I suppose it has been too long."

"It doesn't mean that every bottle is bad," said one of the cousins. "We can check more of them."

Nikolaus picked up his box and bade the vintners goodbye. Out in the sun again, the box was now nearly a golden brown and he remembered how the box used to change when he held it; he had always assumed the glow of the wood meant something good. Too bad for the vintners that it had not worked its good powers on their wine. It occurred to him that the artifact might contain both good and bad influences. Did its owner or its location make a difference?

"Here, Dad, I can hold that for you," Johann offered as they began the walk back toward their car.

Nikolaus relinquished the box and felt his energy immediately drain away. In Johann's hands the box had gone dim again. A heavy weight seemed to press upon Nikolaus's chest. He looked around the village of his youth, seeing the half-timbered buildings and millennia of history one last time before he fell to the cobbled street.

* * *

Johann and Krystal Schenke sifted through the rooms full of their father's possessions. So much to deal with! It was probably the fact of his upbringing during the Great Depression and the War, they suggested to each other. Doing without, having so little as a child, including losing his parents so very young. Maybe that was the sort of thing that led a man to become such a hoarder.

No matter. With both parents gone now and each of the siblings involved in new lives, new relationships, they simply had no choice but to clear it all out. They had agreed—the sale of the apartment in Zurich and what items might be salvageable would be split and used to establish themselves.

"Keep whatever you want," Johann said. "Personally, I'm not interested in any of this old junk."

"I'll take Mother's dishes and the family photos."

"What about that box? The one he found that day—" Neither of them could quite believe how quickly their father had collapsed and died, right there on the street, his old heart condition choosing that particular weekend to take him.

She shook her head. Their father had loved that old box but for them, the memories associated with it would always be painful. "We'll sell it at the flea market."

Two weeks later, set up at the Flohmarkt Kanzlei, she watched with mixed feelings as people took away furniture and kitchenware, clothing, collections of Hummel figurines, coins, stamps … her father, it seemed had collected anything that caught his fancy. A large man in a dated three-piece suit meandered between the tables, looking at every item with concentrated interest but passing most of them. At her second table he stopped abruptly and picked up the wooden box, the one item Krystal most wanted to be rid of.

"What's this, then?" The man murmured, almost as if he were speaking directly to the box, but then he looked up at her. "Do you know the history of this piece?"

He spoke English with a heavy Irish brogue and despite the direct questions he had friendly blue eyes and thick hair that had many threads of silver among the once-blonde mane. She repeated the little she knew about how her father had retrieved the box after a Nazi soldier threw it away and the fact that it had been hidden away in a cellar for decades. The man's eyes grew sharp and he studied every angle of the box.

"It's very pretty," Krystal said, although it wasn't the least bit true.

"Yes …" He stared at the object as he fished into his pocket for some francs and handed them over without realizing it was far too much. He walked away before she could give him his change.

* * *

Terrance O'Shaughnessy caught the early evening flight from Zurich to London, connected to Shannon and arrived home in Galway close to midnight. Only seven p.m. on the American east coast; someone would surely be in the office he intended to call. He picked up the telephone and got the overseas operator.

"The Vongraf Foundation."

"Doctor Ernest Hollingway, please."

The director came on the line almost immediately when Terrance gave his name.

"Mr. O'Shaughnessy! How nice to hear from you again."

"I have a box, which I believe is a mate to the other one."

A quick intake of breath, a stretch of silence.

"Could it *be* the other?"

Terrance considered that. He had held the box on his lap during the flight, studying and contemplating its facets.

"I don't think so. From my recollection of the data you had for it, that one had certain … *other* qualities. I made no notes, of course, but I can give you the dimensions on this one."

He picked up a tape measure and carefully checked height, width and depth of the box that now sat on the desk in his study. He could hear Hollingway moving about, the sound of papers rustling. With each measurement the director uttered a soft *no*.

"The size is slightly different," said Hollingway. "We've no proof that the box—or boxes—have an ability to change their characteristics." Not in that way. Both men knew that they did change in other ways.

"So there are two?"

Hollingway evaded the direct question. "I would like to send one of our researchers to inspect it personally, to take additional data. If you don't mind."

"I'd be delighted. I could bring it there, if that would be more convenient."

The Vongraf director paused only a fraction of a second. "Your choice, Terrance. Your reputation as a collector of unusual artifacts is widely known and we always value your input."

"I shall be on the Friday afternoon flight."

Terrance hung up the phone with a rush of excitement. He had heard rumor of The Vongraf Foundation at the age of twenty, had studied their work despite the low-key nature of the organization and had been thrilled at his previous chance to visit their laboratory once. Of course, that had been decades ago when both he and Hollingway were much younger men. He gave the box a pat on its lid and decided to pour himself a little toddy to calm himself enough for sleep.

The telephone rang before he left his study. The clock over the mantle showed that it was nearing one in the morning. It must be someone from The Vongraf calling back. He hoped Hollingway had not changed his mind.

"Yes?" he answered.

"Mr. O'Shaughnessy? I am calling about a certain artifact which I understand has come into your possession."

The voice was unfamiliar—male, accented, Eastern European perhaps; certainly no one from The Vongraf would make that statement without first identifying himself.

"Who is this?"

"Let us say that I represent a very esteemed collector."

"I've no idea what you mean." Terrance's heart thudded as he worked at keeping his voice level.

"Oh, I think you do. You were in Zurich only this morning ... am I right?"

"What do you want?"

"We would like to see the item, to examine it, to make an offer to purchase it."

"I have nothing that's for sale. Good evening to you, sir." Terrance dropped the receiver onto its cradle before the man could speak again.

His pulse raced and he scanned the room. Clearly, the man was talking about the box—it was the only new item he'd brought home from his recent trip. But to know he had been in Zurich, to know he would be awake at this hour ... to know, perhaps, that he was in communication with The Vongraf Foundation already. Someone was watching him. And that person or organization wanted the box.

He moved through the house quickly, checking that all doors were locked, all draperies drawn. His hand shook as he poured two fingers of whiskey into a heavy Waterford glass. He'd been about to go to bed and leave the box sitting out on the desk. Now he decided that would not be nearly secure enough. He cleared some files from a desk drawer, placed the box inside and locked it, dropping the key into his pocket.

The whiskey went down smoothly and he forced himself to think rationally. He should get the box to the foundation as soon as possible. Picking up the phone he booked the next flight into Washington National airport.

* * *

Two Metro stops from the airport and after a short walk through Alexandria, Virginia's, historic streets, Terrance approached the building. He'd rested little, feeling that every face on the plane, every casual jostle as he passed through the airport, immigration and customs might belong to the voice behind last night's disturbing telephone call. He had managed to reach his goal without incident. The old warehouse of red brick with white trim revealed nothing unusual from the outside but behind that Colonial exterior The Vongraf Foundation housed some of the most modern laboratory facilities in the world.

"Terrance! I'm surprised—I thought you said Friday." Ernest Hollingway ushered him, luggage and all, into his private office.

Terrance told him about the late-night telephone call, the eerie feeling of being observed, the impossibility of sleep.

"My dear man, of course you had to come." The jovial courtesy covered the other man's obvious concern over these new events. "Well, we can begin our tests right away. Of course, you know that we do not keep the artifacts that we test. The box belongs to you and only you shall decide upon its disposition."

"Thank you. I shall give it some thought when I am more rested."

"Of course. We must get you into a hotel, right away."

Terrance picked up his camera bag and unzipped the top. "I want to leave this with you rather than carry it with me through the streets. Pardon my paranoia."

"Of course." Hollingway's eyes fixed on the box as soon as Terrance pulled it from the bag.

"Oh, yes, this is definitely a bit larger than the previous one, although none of us here today were able to see or handle that one. Plus, that one had small stones mounted on it, whereas yours is plain. The first one came through our facility in 1910. But there are photographs—lovely old sepia things—and of course the dimensions of the box are recorded in writing and diagrams were made. Have you had any unusual experience with the box yet?"

Terrance shook his head. "No, although I have had it in my possession only a little over twenty-four hours now." Hard to believe. "I understand there were documented cases of the other box eliciting certain reactions …"

"Oh yes, one owner of the first box claimed that the wood changed color and became warmer as it was handled. Only one of our lab people, the director's secretary, got the same reaction. Some were a bit disappointed in that. I suppose everyone would like to think they have the magic touch."

"Perhaps it's the mood of the holder at the time," Terrance suggested. "As I said, I've not spent a lot of time with this one yet, and what time I had was, shall we say, stressful."

"From our scientific research, we know that the first box was carved from wood taken from a tree struck by lightning. There's a certain molecular anomaly to it. My hypothesis is that the lightning strike infused the wood with a certain receptiveness to the electrical impulses given off by some people. We all have varying sensitivities to electrical charges. My guess is that when the box comes into the hands of a person with the right—for lack of a better term— wavelength, that's when the reaction is triggered. Until we test it we won't know whether your box has any of these properties."

"Well, then, I shall let you get on with it." Terrance pushed the box across the desk and accepted the receipt Hollingway wrote out for him. Suddenly, he could hardly keep his eyes open.

* * *

A band of brilliant sunlight showed around the edges of the blackout drapes in Terrance's hotel room. He stared uncomprehendingly at the red numerals on the bedside clock. It took a moment to realize that he had slept through half a day and all night and that it was now nearing noon of the next day. He rubbed grains of sleep from his eyes and sat up.

Excitement took over—today he might learn the results of the Vongraf study. He rushed through showering and dressing and forty minutes later was being escorted into the laboratory where Ernest Hollingway in white lab coat was examining something under a microscope. He looked up at Terrance with a triumphant expression.

"It's the same," he said. "We shaved a tiny sliver of the wood and I'm thrilled to say that the molecular content is identical. Your box came from the same tree as the first."

Terrance realized he was holding his breath. All his years of travel and the hundreds of hours browsing items in foreign bazaars and jumble sales in a quest for something of true historic and perhaps mystical value.

"Can you tell whether it has the other properties we discussed? Is it—" He couldn't bring himself to say the word 'magical.'

"That is, naturally, the harder thing to prove. As I surmised yesterday, often these artifacts react differently with different people. Would you like to spend some time with it? Handle it a bit more? Now that you are rested you might find a connection with it."

Terrance knew that his eagerness must be showing on his face.

"All right, then. My assistant took the box into my office awhile ago. You know where that is. Go on up, if you'd like."

Terrance climbed the stairs to the same third-floor office where the two men had spoken yesterday. Hollingway's office was at the end of the hall and Terrance could see a light under the door. He turned the knob and walked in.

Standing over the desk, arms braced on each side of the wooden box, was a young man of about twenty, dark haired with a shadow of unshaven stubble. A trancelike fascination surrounded the lab assistant and a greedy smile stretched his mouth. His deep-set eyes were fixed on the wooden box, and he didn't seem to realize that Terrance had come into the room.

Terrance started to speak but the words stuck in his throat. His eyes were drawn to the box. It had turned black.

* * *

"I couldn't think what to do," he told Hollingway. "I simply snatched it away from him and ran down the hall. It seems rather undignified now."

"You say the box was pure black?"

"Like something in deepest outer space. More than black, it was … I don't know how to describe it."

"And yet now it looks normal, just the way it did yesterday. The same as it appeared this morning after I took the scrapings and handed it over to Jason."

"You said the boxes might have different reactions to different people. This young man, Jason … what do you know about him?"

"Well, he's very new here. An eager fellow who wanted the job intently, almost with a passion. Normally, the newer employees do not have direct access to the artifacts until they've …" Hollingway's face went pale as he apparently thought of something. He picked up the intercom and called security.

Chapter 12

Legacies Are Passed

Stealthy, yet lightning fast. That's how the years seemed to get past her. Bertha Martinez stared out her kitchen window at the million golden leaves on her old cottonwood trees. Only days ago those branches had been filled with green. A few days from now the leaves would be scattered to the ground. She hadn't much time to find the right person, the one who would assume responsibility for the item she had taken into her care nearly a century before.

She let go her grip on the linoleum countertop and reached for the back of a chair at the table; from there she could touch the doorframe, after that, the wall in the hallway. A doctor would probably insist that she use one of those aluminum 'walker' contraptions, or he would put her in a wheelchair in a strange institutional place.

"Pah," she wheezed. "I didn't live to my ninth decade by listening to that bunch."

Slowly and carefully she made her way toward her bedroom, passing through the living room where candles and herbs from her last curing still lay on the coffee table; she must have forgotten to pick them up and store them. At the back bedroom she paused. One of her acolytes had taken it upon himself to paint the walls red and to add ritualistic symbols in white. Bertha had dismissed the boy on the spot; she seemed to be getting too many of those in recent years, the ones who thought what she did was somehow connected to witchcraft or paganism. She should have insisted that he at least repaint the room before he left.

In the old days she would have had the energy to do it herself. Now, she could only think about having a nap. But first, she stepped into the hideous red room and switched on the overhead light. By its barely adequate glow she found what she wanted, the carved wooden box that came into her possession when she was a girl. She used the hem of her sweater to wipe off the dust, feeling a bit stronger as she held it and absorbed its loving warmth.

Bertha walked more steadily now, going to her own bedroom at the front of the house, tucking the box into a drawer. Almost immediately, her energy faded and she crawled between the sheets. As she curled into her most comfortable position for sleep she caught sight of her hands, spotted now, with thick veins and knobby knuckles. Her fingers had become so thin that her grandmother's ring no longer stayed on. It lay on the nightstand beside her bottles of herbs and oils. She studied the shape of her hand, almost unrecognizable from the old days …

* * *

Ruben Martinez shouted at the donkey to move faster. The animal kicked, pelting Ruben with clods of soil, dislodging the plow blade from the crooked furrow where the man struggled against the dry earth, trying to eke out a crop of corn or beans or potatoes each year. His cousin Rudolfo made a successful trip to Mexico each year, trading his harvest for the manufactured goods in the south—saddles with trim of Mexican silver, tools of iron, fine carved furniture—but the big hacienda ten miles to the west produced far more than Ruben could ever seem to manage from his small plot.

The land had been granted to the family more than four hundred years ago, but over time Ruben's grandfather, and then his father, had sold off portions of theirs while Rudolfo's grandfather added to and created wealth from his holdings. Ruben sighed. Only on occasion did he feel a stab of envy. Mostly, he could not absorb the idea of treating the land as a business. The land came from God.

Well, God and the king of Spain.

Bertha laughed, from her spot in the shade of the old cottonwood tree, when the donkey kicked dirt once again. Papá would swat her bottom if he thought she was making fun of him. He would whip the poor thing. Last summer Papá had been in a much better mood; there had been rain. His moods seemed directly tied to the weather. *Abuela* told Mamá yesterday not to worry; the rain would start soon and Ruben would laugh again. *Abuela* rubbed at her warped knuckles as she said it.

Thinking of this, Bertha looked at her own hands—soft, brown and plump. What made her grandmother's hands so thin and ugly? She suppressed that thought. *Abuela*'s hands were not attractive but they were filled with love. When

Bertha climbed onto the old woman's lap she always got a hug, a kiss, a warming stroke on her hair. She got songs, old Spanish ballads about love, and stories of the conquistadors and the Martinez heritage from Spain.

A bell clanged and Bertha peered around the trunk of the big tree. Mamá stood on the porch, swinging the short rope against the brass bell that had been a gift at Christmas from Papá's brother. Ringing it was a far easier way to get Ruben's attention from five acres away than standing on the porch and shouting.

"*Cena!*" Theresa called out. The scent of beans wafted from the open doorway.

Bertha scrambled to her feet and ran toward the house. "*Niña, estás creciendo otra vez.*"

Of course she was growing. She would soon be a big girl and would be allowed to attend classes at the one-room schoolhouse in Talpa. She had overheard the discussion between the adults, how now that New Mexico was a state the children would be required to attend school. The classes were conducted in English! The thought of learning the odd-sounding language frightened Bertha a little. Would she know what to do when she got to school?

Abuela couldn't seem to get over the idea that Nuevo Mexico was part of the United States and was called New Mexico by everyone now. The idea of statehood was slow to take hold out here in the territory. Why change the old ways?

"Ah, *Bertita*, there you are," said *Abuela*. "Wash your hands." She put an arm around Bertha's shoulders and steered her toward the wash basin near the back door. "Before your papá muddies the water."

Bertha swished her hands in the basin of water and

started to pick up the scrap of rag her mother kept handy as a towel.

"Eh-eh ... *usa el jabon*."

Bertha picked up the chunk of homemade soap and, feeling her mother's watchful eye, worked her fingers around it until the bits of dirt and the green from the fistfuls of grass she had pulled this morning were gone.

"*Mucho mejor*." Theresa gave her daughter a pat on the head and pointed toward the table. "Don't start until your father is here."

The freshly made tortillas smelled so good that Bertha nearly forgot her mother's instruction. Her hand was halfway to the basket before she pulled it back. Her father's footsteps sounded on the wooden porch, and Bertha planted her hands in her lap as a way of forcing herself to wait.

"I'm done in the field today," Ruben said as he washed his hands in the same water Bertha had used. "That burro and I, we are having words!"

Theresa laughed and gave him a kiss on the neck.

"This afternoon I shall go to town for supplies." He glanced at Bertha as he dried his hands. "Maybe you would like to ride along?"

Bertha was half afraid of the stubborn old burro, especially after her father's 'words' with the animal, but the trip to town was a diversion from playing outside and far more fun than helping Mamá to sweep the floors or wash clothes. Her face lit up and Papá gave her a wink.

Once he loaded his plate with pinto beans and corn tortillas and topped them with *Abuela*'s famous chile salsa, Mamá spooned beans onto Bertha's plate and then the women served themselves. Although she'd felt ravenous earlier, in the excitement of making the four-mile journey to town Bertha couldn't concentrate on food. She nibbled at a tortilla and finished her beans, not asking for more.

The moment Ruben stood, Bertha was at his side.

"Don't forget your bonnet," Mamá reminded.

Bertha submitted to having the cloth strings of the homemade hat tied under her chin.

"Before you start school, you must learn to do this yourself," her mother said. Everything these days revolved around the big event, and Bertha realized she would probably be the first in her family to attend school. The idea gave her a small thrill.

Papá grabbed her under the arms and hefted her up to the blanket on the back of the burro, then climbed up behind her. The animal seemed much happier with this burden than it had earlier with the harness and plow. They set off down the two-rut track that ran past their house.

Talpa barely deserved the designation as a town, although everyone called it that. It consisted of a dirt road flanked by a general store, a repair shop owned by an old man who could perform blacksmithing duties or rebuild a piece of furniture, the one-room schoolhouse, and a half-dozen homes. Ruben brought the donkey to a stop outside the repair shop and tied the reins to the hitching post outside. From a canvas pouch he pulled out a broken piece of harness.

"Stay here," he said to Bertha after he lifted her down from the animal's back. "I will be only a minute."

He called out to the old man and they started discussing what needed to be done to fix the harness, while Bertha stared at the school building. It seemed so big, with a wide front door. You had to climb three steps to get to it, and there was a little pointed tower on top with a bell in it, a bell much bigger than the dinner bell Mamá used at home. The adobe walls looked familiar though, thick and brown like theirs at home, and the window frames and door were painted blue. *Abuela* said that was for luck. She had personally repainted the ones at home when the old paint began to flake away. Bertha felt reassured that the paint on the school door was not flaking.

"*Lista, niña?*"

Her father's hand touched her shoulder and she brightened, already envisioning the wonders of shopping at the place with the hand-painted sign saying The Store. She held her breath as they entered through the door where you could see inside through squares of glass with wood strips between them. If she was a very good girl and didn't actually ask, sometimes Papá would buy her a piece of candy. If she was allowed to choose her own, she would pick the kind that were two for a penny. That way, she could eat one on the way home and have another for later.

The store never failed to fascinate her—surely you could buy anything in the world here! At the front stood the candy counter, with bins of brightly colored jelly beans, fruit-flavored hard candy, peanuts covered with a dark reddish candy shell, dabs of chocolate shaped like stars ... so many that it was hard to choose only one. Bertha knew the selections by heart.

Along an aisle to the right were the next best thing to candy—toys. Wooden tinker toys, shiny marbles, a fascinating wind-up carousel ... there was even a beautiful doll wearing a glamorous long dress, the like of which she had never actually seen on a real person. Bertha yearned for that doll but she knew they could never afford it. She had once asked her father if he would get it for her; his answer contained so much pain that she knew better than to ask again.

Farther down the aisle, the store contained dishes and pans, lamps, bolts of cloth, oil lanterns, and hardware items. Her father was looking at some hinges for their broken gate. Bertha wandered to the store's other side, where another aisle ran parallel, clear to the back. Tins of vegetables and loaves of bread seemed like funny items to buy at a store. Her mother put up the tomatoes, green beans, and fruit from their garden in glass jars, and who would consider buying bread when anyone could bake their own. She skimmed over the odd packages and looked ahead.

Across the back wall of the store was a wooden counter with a window that had a metal grill across it. The post office. Her mother bought stamps here and sometimes mailed a letter to her brother, Uncle Patricio. They told Bertha she had met him, when he returned from the war, but she had no recollection of it. They said she was only a few months old then. Now he was married and lived in a big city called Chicago and went by the crisp-sounding name of Patrick.

Heavy footsteps on the hardwood floor told her that her father had finished in the hardware area, so Bertha scampered to the front, ready at the candy counter where he would see her when he pulled coins out to pay for the hinges. She crossed her fingers that there would be a penny or two left over.

"Mr. Martinez, don't forget your mail!" called the proprietress, a thick-waisted blonde woman named Mrs. Frohlsen.

She was moving around behind the postal counter and came out with a box, wrapped in brown paper and tied with string. Bertha's eyes widened. A package! She remembered only one package ever arriving in the mail; it came at Christmas. She stared down the aisle as the woman came forward, sizeable hips nearly bumping a display of kitchen towels, carrying the package. Her father's eyes registered as much astonishment as her own.

Mrs. Frohlsen handed the box to Ruben and he turned to Bertha.

"Hold this, please, *chica*." He held it out and Bertha took it while he reached into his pocket to pay for the hardware.

On the top of the package were written some words in black ink. She felt amazement well up inside—if only she had already gone to school, she would know what they said. She held the parcel carefully balanced on her forearms. It was nearly as wide as her small shoulders but it wasn't too heavy for her. She stared at every detail of the lettering, wanting to memorize it and remember this special moment.

Automatically, she followed her father outside and across the road where the burro remained tied. He spoke briefly to the man in the repair shop and came out with the harness he had left earlier. Taking the mysterious package from Bertha, he stuffed both items into his canvas bag and slung it over the burro's back, then lifted Bertha astride it and resumed his own position behind her. She watched the rectangular lump in the bag, bouncing slightly with each step. It wasn't until they were nearly home that she realized she'd forgotten all about the candy.

* * *

"Goodness, what could this be?" Theresa said when Ruben set the package on the kitchen table. She peered at the writing on the top. "It's from Patricio."

Consuelo looked up from her *metate*, where she had been busy grinding corn.

Ruben found a reason to go out to the small board shack he used for storage of the farm implements. He always seemed to leave the room when Patricio's name came up.

Theresa cut the string off the box with a kitchen knife, then carefully removed the brown paper and folded it neatly for future use. She lifted the flaps on the cardboard box inside and pulled out some wadded sheets of newspaper. These, too, she smoothed and folded. Out came an envelope with her name written on it. Below that, some sort of rectangular wooden item. She reached in and pulled out a carved box.

It was not much larger than a cigar box, carved in a quilted pattern with some small, dusty stones mounted in each X of the pattern. Not exactly *rustico*, but not very finely done either. She lifted the hinged lid and saw that it was empty.

"Maybe the letter explains," she said, running her finger under the gummed flap and withdrawing a single sheet of white paper.

"Dear Theresita . . ." she began reading. "He asks how we are doing," she said, looking up at Consuelo, then to Bertha. Her eyes traveled side to side across the lines and her mouth made little movements.

"Read it," Consuelo urged.

"He uses some English words I do not know," Theresa admitted.

Consuelo scoffed. "After the Army and now in the big city—he's forgetting his heritage."

"It's mostly in Spanish." She began to read aloud.

"My dear sister, please keep this box and care for it. A

buddy—" Her brows knitted in puzzlement over the word. "A *buddy* in France gave it to me. Believe it or not, I think that this box saved my life during the war. I do not know how to explain it any better than that. Now, we no longer have a place for it in our home but it is dear to me even so."

Theresa looked up at her mother-in-law.

"It's that gringo wife of his," Consuelo said. "You remember how she looked at us when they came to New Mexico after their marriage. The same way she must look at this old box."

"It's not very pretty," Theresa admitted. "Not the sort of thing most women would choose, especially in the big city where *rustico* is not the style."

Consuelo nodded grudgingly and went back to grinding the corn with a vengeance. "No place for it in their home. It's that Deborah, having three children so quickly, who caused that problem. A wonder they have room for all of them."

Theresa winced.

"I'm sorry, *hija,* I didn't mean—" They never spoke anymore of the difficulties during Bertha's delivery, of the fact that Theresa had nearly died. In five years it had become apparent there would be no more children in this house.

"I don't know what I will do with it," Theresa said, reaching to place the wooden box on an open shelf above the cookstove.

"Mamá, *I* can use it." Bertha's face glowed with excitement.

"For what?"

"Um ... for my treasures!"

"What *treasures* do you have, little one?"

Bertha registered a moment's consternation. She raced

out of the kitchen. Two minutes later she had returned with a feather, deep blue, from a jay.

"This," she said proudly. ". . . and I have some ... some other things."

Theresa looked at her daughter. "You'll break it. You heard what Uncle Patricio said in the letter. It is an important thing to him."

"I'll never break it, I promise, Mamá. It will be my greatest treasure."

"Where do you get such words—*mayor tesoro*? *Hija*, you will be a scholar one day."

"So, may I have the box?"

Theresa reached to the shelf. "If you keep it safe in your room where *Abuela* can watch out for its safety as well."

From her mother-in-law's studied indifference, Theresa doubted that this was a guarantee but at least she had somewhere other than the crowded kitchen to keep the box. If Patricio were ever to visit again, at least the box would not have the grease residue of fried tortillas on it.

Bertha held out her hands and carefully took the box. Holding it gently she set it on the table, opened the lid and placed the blue feather inside. She left the kitchen and walked slowly down the hall to the back bedroom.

"She's a smart girl, our little *Bertita*," Theresa murmured. "I wonder how she thinks of these things."

"One day perhaps I shall teach her in the ways of the *curandera*," said Consuelo. "I will soon need a protégé to take over my work."

* * *

Bertha reached under her bed for the carved box. Her

fingers, she realized, had grown long and slender, as had her legs and arms. Her breasts were emerging and a week ago she had been shocked to see blood in her panties, almost panicky until *Abuela* explained that it was a natural event. That day, she began her studies in the ways of the *curandera* and today she was to go along to attend a birth for Donna Salazar who, only a year ago, had been a bride dancing at her wedding and before that, a shy teen whom Bertha remembered from the days when they studied together at the one-room school. Donna in sixth grade had tutored Bertha, grade three, in reading English and doing mathematics.

Bertha sat on her bed and opened the carved box, smiling at the little collection of treasures she had accumulated over the years—a red leaf and a shiny stone and a bird egg, in addition to the blue jay feather she had quickly picked up the day she talked her mother into letting her keep the box. Now, she could use the box for far more important things: her growing collection of dried herbs. She placed the childhood curiosities on the quilt and studied the box itself.

A shaft of light from the window hit the very spot on her lap where the box sat and she noticed for the first time a very faint bit of carving on the inner edge of the lid, perhaps the letters V-I ... But the word, or words, were so faint that she couldn't make them out. As she had several times over the years, she wondered about the age of the box. She ran her fingers over the colored stones that decorated it, realizing now that they were not nearly as valuable as she had imagined them to be when she was five years old.

The inside of the box had never been finely sanded smooth, she could tell, but from use and wear it had obtained a certain patina. As long as there were not deep grooves it would work for storage of her herbs. She ran her fingers around the edges of the box's interior, checking it.

Suddenly a jolt, like an electric shock, traveled up her arm. She fell to the floor and the room faded away.

"*Bertita—Bertita!*" Mamá's voice came down some far tunnel. "Consuelo—come quickly!"

Abuela's voice came to her and Bertha's eyes struggled to open.

"She was unconscious on the floor," her mother was saying.

"Let me see."

Bertha felt her grandmother's gentle touch, the wise old hands cradling her head, subtly feeling for wounds. She cleared her throat and tried to speak but the words came out scratchily.

"I'm okay. I think I am." She rolled to her side and slowly sat up.

Where was the box? She looked around, afraid it might have crashed to the floor and broken, but it sat beside her unharmed. Her mother fluttered like a nervous sparrow but *Abuela* looked deeply into her eyes, a knowing gaze. Something had changed.

Bertha wanted to avert her eyes but couldn't. She realized they would probably never speak of this.

"Come, dear one. It's time to go."

It took Bertha a minute to realize she meant that they were needed at Donna Salazar's home. It was not lost upon her that *Abuela* had used a grown-up endearment. She stood up, willing back a wave of dizziness, and straightened her skirt. *Abuela* busied herself gathering her kit and finding the black wool shawl she'd worn in public since *Abuelo* had died, before Bertha was born.

Papá had already hitched the donkey to the small wagon for them. He would have offered to drive them in the farm truck he'd acquired when Bertha was seven—she still remembered the day he came home so proudly in the used Ford—but the vehicle was perilously low on gas and there was no money right now to buy any.

"Modern conveniences," *Abuela* said, at her side. "Pah! The truck has no gas and the radio brings only bad news."

Bertha couldn't disagree—no jobs in the cities, no money in anyone's hands. She helped her grandmother up to the wagon and climbed onto the seat beside her, taking the reins. More often than not, when *Abuela* cured someone of a deadly illness she came home with a chicken or a sack of potatoes rather than cash. At least they were eating.

At Donna and Arnoldo Salazar's house, the labor was well underway, judging by the high-pitched shrieks they could hear as soon as they opened the kitchen door. Arnoldo sat at the table with a cup of coffee in front of him, his hair standing out at wild angles and a look of anguish on his face. Clearly, he wished he could be somewhere else and didn't have a clue what to do. He pointed toward the bedroom. A female neighbor came out, carrying a damp rag, saying she wanted to refresh it with cool water.

Consuelo took charge and led Bertha into the room where the sixteen-year-old mother-to-be writhed on the bed.

"Open my kit," *Abuela* said to Bertha. "Find the lavender and the *malvas*, then go to the kitchen. Brew the lavender tea and boil the *malvas*."

The old woman turned away from Bertha and began speaking soothing words to her patient, coaching her to breathe rhythmically and helping her to a more comfortable position. Bertha put the malvas leaves into a small pan with fresh water and turned on the gas burner. Boiled, the liquid would make a soothing wash for the new mother after the birth. Meanwhile, she brewed a light tea from the lavender and carried a cup of it into the birthing room.

She held it out to her grandmother but at that moment Donna's face contorted with another contraction.

"She's farther along than I imagined she would be," Consuelo said, indicating that Bertha should set the cup on a dresser that had a picture of the Virgin hanging above it. "The child will come—"

A scream ripped the air.

Bertha watched as *Abuela* gently stroked the swollen belly, a feeling—half awe and half terror—coming over her. She forced herself to concentrate on her grandmother's actions rather than imagine herself in the position of her friend, going through this agony.

"It's coming very soon now," Consuelo said, her voice low and soothing. "You will feel an urge to push."

Bertha stood to the side, unable to watch what was happening under Donna's messy nightgown. Instead, she looked at her grandmother's face. The calm and benevolent expression shifted imperceptibly.

"What is it?" She mouthed the words rather than saying them aloud.

Abuela gave a short jerk of her head and Bertha moved into place. Between Donna's legs a dark blob of a head showed, with a spongy, greenish band around it.

"I need to get this cord away," *Abuela* whispered. "Take the baby as it comes out."

Was it a real baby? Bertha was horrified at the blue-gray color of its face. She stretched out her arms and *Abuela*, in nearly one move, pulled the baby free, placed it in Bertha's hands, and began working on the ropey cord. Bertha didn't see exactly what her grandmother did—she couldn't take her eyes off the warm, sticky little form she was holding. She was vaguely aware of the cord coming away and then she simply hugged the tiny infant to her chest, heedless of the mess to her own clothing. She felt a peculiar energy travel through her arms and hands, flooding through to the little bundle she held. In short moments, the baby began to squirm, then to whimper. When Bertha looked again, its face had turned a vivid pink.

"That's good!" Consuelo's face lit up, her grave consternation gone.

From the bed, Donna lay back against her pillow, panting and trying to ask what was happening.

Consuelo turned to her patient. "You have a beautiful baby girl."

Bertha moved automatically, washing the baby, handing it over to its mother, following *Abuela's* directions. She barely remembered leaving the Salazar house, driving the wagon home or eating the enchiladas Mamá prepared for dinner.

In their bedroom that night, *Abuela* spoke quietly in the dark. "You have a gift, *Bertita,* an ability I have never seen before, even in my apprentice years with my mentor. That baby would not have lived but you made it so. I do not know how you did it, but do not relinquish that gift."

Bertha remembered the tingle in her arms. She thought of the box stored under her bed. She knew where the gift came from. She also knew she must never speak of it.

* * *

A saucepan of chocolate bubbled over the gas flame on the stove. Bertha reached for the shelf and adjusted the volume on the radio, turning down the upbeat horns of Glenn Miller's orchestra. It seemed a constant battle of wills—her mother wanting everything louder, Bertha longing for quiet. The jazzy notes continued, softer now, and Theresa grumbled a little as she shelled pecans at the kitchen table.

A pan of fudge would be their contribution to the gathering at the church this afternoon, a festive time when everyone in the community pitched in to decorate for the Christmas season. Bertha stirred the mixture, judging its consistency.

Jorge Espinosa had asked her to go with him, but she'd demurred on the pretext that her mother and grandmother needed her assistance. Theresa was certainly capable of driving the Ford truck to town by herself; Bertha's real reason was that she had not yet decided whether she wanted Jorge's interest. All these thoughts must be kept to herself, of course. Theresa and Ruben hinted constantly that it was about time Bertha find a husband. Practically every other girl over twenty was already married and most had their first child already.

Abuela alone understood. Bertha had studied with her grandmother for eight years, learning the methods of the *curandera*—how to consult with a patient to learn their ailments, which herbs and roots worked for which illnesses, and when it was best simply to listen. Sometimes, that in itself was a cure. Although the two women never specifically discussed the future, there was a *simpatico* between them, reading each other's feelings, knowing what was in the heart.

The Glenn Miller piece transitioned into a Benny

Goodman number and Theresa's foot tapped under the table. Bertha checked the fudge again and decided it needed a few more minutes. She could step out of the overly warm kitchen for a moment and make a quick trip to the outhouse. Maybe she should marry someone and move to town where nearly everyone had indoor plumbing these days. But she hadn't cleared the back step before a shriek from the kitchen grabbed her attention. She spun around to see what was wrong with Theresa.

"Turn it up! Turn the radio up!"

Her mother's expression showed alarm; Bertha complied.

"*. . . day that will live in infamy . . .*"

Bertha felt her insides go cold. Consuelo stepped in from the living room where she had been sorting herbs.

An announcer came on, repeating what the president had said, giving statistics. There were practically tears in his voice. The three women stared at each other.

"Get your father!" Theresa cried.

Bertha glanced toward the pan on the stove, turned off the burner. She pulled her jacket from the peg by the back door and shoved her arms into the sleeves as she ran toward his workshop.

It wasn't yet dark, and well before the planned hour for it, but everyone in the community had begun to drift toward the church. Father Pedro greeted them and led prayers for the dead sailors in Hawaii, for the country itself. The pine boughs and candles that had been gathered for decoration lay in the vestibule, untouched. After the priest finished, people gathered in clumps, some crying, most wearing stunned expressions. Jorge Espinosa approached Bertha and reached for her hand.

He pulled her to the back corner of the room and stared earnestly into her eyes.

"We're all enlisting," he said. "Me, Miguel, Jaime ... pretty much all the fellows in town."

Bertha wasn't surprised. She'd already heard the whispered conversations.

"I figure we need to, us younger guys, to keep our fathers from going. We'll get over there, show those Japs a thing or two, and then we'll be back."

A sudden and terrible vision came to Bertha. It wouldn't be over that quickly or that easily, she knew. But she didn't say anything.

"So, anyway, I was wondering, Bertha ... while I'm gone ... will you wait for me? I mean, would you—?"

She nodded before he could finish. It wasn't as if he hadn't already hinted around about marriage. She had heard the whispers around town, about herself, the oddball girl who performed cures and like to hang around with her grandmother more than her friends. She knew the words 'old maid' and 'spinster' had been thrown around. And other words, worse ones. There was a fine line between miracles and witchcraft in many peoples' minds and she had to be careful—so careful—in her practice of healing the sick and injured. Having a husband and home of her own would add legitimacy.

"We could go tomorrow for the license," Jorge was saying. "Have a ceremony at the town hall in Taos."

She took his hand. "It's all right. I'll wait for you."

Across the room, a giddy shriek told her that some other girl had decided to go ahead with a quick wedding. Bertha didn't mind. The extra time would give her a chance to get used to the idea of sharing a life with Jorge. Although she didn't love him in the way her parents loved each other, she could imagine that it would work out all right. She met his steady gaze, realizing that he was about to kiss her.

* * *

Jorge Espinosa was among the first reported casualties. Four letters—it was all she had to remember him by, those and the photograph he'd sent of himself in a crisp white uniform and cocky sailor hat. One week after completing basic training, his ship had sailed out of San Diego and been bombed. So much for showing the Japanese a thing or two.

The day she received the news, Bertha went to the bedroom, pulled the carved box from under her bed, and held it on her lap for a long time, absorbing warmth from it, healing the scraps of pain even though they had never coalesced into full-fledged grief. Then she put the box away and went on a cleaning binge through the house, moving furniture and scrubbing the floors for three days, until her mother took her by the shoulders and insisted that she go to bed.

Bertha accepted the condolences of friends. Most of them wore a wary expression, as if by acknowledging that her fiancé could die so quickly, their own loved ones might meet a similar fate. Her parents seemed resigned—they'd come so close to seeing their odd daughter married, and now that hope was dashed. Fewer men would be available after the war and the prettier girls already seemed to have snatched up the best choices.

Ruben sold another parcel of land and they spent the money to install a bathroom indoors and to fit the kitchen with a real refrigerator to replace the old icebox and to place new linoleum tile on the floor and countertop. Bertha told no one that the convenience of the refrigerator meant more to her than marriage. Only *Abuela* understood her detached attitude. Curing—that was her life now.

Two years went by and news of the war only got worse. Her father talked of enlisting—most of the men from town had done so, but the farmers were encouraged to stay behind, to keep producing food. The government paid well for his crops of corn and potatoes, and Ruben commented more than once that perhaps he shouldn't have sold that last parcel. It was a moot point; the land was not theirs now, plus he had no hired men to help with the work. Bertha and Theresa took turns working in the fields with him and watching over *Abuela*, whose health declined week by week.

"I'm old, *hija*. I will die. It is the natural way of things," Consuelo said from her bed, staring into Bertha's face with eyes that were nearly sightless now. "People die."

Like Jorge? Like the men whose names showed up on lists of New Mexicans who were killed or missing every week? Was that the natural way of things? Bertha suppressed the questions for which she would never have answers.

"Go now," Consuelo insisted, "take Margarita Vasquez some of that sore throat remedy, and young Johnny Rodriguez can use some *añil del muerto for his injury.*"

Bertha smiled. Goldweed could be a wonder for sores and cuts, but Johnny's wounds from the war were far more serious. Still, she would offer whatever help she could. As always, before she left to visit a patient, Bertha handled the wooden box and allowed it to suffuse warmth into her hands.

"*Cada remedio tiene su virtud,*" said *Abuela* as Bertha put the box away.

Each remedy has its virtue. Bertha wondered if Consuelo was referring to the box. Although she'd never told her grandmother about her experience with it, the old woman was very perceptive. She opened her mouth, the story wanting to come out.

"I will rest while you are gone," Consuelo said. "We can talk more when you return."

"All right, *Abuela*. You rest."

She climbed into the old Ford truck after telling her mother she would be back in an hour or two. Down the road two miles, she dropped off the throat remedy she'd made from mallow. And in town, Johnny Rodriguez did indeed seem better than the last time she'd visited with him. Touching his wounded arm, the warmth from her hands seemed to provide some relief. His was a shattered bone and the surgeons performed a minor miracle with repairs, rather than amputating, but a lot of the surrounding muscle was gone now and no amount of exposure to the powers of the wooden box would replace it. They had told him he would never have full use of that arm.

Cora, his wife, a girl Bertha had known in school, came into the room and cleared her throat noisily.

"I can do that for him," she said, pushing past Bertha and laying a proprietary hand on her husband's shoulder.

"Certainly." Bertha stood up. The attitude was one she encountered often—from women who no longer turned to the old ways of curing, who would rather have their babies in the modern hospital in Taos than to call upon herself and her *abuela* as midwives. Times were changing.

"Cora, look—my arm is much better," Johnny said. The skin around the wound which had been an angry, infected red when Bertha arrived, indeed looked nearly normal.

Cora stared at Bertha, challenging her.

"I'm glad to hear it," Bertha said. She handed the woman a vial of the goldweed ointment and wished them well.

As the Ford truck rattled along the dirt roads, taking her home, she decided to dismiss the incident at the Rodriguez house. Why women like Cora should feel jealousy toward Bertha was a mystery to her. These were the girls from school who were pretty and they had attracted husbands, men in whom Bertha had no interest apart from her curiosity about how the body worked to heal itself with only the simple aid of the *curandera*. She supposed the occasional antagonism came from lack of knowledge. People who did not understand the old ways could not appreciate them. Words like *spells, witchcraft,* and *conjuring* were sometimes thrown about. Bertha and her *abuela* knew differently. That was the important thing.

She steered the truck along the dirt track that over the years had become their driveway, pulling to the back of the house. It wasn't until she walked into the kitchen and heard voices from the other room that she realized the priest was here.

Abuela! Bertha ran into the bedroom and knew at a glance that she would never have the chance to finish their earlier conversation.

* * *

First *Abuela* and now *Papá*. Bertha stared at the freshly filled grave, beside the older one. Theresa knelt, the knees of her heavy stockings getting dirty as she placed a small clutch of flowers at Ruben's headstone. A month ago, neither of them could have imagined this.

The new tractor he had purchased after the war, the slicing blades of the discs, a freak fall at the wrong moment—Ruben Martinez had bled to death before anyone knew he was in trouble. Bertha, coming home from treating a child's skin rash, had spotted the stalled machine—first with curiosity, then with horror. If only she had been home, if only she had seen the accident. Guilt and regret wracked her each time she thought of it, each time she saw her mother's ravaged face and Theresa's slumped posture in the all-black clothing she now insisted upon wearing.

They would get through it, somehow. Money—the lack of it—was the big concern now. Bertha's income from performing cures was nothing. Five dollars was a typical fee, more often a chicken or some fruit or vegetables from the patient's garden. The nation might be in an economic boom right now, but this was a poor county in a poor state. People had nothing with which to pay. As a farmer, Ruben had not paid into the new Social Security plan. They were two women alone, and they would have to make do. Bertha needed to talk with Theresa about it, to have an earnest conversation, but her mother could not yet speak of the future.

The closest she had come to making a plan had been to insist that Bertha move into the front bedroom. Theresa could not sleep in the big bed in the room she had shared for more than thirty years with Ruben. They switched bedrooms, Bertha finding it strange to leave the one where she and *Abuela* had lain in the two narrow beds, talking often into the night. But that was gone now too, and maybe it was better to assume new roles.

She sensed movement and offered a hand as her mother got to her feet at the graveside.

"Come, *Mamá*, we can go home and I'll make you a nice lunch."

"There are beans. I cooked beans yesterday."

It was all she did anymore—cook traditional dishes as if there were still four people in the house. Bertha often took the extra food to her patients, but they scarcely had the money to feed the county. This was another subject for discussion.

"*Mamá*," she said as she ladled beans from the steaming pot to their plates. "We have to talk about money."

She looked at the hunched form of her mother—barely fifty years old and already her spine was curving. Arthritis, too, was taking a toll and Theresa could hardly lift a cooking pot, much less hoe a garden or drive the tractor.

"Neither of us can do the work of the farm now. Without a crop to sell, we cannot feed ourselves. I think we should sell the land."

Theresa stared at her food. No words. But a tear plopped onto the paper napkin that Bertha had tucked into the neck of her dress.

"This land came to my family thirteen generations ago. My grandfather told me the stories, made me promise to keep it always."

"I know, Mamá, I know." Bertha let the silence grow. "I will make sure that we keep the house."

"Is that it? Is that the best I can hope for?"

Bertha's voice came out barely a whisper. "Yes. I think it is."

With an eighth grade education, Bertha had already been turned away for most of the jobs in Taos. She accepted work cleaning houses but it was not a rich town; no one hired a full-time maid. Besides, her real love was healing.

But the administrator at the hospital had laughed to her face when Bertha inquired about nursing work. "Get a nursing degree," the man had said as he shut the door firmly after her.

Two women alone. They would starve before Bertha found a husband, even if there was such a man who could immediately step in and keep their farm land productive, keep producing crops when the focus on growing things seemed to have switched to big farms owned by corporations in the fertile plains of the nation, not the tiny places of a few dozen acres where the growing season was so short and the land so arid that it was nearly impossible to bring in a crop before winter killed it.

The man who wanted to buy the land had told her these things, and although it made her angry she recognized the truth in his words.

Ten thousand dollars. He'd held a check out in front of her. It was more than city people made in two or three years, he'd said, more than the people of Taos County averaged in ten years. She could support herself and her mother for a long time if she invested the money properly.

He went on about earning interest at the bank and some other things, but Bertha understood little about those ways and cared even less. On the day she slit open the last sack of beans in the cupboard, she decided to call him. He offered an extra three thousand if she would include the tractor. She bargained long enough to make him exclude the house and a city-sized lot around it from the sale. When he handed over the check she turned away.

Tears flowed freely once she was outside the bank where she had signed papers and exchanged the paper check for cash. The 1932 Ford truck refused to start, even though she tried the various tricks *Papá* had shown her. She was about to abandon the stupid thing and walk home when a young couple stopped, sensing her problem.

"Let me tow it for you," the man offered, and before she knew it Bertha was at the car lot making a deal to trade the old truck for a used sedan and some of her newly acquired cash.

She took a deep breath on the way to the house. This sort of thing will have to stop, she told herself. The cash had to last them a very long time. When she arrived at home, driving the new car, it was heartening to see the way Theresa's expression brightened, and Bertha told her mother to get in—they would take a drive just for the fun of it.

Since the war, gasoline was plentiful and cheap; they deserved a little enjoyment from life. They drove out to the Taos Pueblo, which Theresa remembered from her childhood. Bertha had never been there. By evening, when they arrived back at their small adobe house, Bertha could tell that *Mamá* was tired. They snacked on tortillas and went to bed shortly after dark.

The next day Bertha was awakened by a ferocious roaring sound. Two bulldozers and a grader scraped at the land, ripping out the sage and tearing through the small, secret places where her medicinal herbs grew. She raced outside and shook her fist at the driver of one of the huge machines but he only shrugged and said this is what the boss had ordered. She went back into the house, where she rummaged through the things in the bedroom closet that her mother had never sorted, coming up with *Papá's* shotgun and a box of shells for it.

She screamed at the drivers of the big equipment but

no one paid attention until she fired a shot into the air. All three machines stopped; the men stared at her.

"Crazy old witch!" one of them shouted as they ran for their pickup truck and drove away.

An hour later, they were back with the man who had given her the check and the county sheriff.

"Sorry, ma'am," said the sheriff. "This all looks legal. He bought your land and now he wants to build on it."

He informed her that she could keep the shotgun as long as it stayed inside the house. If she brought it out again he would have to take it away.

Within a week, their acres of beautiful land had been flattened smooth, the raw dirt looking pitiful without vegetation. Wooden stakes with bright ribbons tied on them appeared in patterns that marked off squares. Signs went up along the road. Foundations were dug, walls of cinderblock went up. By Christmas, two dozen little houses had sprouted up and their quiet lane had cars traveling up and down it all day.

Bertha noticed that these were young families—husbands who had been to the war, come home to marry, and babies were starting to come. She talked to two of the women who were obviously pregnant, offering her services as midwife. Both of them looked at her as if she were looney, before informing her that they would have their babies the real way, in the hospital with a doctor at hand.

She trudged back into the house and called Donna Salazar, the friend she had known all those years ago in school, mother of the baby whose life Bertha and *abuela* had saved. Donna had been suffering a chest cold and Bertha offered to bring by more of her special salve.

"It's changing too fast for me, and I am not an old

woman," Donna complained once she had greeted Bertha and offered coffee. "Even my own Gracie—she's going to a doctor at the clinic now."

They shook their heads over it. Bertha wrapped her hands around the coffee mug and looked at her slender fingers, with *abuela's* thin gold wedding band on her right hand. She didn't feel like an old woman, either, but Donna was right. Things were definitely changing.

* * *

Bertha pulled the carved box from the drawer in her dresser. The wood warmed her gnarled hands and she flexed her fingers. In the adjacent drawer were her bottles and bags of herbs, meticulously gathered and prepared each season, just as *Abuela* had taught her more than fifty years ago. She plucked out the bottle of *inmortal*, the antelope horns root used for respiratory and heart conditions. But she suspected *Mamá* would also need *cota* for her kidneys and persistent stomach ailments. In her nineties now, Theresa was nearing the end.

Once, that thought would have brought inconsolable sadness to Bertha but she had seen much death in her time. She carried the herbs to the kitchen and began preparing the Navajo Tea from the *cota*, thinking back to that first time she had attended a patient with *Abuela*, the time she saved the tiny infant. Baby Gracie Salazar had grown to adulthood, become a grandmother, died in a traffic accident on her way to Albuquerque to fly in an airplane to California and take the grandchildren to a place called Disneyland. Too many things had changed.

She poured the tea and carried a cup of it to *Mamá's*

bedroom, setting it on the bedside table so she could lean over and help her mother to sit up. Stuffing pillows behind the crooked back, Bertha thought of the many old people—most of her patients these days—who were about the only ones in the county who believed in the traditional *curandera* ways. She had attended so many of them, and she knew the signs of impending death. *Mamá* was in her final weeks; there was really no way around it. Bertha tamped down the terrible feeling that rose in her chest. Relief. Caring for strangers was one thing; living the caregiver role day in and day out for years—it had worn her down.

In the living room, the telephone rang. Bertha started to ignore it, then realized it was surely another patient—only her patients ever called the house and it was the only reason for getting the telephone at all. Perhaps this one she could actually help. She set the teacup down and told Theresa to rest until she came back.

"My father is calling for you," said the voice on the line. Bertha recognized it as Sarah Williams, a woman in her fifties who had shown an interest in studying the ways of the *curandera*. "I've given him the *altamisa* for his fever, but he thinks you can do more. At this point, I welcome anything you want to try. He's driving me crazy."

Bertha smiled and reassured Sarah that she would come soon.

"*Mamá*, I'm going to ask Tina Ortiz to come over and stay with you a few minutes," she said, when she'd gotten Theresa re-settled under her quilts.

"Who is that? Patricio can stay here with me. I'd rather have him."

"*Mamá,* you know Tina. She lives next door. She's been here many times. Uncle Patricio is too far away." She'd given up repeating that Patricio had died more than twenty years ago, still in Chicago, having only visited New Mexico a handful of times after he left.

Bertha went to her own room and gathered her kit, placing some loose herbs into the carved box, carrying an assortment of bottles in the bag that she normally took on every house call. When she looked in on her mother, the old woman was sleeping soundly.

The sedan she had bought in 1950, right after the death of her father, sat in the driveway—well-maintained and rust-free in the high desert climate. She placed her medical kit on the back seat and walked to the house next door. Tall elm trees shaded the front yard, where the Ortiz family was one of the few who had moved into the new development and stayed. Most of the other homes had changed hands several times; Bertha didn't understand this new way people had of moving all the time for no particular reason. Her knock at the door brought no response. Tina must be shopping. Bertha left a note explaining that she should be home within a couple of hours. Theresa could not get out of bed on her own, would not even attempt it, but she might need to be assisted to the bathroom. Thankfully, Tina didn't mind such duties.

Bertha hurried back to the car and drove to the Williams home, where she gathered her kit and greeted Sarah at the door.

"How is he doing?" Bertha asked.

"The fever is down. The *altamisa* really helped, but he still has pain in that leg."

"Don't talk about me—I'm sitting right here!"

Bertha walked in, to find Monty Williams stretched out in a recliner chair in the living room. Close to her own age, he hadn't fared as well health-wise. He'd let a head cold go untreated until he had a high fever, which Bertha and Sarah had been treating successfully. Today's complaint was apparently about his right leg, which was sliced with scars from old war wounds and now gave him pain every time a new weather front moved through.

Bertha set her kit on a nearby table and asked if she could see his leg. "You have a couple of new lesions here," she told him. "Did you run out of the goldweed ointment I made for you?"

But Monty Williams's attention was not on Bertha. He was staring at the carved box.

"Where did you get that?" he asked.

"I've had it since 1925. I was a child when my uncle gave it to me." It was the most explanation Bertha had ever given as to the box's origin.

"I saw one just like it once," he said, his eyes taking on a faraway look. "Germany. Early forty-two. They sent me to Bernkastel, a little town on the Mosel River. A Nazi soldier had that box. I picked up enough German to know that he was telling his buddy the thing belonged to Hitler himself."

Bertha felt a chill creep up her arms.

"Course, it couldn't have been *that* box," he said with a nod toward the coffee table, "not if you've had it since the twenties. Aw, who knows? There are probably hundreds of 'em out there, way they mass-produce stuff these days."

Bertha went through the motions of grinding more goldweed leaves and mixing them with a little olive oil in a vial, leaving the ointment with Sarah for treatment of her father's skin condition. But her mind was on the box and what he'd said.

There were not hundreds of them out there, of that

she felt sure. But even knowing there were two, she had to wonder. Did the other one hold the same kind of power as this one?

* * *

Bertha turned off the gas burner under a pot of boiling water and realized the odd noise she'd imagined was someone knocking at her front door. *Now who could that be?* She couldn't remember the last time someone had come to the door, not counting the time that young sheriff's deputy had stopped by to caution her. Well, that was all the fault of those punks whose taunting had reached the point where they threw rotten eggs at the house and rolls of toilet paper all over the place. He had promised to catch the kids and warn them, too, and it must have worked because they hadn't come back.

She made her way through the living room and peered out the front window to see a shiny vehicle out front, one that looked familiar. She opened the door.

"Happy birthday!" Two candles glowed on top of a small cake, one of them shaped like the number nine and the other a zero.

Beyond the bright flame she made out a woman's face. The chin-length, curly gray hair was familiar along with the short, stout build.

"I couldn't let your ninetieth birthday go by."

Bertha struggled for a moment. Finally, she figured out that it was Sarah Williams, her former protégé. She smiled, more at the fact that she'd been able to recall the name than the idea that her advanced age should be a reason to celebrate.

Sarah took the smile as an invitation to enter. When she pulled the screen door open, Bertha stepped aside, gave a glance around the living room—if she'd known there would be company she might have dusted the furniture. She spent so little time anywhere but the kitchen these days.

"Blow out your candles," Sarah instructed.

The action took Bertha back to childhood. *Mamá* always baked her a cake, and a few times there had even been a store-bought candle on top.

Sarah carried the little cake to the kitchen, going on about how they should eat a piece of it right now.

"How are you feeling?" Sarah asked as she accepted a sharp knife from Bertha and began cutting the cake.

"Oh, you know. All right." People really didn't want to hear about an old woman's aches and pains, even though she knew Sarah asked out of genuine caring and with an eye toward helping if she could. Bertha changed the subject. "How is your healing practice doing these days?"

Sarah took a seat at the table and Bertha brought two clean forks from the drawer.

"I actually have some new patients, can you believe it? After years of thinking that the old healing arts were dying out, I'm finding a lot of these younger ones are looking to herbal remedies and natural methods. Of course, a lot of them just want to walk into the health food store and buy up everything and try it all, willy-nilly."

Bertha nodded and took a bite of the chocolate cake. Her appetite may have dimmed—she knew by the way her clothes fit that she'd lost weight—but her love of sweets hadn't gone away.

"Remember, those of us who studied with you? It was a small group, but I think I am the only one who is still practicing. I've been thinking of taking on a group of apprentices of my own, teach the younger ones so the art doesn't die out. There are two young women and one man who show an interest in learning."

"Not like that one who thought I wanted a red-painted room so I could practice the occult," Bertha said.

She couldn't recall his name but she remembered how he had redone the back bedroom without her permission. That was in the days when she occasionally took in a student for the room and board money that helped with expenses.

Sarah rolled her eyes toward the ceiling. "Oh, yes. Damien, wasn't it? He never quite understood the whole thing, did he?"

"Well, I never understood those things he painted in the room. Next week, I think I shall paint it white again."

She caught the flash of skepticism on Sarah's face.

"I can bring the paint and help you," Sarah offered. "The week after next would be a good time, after I get back from Albuquerque. The grandchildren. I'm staying with them while my son and his wife go to a conference."

Bertha nodded. It had probably been ten years or more that the room had been red. Since her curing days dwindled away she'd had no real reason to go in there. But it would be nice to have the walls white again, as they were in the old days when little-girl Bertha had shared that room with her *abuela*.

"I remember the days when you used to come to our house to treat my father," Sarah said, gathering the empty plates and taking them to the sink.

Monty Williams. The memory leaped into her head, of the day she'd carried her carved box along on a visit to that house. Monty Williams claiming to have seen it before, somewhere in Germany. The same emotion rose in her now, the premonition she'd felt when she realized there were two of the boxes. It reminded her that since leaving the practice of healing she'd not had daily contact with the box. She should look for it.

Sarah left, after repeating the birthday wishes and reassuring Bertha she would be back for another visit. Bertha closed the door behind her and glanced into the living room. Where had she left that box?

It used to stay in her dresser drawer, along with all her bottles of herbs. She walked into the bedroom and opened the drawer, but everything in it was different. After she stopped practicing, she remembered now, she had given her herb collection to her students. But she hadn't given away the box ... had she?

No, she would never part with the treasure from Uncle Patricio.

The idea wouldn't go away, though. What if someone had taken it? Her heart began to race. She *needed* to find that box, to get it into the right hands, not necessarily the hands of a *curandera* but to someone who would understand and properly use the power the box conveyed.

She turned quickly and a sharp pain shot through her leg. She collapsed against the bed.

The room was cold, the sun low in the sky when Bertha woke. She pulled the quilt over herself and drew upon her inner reserves for strength. Her eyes closed once more.

By morning, she felt as if she could roll over. The pain was persistent and she gasped slightly as she reached the edge of the bed and lowered her feet to the floor. Gritting her teeth she used the bedside table for leverage to stand, then the footboard, then the doorsill as she made her way to the kitchen. Coffee. That would revive her.

Later she would call Sarah and request a poultice for the ache in her leg. But Sarah was going somewhere, wasn't she? Bertha couldn't think of anyone else to call. Maybe an idea would come to her once she had finished her coffee.

Outside, the leaves on the cottonwood were brilliant yellow now. When had that happened? In the big field where her father should be plowing under the old crop, there were tall trees and walls and the roof of a house showed over the wall. That didn't seem right either.

She started to fill her old metal coffeepot with water and then remembered something. She must find the wooden box. She abandoned the coffee for the moment and made her way, a few feet at a time, to the red bedroom where she found it. With the box in hand, she carefully took it to her own room and put it back in its rightful place. Then, at once, she needed to rest.

Somehow, another day passed, and maybe another. She lost track. She thought she should be hungry, but it seemed too much effort to go to the kitchen for food. She pulled the quilts over her thin shoulders and slept.

The next time she opened her eyes, the room was light. From outside the room came a small sound. Perhaps Sarah had come back. Bertha tried to sit up, but couldn't manage it; the wooden headboard bumped against the wall. Another small noise from another room—she struggled again but couldn't seem to speak. All that came out was a low moan.

She stared toward the door and saw it swing inward slowly. Please, be Sarah. Prayers she barely remembered from her school days came back to her in a rush and she ran through them. Send me the person I need for this moment of my life, she asked.

The figure was female, but it wasn't Sarah. This woman was taller, with hair that was not so curly. Around her was an aura of pink and Bertha sensed a person who would be loving, intelligent and compassionate.

"Come, girl," she said when she was finally able to clear her throat. "There is something you are meant to have."

She gave instructions to find the box, to take it and protect it. The woman questioned but did as she was told.

Finally, Bertha could go.

Chapter 13

Lightning Strikes Again

Thunder echoed through the streets of Washington, DC, emphasizing the clouds which had built up all day. Isobel St. Clair held her umbrella against the light rainfall as she walked the narrow sidewalk along King Street up from Waterfront Park. Her daily break from her desk at The Vongraf Foundation provided a welcome respite from paperwork, but she was still nursing tender muscles from the auto collision in New Mexico two weeks ago, wishing she could walk a bit faster to avoid the downpour that would probably begin any moment now. Perhaps more irritating than her few bruises was the idea that Marcus Fitch and OSM now had information from her files.

Security at The Vongraf had tightened over the years, comparable now to that of the strictest protocols in place in the corporate world. To their knowledge, nothing had ever been taken from inside the old building which housed their scientific studies. She reproached herself daily for placing too much trust in the hope that Fitch had not known of her trip west. She had called the man evil—perhaps that was too strong. Perhaps not. He had gone to extraordinary lengths, just short of killing her, to steal her research.

She cut over a block to the north and approached the deceptively simple red-brick building, as always marveling that Vongraf's founders had chosen the location so well, more than two hundred years ago. Outside, those men would still recognize the place. She slid her keycard past the sensor in the lock—okay, the founders would not know what *that* device was for. Beyond the white-painted door nothing would be familiar to them.

In the vestibule she presented her thumb for a fingerprint scan. An electronic buzz activated a sliding door and Isobel stepped into the modern world. Two security guards sat behind a curved teak desk, both men armed, both military special-forces trained.

"Nice lunch out, Ms. St. Clair?" asked Tom.

She nodded and passed her identity card through another reader as she chatted with them. Silently, double doors slid apart and she walked into The Vongraf's state-of-the-art lab. Isobel's double major in chemistry and business administration had landed her the job, but her minor in history had led her to study the foundation's past. She knew from old photographs that the layout and size of the lab had not changed much over the centuries. There were long tables running the length of the room back then, cabinets with tiny bottles of chemical compounds along the walls, administrative offices at the back.

Today, long tables still ran through the room, with beakers and burners in certain spots, chemicals for performing their tests in locked cabinets. Space for a half-dozen scientists and several lab assistants, a Foundation Director, two secretaries, and herself—Assistant Director. As technology advanced, the organization had added electron microscopes, radio carbon dating equipment, DNA testing abilities and more. Isobel knew they would continue to have whatever they needed, thanks to the judicious management of funds by the men who had conceived the idea of devoting their time and resources to the study of the unexplained.

She hurried to her office with the old metal safe which had been there since the beginning. Of course, now The Vongraf Foundation had a state-of-the-art vault in the basement with security measures that went beyond time locks and multiple keys. This one was here purely because of its history. She usually stashed her lunch and purse in it.

Stanley Norman, the director, looked up from his desk as she passed his door. Water now streamed down his windows—she had come inside just in time.

"Isobel? A word?"

She'd dreaded this, Stan's first day back in the office since her misadventure in New Mexico. She readied an explanation of the events.

But his expression conveyed more eagerness than criticism. "My trip to Ireland was productive," he said, motioning for her to take the chair across from him. "I got a lead on one of the boxes."

There was something about these wooden boxes, but she didn't quite know what. The Vongraf certainly had many other phenomena come through their doors—everything from UFO sightings, to animals purported to have ESP, to craters in the earth where no one had witnessed a meteor crash. Sometimes they were called upon to look at electronic devices, such as the data recorders from airplanes, that registered unexplainable results—the Bermuda Triangle effect, as they had dubbed those. With such a variety of projects to investigate, what was it about these old wooden boxes which they had now carbon dated to the thirteenth century? What made every scientist on staff, all the way to the director himself, want to see and touch and feel those ancient artifacts?

Isobel could only guess that the reason was because these were among the very few so-called magical items that they had been able to verify. Over ninety percent of the items they studied either had reasonable scientific explanations for the exhibited behavior or they were proven to be outright frauds. To demonstrate an item's supernatural powers and to be able to reliably replicate it—those were their success stories.

"We had traced one box to a man named Terrance O'Shaughnessy in Galway," Stan said.

She nodded.

"He was a very old man who passed away about a year ago. His niece inherited the box, along with his other property. She lives in the US, and in fact ..." He paused for effect. "She's the woman you went to see—Samantha Sweet."

Isobel felt her excitement rise. "The box in New Mexico is what I wanted to report to you. Its powers are real. I witnessed it. The wood glows when Samantha touches it, her hands become warm ... she achieves a touch, I suppose it could legitimately be called a healing touch. She demonstrated it to me."

Stan Norman seemed puzzled.

"I took pictures," she insisted. "Unless Samantha Sweet has two of them, the one in Ireland has to be a second box."

He gave her a direct stare. "It can't be the same box. The one I went to investigate is still there somewhere, in Ireland."

Now it was Isobel's turn to stare. "Verified, I hope?"

He sighed. "I didn't see it. I talked with an attorney, the man who handled Terrance O'Shaughnessy's estate. He knew of it, he said Samantha Sweet took it with her but that it vanished from her rental car before she came back to the US."

"Samantha didn't mention this to me." Isobel felt a little put out. "The box she showed me came from an old woman in Taos named Bertha Martinez, a woman known from her earliest years as a healer. It's been in New Mexico at least since the 1920s."

Stan ran his hands across the smooth surface of his desk. "We've verified two boxes then. And even though we can't put our hands on the second one just yet it's definitely of interest that this same woman, Ms. Sweet, has handled both of them."

Isobel made a mental note to contact Samantha Sweet again and ask about her contact with the Irish box. She looked at Stan once more. "You know there are rumors of a third. The stories have been around for ages. In one of my history texts there is a sketch of a man in clerical clothing in Rome holding a box exactly like these others."

"Are you thinking what I'm thinking? OSM?"

She shook her head. "I don't know. We suspect close ties to the Church and, yes, the Roman connection could suggest that. But we just don't know, do we?"

"But it makes so much sense. The Church, especially during the Middle Ages was known for hiding and suppressing anything that contradicted their teachings."

"Middle Ages?" she scoffed. "How about the Dead Sea Scrolls in 1947, kept under lock and key for more than fifty years before anyone from the outside got to study them."

"My point exactly."

"But these? Carved boxes that have special properties— how could those go against Church teachings? It's not as if they do anything to contradict the Bible. I just don't see the connection."

"We don't know, yet. But I wouldn't rule out anything. We're scientists—open minds?"

"Absolutely. After all, Bertha Martinez grew up in a heavily Catholic town and was known as the local *curandera*. Certainly, no one persecuted her for the abilities she derived from the box."

"We can't rule out greed and profit either. Maybe OSM really does stand for Office of Serious Money," he joked.

Everything in Washington had an abbreviation that twisted its real meaning into something cute and pronounceable. Isobel knew OSM had been around for a long time and she knew that somehow their goals and that of The Vongraf Foundation were at odds, but the other group operated under a cloak of absolute secrecy. She had documented several historical instances of OSM's involvement during the Spanish Inquisition and, later, the enslavement of those in the New World who would not change their beliefs. Maybe 'evil' was an accurate term.

* * *

A side street off Dupont Circle, a nondescript granite building that blended in with all the other plain-ish, gray-ish ones in the nation's capital, its only identification a small brass plaque near the opaque front door with three simple letters—OSM.

Marcus Fitch gave a nervous glance toward the leaden sky, approached the door, entered a five-digit code on the keypad and went inside. His recent trip to New Mexico had been a disappointment and today he would have to explain to the board of directors his failure to obtain the carved box. He had braced himself with two cups of strong coffee; it might not be enough. Elias was already here, he noticed as he stepped off the elevator and slunk past the director's spacious corner office.

It was inevitable that he and Elias Swift would clash. The eldest of the directors wanted everything done the traditional way. He refused to use the initials OSM when speaking of the organization but rattled out the whole original Latin version, *Officii Studendi potest Mystici*, every time. Marcus found the old man tiresome. The old man found him young and brash and was jealous of his quick movements and confidence.

Outside these walls no one knew what was truly done here. Anyone on the street would assume the acronym stood for Office of … anything—the beauty of maintaining their largest office here in modern DC. There were hundreds of little bureaus and divisions of the government that no one fully understood, not to mention the nearly equal number of lobbyists, special interest groups and law firms that supported the entire structure. Even Beltway insiders couldn't keep track of it all, how could the voters in Little Nowhere have a clue? Marcus liked things that way, thrived on the busyness of it all.

Elias Swift walked past Marcus's cubicle. "Conference room, five minutes," the old man reminded.

Marcus had his list of excuses ready. He could handle this.

Swift stood at the head of the long conference table, refusing to sit until all the other men were present. With his longish white hair, the old man fancied himself in the position of Jesus and the others as his disciples, Marcus thought. It was no coincidence that the Board had always consisted of a President and twelve members. And although the organization's membership now contained a mix of religious, political and business leaders, no woman had ever, in more than five hundred years, served in a place of importance here or in any of the OSM branches throughout the world. Marcus sighed audibly. The rituals all seemed moot—stupid traditions that had no meaning when their real purpose was to attain power.

His thoughts drifted back to the little town in New Mexico where he'd so recently traveled. There, a fifty-something woman possessed one of the carved boxes. He knew it as surely as he was sitting here, although he'd not actually seen the piece.

Isobel St. Clair from The Vongraf Foundation had been there, her presence proof of the rival organization's interest. She'd met with this woman at a coffee place in Taos—Marcus had watched as St. Clair left a funeral service, greeted the woman and then sat at an outdoor table speaking in low tones. Marcus had not been able to get close enough, even with his listening device, to hear them, but through binoculars he saw some sort of paper and an old photograph pass between them.

He had followed St. Clair to her hotel and watched the following morning as she went to the woman's residence, a ranch house out in the country. Isolation was normally good in this situation, but a law enforcement man had also been there. Marcus had hoped St. Clair took the box with her but when he'd rammed her car, running her off the road, then searched, all he got were copies of the documents—no artifact.

At the head of the table, Elias Swift cleared his throat.

"We are coming to the end times," he said. "The world is wholly out of control, with wars on many fronts, starvation and disease wracking the poorest nations, the wealthy and powerful taking more and more for themselves. And why? Because the Church has lost its influence with the people. They have lost their moral code and, therefore, have lost their way."

Beyond the panoramic windows, lightning cracked horizontally through the sky, punctuating his words. Uneasy glances traveled around the table.

Swift let his dark-eyed gaze fall on each man before continuing. "Our worldwide organization was formed with the goal of maintaining the influence of the Church. We cast nonbelievers out of Spain, we sent many priests throughout the New World to convert the heathen tribes, we laid out our set of rules for the masses. And now—that influence is in jeopardy, is being lost daily."

Heads nodded around the table. Marcus held his tongue. Influence? Power—that's what this was all about. They'd lost their power because they were obsolete. Power and influence were now the purview of the up-and-comers of his own generation.

"Goodness and evil are not ancient concepts," Elias said, as if he'd read Marcus's mind just now. "But we need to bring the ancient powers together in order to focus the energy toward our goals."

He let another few beats go by.

"We all know that the powers of heaven can be assisted by a certain earthly source of supernatural energy. Call it magic, or call it mysticism as our founders did. Whatever the original source, we now know that a great deal of it comes forth through a trio of artifacts. Through the centuries our members have witnessed enough events and have followed the stories of many who have come in contact with these three carved wooden boxes.

"We know that one box performs acts of goodness; the woodcarver named this one Virtu. Its powers for good are well documented. One box, interestingly, has powers from the dark side; the carver called it Facinor. This one we have secured in a vault within the Vatican catacombs, in a place where it cannot reach the hands of those who would use it for harm."

To keep Facinor *out* of the hands of others ... or to keep it *within* the hands of themselves? Marcus stared at the old man.

"Manichee, the third box appears to represent a middle path—it takes on the character of its holder, intensifying that person's own tendencies. In the hands of a good person it performs miracles in the same manner as the one called Virtu; in the hands of a man of evil intent, this powerful artifact gives that person the power to carry through with the devil's ways."

One of the other members, a leader in international business, spoke up. "Yes, yes. We know this. Our question now is what do we *do* about them?"

"For centuries we have tried to bring all three boxes to one place. To secure them, as we have secured hundreds of artifacts, including the box Facinor, in a location where they will not fall into the wrong hands, for to experience the power of all three boxes at once would be *akin to a meeting with God*." His voice grew quietly intense at that last statement.

Several stunned faces stared back at Elias; others studied their hands in their laps. The room went quiet until one man found his voice. "I was under the impression that OSM had secured all three boxes long ago. Now we learn two of them are not under our control? And where are the two missing boxes now?"

Elias glanced toward Marcus. "I believe we have a report on one of them?"

Marcus straightened in his seat and began speaking, taking care to show no weakness in front of the more experienced men. He told of the trip west and the close encounter.

"I came back with this," he said, pushing the folder of papers forward. "From the records of The Vongraf Foundation."

Several of the men showed their scorn for the rival organization. Almost from the founding of America the two factions had vied for control of the same targets. These wooden boxes were only part of the long line of items with purported mystical qualities. OSM wished to get these artifacts out of the hands of ordinary people. As for Vongraf—their goals were not clear to the men here. It seemed each time a potentially heretical item could be taken out, these scientists would study it briefly and then give it back to its owner. Back to wreak its havoc in the world.

"In short, we know one of the boxes to be here in the United States, most likely with this woman named Samantha Sweet in New Mexico."

"And we already ascertained a couple of years ago that the other, shall we say, loose cannon is somewhere in Ireland," said the Congressman from the Midwest. "We tracked the movements of a man named Terrance O'Shaughnessy who purchased it from an estate sale and then kept it in his possession. But then two years ago it vanished, just as we were close to finding and taking it from the Irishman."

"We recently learned that O'Shaughnessy was the uncle of this Samantha Sweet," Elias Swift said, dropping the new information like a kiloton bomb on the unsuspecting Marcus Fitch.

Marcus seethed, sucking air through his clenched teeth. A glance around the table told him that none of the others were particularly shocked by this news. No one had thought to tell him this before he went to New Mexico?

"Our problem," said another of the members, "is that none of the boxes has ever gone on public display. Those who hold them in ownership do not flaunt the fact. They keep very quiet about it."

Faces were solemn around the table. What could they report to Rome to help solve the problem?

Marcus glanced at the men who appeared to be deep in thought, his mind racing. Screw the rest of them. If bringing all three boxes together increased their power exponentially—oh, what he could do with that, on his own! He excused himself from the meeting and fled to the nearest Metro station.

* * *

Isobel tamped a stack of papers into a folder and

hurriedly stuck them into her bottom desk drawer, reaching into the antique safe for her purse. She'd spent so much time talking with her boss this morning that she'd nearly spaced out her dental appointment. Two Metro stops away and only thirty minutes to get there. She rushed to the station, ignoring the first fat raindrops to hit her on the head. *Forgot my umbrella*, she berated herself. *Oh, well, the dentist doesn't care how my hair looks.*

The lighted board overhead showed her train arriving in one minute. She huddled near the covered bank of benches and watched it roar to a stop with a whoosh of air. Doors slid open, people pushed out, Isobel edged her way inside the crowded late-day car. A man who'd seemed intent on getting off the train backed inside again, letting Isobel pass him. It was only after the doors closed behind her that she realized he was staring intently at her. Marcus Fitch.

Her pulse thrummed, pounding in her ears. What was he doing here in Alexandria?

"Ms. St. Clair," he said, his voice low, almost seductive. Those pale blue eyes never wavered.

She inhaled. "Mr. Fitch."

"I was on my way to your office. I'm glad I caught you," he said.

Like a rabbit in a trap?

"I wanted to apologize for that silly accident a few weeks ago."

Silly? Accident? The man had deliberately rammed her rental car, searched her possessions while she was trapped, and eluded the police. She tried to move away from him but the car was packed with people and there was simply no place to go.

"I have a peace offering," he said.

"I'm not—"

"The whereabouts of the other wooden box. I know exactly where you can find it."

She stopped edging away.

His gaze took in the nearby passengers. "We need to talk privately."

The train was slowing. People began pushing toward the doors, easing Isobel along into their tide. She needed to move aside, to stay aboard until the next stop. Fitch pressed against her, touching her elbow. When the door slid open his grip tightened and he steered her onto the platform.

"This way," he said, "there's a coffee house that will be quiet right now."

"What about this other box? Where is it?" Her appointment would have to be rescheduled.

"You know enough of my organization to be aware that we are associated with the Vatican."

He said it as though he were the head of the entire OSM, and she strongly doubted this was the case. Even more doubtful was that this man had access to the Vatican. Still, she might learn something valuable.

The rain had not materialized this far north yet although the air smelled of ozone and the clouds were darker than ever, giving a twilight feel to the late-afternoon summer sky. His hand touched her elbow once again and she found herself walking beside him down a set of stairs to street level. He tilted his head to the left and she followed.

"That woman in New Mexico," he said. "She owns one of the boxes, doesn't she?"

Isobel hoped her stare did not convey what she was thinking. *You know she does.*

"We at OSM would like to examine that box, just as

your staff at Vongraf was able to do." But his expression showed nothing but raw greed. This man wanted the power of the boxes, not their potential for advancing science.

"The Vongraf Foundation has only examined one box of this sort in our entire history, and that was in 1910."

"Don't play games with me, Ms. St. Clair. I'm not the type." The soft tone he had used on the train was gone. A steely glint shone in his stare. His jaw clenched.

She had a brief, sickening thought that she might have just revealed new information to him. Then decided she hadn't. Somehow, he'd known of their earlier work.

"How did you know I would be going to New Mexico?" she asked.

His expression turned colder yet. In a split second he gripped her arm and shoved her into the recess of a doorway. A shop, she saw, that had been boarded up for a long time. Suddenly she realized they had walked into a derelict neighborhood with few people around.

"I'm not here to answer your questions," he hissed. "You will answer mine. Did you bring that box back from New Mexico to study? You have it in your lab, don't you?"

"No! I left—"

"I want that box." His voice went quiet, deadly. "I will have it. Together with the other, their power will be incredible."

The blue eyes were glacial ice now. Isobel felt her first real shot of fear.

"Move aside," she demanded. "I have an appointment."

"Your only appointment is with me. We'll go to your office, you will escort me inside, and you will give up the box and any notes you have about the locations of others."

She thought of The Vongraf's security measures—the

scanners, the military-trained guards, the impenetrable vault where her research notes were kept—and she nearly laughed in Fitch's face. The icy eyes stopped her. They bored into her with a no-nonsense intensity.

He gripped her arm again and this time she flinched as his fingers dug into a muscle that still ached from the car crash.

"That's better," he said, his tone almost crooning now. "Let's find a car. Much less crowded than the Metro."

He yanked her from the doorway where any observer might have thought them lovers who were pressed against each other. She felt her resolve harden. There was no way she would get into a car with him. The man was mentally on the very edge. He *said* he wanted to get into the Foundation's vault, but he would not hesitate to kill her. She knew this, right to her core.

"The train is fine," she said, matching his pace and working to keep her tone cooperative. "I won't try to get away. After all, you've offered to share information on the other box with us, right?"

"Facinor," he said. "It's the name of the box in Rome." He slowed his pace slightly but the grip on her arm was still quite firm.

Up the stairs at the Metro station once more. Onto the train returning to King Street. Pressed into the rush-hour crowd. Isobel looked at the bored faces for one that might help her escape Fitch, but people on their way home from work tend to operate in their own little worlds. At the station she might have the chance to run from him. She knew the area and had friends among nearby shop owners and restaurateurs. Mentally planning the steps (swing purse at his head, dump the high heels, run to the sports bar at the corner—it will be crowded this time of day) got her through the short ride. But when the doors opened, Fitch took her hand and entwined his fingers so that he could easily break hers if she made any sudden move away from him.

All right, she thought. Plan B. It was the better one anyway.

Rain fell steadily, soaking her thin blouse, drenching her hair. Somewhere near the river, lightning cracked, shuddering the leaves on the trees. Her nerves felt raw, her skin prickling as if all the tiny hairs on her arms were standing on end.

Fitch seemed unaffected by the storm and he was familiar with the route, which didn't calm Isobel's anxiety at all. Obviously, he had been watching her much longer than she'd ever suspected. He dropped her hand only after she inserted her key card at the outer door. At the fingerprint scanner in the vestibule, she felt Fitch tensing up.

"This is as far as you'd ever get on your own, you know," she told him, "even if you managed to steal or duplicate my key."

"I wouldn't bet on that," he said under his breath. "A thumb is pretty easy to remove."

A shiver coursed down her spine. The man truly was ruthless.

Beyond the second door, when the two armed guards came into sight, Isobel sneaked another glance at Fitch's face. This time the security measures surprised him. However, if he ever decided to break in here on his own, he would come prepared. Anyone willing to chop off a woman's finger probably wouldn't hesitate to arrive armed and ready to take out two guards. Today's visit was a test—surely he knew that she did not actually have the carved box on the premises.

"Afternoon, Ms. St. Clair." Tom, the larger of the two guards, raised one eyebrow. "Your dental appointment went quickly."

This was her moment. "It was *devil-dog* excruciating."

An AK-47 appeared from behind the long desk, barrel pointed directly at Fitch's chest. Mack shouted an order for the stranger to put his hands on his head. Tom's Glock was out of its holster, the guard circling the desk, telling Isobel to step out of his line of fire. Fitch sent her a glare of pure malice but slowly raised his hands.

Their code word had worked. Each Vongraf employee had one, just another part of the heightened security measures. Isobel silently thanked the board of directors who had insisted upon them.

She watched as Tom snapped handcuffs on Marcus Fitch, marching him to a special room where she had a feeling he would be interrogated far beyond what the police would then do when they came for him. As the door closed on Fitch, she remembered to breathe.

She'd barely had time to retreat to her office and exchange her soaked blouse for a dry lab coat before the police arrived. Fitch, who now sported a red knot on his left temple, was taken away and two officers stayed behind to get Isobel's version of the story. It took far longer to repeat the details of her abduction and forced return to the office than for the events themselves to unfold earlier.

Eventually, there were no more questions. Thankful for the reprieve, Isobel returned to her own office. There stood the framed photo of her predecessor, Aurora Potts. The woman in the Edwardian-era dress and hat looked out at Isobel with a great deal of wisdom. Outside, the lightning receded into the distance and eventually the rain slowed to a gentle patter as nightfall came on.

For now, Aurora seemed to say, *we can only proceed with our own investigations, apply scientific tests to prove or disprove the claims presented to us.* One day, Isobel felt sure, a lead would come that would take them to the box currently somewhere in Ireland, and maybe another lead would take them to Rome. Or beyond.

The world was becoming a much smaller place. Facts, suppositions and stories that once required journeys of thousands of miles, weeks or months of time—now they could be found with a few keystrokes on the Internet. She thought of the box she had so recently seen in New Mexico. Right now they could only guess at its history; perhaps it had originated continents away from where it sat now.

Of one thing she felt certain—if there *were* three boxes in existence they had most likely come from the same source, that same woodcarver whose secret had remained enigmatic for centuries. Part of the thrill of discovery was the way in which those secrets tended to unfold.

Excitement grew in her belly. To one day have all three of the boxes in one place, to study them, take the necessary samples to prove their origin, it would be a scientist's dream. She stared at Aurora again and the eagerness intensified.

She could feel it, deep inside, the anticipation that they were nearing a pinnacle of some type. Call it the end of days, call it a zenith of sorts. She envisioned a time when humans would be able to learn unlimited amounts, to explore beyond the physical realm, to have knowledge of both the scientific and the spiritual without restraints from the established scions of either. Knowledge, rather than greed or misplaced hero worship, would become the hope for mankind.

Isobel walked through the lab admiring its polished steel tables, the gleaming glass containers and whirring machines. Out into a night that seemed filled with stars and hope all at once.

A full moon broke through the remaining ragged bits of cloud, bathing Vongraf's brick walls in light, illuminating treetops in a nearby park, creating a shimmering stripe of silver on the river, blocks away. She sighed, releasing the last of her tension. Her mission would continue but the storm was gone.

Author Notes

Readers who have followed my Samantha Sweet mystery series have been treated to many inside experiences with one of the three boxes, the one passed along to Samantha by Bertha Martinez in the latter chapters of *The Woodcarver's Secret.*

In crafting this story I have blended real places with fictional events and placed some real events in fictional places. The actions and words of actual historical persons have been fictionalized here. A few highlights:

The Spanish Armada's plan to invade England was practically doomed from the start, the leaders being outnumbered and acting upon bad advice about the weather. I could only imagine what one lone Spanish patriot might have attempted in the effort to assist his king.

The port city of Vera Cruz was once the largest city in Mexico, the landing point for nearly all Spanish trade ships during a time when the king of Spain issued decrees regarding the New World. The raw materials of Mexico, especially gold and silver, were taken to Spain in huge quantities, with all resulting manufactured goods being made only in Spain. Throughout the 14th century, even simple goods such as rope, cloth and paper had to be brought to Mexico by ship. We know from historical accounts that many of these ships and huge amounts of treasure went down in stormy seas.

The trade routes along El Camino Real have a long and fascinating history spanning three centuries and two countries. In a time when many Europeans ventured no farther than a few miles from their home cities, ordinary people in the North American southwest became traders and regularly made the year-long round trip of 1,600 miles from what is now northern New Mexico to Mexico City. Today, a visitor's center south of Socorro, New Mexico, houses interesting displays and the largely unchanged landscape gives a very accurate picture of the *Jornada del Muerto*, the Dead Man's Journey, where water was scarce and hostile Indian tribes were not.

The wine cellar described in this story exists today in Bernkastel, Germany, in the wine region along the Mosel River. According to the stories, a small side room actually was bricked up during World War II to hide the rare wines; the room's existence was revealed long after the war by a former winery employee before his death. Other landmarks in Bernkastel include the 'Pointed House', the Doktor Fountain, and the statue of the bears who in folklore so famously saved the lost woman and her children.

This book was many years in the making as I have incorporated locations and tales from my own travels over the past two decades. In addition to my home region in northern New Mexico, I offer my thanks to those places I have visited: Galway, Ireland; the cities of Seville and Cordoba in Spain; the Forbidden City in China; the coastal areas and beautiful Caribbean waters of Belize (subsequent to the timeframe of this story it was known as British Honduras for a little over a hundred years) and Panama; the cities of San Antonio and Galveston, Texas, where the Republic of Texas was born; many Rhine and Mosel river cities in Germany including Bernkastel/Kues; poignant and emotional visits to the battlefields and cemeteries of Germany, France and Luxembourg; the city of Nuremburg with its infamous courtroom and Nazi parade ground; the Caribbean coast of Mexico; Rome and Vatican City; and to dear friends Jim and Debbie Pawlik who introduced us to Alexandria, Virginia. Many guides walked with me through these places, during many trips, over many years. You answered my countless questions, despite the fact that neither of us knew at the time exactly how the information would eventually come forth in a story. Thank you, all. You have my undying gratitude.

Connie Shelton, February, 2015

* * *

**Follow Samantha Sweet's modern-day encounters
with the magic box in the
Samantha Sweet mystery series.**

THE SAMANTHA SWEET SERIES
Sweet Masterpiece
Sweet's Sweets
Sweet Holidays
Sweet Hearts
Bitter Sweet
Sweets Galore
Sweets, Begorra
Sweet Payback
Sweet Somethings
Sweets Fogotten
The Woodcarver's Secret

**For the latest news on Connie's books,
announcements of new releases, and a chance to
win great prizes, subscribe to her monthly email
newsletter. All this and more at
conFvshelton.com**

Connie Shelton is the author of two bestselling mystery series, as well as several award-winning essays. She taught writing courses for Long Ridge Writer's Group and was a contributor to *Chicken Soup For the Writer's Soul*. She and her husband live in New Mexico.